THE SENTINEL

A REX CHASE NOVEL

BY TIM WHEAT

WWW.TIMWHEATBOOKS.COM

The Sentinel: A Rex Chase Novel

Copyright: Tim Wheat
ISBN: 978-0-9896350-3-5
Published 2014
ERC Press

To Mom and Dad

Prologue
St. Thomas, Nevada. November 7, 1914

"I got you."

"Did not."

"Did too."

"Did not."

"That's enough boys. If you can't play nice then you shouldn't play together at all." Lindsey Baxter scolded her two young sons before addressing her husband. "Jeff, do something about these boys."

"Boys," their father lay on the ground and raised his head while tipping the brim of a large straw hat. "Do as your ma says."

November weather around the sleepy mountain town could often follow a wide range, but this particular day was sunny and eighty-three degrees. Not a cloud interrupted the brilliant blue sky, and rains in the previous weeks had caused the nearby Colorado River to swell. These rains had brought the family ten miles south of their home.

"Didn't you bring us down here for the fabulous hunting? Why are you just lying around sleeping?" Though she had grown up in the West, she held no love for the great outdoors. "I don't understand why you need me here at all."

"Linds, first, it's two in the afternoon. Even in this beautiful weather, the animals are going to nap. Second, the boys are eight and six; they can hunt with me in the morning, but are too tired by night. Last, I need you here because I love you."

She smiled at his final remark. Though he had manufactured his first two comments, he saved himself with the last. Her demeanor lightened as she spoke again.

"Believe me, if I didn't love you we wouldn't be here. I thought the rain was going to make deer hunting a breeze. We're already on our third day and I haven't even seen one."

"Well, we've had a couple of setbacks, but I'll leave the boys with you tonight and go out on my own. Willy's spooked three doe already. Don't worry; we'll be on our way home tomorrow morning." Confidence oozed from Baxter's delivery.

"I think you'd better get going then. I'm ready to sleep in our bed." Lindsey stood over her resting husband and gave him a light kick to the rear. "Let's go Mr. Great Deer Hunter."

"Fine, fine." Jeff stood and dusted off his Levis. The southern drawl of his youth became pronounced as he grew annoyed. "I'm tellin you though darlin, the deer ain't runnin this time of day. I'm just gonna get out of sight and lay back down for a nap until it's time. You know I'd rather be here with the three of..."

At that instant a tremendous thunderclap pierced their ears, and a bright flash of lightning raced across the sky, terminating in the nearby canyon. Instinct caused both Lindsey and Jeff to grab their ears, while their two young sons became quiet, looks of wonder adorning their faces. After a respite of thirty seconds, Mrs. Baxter's question vocalized her concern.

"What was that?"

"Dad. I saw it. I saw where it landed. It's just down in the canyon. Can we go see it? It must be a meteorite, or a UFO, or even an alien." Their oldest son had a vivid imagination.

"Tone it down a little Willy. Stop scaring your brother." Jeff's drawl disappeared as he became serious. "I couldn't see where it landed. Did you get a good look from over there?"

The two boys had been playing fifty yards away from their parents, and had a better view of the canyon. Both replied in unison.

"Yes."

"OK then." He clapped his hands, playfulness returning to his voice. "Looks like a little family adventure; you coming Linds?"

"No thank you. Just being out here with you wild men is enough adventure for me. I don't need to chase down any aliens or meteorites. You boys have a nice hike down into the canyon, though. Don't forget to bring back a deer with you this time. I'm ready to go home."

"When we discover gold that has fallen from heaven and disappear down the Colorado without you, you'll be sorry." Jeff packed water onto their mule, and checked the saddle's buckles. "We should be back by the morning though, babe. Just a quick hike down tonight; we'll bag ourselves a deer, and by this time tomorrow, we'll be on our way home."

Lindsey smiled as the rugged looking man took her face in his hands and stole a passionate kiss. Though they had married almost twelve years before, and had suffered through the deaths of three of their five children, love still existed in droves. She couldn't imagine her life any other way.

"Be careful. I thought I heard a mountain lion last night."

"I heard it's the grizzly bears that will sneak up and eat little boys. You and I should be fine, but they love tender little boy meat." Jeff teased his young sons whose faces showed genuine concern.

"Be nice, Jeffrey." Lindsey feigned disapproval, though his ability to relate to the children was one of his most endearing qualities.

"Dad, you're just teasing." The older of the two boys accused his father while adding, "We don't even have grizzly bears this far south."

"I don't know. Lots of old timers say that grizzlies used to roam the mountains all the way down to the Mexico border. Just to be on the safe side I suppose I could pack the forty-five caliber Colt and take it with us. We could use…"

"You sure won't take my Colt." Lindsey said, an indignant countenance dominating her face. "How dare you even suggest leaving me out here unprotected?"

"What do you think boys? Should we take the Colt with us, or leave it here for mommy to protect herself?"

Both children paused, and seemed to contemplate the question with intent. The younger of the two furrowed his brow, pretended to stroke his nonexistent chin hair, all while watching his older brother. At eight years of age, the eldest of the Baxter boys was an intellectual, and he arched his left eyebrow before speaking.

"I think we should be able to protect ourselves from grizzlies with the shotgun and the rifle. Mom should keep the Colt just in case. It's just a forty-five anyway. A grizzly bear would run right through that."

"Thanks a lot." Lindsey said. "I feel much better now. You were right, though, nobody has seen grizzly bears this far south in a long time."

"It's all settled then. We leave mommy to the grizzlies and we'll go collect our gold from heaven."

"Do you think it's gold papa?" The younger of the two boys spoke with hope, and his eyes shone.

"Gold doesn't fall from the sky stupid. Dad is just playin with…"

"That's enough." Jeff interrupted his eldest son's sentence with a simultaneous rap to the back of the head. "You don't tell people they are stupid, and it's playing, not playin. Your mother works hard for you boys to speak right, unlike your ignorant old man. Now apologize to your brother."

"I'm sorry." Both boys stood, their heads down, looks of dejection on their faces.

"So. Which one of you wants to shoot the rifle first?" Their demeanors changed in an instant and his two young sons raised their hands, clamoring for his attention. Jeff smiled at their eagerness. "I guess we'll have to hike down this canyon and see if we can find ourselves a deer."

"Do you think we'll find gold too?" The younger of the boys flashed a sweet and expectant smile.

"I sure hope so son. I sure hope so."

***

Though the trek down the side of the mountainous terrain was not treacherous, the three Baxter men made slow time. Jeff was proud of his two young sons. Neither complained, and they listened when he gave them direction. Along the way they had seen an abundance of wildlife, including a close encounter with a mountain lion which still had the boys buzzing with excitement.

"Dad. How many mountain lions do you think live in the canyon?"

"Yeah, do you think that the mountain lion heard us talking about him?"

"Do you think the mountain lion is going to attack mommy now?"

THE SENTINEL

The questions hadn't stopped, and though Jeff had spotted the beast before they were in any real danger, the boys had become enthralled.

"Take it easy guys. I doubt we see any more mountain lions. If we do I don't think they'll speak English. I doubt he goes after Mommy because she has the Colt and those cats aren't stupid." He attempted to divert their attentions. "How far do you guys think before we get to our sky gold?"

"Not far dad" said his eldest son.

"Nope, not far dad" echoed the younger.

"That's good, because it's almost prime deer hunting time. I'd be willing to bet that's what our buddy the mountain lion was out here doing."

"That's what I think too."

"Three."

Jeff chuckled as they rounded a bend in the trail and the canyon floor opened. His sons bolted to the edge of the small stream that had dug through the rocks over millions of years. Without warning, though, their mule stopped in its tracks, refusing to go any farther.

"Come on old girl." Baxter pleaded with the stubborn animal while stroking its neck. "We still have to go back up in a little while."

"Dad."

"Dad."

"Come look over here."

"Come look over here."

Laughing as he tied the obstinate beast to a bush, Jeff turned to look at his sons. They stood near the edge of the small stream, but that wasn't a problem. At their feet, however, was a mule deer, steam emanating from its fatal wounds. Without thinking, and with incredible speed, he removed his Springfield M1903 rifle from its leather holster.

"Boys. Get back here right now." He had received training on the rifle at the tail end of his military service, and upon his honorable discharge, had kept the accurate weapon. He now turned, and for the first time in his life, used the M1903 with deadly intent. Horror filled his very existence as he took aim at the massive beast sprinting toward his two young sons. "BOYS."

Both young men stood, almost a hundred yards away, frozen in fear. Charging in their direction at a speed approaching thirty-five miles per hour was a massive, angry grizzly bear. Neither boy moved as the incredible brute bore down upon them. All they heard was the beating of their own hearts, and the splashing of their impending attacker's immense paws. Death, it seemed, was upon them.

Gunshots rang out, but the advancement of the centuries old killer failed to slow. Baxter had fired four of his five shots, and with the immense animal bearing down on his children he aimed with desperate purpose. Staring down the battle sight of the military weapon he filled his lungs and held the air a moment before blowing it back out. Calm settled upon him as he pulled the trigger.

Hurtling through the air at twenty-eight hundred feet per second, the 30.06 caliber projectile was true. It crashed into the side of the enormous bear, just behind the shoulder blade, with the kinetic energy of almost one hundred arrows. Slamming into the shallow waters of the stream, the great beast roared as its body slid to a stop.

Death averted, the brothers snapped from their frozen state and ran toward the man who had saved them. Baxter moved with speed and determination, covering seventy yards before his sons managed thirty. He dropped his weapon and showed no shame as he wept and scooped the two boys into his arms. They had never seen their father cry, and both soon followed.

After a full minute Jeff set his two sons down and what he saw next chilled his soul. Thirty yards ahead, the magnificent grizzly bear stood. Satan himself seemed to appear behind the animal's eyes as the great beast shook the tremendous head millions of years of evolution had afforded it. Fumbling to pick up his rifle Baxter commanded his children.

"Run boys. Run."

In the waning light of the day Jeff struggled to re-load the bolt action weapon he wielded. The bear closed distance with incredible speed, and before Baxter had time for a shot, the fifteen hundred pound beast buried its head in his stomach.

All of the breath left his body and the Springfield rifle flew through the air, landing fifty feet away. The two children watched in abject horror as the bear slashed at his body, using its razor sharp claws as primeval weapons. A blood curdling scream emanated from deep within their father, and pierced the late afternoon sky. Then, in almost the same instant, the sound stopped as the vicious bear grabbed the helpless man in its jaws by the throat, tossing him twenty feet.

Without mercy, and though Baxter's body made no attempt to move, the bear pressed the attack. Then the two boys witnessed something they would never forget. As their father's killer advanced on his lifeless body, an apparition appeared. The gray haired man, wielding nothing but a bowie knife, leapt on the back of the great beast and began attacking it with the fervor of a banshee.

Roaring, the monster stood to its full height of almost ten feet. The gray haired man loosed his grip, and athletically dropped to the ground. He pressed the attack with his knife again, plunging the blade deep into the massive animal's back, just above the tail. Its claws lashed with killer intent as the grizzly pivoted and returned to all four legs.

The gray haired apparition was faster, though, and dropped to his back. Lying flat on the ground he slashed again, working the knife deep into the beast's inner right thigh. He wielded his instrument of death with precision, and used the momentum of the enormous animal's movement to pull himself free of its clutches.

Its injuries were severe and the grizzly halted the fight, moving off ten yards. Both boys stood frozen, almost unable to fathom everything that had happened in the previous minutes. The bear grunted and groaned as it sat on its haunches and began licking at the large wound on its inner thigh. Blood spurted from the fatal injury to its femoral artery. Time was no longer on its side.

With an immense serenity their gray haired savior approached the terrible animal. As he neared, it fell to the ground, mere seconds from death. Baxter's two sons watched as he took the ferocious beast's massive skull in his hands and spoke to the bear in a language they couldn't understand. He caressed the animal's head with great care while he spoke into its right ear. Though they did not understand, his tone was soothing, and after thirty seconds the dreadful creature stood, and ambled into the nearby stream.

His well-tanned skin glistened with sweat and he watched the bear until it had disappeared under the current. Quiet filled the canyon, and the sound of his own breathing was all that he heard. Turning, he moved toward the young men, and though their terror had subsided, the brothers still stood, frozen in place as he approached.

"You boys have names?" He delivered the question with the slightest hint of a southern accent and the eldest son replied.

"My name is Willy, and his name is Tad."

"And your father's name is Abraham Lincoln then, I presume."

Willy knew that the 16th president's children held the same names and his reply was simple.

"No, his name is Jeff."

"OK then." The man's smile was whiter than any they had ever seen before, and his eyes were bright blue. "Let's see if we can help him."

As the three moved toward the body of Jeff Baxter the scene was horrific. His bowels protruded from the injuries inflicted by the bear's slashing claws, and great puncture wounds were evident in his neck. Their father's face was a mask of blood, and Tad shook as he cried.

"Papa. Papa. Wake up Papa."

"Shhhhhh." His voice was soothing and without knowing why, the brothers afforded the stranger an implicit trust. "I think he's going to be alright boys. All you have to do is have a little faith. Just stay right here and don't move. I'll be right back."

The Good Samaritan leaned over, held the body of the wounded man in his arms, and carried him toward the stream. A stillness fell over the canyon. Just the solitary sound of water gurgling across the rocks disturbed their tranquility. Willy and Tad obeyed and held their ground as the apparition slipped into the water with their father.

Their rescuer disappeared, Jeff in his arms, under the water, and after a minute passed, the boys became apprehensive. Tad nibbled on his fingernails and fidgeted while scanning the area for predators, whereas Willy's curiosity rose as he took a few steps toward the stream. He craned his neck, attempting to make out the men's outlines in the mountain runoff.

"Willy, he told us to stay put. I think we should stay put." Tad had spoken and for the first time in his life, Willy obeyed him.

"You're right Tad. I'm sorry." Five minutes passed, and the brothers' apprehension soared. "It's been almost five minutes. I haven't seen hide nor hair outta…"

At that moment a soaking wet mass of tousled gray hair emerged from the water. Each deliberate step brought him closer as he made his way across the current and approached the two boys, the lifeless body of their father still in his arms. Gone, though, was the mask of blood. More important, however, was that the wounds to his belly and neck seemed to no longer exist. Looks of astonishment were clear on the sibling's faces as the man spoke.

"I think he's going to pull through boys. We should get him home, though. Do you live around here?"

"What did you do to him?" Willy said, asking the question both children wondered.

"It was nothing," said the stranger. "I learned a few things from a great Navajo medicine man a number of years ago."

"We're from St. Thomas." Tad said.

"St. Thomas? What in the blazes are you doing way out here?"

"We are out hunting for deer," Willy said. "Father thought we would have good hunting after the rains."

"Your father is a wise man. I suppose I will take you all the way back to St. Thomas then."

"Our mom is at our camp at the top of the gorge," Tad said. "You could just help us up there, and we'll..."

"Shhhhhhh," Willy said. "Remember what father told us?"

"Oh yes."

"Your father told you never to go with strange men, or bring them to your mother." He said the words as the boys nodded their heads. "Like I said before; your father is a very wise man. Just once, though, I think it would be in his best interest if we got him to safety. I'll place your dad on the mule, get him as comfortable as I can and we'll get on up the mountain."

"Won't it be dark soon?" Willy asked.

"I suppose it will be young Willy, but that doesn't matter. We'll have a full moon to navigate by tonight and the two of you can ride on the mule as well. We'll be in camp before you know it."

The boys relented and within minutes loaded the mule.

"What about the deer?"

"Yeah, what about the deer?"

"Yes, the reason for all this trouble; a lousy deer." He blew a deep breath out and seemed to assess the situation. "I suppose I could field dress it in five minutes or so and we could load it onto the mule, but you boys would have to give up your seats."

"That's what I want to do."

"Me too."

"Then that's what we'll do."

***

Neither boy complained on the entire return trip to camp. The man with gray hair set a grueling pace, expecting the brothers to fold, but they surprised him by continuing to move forward. He garnered a respect for this family he had not afforded most in recent years, and when they arrived in camp, the mother didn't let him down either.

She was a fiery woman who listened to the imaginative story of her sons while keeping a wary eye on the stranger in their midst. He unloaded the still unconscious Jeff Baxter into her personal tent, and though she was cautious, something about the unfamiliar man instilled trust. Both boys yawned and seemed exhausted from the day's ordeals. Adrenaline kept them awake, however, and as Lindsey tended to their father they sat with the stranger by the fire.

"So you boys were just down to hunt mule deer huh?"

"Not just mule deer. We saw gold fall from the sky." Tad's exuberant description caused the other two to laugh.

"I told you it wasn't gold Tad. Scout's honor though, we saw a meteorite or something shoot through the sky, clap like thunder, and land in the canyon," said Willy. Excitement dominated his voice before lamenting. "We forgot to see if we could find it."

"Do you mean these?"

From his pocket the gray haired man pulled two smooth objects. The glow of the fire coupled with the gleaming full moon, danced across their glossy finish. Colored a deep black, the objects seemed to have inscriptions upon them.

"You found them. Are they meteorites?"

"Are they gold?"

"No. No. They aren't gold." The stranger laughed as he moved the two objects in his hands. "It's going to be a little hard for me to explain to you what they are."

"Can I hold one?" Said Willy.

"Can I hold the other one?"

"Well, I don't see why not. Be careful, though, they're delicate."

"They came shooting from the sky and crashed to earth without getting a scratch. How delicate can they be?"

"Very astute Willy, very astute indeed."

He handed each boy one of the oval shaped objects and their faces told the entire story. Tad's expression changed very little as he felt the heat of the item. Willy's expression, however, bordered on awestruck.

"It's heavy. Way too heavy for its size. I mean, this rock is about twice the size of an egg, and the same shape, and it must weigh ten pounds."

"It weighs an exact three thousand, nine-hundred grams, or nine pounds, give or take." said the stranger. "Also, it's not a rock."

"What's a gram?" Tad said.

"They use it to measure stuff in Europe." His brother replied with haste so he could ask more questions. "If it's not a rock, what is it? Why is it so warm? What do these markings on the sides mean? Why does it feel like mine is pulling itself toward the other one? Why would…"

"Take it easy Willy. You'll blow a gasket. I'm going to answer your questions, but I want to show you something while I do. You'll have to give them back to me, though."

Tad handed his object back, but Willy held onto his with reluctance, wanting to inspect it more before submitting. The deep black color of the two mysterious eggs seemed to blend into the night, and the boys watched them with intent stares. As the stranger stood, he spoke with a purpose.

"You see boys, these two objects are quite important to me. A very long time ago I used them to help achieve a specific goal." As he spoke the stranger touched the two objects together, twisted each a turn counter to one another, and released them. To each boy's surprise, they began orbiting one another in the sky. "You see, they aren't rocks at all. Have you ever seen a rock do that?"

"You're doing a magic trick." Willy hesitated as he spoke the words.

"I love magic." Tad said, youthful exuberance obvious in his countenance.

"This isn't magic boys. This is science," he said. "These eggs are made of a very exotic element, and this element is made of almost pure energy. The reason they feel warm to the touch, is that the energy stored inside always keeps them warm. These particular objects always come in matching pairs, and when I touch them together in a specific way they become active."

"So that's what the writing on the sides explains? How to activate them?" Willy asked.

"Very thoughtful Willy. See, you understand them quite well. They are warm because they are energy, and they are attracted to one another because of the same energy."

"I noticed that they are moving around each other in a specific pattern. What would happen…"

A long snore from Tad interrupted his question. All the non-stop activity of the day had taken their toll on the youngster. The stranger laid the boy's head on a rucksack used as a pillow before continuing.

"They are moving in a pattern Willy. It's the sign of infinity they are making. Do you want to see something neat?"

"Yes."

"OK, come here."

Willy stood and walked to where the two objects moved through the sky.

"Without touching the other, I want you to take one object out of its orbit, and touch their main inscriptions together."

"I don't understand."

"Watch me. I'll do it once, but it takes a total of three times in short succession." The stranger pulled one of the objects from the sky, and as the other still circled, allowed their largest inscriptions to glance off one another while releasing the original object back into its orbit. "Do that three times, and you'll see something magnificent."

Anticipation mounted as eight-year-old Willy grabbed the energy mass from the sky. He held it in position as the other came into solid contact. Three times the objects touched, and he released his grip.

Both of the glimmering black orbs vibrated in midair before coming together. Willy took a step back as they hovered side by side in the sky for what seemed an eternity. It was almost imperceptible at first, but then the two objects moved up, separated, relocated opposite one another, and proceeded to outline the shape of a box in the air. Coming back together they hung for one precise second longer. What happened next caused the youngster's jaw to drop.

In the sky, as clear as if she were standing in their midst, appeared a little girl. She wore a green dress, which showed from underneath her wool coat, scarf, and mittens. Her cheeks were rosy, and she smiled as she held two identical objects in her hands. She threw them in the air, and attempted to bat them to the ground.

"What, what, what... What is happening?"

"Don't be afraid." The stranger's voice was soothing and he could see the young man's demeanor shift. "What you are seeing is a representation of another person who has found a set of these bundles of energy." At that time a large man entered the picture, seemed to scold the girl, and she hid the objects in her pocket. "Would you like to see another?"

"Yes."

"You've got it." The stranger reached out, motioned with his finger, and the scene in the sky changed. A single object resting on a shelf in a cave replaced the girl. "Now that one. That's the one right there."

"What do you mean?" Willy asked.

"Thirty nine of these objects exist; nineteen pairs and one all alone. It's the key to the whole thing. They are all attuned to each other as well as to the earth itself, and if you can't tell from the holographic image that one is quite a bit larger than the others. The big one fell from..."

Lindsey Baxter cleared her throat as she stepped from the tent. The stranger who had saved their father's life snatched the two floating eggs from the sky, and the images disappeared. As his mother walked over, Willy met eyes with the stranger who winked, and held a finger over his mouth. He understood, and vowed to himself that neither he nor Tad would utter a word. It was a vow he was willing to take to his grave.

✷✷✷✷✷✷✷✷✷✷✷✷✷✷✷✷✷✷✷

1.

"Come on Rex," Angela Ahiga plead with her husband's best friend. "You've been moping around and burying yourself in work long enough. You need to get out and have a little fun."

"You have an unhealthy obsession with my personal life." Rex Chase shouted as he leaned under the hood of the Packard Six, his hands covered in oil and grease. Somehow he hadn't noticed the alluring woman enter his expansive garage and remove her coat. "When I need to relax I come out here and work on the Six. How did you sneak in here anyway?"

"Working on that beat up old car doesn't count as having a good time, and you have the radio turned up loud enough for a freight train to sneak past." Angela's face went from a smile to a pout as she lowered the volume on the old Automatic radio. "Please come with us. It's going to be so much fun."

"You know something." Chase stood and looked around the room before grabbing a shop towel and cleaning the filth from his hands. "Even with the radio, it was much quieter in here about five minutes ago. I'll have you know, too, that this beat up old car is a luxury vehicle. I could have sworn I released the hounds."

"Yeah, like those two ferocious animals are going to do anything." Sarcasm dripped from her words as they both took notice of the pair of sleeping golden retrievers lying on a large rug. "Don't change the subject. Please, come with George and me to the awards ceremony. He has his heart set on you being there. He's just too obstinate to come in here and ask you himself."

"He can be a stubborn old goat. The two of you don't want me third wheelin it with you anyway. I can see all the understanding looks already." Rex walked around the side of the vehicle as he impersonated the fictitious group of sympathizers. "Look at that poor Rex Chase sitting all by himself. He just can't seem to get his act together."

"Nobody is going to say anything like that. You've achieved more and worked harder in the last year than anyone I know. Besides, who says you're going to be just a third?" Angela said, a sly grin crossing her face.

"Nope. I'm not getting set up on a blind date." Chase's voice was firm.

Since the death of Mary Elizabeth he had sworn off women. Instead, he had returned to Massachusetts and focused on his work. Evil and bad luck had erased Bobby Poppen's formula, and Rex, in its absence, had devoted himself to advancing the physics. Scalar energy could still be used to an extent, and his name in the world of science had exploded.

"Don't give me that line Edward Rex Chase." Angela had heard Rex's mother use his entire name once, and attempted to utilize a similar maneuver. "It has been well over a year since you've been on a date, or even talked to a woman other than your mother and me. My friend Sarah is beautiful, smart, and when I told her about where you lived she still agreed to meet you."

Chase smiled as he feigned indignation.

"How could any woman not want to meet a man who owns all of this?"

Rex motioned out the window toward the cabin he now called home. After Chase's return from Morocco, Patrick Castle had shown his gratitude by giving Rex the place to live and the remnants of the Packard Six. The old dwelling on Populatic Pond was damp, and smelled from decades of negligence, but Rex had made himself a sufficient living space.

"Yes, women love the smell of mildew," Angela said. "Maybe you should have cleaned the house up a bit before you built this gargantuan garage."

"I don't spend that much time in the cabin. You see, it's so comfortable out here in the garage, and I like to go hunting with the pooches."

"You have lived out here, in the woods, for a year and a half," Angela motioned her arms. "You're telling me you've never had time to clean up the house? No woman wants to date a man who lives in a garage. What if I came over and helped you? Would you come with us then?"

"I just don't want to lead anyone on or anything. I'm not interested in…"

"I know the story Rex." Angela moved around the side of the car and placed her hand on his shoulder. "It's OK. You can't spend the rest of your life hiding in here working on your car, or burying yourself in the lab for weeks. She wouldn't want you to be doing this. She would want you to live your life."

Chase shifted his weight and scratched the back of his head.

"I know that. I still see her in my dreams, though. Every night it's like I meet her all over again. I just can't seem to shake it. I…" Rex cleared his throat as the words left him.

"Believe me, I understand. You aren't the only person who lost someone you know. I lost my twin sister and my father."

"I know. I know. You don't have this memory of mine, though. The picture of her in my head is as vivid as if she were going to walk down that lane any minute. How can I just turn that off?"

"Why would you want to turn it off? Nobody is asking you to do that." Tears filled Angela's eyes as Chase averted her softened gaze. "You never forget your first love. I was lucky with George, but not everyone is. You can't use it as an excuse forever, though, because you'll end up an old man whittling sticks by himself on the front porch of your dump."

"I don't even like to whittle." Chase smiled as he looked at his best friend's wife. Her long blond hair curled past delicate shoulders, and though she wore a simple green dress, her beauty was radiant. A natural exquisiteness seemed to emanate from her very soul. "You'd waste a day to come over here and help me clean up this place?"

"I'm out here now, and if you kept the cabin as clean as the garage you wouldn't have any problem." Angela wiped the tears from her eyes as she scanned the immaculate workspace. "It's like an operating room in here, and hot. I don't see a fireplace or anything. How is that possible?"

"I am a pioneer in the field of sustainable energy." Chase was happy to change the subject and motioned for Angela to follow as he moved toward the north wall of the building. "I forgot the two of you haven't been out here since I made one of my latest findings. Speaking of the two of you; I assume Chief is around here somewhere."

Since their marriage George and Angela Ahiga had been inseparable. Chase knew Chief would not have let his wife drive into the countryside by herself on the cold November day. The early winter of 1938 had proven to be one of the coldest and snowiest in more than thirty years, and Rex hadn't had much company.

"You assume right. I'm not sure where he is, though. He got out of the car at the same time I did, but I made a beeline through the snow straight in here." Angela followed behind Rex. "I could make an educated guess, though."

"I could too."

Chase's property sat on the St. Charles River which bordered the northern section of Populatic Pond. Months before and within a short walking distance Ahiga had spotted a prime ice fishing site. Now, though the temperature dipped below zero, and snow drifted higher than three feet, they both assumed him to be checking the spot.

"Alright, check this out." Chase had led Angela across the expansive garage and approached the only wall without windows. He took hold of a wrench, which seemed no different from the others, and moved it a quarter turn to the left. Mrs. Ahiga watched in wonder as the entire wall melted into the ceiling.

"So you don't even use any of the tools on that wall?" Angela said.

"Ha. That wall is the least cool thing I'm about to show you." Chase used the new term he had just heard on the radio before moving into the room. "First of all, stay where you are until I tell you to move."

"Why would I stay in the uncool room?" Angela said. "I want to see all of the..."

The large wooden entry door flew open and George Ahiga's wide frame almost spanned its width. A frigid blast of air burst through the room and the two startled canines leapt from their slumber, baring their teeth and barking. Chief entered, shaking the snow from his boots, before bellowing.

"Easy mutts, I brought you guys something." The two dogs recognized their master's friend and their collective demeanor took a one hundred and eighty degree turn. Chief laughed as he removed his coat and the friendly beasts clamored around him. They seemed to have smiles on their faces as they danced in place, whining while pleading for his attention. Ahiga knelt to the ground and spoke in a voice he reserved for the two golden retrievers. "Hey there big dogs. I got you a treat. Yes I did. Yes I did."

George laughed as he petted the animals with his right hand while concealing something behind his back with the left. Axl, the male, moved to the right and sniffed the air, a frenzied look on his face. Belle, the female, went one step further and buried her snout into the massive left elbow of Ahiga.

"Alright. Alright." Chief pulled a large fish from behind his back, and threw it across the garage onto the floor. "Take it you beggars."

Both animals slipped across the concrete surface as they scrambled to be the first to the fish. They growled at one another upon reaching the flailing animal before devouring it together. Scales and blood splattered on the floor, and almost as soon as the fish had appeared, the dogs consumed it.

"Are you kidding me man? You just walk in here and throw a fish on the floor?" Chase pretended to be offended.

"Don't you feed those two?" Ahiga beamed as he stood and walked across the room toward his wife. Approaching her, he swept the woman of his dreams off her feet and cradled her in his massive arms. A few seconds passed as they shared a deep kiss before he placed her dainty frame back on the ground. "You wouldn't believe what just happened out there babe."

"You caught a fish?"

Rex and Chief both laughed as George replied.

"Well, yeah, but it was crazy. I walked down to my spot, drilled a hole and that largemouth bass swam right to the surface. I just stuck my finger in his mouth and pulled him out. We need to move out here ASAP."

"And then you had him slaughtered by my dogs, leaving a bloody mess in the middle of the floor," Chase said before Angela could protest. "Before you move out here, though, you're going to clean that up."

"Whatever you say buddy. I just figured since your house was such a dump the garage would be too." Chief took in his surroundings. "This setup is amazing, though. I know we haven't been out here in a while, but I love what you've done with the place."

"We'll talk about moving out here later." Angela took her husband's hand before continuing. "You should have seen what he did with the wall a minute ago. Show him Chase."

"It's not that big of a deal. The other things I have to show you are a lot..."

"Come on man," Chase's oldest friend interrupted. "The lady says it's worth it. Let's see."

"Fine." Chase rolled his eyes before moving to the other side of the wall and returning the wrench to its original position. The barrier creaked as it moved from its spot in the ceiling before coming to a stop on the floor. "There. Now you've seen the wall."

"Pocket walls huh? We have pocket doors in our house baby. It's not all that different." Ahiga said, a smile adorning his face as he squeezed his wife's hand.

"Well, I think it's pretty cool, and ours aren't automatic," Angela said.

"Cool, huh? Are we hanging out in jazz clubs now?" George quipped.

"Alright. Alright. If you thought that was cool, what you're about to see is downright freezing." Chase had turned the wrench and the wall once again returned to its spot in the ceiling. He moved into the adjacent room and spoke with conviction. "In the last few months I've been making serious breakthroughs. At first, I thought it would be impossible to do most of these things, but I had an epiphany a while back when I was building this wall."

"Hey man, it's hotter than hades in here. Do you think we could crack a window or throw a little snow on the fire or something?" George adjusted the collar of his sweater. "I'm sweating to death over here."

"Angela, you stay there. Chief, I want to show you this real quick."

Chase motioned his friend over, a pleasant look on his face. George released Angela's hand and moved forward. His stride was smooth, and his movements easy, until, without warning, he ran into an invisible barrier. Ahiga's expression changed as his nose crumpled and his knees buckled. Almost falling to the floor he stumbled backward and exclaimed.

"Come on. You could have warned me." Ahiga's voice was almost drowned out by the laughter of Chase and Angela. "Ha. Ha. Ha. You guys are hilarious. I think I might have broken my nose."

"I thought that technology was unattainable." The three friends took notice of the voice. Leaning against the rear of the Packard Six, stood Leonard, a wide grin on his face. "The last time I saw you, you told me that couldn't be done."

Chase walked across the garage, and Ahiga winced as his friend approached the invisible wall. Instead of smacking into the barrier, though, Rex moved as if impeded by nothing. George reached out with his hand and extended his fingers, but they would not pass. He leaned his ample frame against the hidden obstruction, an awe inspired look on his face.

"They didn't tell me you had come too." Chase hugged his middle aged mentor before continuing. "I'm sorry I haven't been into the city for a while. I've gotten so engrossed in my work out here that I…"

"Don't worry about it. We've been busy too." Leonard motioned toward Chief and Angela. "When George told me he was making the trip out I asked if I could tag along."

"Excuse me. George wasn't taking a trip anywhere." Angela scowled as she corrected Leonard. "We made the trip so that I could invite Chase to the ceremony for the General. You two are tagging along with me."

"I stand corrected." Leonard laughed as he moved to the force field, testing it. "Tell me how this is possible and why you can walk right through it."

"That's what I've been trying to do." Chase moved past the other three before continuing. "It's going to be hard to explain, but before I do, you have to see this."

Rex had retrieved a lockbox from under a long wooden table, and his nimble fingers worked the combination. Opening the box, he pulled an article out, and then moved back toward the other three. He removed a small sheath from the item, revealing it to be a syringe, before speaking.

"Do you mind Leonard?"

"If you mean that you'd like to stab me with that needle then I do mind. I mind a lot." Angela squealed as the silver haired man used her to shield himself.

"Come on. I'm not going to stab you with it ya big baby." Chase waved the syringe in a stabbing motion. "I'm just gonna give you a little pinch."

"No way. No how." Leonard cowered behind Angela Ahiga as both Chief and Rex howled with laughter. "Unless I'm almost dead, I don't do needles."

"Fine. Chief. Do you mind?"

"Using my wife as a human shield," George said. "I bet if he asked to shoot you in the foot you'd let him try that."

"I am much less fearful of guns than needles. You are correct."

Everyone laughed as Chief rolled up the sleeve to his sweater, revealing a muscular arm. Choosing a vein would be easy as the blue/green vesicles were prolific under his skin. Chase picked a large example, and administered the contents of the syringe.

"OK Chief, follow me."

Chase walked back toward the work bench, throwing the plunger in a waste receptacle.

"Nope. You got me on that once. I'm no dummy." Chief said.

"Be as careful as you want." Chase spoke with his back turned as he worked the controls to a panel on the wall.

George hesitated as he moved forward, testing the area he knew the invisible field to inhabit. He met no resistance, though, and approached Chase, his movements unhindered. A large smile covered his face as he turned to the others.

"I love party tricks."

"Now, put on those gloves, go back over and pick up that tire iron and throw it at me." Chase said without looking up from his work.

George obeyed, put on the gloves, moved unimpeded across the garage, and picked up the iron. He looked at his wife and Leonard, who shrugged his shoulders, then scratched his head. Pulling back, Ahiga threw the tool with all his might. It reached the area of the field, and bounced off, clanging on the concrete floor.

THE SENTINEL

"Ok, so the tire iron can't go through it, and whatever you gave George made him able to go through it. Are you going to explain this to us now?" Angela didn't always like the way Rex tried to drag things out.

"Yep. Chief, take off the gloves, pick up the iron and bring it over here." Chase finished what he was doing, and turned, leaning against the workbench.

George picked up the tire iron as ordered, passed through the barrier with no complications, and brought it to Chase. Holding out the tool he attempted to hand it to Rex.

"Here you go man."

"Leonard, do me a favor and step away from Angela for a minute." Chase nodded as he took the tire iron from his friend, and held it. "I'm going to throw this at you, OK?"

"Well, it's not going to get through the field right?" Leonard said.

"What do you think?"

"Just throw it."

Chase laughed as he tossed the tire iron underhanded in the direction of the older man. The other three watched in anticipation as the tool moved through the air. As it neared, Leonard winced, but expected the force field to do its job. Then, the heavy metal object floated through the barrier and hit him in the nose. Chase and Ahiga guffawed as their superior in The Organization held his face in his hands. Angela seemed annoyed at the display and reached out, testing the invisible shield again. It was still in place, however, and her hand did not pass.

"So now that you've had your fun can you tell us how this works? It wasn't that long ago you told me the math was impossible." Leonard stood; his head leaned back, while attending to a bloody nose. "Also, can I get a vial of that stuff for the Plan CF guys?"

"I already sent the formula to the lab. The CF guys should be getting it soon if they haven't already." Chase laughed before continuing.

"I'm sorry guys, but I've always found demonstration to be the quickest way to facilitate learning. Here comes the boring part." Chase walked toward where the barrier met the physical wall and stood. "First of all, I abused myself with the math for a year. I don't know who Hoff had working for him, but they must have been incredible. Without Bobby's equation, though, I just couldn't find a way to make the scalar energy work the way I wanted."

"So you've figured out his equation?" Angela asked.

"No, not at all," Chase said. "One day, though, I was working with my dad on this retractable wall, and we were discussing quantum physics..."

"Same thing my dad and I talk about," George mused.

"Yeah, well, we were talking about quantum physics, and then he reminded me of something he and Bobby had determined."

"Gravity doesn't exist," Leonard said.

"Yep, which in itself, wasn't that helpful, but when I put it in the context of what I had asked Bobby to do, I had a revelation. He had solved large portions of the E^8 problem by assuming it didn't exist, and had then extrapolated his equation from that."

"So you've figured out the equation." Angela said.

"No, I haven't." Chase took a deep breath before continuing. "I began working on the E^8 problem, and realized a few things right away. One was that Bobby was a certifiable genius. Two was that I still couldn't make the calculations to run a moving object, or create antenna like they did on Hoff's ship. The third was that a very special kind of iron is needed to make the energy possible. I don't know if Hoff knew this, or if he just got lucky."

"I'm lost."

"Me too."

"That's why we did these quick experiments. Why do you think the tire iron acted the way it acted?"

"Because of what you injected into George?" Angela said as she raised her eyebrow.

"You're on the right track. I didn't inject anything into the tire iron, though, so why did it hit Leonard in the face when I tossed it?"

Leonard stood, still holding his nose, and the three shared looks before he spoke.

"I think it's safe to assume that we don't know."

"I've begun calling this special iron Castleinium. It is an isotope of the normal element, but something about its makeup causes it to behave in odd ways. If you'll remember I asked for one ton of the stuff from the Arizona mine." Chase paused as Leonard nodded his head. "Well, I took a page from the Dietrich Hoff handbook and built a stationary antenna from it."

"Wait a minute. I thought you said that you couldn't do the calculations." George said.

"No, I said that I couldn't do the calculations that would make it possible to make scalar energy mobile. It took me almost a month, but after I built the receiver here, I finished the math, and now live in the first scalar powered domicile."

"So a massive scalar weapon is still possible?" Angela said, her voice tinged with fear.

"It's possible, but we're certain Hoff killed all the men who worked on his project." Leonard said.

"Until just now, I was the only person who knew about Castleinium. Whereas before I believed the magnetic field played a large part in functionality of a weapon, I now know it to be in conjunction with the metal."

"So we didn't do anything when we blew up those other weapons?" George asked.

"Well, we didn't do as much as we theorized, or in the way we theorized it."

"I don't think I ever theorized anything." Everyone laughed at George's observation. "You have to start speaking English for me man."

"So changing the magnetic field does change the math, and because of that, the chances of someone building another large scale weapon are astronomical. If you couple that with the chance that someone else has discovered Castleinium, the odds become even more stacked. We should be just fine, for now."

"So talk to me about our experiments here." Leonard said.

"What I've been able to do is to isolate Castleinium and mix it into an injectable solution. When I put it into Chief's bloodstream he was able to penetrate the shield."

"How did that work with the tire iron then?" asked Angela.

"Yeah, and how long does it last?" asked Chief.

"So far, I've injected myself once and it still works. It hasn't seemed to decay at all. We'll see more trials when the Plan CF guys get a hold of it." Chase answered his best friend's question first. "I also invented these one-time use syrettes."

"The same as a morphine syrette." Chief grabbed a handful off the nearby workbench and stuck them in his pocket. "In case you ask me to watch your place or something."

"Don't go handing my house key out to everyone." Chase laughed before continuing. "As far as the tire iron goes, anything you are touching or holding seems to come through the field. Once Chief and I had touched it, something about the oils in our skin affects the other object. I haven't studied it as much as I'd like yet, because I have so much other work to do, but that tire iron will pass through the force field until the oils from our skin cease to give it the ability."

"So you're just skipping to human trials on the syrettes?" Leonard asked.

"It's pretty much just an iron and saline solution. It might need to be modified to work in different men, but the solution itself is pretty benign." Chase gave a succinct answer and the others seemed to accept his assessment.

"I guess the reason you don't have a furnace or boiler or wood stove out here," Angela gestured around the room, "is because you're using scalar heat?"

"See those light fixtures on all the walls and the ceiling?" Chase motioned around himself and the three others took notice of the room. "I made all of those myself. They are a combination of heat and light using scalar power. The amazing thing is that I don't need any wires to connect any of it."

"Could you do this all over the world?" Leonard asked.

"I can do this anywhere that is stationary."

"If you had Bobby's equation could you jump that hurdle?" Angela asked.

"I believe I could."

"So then you could fly to the moon, through the ocean, and travel through time."

"I could do all of those things. Right now, in theory, I could still travel through time."

"You could? How? I thought you said the energy couldn't move?" Leonard's tone was incredulous.

"Well, if we want to get technical, you can stay in one spot, and bend time around yourself. The calculations would be immense, and I don't know how long it would take me to do them. For a comparison, though, it took me almost two weeks to figure out the lights in here. Time travel is about 10^{27} times as difficult."

"I'm guessing that's a huge number." George flashed his pearly white grin.

"That's understating it buddy. That number is one octillion." Chase scratched the stubble on his chin before continuing. "I mean, if there were a million other guys just like me working on the problem we could solve it in three-hundred and eighty-five quintillion years."

"But if you solved it, the power is available?" Laughter by all met Leonard's question.

"Yeah, I suppose. You'd have to calculate the power consumption, and that's in the googol of joules, but scalar energy is, in theory, limitless. Forward in time is pretty easy, too. We would just speed you up until those around you had moved ahead a certain amount of time, then slow you back to a stop. It's like a movie reel. Backward in time is a lot more difficult."

"It's not like a movie reel?" Angela inquired.

"No, and this is just me talking, but it would take something called a wormhole moving through a multiverse. At least that's my idea."

"Lost again."

"Me too."

"Can you explain that last part?" Leonard prodded for more information.

"I'm not sure why we're even talking about this. A multiverse is the idea that our universe is one of many, and that it is also being mirrored by others. If you were to create a tear in space time, say, when you passed the speed of light, you could travel to another portion of the multiverse, and then back through the tear, or wormhole. You would not age much going forward, and backward would be almost instant."

"So if someone had torn space time seventeen million years ago we could travel back through the hole?"

"I guess Leonard. I can't imagine a machine that would keep our bodies from flying apart, and I wouldn't know how to do the calculations to make sure you'd appear in the right year. Also, I don't know how we could calculate where the opening in time would be. The math is astounding. For now, we can..."

"Sorry," George interrupted. "So if you were to tear a hole in space time in this room, you could jump through it, end up in the future, then turn around and jump back through it and be here?"

"No, you would be torn to pieces, but if you had some sort of protection..." Chase paused as he thought. "Yeah, that could work, though you might be traveling to a different part of the multiverse. You might not stay in our timeline. It's conceivable you would jump through a wormhole, and meet your alternate self in a different universe."

"You're saying that the power to do this exists within scalar energy?" Leonard asked again.

"Yes, but, again, the math is not even imaginable for us. Maybe if we had Bobby's formula and used the theory of everything to its potential we could understand all of these things, but we don't, so we can't." Chase's tone had shifted to annoyance, so the others stopped pressing.

"I tell you what kid, you should be writing fiction books about this stuff. Changing the subject, though, I have something for you." Leonard pulled a piece of paper from his pocket and handed it to Chase.

Rex unfolded the cardstock and studied its contents. His brow furrowed as he read and the others watched. A few seconds passed, and Chase's demeanor soured.

"Is this an order?"

"I'm afraid that it is. Your friends and I have been tracking some disturbing events throughout the world, and since you haven't been in contact for some time, the General needs to see you in person." Leonard said.

"Why can't I just come to his office? Why do I have to come to this ball, or awards ceremony, or whatever this is?" Chase was angry and he let it show. "I have a lot of work to do here. We can change the world, but I have to be able to work."

"Don't be a sourpuss." Angela was excited and made no attempt at hiding it.

"Did you know about this?" Chase held the General's letter in the air.

"Nope. I wanted you to come out with us and have a good time because we love you, but since you're such a stick in the mud, I guess I'll settle for you being ordered to go." An ear to ear smile graced her face as she clapped her hands together once and hopped up and down. "Sarah will be so excited. I've gone on and on about you to her Chase so you can't let me down. I've told her all about…"

"This is a nightmare." Chase rubbed his eyes as Angela bubbled on in the background.

"Since when is going out with a beautiful woman a nightmare?" Chief put a heavy arm around his friend. "We'll double date. This'll be fun."

"It'll be something. That's for sure."

Chase listened as Angela brimmed with details of the party. She listed who was attending and the evening's scheduled menu. Leonard and Chief laughed as they enjoyed

Rex's discomfort. Sarah was going to be delighted to meet him and he was going to love her and they were going to have the greatest of times, and the information never seemed to stop. At least he wouldn't have to make any plans of his own.

****

2.

He had worked as a busboy many times before, but the young man despised his current assignment. Day after day he reported to work and suffered in silence through the racist brow beatings given by his co-workers. The owners of the small catering business were a kind older couple, and he liked them. They, however, seemed ignorant to the transparent racism of their employees.

"Hey Nip." He cringed as a repeat offender walked in the employee entrance, flanked by another tormentor.

"Hey Tommy. I've asked you not to call me that."

"Oh, we're sorry Buddhahead. It's a lot easier than your real name, though. What is it? Wang Dong Ping Pong Chong?" The two teenage boys cackled as they congratulated each other with slaps on the back.

"First, I'm Catholic, not Buddhist. Second, I'm a Boston native just like you two Gai-jin's. Third, my name is Larry, and you know that Carl."

"OK, first, your name is Fuji Samurai Tokyo. Second, if you want to slur someone in America you have to use English. And third of all, you have slanty eyes." Tommy used his fingers to pull his eyelids to the side and mocked Larry while he danced around the employee room to the delight of Carl. "Ohhhhhh. Sank you. Sank you so much." Carl howled louder as Larry's face grew red with rage.

"Laurence? Laurence, are you back there?"

"Yeah Mrs. Prepot." Larry answered the call of the matriarch while glaring at the now complacent Tommy. "We're in the busser's break room getting ready for work."

"Excellent, Laurence. That's excellent."

Linda Prepot had spent her entire life in the service of others, but the small catering business she and her husband now owned would be her last. Arthritic gnarled fingers were a testament to her seventy-five years and osteoporosis bowed the old woman's back. Her husband, David, wasn't an ideal picture of health either. They ran a successful business, however, and since she had no children of her own she often treated the younger busboys like she were their grandmother.

"Are you fellas ready for a busy evening tonight?"

"Yes, Mrs. Prepot." All three teenagers replied in unison.

"Excellent. Excellent. Try to stay ahead of things out there boys. I want water glasses full and dishes cleared. Remember, Thomas and Carl, to watch Laurence. He knows what needs to get done and when to do it. Tonight is just a warm-up for the big one tomorrow."

Larry cringed at the praise from the woman. He knew the other two would be more incensed than usual after she lauded his efforts. He also cringed at the work ahead. Tonight, as she alluded, would be easy. A banquet of two hundred guests wouldn't fill a quarter of the dining area. Tomorrow night, however, would be different. He would have to work like a dog then, as the scheduled ceremony had an invitation list of nine-hundred.

"Oh Laurence. Laurence." Tommy mocked their employer in a high pitched voice as she had left the small break room. "I wish I were a thousand years younger so I could ravage your gorgeous little yellow body. I think..."

Larry acted on instinct rather than the self-control he had shown for months. Moving with more speed and precision than either of the other young men had ever seen, he removed a switch blade from his back pocket, grabbed Tommy by the collar of his button down shirt, and pinned the larger boy against the wall. Bringing his knee into an uncomfortable position near the tormentor's groin he also pressed the sharpened steel blade against Tommy's pale white neck.

"You know something Tommy," he said. "Less than a quarter inch away from the tip of my blade is your jugular vein. If I were to have an accident, slip and nick that vein, you would bleed to death right here on the floor before anyone could help."

Larry felt something warm on his knee and without averting his eyes from the terrified coworker addressed Carl.

"You see that Carl. I push back just a little and your big bad friend here pisses in his pants. It's gonna be a long night at work squishin around in your piss pants. I think I'll call you Polly from now on. Polly Pissy Pants. Whatya think of that name Carl?" Larry looked at his other tormentor who stood frozen a few feet away. He hadn't moved an inch to help the other racist busser. "Focus Carl. I said, whatya think?"

"I, I, I, I, I don't know Larry. W,w,w,w,what do you w,w,w,w,want m,m,m,m,me to s,s,s,s,s,say."

"T,t,t,t,t,t,talk much Carl? You've got to be kidding me with this garbage." Larry laughed in a tone that chilled the other two to their bones. "So from now on we have Polly and Stutters. You guys like your new names?" Neither boy responded to the question so Larry shouted. "I said do you like your new names."

"Yes sir."

"Y,y,y,y,y,y,yessssssssssssir."

"Unbelievable." Larry released his grip on the larger of the two offenders and returned the blade to its place in his pocket with deft precision. "You're gonna want to throw an apron on over those pants Polly."

Larry turned and left the room feeling quite satisfied with how the night had begun. He entered the dining area as if nothing had happened and started setting up for the evening. They had done most of the preparatory work the night before, but he went about some of the last minute details. As he began setting butter and bread baskets down on the tables his two coworkers emerged from the back and began to help. He flashed a fiendish grin as he relished the fact neither could look him in the eye.

"I don't know why I didn't do that months ago."

Larry spoke out loud to himself, but he knew the reason, and though accosting the two young men had felt good, he knew it to be the wrong strategy. He had strict orders to keep a low profile, and the role of submissive Japanese American was his best play. The past was the past, though, and he would use his newfound respect at work to his advantage.

****

3.

Coarse sand from the platinum white beach seemed to flow like liquid between his toes. He sipped on an ice cold rumrunner and enjoyed the tropical breeze wafting across his face. Shifting his weight in the beach chair, he pulled his feet from the sand and let out a contented sigh. A stunning woman moved in his direction and he blinked as she stole his attention from the blue green beauty that was the ocean.

Her long blond hair fell around bronzed shoulders and finished in curls near two dimples nestled in the small of her back. She wore a tight white bikini that left little to the imagination and his eyes followed the ample curves of her body as she neared. He sipped again from the island concoction while being mesmerized by her lithe legs. Nothing could be more perfect than this moment.

"I've been watching you all morning, but was too shy to say hello." Her translucent green eyes shone as she toed the sand near his beach chair.

"Hello, my darling." He stood with a purpose, brushing the silicates from his tanned lean frame. As her eyes followed his movements he took the wonderful hand she offered and kissed it. "I've loved you my entire life."

"Oh my." She giggled while covering her mouth with the other hand. "I don't know how but I've always loved you too. You're the man of my dreams…"

He awoke with a start. Instead of a beautiful blond woman, solitude now accompanied him. A crack in the eggshell white ceiling above seemed to stare at him, and he worked to will his ancient bones from bed. Time catches everyone and at his age he should have been happy to be alive and sane.

Still, though, the recurring vision he had night after night haunted his very existence. Every morning after the dream he would enter his small dark kitchen and fix breakfast. Even ten years prior the task would have taken him fifteen minutes, but now lasted an hour.

"I have to take a dad gum nap after eating breakfast." He spoke to himself while clearing the table. "When I was twenty I could climb mountains."

He exited the kitchen and lowered himself into the medical lift chair. Pushing the button to his right the Ameriglide moved on a gradual plane from the upright to seated position. It was already nine o'clock in the morning and flipping on the thirty-two-inch television no longer consisted of flipping anything. Instead he pushed a button on a controller and pictures began showing on the screen.

"Nine o'clock huh? I guess I'll start out by checking on the market."

The old man preferred to read the newspaper, but since he had reached the age of ninety his eyes had failed to the point he could no longer make out the words. Even when his only friend made every effort to help he had still failed. On the table to his right sat an electronic device given him the year before. On it, he could zoom in close enough to still be able to read the paper. Technology would never cease to amaze him, even though he had spearheaded technological masterpieces his entire productive life.

"I don't feel like messing with that thing right now Felix." A tiny Pomeranian jumped onto his lap and nestled in, between his legs. He stroked its matted brown and black fur while switching channels on the television. "You know Felix, I can't remember what channel it is that I watch for market news." He laughed at his failing memory. At his age there wasn't much he could do about it. "Oh well. I guess we'll stop here."

The little dog's ears perked up as the old man had stopped on a replay of the Westminster Dog Show. A parade of miniature dogs just like his Felix ran in a circle around the arena. He watched in fascination as the judge picked a few animals from the group and then set them on a table.

"What do you think he's doing to those little doggies? Huh pooch?" He smiled as his companion nestled back into the crease in his sweatpants. "I think I'll watch this for a while. Whatya say we make you a show dog?"

****

4.

Time had dragged the entire evening. Sometimes, like tomorrow night, the work would keep the three men busy. Tonight, though, the diminutive crowd wasn't even enough work for one bus boy, let alone three. Larry stood in the back of the room and puffed on a Lucky Strike while he watched the two others work. His job had been simple tonight, as Polly and Stutters had increased their productivity tenfold.

Five servers worked the party as well, and he wondered how much money they made. Earlier in the year the United States Congress had passed a bill, and he had received a wage increase from fifteen to twenty-five cents per hour. At the time, he had celebrated, but over the course of several shifts he noticed that nobody else seemed to revel in the raise. It figured the kind older couple would be racist as well, they just hid it better.

Larry yawned, stretched his arms to the sky, and then brought the left down to pat his belly. The old woman sure could cook. Dinner had been an appetizer of clam chowder, followed by pot roast with mashed potatoes, green beans, and carrots. The guests' current dish consisted of Prepot's famous Boston Cream Pie which they ate while being regaled by a funny man at the head of the room. Larry paid the diminutive character little mind and instead lit another cigarette. Inhaling, he savored the sweet tobacco smoke filling his lungs.

"Hello Itsuo. Do you mind?"

Without moving his eyes from the performer ahead he offered his Zippo to the woman. She leaned over with grace and lit the thin tobacco product. A few seconds passed before she spoke again.

"Do you know who I am?"

"I do."

"Perhaps you could tell me about your name?"

"Itsuo was my father's name." He buried his left hand deep into the pocket of his jeans as it failed to stop shaking. "Translated into English it means 'fifth male.'"

Larry's father had been the fifth of twelve male siblings born in the harbor town of Yohohama, Japan. He had married Larry's mother in 1913, and a short time thereafter she had bore him a son. The young Japanese man had lied to the boys earlier about being born in Boston. When he had been two months old his father had died in a tragic accident. His mother, being widowed at such a young age, had fallen in love a short time later. In itself, that was not odd. No one presumed young women should fend for themselves, but she had done something nobody expected. His mother had fallen in love with a white man.

"Very good Haruko. Don't be afraid of me." Her voice was as beautiful as a songbird's. "I will ask you questions, and you will have the answers. Now, tell me about your real name."

"Haruko means 'First Born,'" Larry said. "I was the first born son of Itsuo and Tamiko Nishizawa."

"Thank you Haruko. Tell me about your mother."

"My mother's name means 'most beautiful child.' She married my stepfather a short time after my birth, and they brought me here to live in Boston. He died when I was six, and now my mother works herself to death in the fish packing plant. You are Izanami?" Larry's voice quivered as he showed the name proper reverence.

"I am." She said. "I trust you Haruko, or would you prefer me to call you Larry?"

"Larry would be best ma'am." He still had not looked at her face. "Nobody calls me Haruko."

"It's a shame. To have such a noble name and have it replaced with Larry." Her tone became serious. "Are you prepared for action Larry?"

"I am ready and willing to do anything you request of me."

"Good. Good." She smiled, showing a perfect compendium of teeth as she slipped a piece of paper into his front pants pocket. Without stopping the momentum of her hand she grasped his manhood while whispering in his ear. "I hope we meet again under different circumstances. You're cute."

Then, as fast as she had appeared, Izanami left. Larry removed his left hand from his pocket and both upper appendages shook as he lit another cigarette. Cursing and muttering to himself he grabbed an apron from the nearby cart to hide his growing erection. Minutes passed as he reveled in the calming effects of the tobacco. He pulled out the folded piece of paper and read it. All his preparation and training were about to be tested and a wave of excitement mixed with anticipation coursed through his body.

"Laurence honey. Laurence. Do you think you could take the garbage in the kitchen out for me please?"

"Yes, Mrs. Prepot."

"Thank you honey."

"No problem," he said before murmuring under his breath. "I don't have much time left trapped in this stink hole."

****

5.

"How is it possible my men have a combined IQ of almost three hundred and fifty, but neither of you can work a bow tie?" Lucille Chase finished tying the formal wear and took a step back from her only son. "You are going to be the talk of the girls tonight."

"Ugh." Chase groaned at the thought of young women giggling and hiding their faces to speak to one another. "I just want to get in and get out mom. I don't think this monkey suit is even necessary."

"This is a black tie event Edward." Luce smiled as she brushed some nonexistent lint from her son's lapel. "You can't just show up in your dingy old mechanic's outfit."

"I don't see a thing wrong with cavorting around in my dingy old mechanic's coveralls." Chase flashed his brilliant white grin as Luce shook her head.

"The President of the United States is going to be there, not to mention Angela informed me you agreed to meet a certain young lady," she said.

"Believe me mom," Rex's smile vanished. "I am not out looking for a woman to settle down and make babies with. I have too much going on right now with my work. I'm on the cusp of some fantastic things. You should..."

"I'm your mother Edward," she interrupted. "You don't have to lecture me about how much work you have to do. Remember, I was a professional in my early twenties once too." His mother smiled and winked at him as she moved from the parlor into the kitchen area. She was a beautiful woman in her forties, but looked to be in her twenties. Her long brownish red hair curled just below her shoulders, which still held the muscular lines of her youth. Their new home on the St. Charles

River had made a daily regimen of rowing a breeze. Chase followed her into the open kitchen area as she continued. "You can't live your life under a rock though honey. It'll be good for you to get out there and meet a few people."

"But I don't want to meet any people mom." Chase sighed as he unwrapped a caramel. "I just want to be left alone."

"Hogwash," Luce said. "You have always been, and will always be, a social creature. Locking yourself up and letting that mind of yours rehash the events of a year and a half ago won't do you a darn bit of good."

"It just won't leave mom. I can't get it out." Rex fiddled with the caramel wrapper in between his thumbs as his mother approached and brushed the hair from his eyes.

"You've always had a kind heart Edward," her voice soothed the young man. "If you don't ever let anyone else in, how can it heal?"

"I don't know mom. I don't know."

Just as Rex finished his sentence the front door flew open and Alexei Chase hurried to enter. A cold wind rushed through the house as he kicked the snow from his boots and loosed the scarf around his neck.

"The wind chill out there has to be negative one hundred and twenty," Alexei exaggerated, and as he turned, an enormous smile crossed his face. "Rex, I didn't see the Six out front?"

"Nah dad. I came in on the runabout."

"On the river?"

"I told him he was insane. I can't believe the ice didn't beat the hull to pieces," Luce said.

"The big boats moving up and down the river have kept it pretty clear. I didn't have much of a problem at all. I mean, it was cold, but I think I have a better chance of getting stuck out in the snow in the Packard."

"I suppose you have a point." Alexei had removed his winter clothing, and now stood with his family. "You should ride with us to the ceremony, though. We can't have you meeting Sarah looking like a homeless man who lives on his little boat."

"So you're in on this too?" Chase rolled his eyes.

"I'm not in on anything. I've met the young lady a few times and she's pleasant, charming, and smart." Alexei leaned closer to Rex. "She might even give you a run for your money."

"If it's all the same to you dad, I'd rather just go in the runabout. I have the top on and everything, it isn't all that cold," Chase lied. "I'm told the weather should be letting up at any time. The clouds should be blowing over and the winds dying down."

"I'll believe that when I see it." Lucille Chase shrugged her shoulders and clutched herself. "That wind chills me to the bone. When do we need to leave Alexei?"

"In an hour or so."

"I need to finish up then." Luce approached Rex and kissed him on the cheek. "This is the last thing I'll say about it Edward. Promise me you'll keep an open mind."

"She can't be that ugly mom." Chase smiled from ear to ear and winced as his mother smacked him in the arm.

"Be nice. It's good to see you smile though dear."

Alexei watched his wife leave the room and Rex's smile was almost an embarrassed one. After all their years of marriage it was still apparent the elder Chase adored her. Clearing his throat Rex broke the short silence.

"So Dad, how do you like the new place?"

"Like it? I love it." Alexei patted his son on the shoulder as he moved toward the kitchen. "Shall we have a drink?"

"Sure."

Alexei removed a bottle of Wild Turkey 101 from the cabinet over the sink and began pouring it into two glasses.

"I'm having an Old Fashioned. What's your fancy son?"

"I'll just take mine neat Dad."

"Neat? You don't even mess with ice cubes anymore huh?"

"No sir. To be honest, I didn't have a means of refrigeration at my place for a long time. I kinda got used to it."

Alexei laughed as he finished mixing his cocktail. Turning, he handed the amber colored liquor to his son who downed the three ounces.

"Just like that. Goodness gracious boy, I haven't even taken a drink of mine yet." Before Chase knew it his father had grabbed the bottle and poured another three fingers into the glass. "Are you that nervous?"

"I'd be lying if I said I wasn't." Rex attempted to change the subject. "Anyway, so the new house is good?"

"It's fine to be nervous." Alexei's smile was easy and genuine. "You'll be just fine. The new house is amazing though. Patrick's generosity in bequeathing it to us is amazing, and we have taken full advantage of the amenities. I hate to think how much money that man must have to just give away a couple of houses."

"He's also funding my work." Chase took another sip of his drink.

"Of course." Alexei sipped his cocktail before replying. "I spoke to The General today and he tells me you've proved time travel possible?"

"No I haven't." Chase furrowed his brow. "I don't understand the obsession with this."

"Nobody is obsessed son." Alexei said before laughing and pouring himself another drink. "It's kind of a big deal if you've proven time travel to be possible, though."

"Well, someone misinformed you then." The annoyance was evident in Rex's reply. "I know that it's possible, and I know how to prove it, but the proof would take me an infinite number of years."

"But the power exists, and the science exists?"

"It's all in theory dad. It's all in theory."

Chase finished his second drink and placed the empty glass on the counter.

"I've gotta get moving or I won't be on time. I'll see ya there pops."

"We'll see you in a few."

☆☆☆☆☆☆☆☆☆☆☆☆☆☆☆☆☆☆

6.

George shivered as he stood on the front porch of Sarah's home, watching a myriad of vehicles make their way toward Harvard Square. He and Angela had stopped to pick up his wife's best friend, but he had grown tired of waiting indoors. It was too hot inside, and the wind outside had died down, making the near zero temperatures tolerable.

Clouds had given way to clear skies which allowed the stars to twinkle overhead. George's breath crystallized in the air and seemed to be suspended in the frigid winter atmosphere. Orion the Hunter was visible and he closed his eyes, remembering all the different times and places he had seen the constellation. It comforted him knowing that no matter what was going on in the world, the stars paid no mind.

Chief startled from his reverie as a door inside slammed and he heard the two women giggling. Angela and Sarah had split a bottle of champagne, and were a little tipsy. He smiled as he could see them through the large picture window. It wasn't often his wife let her guard down like this, and as he opened the front door, he appreciated that she was having fun.

"Angela Ahiga. I do believe you are drunk."

Both women laughed as they helped one another with their coats.

"I know, I'm such a lightweight." Angela wore a long black dress with a deep v-neck that cut between her breasts. George eyed her as she continued. "Just one more drink the rest of the night. OK?"

"I'm not babysitting you."

"Me neither."

All three laughed in unison as George held the door for the two women.

"I am going to be the envy of every man there." Chief closed the door behind him as they descended the front stairs. "Walking in with the two of you on my arms is like hitting the jackpot."

"If you play your cards right you might hit the jackpot later." Angela attempted to deliver the private message in a whisper, but was neither quiet, nor anywhere near her husband's ear.

"Gross." Sarah wrinkled her nose as they walked down the sidewalk. "You two can keep that stuff to yourself. George. Would you mind if we took my car tonight? I haven't driven it in a while and it could use the work."

"You've got it."

George's enthusiasm was noticeable as they approached the 1931 Marmon 16. He marveled at the deep maroon vehicle he couldn't dream of affording, and opened the rear suicide door for the women. Sarah and Angela laughed as they entered the automobile, but George no longer paid them any mind. He closed the door behind the girls and made his way to the driver's seat.

Skilled craftsman had made the vehicle's seats from the softest leather Chief had ever felt in his life. Though the two women were making an awful racket a few feet away, all he could hear was the roar of the sixteen cylinder engine coming to life and the deep throaty rumble of its exhaust. It wasn't every day he would have an opportunity like this. Without realizing it, he had been sitting, listening to the engine for more than a minute when Sarah snapped him from his daydream.

"George. George." Sarah laughed as she yelled his name. "She's a V16 with two hundred horsepower, but you've gotta put her in gear and give her some gas."

THE SENTINEL

The trio laughed in unison as George worked the three speed selective transmission. Both women giggled and told stories as Ahiga guided the vehicle through traffic. He engrossed himself in the experience of driving the 16 cylinder beast, and unlike his passengers, could think of nothing else. A marvelous machine always intrigued him and after ten minutes on the road he adjusted the rearview mirror and spoke to the women in the back.

"How in the world did you get ahold of a car like this anyway? Nobody, and I mean nobody, has a Marmon."

"Well, my daddy had a lot of money and just happened to know Colonel Marmon during the Great War. I believe he even gave the colonel a loan. So when it came time for a car, I got a Marmon."

"That seems reasonable." George said. It seemed like someone gave all his friends a car. "Angela hasn't ever told me where your father lives, or what he does."

"Honey. Be polite," Angela said.

"It's ok," Sarah replied. "He died a little over a year ago. He was often away from home for long periods of time, and one day one of his aides just reported to me that he died. My mother passed when I was young and nannies raised me anyway. He didn't even have a funeral."

"I'm sorry to hear that." George's voice was solemn as he yielded to oncoming traffic in order to make a left-hand turn. The Marmon's powerful engine pushed the vehicle through a narrow space as Chief gave it an ample supply of gasoline. "Can I give you a quick word of advice, though?"

"I'm always willing to listen to advice." Sarah's tone was receptive.

"Rex is my best friend, and he's great, and I love him, but I wouldn't talk about your dad's death tonight."

"As if that's how she would introduce herself." Angela scoffed as she teased her husband. "Hello, my name is Sarah, and my dad is dead."

"That's not what I meant."

"I know you didn't George." Sarah giggled at Angela's joke. "I didn't even know my father all that well. I know about Mary Elizabeth, and I know she was killed right down the street from where I live, and I know about Bobby Poppen. I don't plan on discussing any of that. This is a get to know you evening."

"OK, I'm glad that's settled because we're here already." he clapped his hands as he made the announcement. Two young men opened the doors for the women as Chief handed the keys to a young Asian man, along with a twenty dollar bill. "Keep it close my man. It's cold out tonight."

✱✱✱✱✱✱✱✱✱✱✱✱✱✱✱✱✱✱

7.

"Laurence. Laurence."

Mrs. Prepot's voice snapped the young man from his trance.

"What?" Larry responded in an annoyed tone.

"You seem distracted honey. Most days you would have all the setup prep done already. I need you to be doing your very best tonight. The President is here."

"It's still five minutes before my shift even starts," Larry said, his voice tinged with anger. "Why don't you worry about those two delinquents who are always late and leave me alone?"

"Well, I never." Mrs. Prepot covered her heart with her hand and blinked hard once. She considered another question for her premiere busboy, but thought better of it as he gave her an icy glare. She continued in an almost sheepish tone. "Laurence. In five minutes, I would be very pleased if you would get all the setup prep work finished and then report to the front to help park cars."

"Yes ma'am. I'm sorry ma'am. I didn't get much sleep last night." His tone softened and he looked toward the floor.

"That's ok honey. We all have a bad day every once in a while." The old woman ruffled the young man's hair with her gnarled fingers before turning to leave. "Don't forget to grab your coat before you report out front. It is cold outside."

Larry had arrived at work fifteen minutes early, as was his custom, hung his coat, and sat down in a corner of the breakroom. Mrs. Prepot had been correct. Most nights he would have punched in and gone straight to work, but tonight he had a lot of things on his mind. Now, though, it occurred to him that perhaps he should act as normal as possible.

Begrudgingly he stood to exit the room, but as he did the back door opened. Tommy and Carl burst through the opening, slamming the door behind them. Various garments covered both young men from head to toe, except for one tiny horizontal slit through which to see. They began shucking their coats and shaking off the chill, not expecting anyone else to be around.

"Good evening boys." Larry's voice pierced the air like a knife. "I do believe you're even a couple minutes early tonight."

The pair froze in place and turned to meet the sinister gaze of their coworker.

"H,h,h,h,hey L,L,L,Larry. H,h,h,h, how's it going?" Carl said.

"Stutters." You could hear the smile in the young Asian man's voice. "I thought maybe that was going to be a one-time thing. You wetting your pants too, Polly?"

"No." Anger bubbled in Tommy's voice.

Larry continued to smile but closed the gap between himself and the larger man. Grabbing his former tormentor's testicles with his left hand while pinning him to the wall with his right, he once again felt the warm liquid. He could get used to this kind of control over people.

"That's what I thought Polly." Larry released his grip. "Mrs. Prepot wants me to go outside and help park cars. You guys are in here by yourselves tonight."

"B,b,b,b, but y,y,y,y, you usually s,s,s,s,set everything up." Carl said.

"Don't be a couple of crybabies. I did just about everything last night anyway. All you have left to do is the server alley stuff, water, and butter. I'm not setting up anymore tonight. You two are on your own."

"That's not what Mrs. Prepot told me." All three boys turned to see one of the waitresses standing in front of the entrance to the server alley. She spoke again in a thick Bostonian accent. "What are you guys doing in here anyway? I can't even get started until you get this prep done."

"Maybe you should mind your own business before I cut out your heart and eat it in front of everyone." The words brought a gasp from the other two boys, but the surly waitress took it in stride.

"Look, I don't care what kind of bad night you've been having. We have work to get done out here and unless you want me to get Mrs. Prepot, I suggest you get to it."

A fury bubbled inside Larry as he approached the woman, menace in his eyes. His plan had been to play it slow tonight, but now his temper had the best of him. He seized her arm, pinned her to the wall by the neck, and growled in her ear.

"I told you I'd have your heart."

"Please." Her voice exuded calm. "I grew up in Southie with five brothers."

Larry felt the sharp point of a blade dig into his groin area. He released his grip on the waitress and relaxed his demeanor.

"I'm sorry Luanne. You're right. I've had a bad day."

"Yeah, everyone is a tough guy until I get my blade out." She put pressure on the steel instrument, backing Larry up. "I've found most aren't as tough as they think. Now, get to work."

All three boys watched as the woman returned the switchblade to a pocket in her apron and left the room. Emboldened, Tommy took a few steps in Larry's direction as he spoke.

"I don't think..."

Larry interrupted the larger man's sentence with a vicious body blow that sent the air rushing from his co-worker's lungs. He followed the punch with a kick to the knee that left his adversary sprawled on the ground. With speed and purpose the young Asian/American dug his boot into Tommy's neck.

"That was the last time I'll be caught off guard. I promise she'll get what's coming to her, and so will the rest of you. I have some business to take care of. Get this place set up."

Larry snatched his coat from its hanger and was out the back door before he even had it on. Mrs. Prepot needed him to park cars, and he wished he wouldn't have just had the altercations inside. Within an hour or two, though, none of it would matter. He took his place in the short line of overworked valets just in time for one of the most beautiful automobiles he had ever seen.

All sixteen cylinders of the deep maroon vehicle purred in time as its driver brought the car to a stop. The two valets ahead of Larry opened doors for the passengers in the back and two beautiful women made their exits. Larry did his duty as well, opening the door for the driver. To his surprise, a mountain of a Native American man stepped from the luxury vehicle, an infectious smile spread across his entire face.

"Keep it close my man. It's cold out tonight."

Larry looked down to see the man had handed him a twenty dollar bill along with the keys to the auto.

"Yes sir. Right away."

Perhaps he had delivered the reply with a little too much gusto because the other man gave him a strange look before attending to the two women. That didn't matter to Larry now as he slipped into the driver's seat and brought the engine to life. A short distance away was a special lot reserved for high rollers and the luxury car hummed as he guided it to its spot.

THE SENTINEL

The Marmon came to a stop and idled, its exhaust emitting a deep throaty growl.

"I could get used to a car like this." Larry mumbled to himself, killed the engine, and pocketed the keys.

As he stepped from the vehicle into the cold, an odd sound wafted across the water. Larry shivered, put his hands in his pockets, and bunched his jacket around himself. In the summer it wouldn't be odd to hear a boat coming down the river, but at this temperature, it was almost ludicrous.

Larry squinted while scanning the dark waterway, and as the sound grew louder he saw the culprit. Running full tilt down the middle of the St. Charles was a small runabout, a shadowy figure at the helm. Mesmerized, Larry watched the diminutive watercraft as it screamed up to the unmanned docks. The driver showed considerable expertise as he cut the engine at the perfect instant and leapt from the boat to the wooden pier.

Two minutes passed as Larry watched the tall man secure his craft and begin walking in the direction of the gala. As the man approached, he removed his hood and ran a powerful looking hand through a thick mass of tousled yellow hair. Even in the darkness of night he could see the deep blue eyes and when the man smiled, Larry realized he had been staring.

"My friend, would you mind keeping an eye on my boat tonight? You never know when some crazy person is going to try to steal it." The stranger spoke with supreme confidence, offered a handshake, and Larry took it.

"Yes sir."

With that, the shadow man moved up the hill. It wasn't often others impressed him, but now was one of those times. He looked into his hand to see what the stranger had given him before mumbling to himself.

"Fifty dollars? I should have been a valet."

****

8.

Waves rolled onto the pristine white sands as the man sipped from his cocktail. Warm and smooth, the coconut flavored rum slid across his lips and warmed his belly. A number of seagulls flew high overhead, the only dots on the flawless blue sky. This day could not be any more perfect, but then it became so.

Her long bronzed legs were the first thing to grab his attention, followed by her flowing blonde hair. Even from a distance anyone could see she was a remarkable beauty. The man lowered his sunglasses in order to take in her full exquisite splendor, a move that did not go unnoticed.

She altered her path, the lines of her form fitting bathing suit accentuating the ample curves of her body. A slight smile curled upon her lips revealing small dimples. Mesmerized, the man stared as she approached, stood before him, and spoke.

"Knock, knock, knock, knock."

He furrowed his brow at the strange greeting before breathing in and formulating a response. Just as he attempted to speak, however, she interrupted.

"Knock, knock, knock, knock, knock, knock, knock. Hey. Are you in there old man? You'd better not be dead."

Perplexed, the man rose from his bamboo beach chair and responded.

"Knock, knock, knock, knock, knock, knock, knock, knock, knock."

His lips moved and his tongue formed the words, but he had no control over them. She seemed to take his reply in stride, however, and responded with a brilliant smile. He watched as she moved closer, her perfect form brushing against him as she leaned close to his ear. Her breath made every molecule in his body come alive and her hair tickled against his neck.

"I love you. Knock, knock, knock, knock, knock, knock, knock, knock."

The old man startled awake. The dog show still blared in front of him and Felix lay at peace in his lap. Behind him, though, the cause and explanation of the strange dialogue in his dream continued.

"Wake up in there old timer. You can't die on your birthday." The visitor's voice was loud, but friendly, as he knocked again.

"Give me a minute," came the perturbed response as he cleared his throat and set the miniature dog on the floor. "I'm a hundred years old."

Reaching to his left he grabbed a cane and labored to hoist himself from the mechanical chair. It would have taken too long to let it do the work for him. He made his way to the door before unchaining the lock and opening it for his guest.

"What were you doing in there? I thought I was going to have to use my ninja skills to kick the door down." The visitor smirked before noticing his friends clothing. "I see you're all ready to go."

"Ninja skills?" The old man laughed before taking notice of his attire. He was a mess. His yellowed a-shirt, or "wife beater" as he had heard them referred to, showed fresh stains from the morning's breakfast. One section of his navy blue sweatpants had crept up his leg exposing his pale leathery skin, long black socks, and fuzzy yellow slippers. And the coup de gras; it seemed he had wet his pants a bit during his nap. "It's a helluva thing getting old Timmy, a helluva thing."

He laughed again before turning and making his way toward the bedroom. Thirty years had passed since he had met Tim Wheat. Though four and a half decades separated them in age, the two had become fast friends. Now, Wheat was the only friend he had left in the world, excluding Felix. The younger man helped the older to a seated position on the edge of his bed before speaking.

"Whatya think of those Cubbies last night? Pulled another one out in the bottom of the ninth. I think this is the year."

The old man smiled as his friend helped him with his socks. He and Wheat shared a love for the Chicago Cubs. He hoped beyond hope he'd live long enough to see them win a World Series.

"Well Timmy. My dad lived to be 103 years old and never saw them win one. I like some of those young arms we've got now, though, including that kid with the long blond hair." Wheat's oldest son was a rookie pitcher with the big league club, and his younger son had flown through the minor leagues after being drafted out of high school. "When are they going to bring up your younger one?"

"He's hitting .415 with an ops of 1.249 at AA, but he's just 19. They'd like him to get a full season in there, but those kinds of numbers at second base are pretty special. Arms up." Wheat made the command and before the old man even had his appendages extended, removed the a-shirt with his left hand. In the blink of an eye he replaced it with a button down black dress shirt from the closet.

"You're getting pretty good at this Timmy."

"You know, I think I went into the wrong profession. I should have been a nurse. Do you want help with your pants?"

The old man cringed. His general health was good, but getting himself dressed was a major chore.

"No thanks. Just hand me the pants, something to clean up this piss and the underwear, but stay in the room in case I need you." Wheat obliged before turning around. The old man grunted and groaned as he struggled to remove his sweatpants. "So, what do you have planned for today?"

"Oh, you know, standard birthday stuff. I figured we'd put away a bottle of Glenlivet before we left here. Then I was thinking we could hit a couple of strip clubs, maybe score some real high quality drugs. After that, I think we'll just play it by ear."

The old man smiled, but played along.

"You know what? Instead of strippers this year, I was thinking we could score some ultra high class hookers instead. Unless you don't think it's in the budget."

"For you my friend, there is no budget."

Both men laughed as the older finished putting on his pants.

"In all seriousness, though, what is the plan?"

"How does the Cantor Oyster House sound? I know how you love oysters."

"Holy smokes Timmy. You'd get off cheaper with hookers and drugs," the old man said.

"Well, June 30th comes once a year and I figured since you were turning one hundred we'd make it extra special."

The old man finished putting on his pants and stood with the help of his cane. His jovial tone became more nostalgic.

"I tell ya what Timmy. It seems like just yesterday I was in college drinking beer and chasing girls. The years fly by my friend."

THE SENTINEL

He didn't know how right he was.

****

9.

White foam swirled in the wake of the 1929 Chris Craft Cadet. The eighty-two horsepower Chrysler power plant throatily idled as the watercraft's pilot guided the vessel through the icy waters. Katsuo Takahiro took notice of the steam emanating from the smaller craft he was pulling alongside. It seemed another man had braved the St. Charles that evening.

He brought the twenty-two foot craft to a stop and leapt the small gap to the pier. As he tied a bowline, the stocky Japanese man remembered a lifetime ago when his father had taught him the knot. Days had been so much simpler then.

With the boat secure Katsuo retrieved a pack of Lucky Strikes from his raincoat. Cigarettes were one thing the Americans did right. He flicked a windproof Zippo lighter, illuminating his weathered and scarred face and inhaled, allowing himself to reminisce.

The water had been his home for as long as he could remember. His mother had once shown him a picture of himself as a toddler and his father on the docks in Yokohama, Japan's largest port. By the time he had turned five years old he was making daily trips to sea, and by the age of ten he had been skilled enough to captain his own boat. Almost fifty years had passed since those good times.

Katsuo snapped from his reverie as a luxury vehicle came to a stop in the parking lot ahead of him, a slight squeaking emanating from its brakes. He breathed deep the flavorful smoke before allowing himself to return to his daydream.

Life had been good for the young Takahiro family. By 1904 their number had grown to eleven and the fishing had been superior. He remembered well the day his father had sat him down and instructed him to continue the family business. Even more ingrained in his mind, though, was the sound of his mother's cries just a few months later.

His father's death in the Russo-Japanese war had brought the family great public honor. In private, though, Katsuo and his mother had loathed the Japanese military. Its influence seemed to be permeating every walk of life, and the family attempted to steer clear of its control.

Over the course of the next eighteen years Katsuo worked from sunrise to sunset, three hundred sixty-five days a year, to provide for the family. He had shunned all advances from would be girlfriends to start a family of his own. His brothers and sisters hadn't all agreed with the way he ran things, but none of them starved, and none of them had to sleep in the streets.

September 1, 1923 was a day he would never forget. Yasuhiro Takahiro, his youngest brother, had joined Katsuo in the family business at the age of five, and hadn't missed a single day's work in thirteen years. He was the pride of the entire family, and though that day had been his eighteenth birthday, it had begun like every other.

Katsuo and Yasuhiro had woken up before the sun had risen, kissed their mother goodbye, and driven to the docks. That time of year the fishing grounds were often four to five hours out to sea. They were planning on staying a few days until their holds were full, but the elder Takahiro had something different in mind.

They had been making way for two hours when strange noises began emanating from the engine compartment. Katsuo was the mechanic of the two and upon investigation had decided to turn back. Yasuhiro, not one to argue with the only father he had ever known, had returned without incidence to the stern of the boat, and read a book.

Their journey home had been lengthy, but as they pulled into Yokohama harbor Katsuo could see everything was going to plan. Yasuhiro still sat nearby, reading a book. The youngest Takahiro was hard working and brilliant. The University of Tokyo had accepted the young man to study physics, and Katsuo planned on telling him in just a few short minutes.

Katsuo opened his eyes for a moment. The cold November air had whipped across the St. Charles and sent a shiver up his spine. Noticing nothing else awry he puffed from his cigarette before letting his mind drift back in time and thousands of miles away. It was almost like it was happening all over again.

"Yasuhiro. Pull your nose out of that book and get to the bow. The current is a little rough today, I'm going to need you to tie a bowline and get us secure."

The younger brother arched his eyebrow, closed his book, and did as Katsuo ordered. His brother was such a good pilot he couldn't imagine how bad a current would have to be for him to make such a demand.

"Alright old man, you must be losing it though. This chop isn't even a foot."

Katsuo feigned anger, but inside he felt like a little kid.

"Just get up there and do as you're told."

"Ok, Ok. You don't need to get all worked up. I don't want you having a heart attack on me." Yasuhiro flashed a smile as he tied the knot and readied himself to leap onto the pier. A large luxury steamer, the *Empress of Australia*, sat nearby and hundreds of well-wishers crowded the area. "That is one huge ship. How long do you think she is?"

"I'd say a hundred two ken."

"Wow, almost a hundred ninety meters. I bet we could make a lot of money with a ship like that."

"You and your meters. Give me the shakkan-ho units any day."

"Meters are so much easier though. I'm telling you in a year or..." Yasuhiro's voice trailed off as they neared their slip and something seemed to catch his eye. "Hey do you see who's up there?"

"No, who is it?" Katsuo worked hard to conceal his excitement.

"It's Mom." His younger brother said. "Everyone else is here too. I knew you'd been acting funny the last week. Wait a minute, is our boat even broken?"

Their entire family had not been in the same place at once in many years. Yasuhiro had begged Katsuo to get everyone together for his birthday, but the elder had used every excuse available. It was going to be a wonderful day. He watched as his youngest brother leapt the ten foot gap to the dock with ease and tied the bowline.

If there was one thing the entire Takahiro family could agree upon, it was their love for Yasuhiro. As Katsuo finished shutting down the engine and made his way to the front of the boat, he couldn't help but smile. He looked down upon his family and a calm settled upon him like he had never felt before. It was a calm that would last but a few seconds.

"You'll never have to work on this boat again my brother." He mumbled the words to himself.

At 11:58 a.m. a sixty by sixty mile segment of the Philippine oceanic plate fractured and slammed against the Eurasian continental plate. The ground quaked as sixty petajoules of energy exploded across the landscape and Katsuo fell backward onto the deck of his boat as a thunder unlike any he had heard before reverberated in his chest. He struggled to stand as the shaking continued for what seemed an eternity.

As he fought his way to the port side, he saw a horrific site. The pier near the ocean liner began collapsing in sections. Screams of the fallen now joined the deafening thunder and just when it seemed the shaking would last forever. It ended.

Katsuo gained his footing as the boat stopped bucking. Four minutes had passed and he feared what he would see as he looked over the side of his fishing trawler. Summoning his courage he approached the edge and gained visual confirmation of his fears.

The pier where his entire family had once stood now lay in shambles in the water. Screams for help had already diminished to feeble cries and an eerie quiet settled across the entire bay. Katsuo was on the verge of tears when he heard a hoarse call for assistance.

"Brother. My brother. Are you alive?"

He rushed to the edge of the vessel and his heart leapt into his throat. Hanging by his left hand from the bowline was Yasuhiro, the limp body of their mother gripped in his right. He had a large gash underneath his rib cage, but still managed a smile.

"She's still breathing Katsuo, but I can't climb with one arm. Could you pull us up?"

"Yes."

Katsuo shouted the word and pulled at the line with all his might. At five feet six inches he was short, but a life of hard work had turned his body into a sculpted muscular specimen. He fought the dead weight below for a full minute, using every ounce of his two hundred pounds, but made little progress.

Then an idea jumped into his head. He leaned over the edge again.

"You're too heavy. I'm going to hook you up to the pulleys for the nets, though. Just give me a second."

"Take your time." The muscles bulged from Yasuhiro's arms and he managed a smile, though the exertion was taking its toll. "I can hold on like this all day."

Katsuo had never moved faster in his life. In less than two minutes he had the rigging all set up to hoist his remaining family to safety. Happy that the plan was ready to implement, he attached a clip to the broken bowline and leaned over the edge. It was the last time he'd see his brother and mother.

"I've got you. Up you come. You're going to the University of Tokyo to study physics."

Yasuhiro looked up, a weak smile adorning his face, then disappeared. A forty foot wall of water slammed into the aft of the boat, lifting it high into the air and tossing it like a rag doll. Katsuo collapsed to the deck, banging his head against a crate and losing consciousness.

The sound of a car horn jerked him back to the present. Katsuo Takahiro stood on the dock on the icy St. Charles River, a different man than he had been back then. He pulled another Lucky Strike from the package and lit it, stroking the long jagged scar on his cheek before flipping the Zippo closed.

He had spent a year searching for the bodies of his family, but to no avail. The Great Kanto Earthquake took everything he had worked years to build. Indigent and living on the streets, Katsuo could think of one course of action. He joined the ranks of those he had hated, the Imperial Japanese Army.

It was in the army that he found his true calling. A natural leader of men, Katsuo had experienced a meteoric rise through the ranks, achieving the grade of colonel with astonishing speed. He completed every mission and every task with flawless precision and in record time.

Although he had spent many years at sea as a fisherman, Katsuo was not an unintelligent man. He had often read books to pass the time on long trips, and in the army he found that he also had a knack for speaking other languages. Inside of two years he had learned English, Russian, German, French, Italian, and bits of Chinese.

His most difficult mission had begun four years before. Command had brought him in and told him he would be going undercover. Posing as a fisherman, his new job required him to spy on American naval installations.

Katsuo took another drag of his cigarette as he thought of all the degrading jobs assigned him on American fishing trawlers. Though it had been obvious to everyone he was a knowledgeable, hardworking fisherman, racism left him the worst tasks. Humiliation and denigration had filled every day of his life in the U.S.

All of that had changed eighteen months before in Seward, Alaska. A new assignment had taken him to a more northern region to assess American capabilities, and the summer in Alaska had proven to be rather pleasant. Katsuo had been staying in a small boarding house run by the only pleasant American he had ever met. One day she had knocked on his door to deliver a phone message. It was one word, followed by an address. The word was "Yasuhiro."

Katsuo had reported with haste to the address which turned out to be a Catholic church. Upon entering he had seemed to be by himself, but then he heard her voice for the first time. It was a voice he would never forget.

"Over here in the confessional. Please have a seat. I believe I can help you find Yasuhiro."

As far as the Japanese Army knew, he was dead. The woman in the confessional had arranged for him to be head of security for Mitsubishi and he had proven to be an efficient leader. After a short period of time she summoned him to another meeting and he feared his benefactor had bad news. That day, though, was the day Katsuo Takahiro became the owner of Mitsubishi.

He had tackled his job as owner with his usual fervor and within months had developed new ideas, and set the company on new naval and aeronautical paths. His most important development, though, was the manufacturing of a new airplane. The Navy Type 0 Carrier Fighter was not being sold to the Navy yet, but initial testing was promising and the company had churned out a few dozen of the aircraft.

Katsuo took a final puff from his Lucky before dropping it to the dock and putting it out with his boot. He shrugged his shoulders and shivered, peering through narrowed eyes at the gala going on above. Tonight was the night he made his play to be the most powerful man in Japan. Tonight was the night he brought the Americans to their knees. Most important of all, though, it was the night that would bring him one step closer to reuniting with the brother he had given up for dead so many years ago.

"Yasuhiro." He said the name aloud in excellent English. "I'm coming my brother. I'm coming."

****

10.

"It was good to see you again Al. My wife is giving me the evil eye though. I'll get a hold of you if anything comes up."

"Sounds good buddy. I'm itching to do something."

George almost crushed the hand of Al Scherzer as they shared a handshake and then parted ways. He wasn't exaggerating when he said Angela had been giving him the evil eye. It had been thirty minutes since their arrival and they were still the only ones seated at the table. The two women got along well, but it was beginning to look like the Chases and Leonard weren't going to show. George shrugged as he approached.

"I'm sorry about that baby. Al's a bit of a talker."

"It's ok. I'm more worried that the waiters already served the first two courses and nobody else is here yet."

"What are you talking about? There must be hundreds of people here." George took his seat, flashed his million dollar smile, and Angela's heart fluttered much the same as it had a year and a half before, but she feigned incredulity.

"George, first you leave us here for thirty minutes on our own, and then you make jokes." Angela smiled before continuing. "I forgive you, though. Who is Al anyway?"

"Al Scherzer is one heckuva a guy and one heckuva pilot. He's a puddle jumper over in the Pacific I worked with when I was still in the Army, and just so happens to live over by Alexei and Luce now. On a side note, the man also drinks scotch like it's his job. I swear if I would have..." George paused and stood, a wide grin on his face. "Speak of the devil, so nice of you to join us."

Alexei and Luce Chase had arrived arm in arm, but disengaged to greet the others. George and Alexei shared a powerful handshake that neither got the best of, and then George gave Luce a hug.

"You look gorgeous tonight Mrs. Chase. If you weren't with this mountain of a man right here I'd ask you out to the dance floor forthwith."

Lucille Chase had known George since he was a little boy, and knew his words were in jest.

"I don't know if Alexei would be too keen on that, nor your beautiful wife, I presume."

"You presume right. This is my friend Sarah."

Angela smiled as both women showed their respect by curtseying to Lucille while Alexei kissed their hands. The small group took seats around the table. Angela was the first to talk.

"It's so nice to see you Lucille. I'm always bugging Rex to get out of that garage and invite all of you to dinner, but I've been rather unsuccessful. Is he planning on being here? Have you seen him?"

"I've seen him alright. He had a tire iron thrown off my face not too long ago." Everyone at the table turned to see Leonard, arm in arm with a woman. "Don't get up everyone, we'll come to you. I'd like to introduce you all to my wife Marilyn."

Well defined looks of shock crossed the faces of everyone at the table, save Sarah. The others had gotten to know Leonard very well over the course of the last eighteen months and he had never so much as mentioned having a wife. Alexei Chase stood, took the matron's hand and was the first to break the silence.

"It's a delight to meet you Marilyn. I'd like to introduce you to my wife Lucille."

The two women exchanged pleasantries as George stood and approached his friend's wife.

"It's a pleasure to meet you. My name is George Ahiga. I'd also like to introduce you to my wife Angela and her friend Sarah."

Marilyn acknowledged the other ladies with pleasantry before taking the seat Leonard had pulled for her.

"I'm sorry to just burst onto the scene like this everyone. I don't care to get caught up in my husband's work, but dinner with General Reagan AND the President of the United States? I couldn't sit this one out."

The ice broke as everyone at the table laughed. Considerable banter and much jovial ribbing amongst the men dominated the next thirty minutes. Most enjoyed the appetizer of baked oysters with breadcrumbs and garlic, and all exclaimed that they didn't know how they could even eat a meal after that. Then, he arrived, startling Lucille Chase by kissing her on the cheek.

"Hi mommy."

"Edward Rex Chase." Luce used his full name and a scolding tone of voice. "Don't sneak up on me like that again or I'll pinch your nose in this oyster shucker."

Rex smiled, but swallowed hard as his father and Leonard both stood to shake his hand. He couldn't believe how jittery he was just to meet a woman. Stealing glances from the corner of his eye he could see her fixated gaze and a knot formed in his stomach.

"Rex, I'd like to introduce you to my wife Marilyn."

Leonard made the introduction, and Chase acted as if he had met her a thousand times before.

"It's wonderful to see you again ma'am." Chase felt flushed as he kissed her hand. Everyone at this table, except maybe Sarah, knew full well he had never met her before. Marilyn smiled before replying.

"It's is a pleasure to meet you. I have heard so many good things."

Chase's lips pursed into a tight grin. His head was spinning and it seemed all that time he had spent pacing back and forth in the lobby had been for naught. Then, George stood, and as he did, so did Angela and Sarah. Rex, using his peripheral vision, took in her feminine features.

She was stunning, and to a degree, that eased his anxiety. Even as his best friend crushed his outstretched hand in an unyielding shake, and scolded him for being late, Rex Chase found control. He had always felt comfortable around beautiful women and today would be no different.

"Buddy, I am serious." George patted him on the back. "You are L-A-T-E, LATE."

Order restored in his mind, Rex continued to evaluate his blind date even as he chatted with his friend.

"I apologize, the river was a little unyielding tonight and then I ran into the lady running the show out there, Mrs. Prepot." Something he had said amused the beautiful woman because he noticed the slightest curl of her full crimson lips. "I got here as fast as I could." He noticed that she averted her eyes and smiled. Chase was playing a game he hadn't participated in for quite some time, and to his surprise, it felt good.

"No problem. I still think you're crazy for driving that thing here anyway." George was oblivious to the couple's inaudible communications. "I noticed you're still limping a little."

"Yeah," Chase rubbed his left hip that had given him trouble ever since leaping from the Six a year and a half earlier. "The doc says my hip might never be the same. It's been feeling a little better as of late."

"How's that golden arm doing?" Leonard said.

At some point in their escapades of eighteen months before Chase had injured his shoulder as well. Once he had been a fireballer, propelling a baseball at speeds nearing one hundred miles per hour. Now, he had a difficult time throwing an object twenty feet overhand without suffering.

"I'm afraid my shoulder is broken. The doc thinks I've torn my rotator cuff or something. He could go in there, poke around, and then might repair it, but it looks like I'm going to have to live with it too. Now that I think about it, though, it's been feeling a little better the last few weeks as well." Chase flexed his right shoulder before addressing George. "So are you going to introduce me, or do I have to do it myself?"

Angela pushed her way past George and embraced Rex in a warm hug.

"I'm so glad that you're here." She released him before stepping back. "I'd like to introduce you to my friend Sarah."

Chase stepped forward and took the beautiful woman's hand. Her opaline eyes shone and as he stooped he could see himself reflected in them. The knot in his stomach had disappeared now as he took notice of her long tanned legs and opened his mouth to speak.

"Sauf pour ma mere vous sont facilementla plus belle femme dans la chambre."

The French flowed from his tongue as if he had lived in the country his entire life. What happened next surprised everyone.

"Merci. Vous parlez magnifiquement."

Rex hid his astonishment well, flashed a toothy smile, and changed gears.

"Es ist immer wieder toll miteiner Frau, die ist sehr schon und gut gesprochen."

His German had passed as native before, and as the table watched she replied.

"Ich bin geschmeichelt. Ich habe dich beobachtet und aus dem. Raum fur die letzte Stunde. Warst du sehr nervos?"

The astonishment on Rex's face was as apparent as the wide grin on his mother's. He composed himself in an instant, though, before continuing in a language very few still spoke.

"Ut enim tempus. You'll 'accipe coeptus?"

"Tusoluer ehabes, et tempus?"

Her reply was immediate and Chase felt a fire he thought had died. He cocked his head to the side and curled the corners of his mouth upward before uttering his reply.

"Imo."

An uncomfortable silence fell over the table for a few moments. Chase, however, couldn't have felt more comfortable. Intrigue permeated his entire being and for the first time since Mary Elizabeth, he wanted to get to know someone of the opposite sex. His reverie ended as George spoke in a terrible Australian accent.

"Alright mates. Let's put some shrimp on the barbie. Maybe we can play with our didgeridoo's and see if we can catch a dingo."

"Nobody wants to see your didgeridoo honey." Angela said, raised a champagne glass, and proposed a toast. "Here's to a wonderful evening."

A cheerful laugh went up around the table as everyone celebrated the toast and dinner began to arrive. The evening's photographer witnessed the occasion and forever immortalized it with his camera. It was going to be a memorable evening.

****

11.

No matter their nationality, the young Japanese man despised politicians. As he looked around the table he saw powerful, dignified business owners accommodating a group of clowns. That's how he felt about the men who made decisions with the lives of others, though they themselves often held few qualifications to make such decisive choices.

He watched in utter disdain as the powerful men with whom he had aligned himself cowered to the Americans. Each of them had expressed their distrust in private, but now, in public, they fell in line.

"Conformist bastards."

Spoken in a hushed voice, the words never even reached his own ears in the packed hall. Checking the Kaigun Koukuutai naval aviator watch on his left arm he took notice of the time. It wouldn't be long now.

Growing up as an orphan on the streets of Tokyo, he had learned to fend for himself at a young age. He had no recollection of his mother or father, and didn't know whether they were dead, or if they had abandoned him. Neither was of any consequence now.

Joining the Imperial Navy at the age of sixteen had been simple. Though his formal education had been lacking, his worldly experience, and desire to excel, had propelled him through the ranks. At the true age of seventeen he had already entered a flight program, and soon earned his own stick.

It was in the air that he had found his true calling. Nobody could match his skill, and very few could match his knowledge of tactics. With the advent of a new fighter he was confident their interests could be protected from the air. A few years before his confidence had not been so high.

THE SENTINEL

He had been flying on his own for less than three months when he began making bold recommendations to his superiors. Engineers had based Japanese aircraft of the late twenties and early thirties off of defunct British, German, Italian, and American designs. They were anything but state of the art.

In his spare time he had devised a long-term plan for Japanese air supremacy, based off of national innovation and hard work. They would no longer ride the coat tails of the West. Fortune smiled upon him and his superiors accepted a number of his recommendations as brilliant. By the age of nineteen he had risen to the rank of Major, and on his twenty-first birthday, he had taken command of his own squadron as the youngest Colonel in Japanese history.

Everything seemed to be moving along as planned when it had all come to a screeching halt. A tryst with a powerful public official's eighteen-year-old daughter, in a coatroom, at a gala attended by the Emperor himself, had seen to that. His superiors credited others with all of his hard work and brilliance, they stripped him of command, and he became a pariah in the military he had once loved.

An honorable suicide seemed his only course of action, and he had been within minutes of doing so when life had changed. Katsuo Takahiro had approached him with an opportunity to salvage his career, his reputation, and seek revenge on those who had taken from him. The intense training of the last eighteen months had been constant, but now he was here to begin reaping the rewards.

Pulling a picture from his pocket the young aviator scrutinized the photograph again. His mission today had a number of objectives, and these two men, if at all possible, were one of them. Though an airman at heart, incursions into

Chinese and Russian territories had baptized him in battle and proven him a worthy ground warrior. Today he would have to use every bit of his training and experience.

He continued to scan the room for his remaining targets when his eyes landed upon them. The one with the blue eyes had caught his attention first, and seated at the same table was the man with the gigantic arms. It just might be possible to complete all of his objectives. Grasping the omamari around his neck the seasoned young warrior mumbled the Samurai creed.

"I have no parents. I make the heavens and earth my parents. I have no home. I make the Tan T'ien my home. I have no life and death. I have made the tides of breathing my life and death..."

****

12.

"That is not a true story."

Rex hadn't had this good of a time in months. He was going to have to thank The General later. Right now, though, he had Angela's accusation to confront. Feigning hurt feelings he replied.

"I swear every word of it was true, ask Chief."

"He's not lying. That crazy little guy jumped out of our plane with no chute on and lived to tell about it. I still haven't figured that out."

"Well, he pushed out one of those crates right before he jumped. He must have hitched a ride on one of those." Before the words were even out of his mouth, questioning eyebrows raised around the table.

"Landing on a box, that has a parachute, when you don't, is, well, impossible my boy." Alexei beamed. It wasn't often his intellect exceeded that of his son.

"Improbable? Maybe. Impossible? I don't think so." Every eye at the table shifted to Sarah. "If I learned anything from Dr. Schoof's book it's that through the use of scalar energy, the impossible becomes, well, possible."

"Which book would that be?" Rex Chase's interest piqued. She wasn't just a little smart.

"Oh, I'm not sure I recall the name. *Scalar Waves in Nature*? Perhaps?"

"You know I theorized a lot of what went into that book. Nicholas and I were…"

Alexei Chase kept speaking, but Rex no longer paid him any mind. His cheeks hurt from how much he had been smiling, but it was a good hurt. Across the table Sarah seemed engrossed In the elder Chase's speech and Chase felt a slight tinge of something he hadn't thought possible. He liked this girl.

"How could it be possible?"

Rex interrupted his father's braggadocios and met her softened gaze. Sarah's blue green eyes sparkled as she tilted her head to the side and formulated a response.

"I'm assuming they made that submarine you were talking about earlier from this special iron. With that much of it in the area that little weasel would have needed a small amount of the ore on his person to be able to perform some wonderful tricks. I mean, in theory, he could have levitated. Right?"

Though she finished with a question, Chase could see the confidence oozing. Her crimson lips curled upward and he wondered if they felt as soft as they looked. Perhaps he had met his match this evening.

"I suppose it was possible, but good old Hans wasn't what I would call a renowned physicist."

"Not by a sight, speaking of sights. You should see the car Sarah has. It's a Marmon."

George had changed the subject, which was fine with Chase. He was about to impress her.

"The 1931 Marmon Sixteen LeBaron Limousine. It has a naturally aspirated, forty-five degree, Aluminum V16 with a displacement of four hundred and ninety-one inches. The two hundred horsepower engine with a Stromberg DDR3 carburetor can push that fifty-two hundred and ninety pound steel beast a hundred six mph, and its three speed manual transmission can handle it too. That's a fine automobile."

Feeling rather hot to trot Chase noticed Sarah seemed a bit bored.

"Four hundred ninety-one point one."

"What?" Chase said.

"The displacement of the engine is four hundred ninety-one point one inches, not four hundred ninety-one."

Alexei Chase led in the collective roar that went up from the table. Rex felt a little sheepish, but met her eyes again. He could see the apology in them. She was just testing him. It was working.

"Ladies and gentlemen. I would now like to introduce to you, the President of the United States of America."

The voice seemed to come out of nowhere and everyone forgot what had just happened and stood to clap. The President took to the podium at the front of the room while The General followed a few steps behind, stopping to shake the hands of numerous dignitaries. "Hail to the Chief" echoed throughout the room and Chase moved his chair around the circular table in order to be better positioned to watch.

He was now standing between Sarah and Angela. The former smiled even as she continued to clap. Rex returned the pleasantry while leaning toward his best friend.

"Who are all the Asian guys The General is shaking hands with?"

"Are Japanese people Asian?"

Chase laughed, but continued clapping.

"Sorry. Who are all the Japanese guys The General is shaking hands with?"

"Those are some big timers up there. You've got the owners of Nissan, Suzuki, Toyota, Kawasaki, and the Japanese Ambassador to the U.S. That's why we're here. The General is being honored for his humanitarian efforts with these guys."

"Huh."

The President cleared his throat and the din began to die down.

"I told John my voice was a bit scratchy tonight, so I scrapped my speech. I'd like to introduce to you. General John Francis Reagan."

The band began playing, and those who had sat down stood back up as everyone clapped once again. The President stepped aside as The General shook his hand and took the podium. Chase beamed. The General was getting more applause than The President.

"Thank you. Thank you. Please. Please." The crowd began to sit and the ovation became a transitional murmur. "Thank you so much. I'd like to thank The President as well for attending this evening even though he witnessed six men assaulting his mother-in-law earlier today."

Absolute stunned silence filled the room. Chase shifted in his chair, but saw the tell he had noticed while playing poker with The General. When he was trying to keep a straight face his left eye would always develop the slightest of twitches.

"That's right. I asked him if he stopped to help, and you know what he said? He said, 'Nah Johnny. They didn't need my help. She's a tough old broad, but six should have been plenty.'"

Laughter replaced nervous silence as The President and everyone else in the room enjoyed the joke. Chase chuckled while he looked to his right and exchanged a glance with Sarah. It was going to be a great night.

The Sentinel

13.

Laughter had never been prominent in Larry's life and the sound of it filling the room had him feeling uncomfortable. Nerves caused his hands to shake and he checked his watch as he worked his way through the room. His days of bussing were about to come to a close.

As he approached the Japanese Ambassador's table, an anger boiled inside. Even on a night like tonight the Japanese dignitaries sat ostracized, away from the larger group. Tucked in behind a large pillar, one of the men didn't even have a view of the current speaker.

Without making it obvious, Larry studied the man. His countryman showed no interest in the speech being given and something about him seemed familiar. Perhaps he had seen him at a local restaurant or something. Checking his watch again the young busser knew it was almost time.

The Type 26 revolver tucked in his apron had seemed an odd choice for the job. Though the weapon was reliable, it was not modern, and held a reputation as being an inaccurate firearm. That was of no matter tonight, though, as his quarry would be within an arm's length.

Larry kept his focus on the front of the room as he came around the circular table. The President of the United States of America was in for a rude awakening tonight. He set his buss tub down on the ground, wiped his brow, and felt the weight of the 9mm revolver in his apron.

"Take one step to your right."

The voice was almost imperceptible, but the foreboding tone was undeniable. Larry looked at the man who had spoken. Then it hit him.

"Shin Shou."

A sinister yellow smile came across the other man's face as Larry assessed the situation. Officials in Japan proclaimed that Shin Shou had committed suicide after his disgrace, but other reports suggested he still lived. Those same reports painted the picture of a man changed. Shou was no longer an arm of the military industrial complex. He was a ruthless and efficient mercenary. Larry now recognized him as the man who had overseen some of his training.

"You should take a step to your right."

Larry obeyed as confusion flooded his mind. The only thing he was certain of right now was his mission. Izanami had given him orders and he meant to carry them out. He peeked around the steel pillar. Twenty yards separated him from his quarry. Then it happened.

A series of devastating explosions rocked the 19thcentury ballroom. Time seemed to slow as the young Asian/American counted the blasts. They seemed to be concentrated at the head of the room and after the eighth concussion in less than two seconds, they ceased.

A deep rumbling noise replaced the violent sounds of explosives. A horrified look crossed his face as he watched the stage at the front of the room seem to float in midair for a moment and then disappear. His prey, the President of the United States, along with everyone else on the stage, had disappeared. Acrid plumes of dust and smoke rose from the basement below. Larry had never seen such devastation firsthand.

Four seconds had passed now and he became aware of another sound. Turning his head a few inches he witnessed the source. Shin Shou wielded the Type 14 Nambu 8 mm pistol with

THE SENTINEL

deadly accuracy, assassinating the four industrialists seated at the table.

The other man's expertise with the weapon was devastating. He had unloaded the eight round box magazine into the heads of his targets and reloaded in less than three seconds. His expression, however, hadn't changed. The sinister yellow smile seemed painted on his face.

"Haruko. Haruko."

Eight seconds before the world had been a very different place. Larry snapped to attention as Shou addressed him.

"Yes sir."

"Kill the ambassador."

Larry hesitated. Killing fellow Japanese was not his mission. Still, Shin Shou's reputation demanded more respect than any politician ever could.

"Kill him."

His training kicked in and Larry pulled the Type 26 from his apron. Women's screams and the cries of the injured permeated his head as he raised the weapon. Confusion was king, and though shots were fired, and those around him killed, the ambassador still sat in his chair, a look of shock adorning his face.

Larry gripped the six shooter and brought it to bear on his new target. He had never killed anyone before and as he pulled the trigger again and again he relished the moment. The ambassador sat a mere ten feet away and all six of the assassin's bullets entered his chest within a second.

"Well done Haruko." Larry felt the Type 26 being loosed from his hands, even as he continued to pull the trigger. The 8mm Nambu replaced it. "Now, go."

Endorphins surged through his entire body as he dashed toward the employee break room. His head cycled through questions. Why had both he and Shou attempted to kill the President? Why kill everyone on the platform when Larry had been willing to accept the suicide mission? Why kill the Japanese men at the table?

None of that mattered now, though, and self-preservation was the new goal. Larry broke into an all out sprint, smiling and laughing as he began to whistle the popular Art Tatum song *Tea For Two*.

****

14.

At the first sounds of the explosions Rex's instincts had taken over and he threw the heavy steel table on its side, shielding his friends and family from the blasts. As if choreographed, each man had ushered their significant other into a protected position. No one uttered a word, yet they had worked as a team.

As the first shots rang out Edward Rex Chase stood tall. His 6'4" frame gave him a good sightline and as The General and the President disappeared into the basement he scanned the room for gunmen. They had fired eight shots in quick succession.

Then, gunfire erupted again, and he identified the source with ease. From behind a large steel column across the room a revolver spewed lead point blank into the chest of the Japanese ambassador. The gun cycled and then went empty as a young Asian man dashed toward the kitchen area.

In an unexpected turn, all eyes focused on Rex Chase. He looked at the other three men and a pride surged within. They were looking to him for leadership, and that's what he was going to give them.

"Who's armed?" All three men answered Chase's question without uttering a word as they pulled pistols from their tuxedo jackets and Marilyn removed a small snub nosed Colt Detective Special .38 from her clutch. Rex smiled before continuing. "I left mine in the boat. Dad and Leonard take the girls and get them out of here."

"I think we should check on the President and the General." Leonard's opinion was what Chase expected.

"The President has more bodyguards than the women do. Plus it's going to be hard to see in here for a while." A large cloud of dust was flooding through the room. The two older men nodded as Chase motioned to their left. "Chief, that six shooter didn't fire those first eight shots and there is a huge hole in the wall over there. I want you to keep an eye on that while I go after the other guy. Anyone have any questions?"

"Nope." The trio replied in unison.

Alexei and Leonard had already begun to help Marilyn and Luce to their feet. Chase swung his gaze to Sarah. She looked frightened and it pained him.

"Don't be scared. These two guys aren't going to let anything bad happen to you." He caressed her soft cheek with his left hand since he had helped her up with his right. "I'll be back in a jiff."

Tears filled her eyes and she nodded without saying a word. Chase took one last look at the beautiful opaline orbs and rubbed his hip. Running hurt.

"Rex, I think you should have this." Marilyn handed him the snub nosed .38 and he took it. "It's not much, but it could get you out of a jam."

"Thanks. I just need it to get me to my boat."

Chase bounded across the room, ignoring the cries of the terrified and wounded partygoers. Ninety seconds ago he was having the best night he'd had in a long time. Now, he was chasing after an unknown enemy. At least his hip seemed to be feeling better.

15.

His heart was racing as Larry burst through the double doors into the server alley. Huddled on the floor in the corner were all the servers. He sneered upon approaching them.

"Luanne."

The waitress stood, her confidence from hours before diminished.

"I don't have time to eat your heart."

Larry raised the semi-automatic 8mm pistol and shot the woman in the bridge of the nose at point blank range. Time seemed to slow once again as he felt the liquid splatter on his face and watched her left eye bulge from its socket. He licked his lips, tasting the saltiness of her blood.

"Interesting."

Hysterical screams from the other women on the floor brought the killer satisfaction. They had all known him as their quiet little Asian whipping boy. Now, though, it was time to escape.

He exited the server alley into the breakroom where they changed clothes and what he saw brought him delight. Standing in shock, mouths agape, were his former tormentors Tommy and Carl.

"W,w,w,w,w,w,what is g,g,g,g,g,g,g,g going o,o,o,o,o,o,o,on out there?"

Larry flashed a menacing grin.

"I'm what is going on, that's what." He raised the Nambu before continuing. "On the floor maggots."

Both boys stumbled backward over each other and fell in a crumpled mess to the floor. This brought the fledgling killer great satisfaction. He approached, stood over them, unzipped his pants and began urinating on the pair.

"Polly and Stutters. You racist punks. Look at me." His voice seemed from another world, and the two boys who had covered their heads turned to look. Larry sneered. "Now open your mouths."

Carl and Tommy's subservience was complete and their bodies repulsed the warm liquid. The two gagged, coughed, and sputtered, all to the delight of their captor. Larry loosed a maniacal laugh as he finished relieving himself.

"I hope you both kissed your mothers before you left home tonight."

Larry released years of built up anger and frustration as he unloaded his remaining seven shots into the pair, though he should have conserved ammo. He doubted Shin Shou had given him the pistol so that he could execute his workplace enemies. His neck ached and he stretched before exiting the room. In the last forty five seconds he had gone from a complacent young man to a heartless killer. It felt good.

****

16.

Sweat poured down his face, but the positives of wearing a gas mask far outweighed the negatives. He wiped dust from the circular eyes and continued to scan the crowd. Beams of light from the fixtures above cascaded through the murky billows and made objects difficult to distinguish.

Then, through the cloud, a tall man appeared. He was moving with incredible speed, more speed than Shin had anticipated. The room sat in utter disarray and the trained killer waited for his opportunity. It wouldn't be prudent to unleash a rash of bullets from the Type 100 submachine gun he now wielded.

Shin Shou recognized the man as Rex Chase. Even through the mask and the dust he could see his adversary's telltale blond hair. He had heard some tall stories about this physicist, a man who wasn't even a soldier, but fought with the ferocity of a goshawk defending its nest. It would almost be a shame to gun him down in this manner.

His opportunity to shoot, though, was coming to an end. The 6'4" American moved like an Olympic hurdler across the room. Obstacles which the Japanese killer had supposed would bring opportunity for a shot, instead served as a testament to the other man's athleticism. Chase moved with a purpose, and in a few short seconds the window had passed.

Shin lowered the Type 100 and watched as the double doors to the kitchen swung shut. It wasn't often in his life he hadn't been able to fulfill all of his mission objectives, but that's why plans always had backups. Now it was time to make an escape.

****

17.

Chase burst through the double doors into the server alley to the screams of the ladies still huddled on the floor. What he saw next chilled his soul. One of the women lay dead, executed at point blank range with a single shot to the face.

"Which way did he go?" The sound of women sobbing met his question. He didn't have time for this. "WHICH WAY DID HE GO?"

One of the women pointed to a door leading out the back and he hurried to it. Pausing a brief second at the exit, he heard nothing and pushed his way into the breakroom. Another sinister sight lay in a crumpled heap feet away.

It looked like the two men on the floor had cowered in the corner and the unmistakable aroma of urine filled the room. Chase knelt beside them and put his pointer and middle fingers on the smaller one's carotid. His chest was still rising and falling, but his pulse was hypokinetic.

"Hey kid. Wake up."

His voice had stirred the injured man who opened his eyes.

"L,L,L,Larry. He p,p,p,p,pissed on us."

The young man's voice was mournful and his extremities began to convulse as his heart attempted to push blood through his injured body. Chase held the young man's hand and watched him move onto a different plane. It seemed that death never came from where one expected.

Just then the women's screams from the server alley put Chase's body on full alert. He leapt from his position next to the fallen men and as the door to the breakroom opened drew the snub nose. Its two inch barrel didn't leave much room for error. He trained the .38 special on the person entering the room, and pulled back the hammer as he aimed.

"Rex. Rex." Sarah entered, tears pouring down her face as she sniffled and smeared them. "Please. Rex."

In that instant Rex Chase's heart melted. He had known her a short two hours but the sight of her beautiful green eyes drowned in tears was more than he could bear. Pocketing his revolver he closed the gap between them and took her in his arms.

"Shhhhhhhhhhhhhhhhhhhhhhh. I've got you." His voice wavered as her body trembled in his arms. Emotion threatened to overwhelm him as he spoke again in a hushed tone. "Shhhhhhhhhhhh. What are you doing in here? I thought you were going with my dad and Leonard."

"I,I,I,I,I just got so scared and then you ran away before I got to say anything and there was a lady in the other room with no face..." She pulled away, wiped the tears from her eyes, then continued. "I,I,I,I just felt like we couldn't end tonight like that. I'm terrified."

"It will be OK." Chase's guard was down, and it shouldn't have been. They were still in a dangerous situation and he reassessed their options. "What I need you to do is follow me out that door. We'll get to the front of the building and find the others."

"Alright."

Her voice still quivered as Chase reached into a nearby locker and grabbed one of the valet jackets. He wrapped the heavy coat around Sarah then guided her to the back door. Just before he opened the steel exit she spoke once more.

"Please don't ever leave me like that again. I feel safe when I'm with you."

✼✼✼✼✼✼✼✼✼✼✼✼✼✼✼✼✼✼✼

18.

A frigid northwest wind whipped down the St. Charles River, across the small docks, and up toward the maelstrom. Larry cursed under his breath as the icy breeze chilled him to the bone. In his haste he had forgotten to grab a coat.

Patrons of the ball were fleeing the building at an alarming speed. It made Larry's escape almost certain. As he scurried to the docks, he took one last look back.

"Like a bunch of cockroaches."

He stepped onto the wooden structure that jutted into the water a new man. All of his hard work and training had paid off. Though the appearance of Shin Shou had been unexpected, it must have been in Izanami's plan.

His heart still raced as he approached the small runabout and began releasing its hold from the cleat. The small marina held two boats in its docks while he had expected just one. Perhaps Shou would be escaping down the river as well.

"I don't believe that is yours."

Startled, Larry dropped to the pier and pulled his semi-automatic. An unfortunate realization formed in his mind and he felt a little silly since the Nambu contained no ammunition. The man in the shadows didn't know that, though.

"Take it easy young Haruko." The stranger stepped away from the pole he had been leaning against and into the light before continuing. "I am not your enemy."

Larry stood and tucked the Nambu 8mm into his waistband. Though his senses had been on full alert he had somehow missed the mountainous man who now stood before him and used his birth name. He looked like he had seen his fair share of battle.

"Then you are my friend?"

"You could say that." The stranger reached into his pocket and extracted a Zippo lighter and a pack of Lucky Strikes. Larry watched as his elder worked the windproof lighter and breathed deep the tobacco before speaking again. "You could also say that I saved your life."

Confusion now reigned in the young Asian/American's head. He studied the older man's demeanor for information, but saw none that was helpful. Larry shivered from cold once again before retorting.

"I was ready to give my life for the Emperor. I didn't need a savior."

"Perhaps this is true." The man breathed in the tobacco smoke again, the glowing red ember casting light on the jagged scar which dominated his face. "I didn't think it would hurt to have Shin in on the operation as well. He goes about his job with a certain efficiency I've become accustomed to."

Larry began to feel uneasy. Something about this situation wasn't right. He should have been escaping down the river by now, not standing on the dock chatting.

"What do you want from me?"

"Do you know who I am?" The stocky Japanese man stepped closer, his black eyes burning through Larry's skull.

"I, I, I, I'm not sure." It was Larry's turn to be afraid and the inflection in his voice made it apparent too.

"Don't be afraid young man." The hateful eyes never wavered as the shorter man took two steps back and extended his left hand. "I'm Katsuo Takahiro."

Larry could feel all the blood drain from his face. He had heard stories of the legend of Katsuo Takahiro. He had wandered the globe searching for his lost brother, killing anyone who meant him ill. What was he doing on this dock, at this time, on this night?

"It's very nice to meet you." Larry extended his hand and grimaced as the other man almost crushed it.

"I assume the ambassador is dead."

"Yes, I shot him six times in the chest."

"Excellent, Haruko. How about the other four men, are they dead as well?"

"Yes." Larry hung his head before continuing. "Shin shot each of them twice in the head."

"I guess it's a good thing he was a little more industrious with his ammo than you." Katsuo howled and Larry followed suit before the situation once again became tense. "What of Yasuhiro?"

"What?" Larry stammered but managed to hold himself together. "I don't know anyone named Yasuhiro."

It happened so fast the young man hadn't even the time to react. In one swift movement Katsuo had pulled an 8mm pistol which was identical to the one in Larry's hand, and shot the fledgling killer point blank in the forehead. A loud crack pierced the night air followed by the thump of a body.

The sound of the bullet tearing through the walls of his head brought him an odd calm. Larry felt no pain as he lay on the weathered timbers, his body angled in an unnatural manner. He could see blood running across the bridge of his nose and he commanded his hands to remove it, but they no longer served him. As his killer walked away, the young man felt his breathing coming in fits and witnessed his arms shaking independent of his mind. He looked to the night sky, found the unmistakable form of Orion the Hunter, and wondered how many men before him had done the same.

It was a beautiful night to die.

✳✳✳✳✳✳✳✳✳✳✳✳✳✳✳✳✳✳

19.

Confusion had morphed into panic, and underneath his mask Shin Shou grinned. He checked the bodies of the slain men before him. They were all dead and that was good. He had completed his primary mission.

Time was of the essence, however, and he set about retrieving the extra ammunition he had hidden for the Type 100. He had chosen the unproven and unwieldy weapon for one reason. It used the same 8mm projectiles as the semi-automatic Nambu pistol. The small caliber would have been underpowered in the jungles of Asia, but in these close quarters its strengths would excel.

Posing as a security guard for the ambassador had afforded him early access to the ballroom and their seating arrangements had made concealing both his weapon and ammunition effortless. The killer cursed under his breath as he stood on a chair to reach the stash. If he were just ten centimeters taller the world would be a simpler place.

The bandolier over his shoulder and Type 100 secured underneath his trench coat, the Japanese subversive removed his mask. An arctic wind whipped through the ballroom, causing the settling dust to flow around his feet. A slight cough slipped from his throat and he decided to play it up, hacking as he walked.

His escape route lay forty yards away. Outside the gaping hole in the wall he had stashed his getaway car, a 1932 Ford Model 18 convertible. The mass produced vehicle had seen its fair share of abuse in the last seven years, but would still serve his purposes today.

Shin laughed to himself as he continued to feign a cough. The old girl was a little rusty, but he had modified the engine, coaxing another twenty horsepower from its eight cylinders. He guessed it would approach 100 mph now. It was a perfect getaway car, inconspicuous and fast.

"Excuse me sir?"

Shin pretended not to hear the man addressing him. With an exaggerated cough he tucked his chin into his lapel and squeezed the Type 100 with his right hand. A scant few yards stood between him and a clean departure.

"Sir. Sir."

Shin could see the other man approaching from the corner of his eye. Escape was going to get a little bloody. That wasn't always a bad thing. He smiled a yellow grin as he brought the Type 100 up, popped in the side load magazine and coaxed a bullet into the chamber.

The unmistakable chatter of submachine gun fire now added to the surrounding pandemonium. Shin Shou had begun pulling the trigger a second early. He meant to cut his pursuer in half.

***

George heard the rat-tat-tat-tat-tat of the weapon simultaneous to seeing the flame erupting from its barrel. Instincts took over as he dove to the ground and tucked into a roll, bullets whizzing by inches above. His ears detected a pause and he deduced his enemy's exhaustion of the 30 round magazine.

Without missing a beat he completed his roll and delivered a well-aimed punch to the other man's abdomen. Ahiga used every ounce of kinetic energy available and the effects of his strike were instantaneous. He knocked his adversary backward, a replacement magazine clutched in the man's left hand, the submachine gun in his right.

Chief gathered himself to press the attack. He had hit the antagonist with all his might and there weren't many alive that could take his best punch. As he dug his feet into the rubble and scanned the ground for his own weapon, he witnessed something he hadn't expected.

Instead of falling onto his back, the stocky Japanese aggressor dropped to his rear and diffused the momentum in a backward roll. George watched in amazement at the speed and agility of his adversary. Within a moment the other man had regained his footing and replaced the magazine in his weapon. He brought it to bear on Chief, flashed his toothy yellow smile, racked the slide, and spoke.

"No one's ever hit me that hard in all my life. It would have been a good fight."

A hail of bullets cascaded from the barrel of the unwieldy rifle. George, however, had not been content with standing still. Just a few feet away an overturned table seemed a promising source of cover. He dove for its protection and as he slid to a stop, projectiles slammed into the steel. Dimpled perforations appeared inches from his face, but the 8mm lead lacked the power to puncture his sanctuary.

The assault paused, and George noticed it had stopped a tiny bit early. Moments before the hail of bullets had continued longer. Doubt crept into his mind. His opponent would soon approach and finish him off. Option after option of what to do next cycled through his brain, and all of them were bad. He had lost his Colt M1911 somewhere in the fray. At least with it he would have stood a fighting chance.

Instead of more gunfire or an approaching enemy, though, he heard swearing. Chief poked his head around the steel table and what he saw gave him new life. The Japanese rifle had jammed.

Ahiga closed the gap between them with lightning speed and attempted to deliver another bone crushing punch. He had underestimated his enemy, though. The other man sidestepped and raised the butt of his weapon.

George felt the smooth wood dig into the skin behind his ear. The entire world got knocked on its side as he tumbled, out of control, onto the ground. He was shaken, but not out. Clamoring to his feet he saw the other man removing his trench coat and placing a pistol on the ground. He looked mad dog angry and Chief could relate.

"I don't think I'll shoot you. My name is Shin Shou. Tell me when you are ready to fight."

George gained his balance and wiped a small trickle of blood which emanated from his nose.

"You can call me George, and I can't remember a time I wasn't ready."

✱✱✱✱✱✱✱✱✱✱✱✱✱✱✱✱✱✱

20.

"What's going on? We heard more gun fire." Rex and Sarah had scampered to the front of the building to find Leonard, Marilyn, Alexei and Luce standing in a circle near the entrance, worried looks on their faces. "Where's Angela?"

Leonard responded to the question with a nod toward the structure they had just evacuated.

"When the shooting started she ran back in."

"All I asked you to do was get the women out front to safety." Rex's annoyance was evident. "Now I have to go back in."

"No." Lucille Chase and Sarah exchanged looks as they spoke the word in unison, the latter still clutching his arm.

"I'll be back before you know it." Chase flashed a smile to his mother even as he took Sarah's cheek in his hand. "Don't worry. My dad and Leonard are more than capable of protecting you. I have to help Chief and Angela."

Before the final word had even left his lips a single gunshot cracked on the riverfront. Women shrieked once again as the crowd of one-thousand people clamored about. They were like cattle in a pen with no one to direct them. Chase's head snapped to attention as he made out the silhouette of a man in a trench coat climbing into a small boat. He had to act.

"Alright, the new plan starts right now. Since nobody seems to want to leave anyone we'll separate into couples." He could already see acceptance in the ladies' eyes, and protest in the eyes of the men. "Leonard and Marilyn, I want you to find out what is going on with George and Angela. Be careful, though, that was automatic gunfire in there. Mom and Dad get in your car and try to keep track of us in the water. You might want to stop by the house and pick up the chopper."

Rex referred to the Thompson submachine gun by one of its many nicknames before focusing once again on Sarah.

"You're coming with me."

Rex Chase started down the hill, without waiting to see if they executed his orders and Sarah followed close behind. The winter wind seemed to crystallize in his lungs as he breathed deep and held it in. To his surprise, his hip did not protest the endeavor, and Sarah ran like a gazelle.

They crossed the reserved parking lot and bounded onto the weathered docks. Ahead of them lay a solitary corpse and Chase identified the slumped over body with ease. The shooter had been a patsy and someone had executed him for his efforts.

He and Sarah didn't even break stride to leap over the fallen killer. She had impressed him before and he was even more so now. Without a word being uttered by either, she hurdled into the boat while he untied it with expert speed. Within seconds the 65 horsepower Chris Craft B motor sputtered to life and he navigated into the channel.

Who was the man in the boat up ahead? Why had he killed the boy on the dock? Were the President and the General still alive? Why had they killed the ambassador and the Japanese businessmen? All these thoughts raced through his mind as he began the frigid pursuit.

✳✳✳✳✳✳✳✳✳✳✳✳✳✳✳✳✳✳

21.

As if built from the same mold on opposite sides of the Pacific, the two men were physical equals. George sized up his opposition. Shou seemed comfortable as they circled one another in silence, waiting for the other to make a move.

George was the first to act. He closed the gap between the two in blinding fashion, throwing a sledgehammer left jab which the other man dodged. Chief slowed his pursuit, held his right hand back, and waited for the counter. He was not disappointed.

Shin was fast, faster than Ahiga had surmised. Before George could react he had taken a right cross to the jaw and could see the left hook coming in behind it. Relying on his experience Chief stepped into the punch, diffusing its effectiveness and wrapped his mammoth arms around the Japanese hitman.

They were face to face now and Ahiga squeezed with all of his might, attempting to toss his opponent to the ground. Shin's defense was strong, though, and a grin crossed his face.

"You're stronger than I thought." Saliva spat from behind his yellowed teeth. "That will make this all the more satisfying."

Shou dropped his weight downward while throwing his left arm across George's body. The move caught Chief off guard and he lost his balance, allowing the Japanese assassin onto his back. In hand to hand combat, giving up your back often would result in death. Chief relaxed, let his training kick in, and countered.

At the same time Shin attempted to wrap a meaty arm around his neck, George dropped his chin and lashed at the other man's knee. The force of the kick brought a howl from

Shou and caused him to lose his grip. Chief moved with blinding speed, using the advantage to grab Shou by the arm, flip him over his shoulder and slam him onto the ground.

His enemy landed with a thud and Chief could see the air evacuate his lungs. The fight was thirty seconds along, but George saw his opportunity. Without releasing his grip on the arm he pulled upward with all his might, hoisting the 220 pound man into the air.

Chief dropped to the ground while at the same time wrapping his arms and legs around his enemy. He had him now. With one arm high in the air and the other pinned against his body, the Asian fighter would not escape. Then, as he squeezed the life from his adversary George felt it.

The first blow felt like it had come from a dream. He blinked hard and squeezed even harder, the veins bulging from his muscular arms. His limited field of vision made it difficult to assess the new danger. Then he felt his grip lessen as Shou bludgeoned his head again.

George was in trouble. He tilted his head back, just in time to see a dull red brick stained in bright red blood. It slammed off his forehead as he let out a deep gasp.

He could feel Shin Shou escaping the death hold, but there was nothing he could do. The other man had been fighting for his life and had somehow gotten his right hand on a brick. George strained with all his might, but consciousness was leaving him.

He saw Shou stand, walk over to his coat, and put it on. A feeling of helplessness was all Chief could muster as he drifted off to what he assumed would be his final sleep. Then, the scene in front of him changed.

Out of nowhere Angela appeared, waving a broom above her head and screaming. Adrenalin surged through

George's almost unconscious form, but it wouldn't be enough to fend off the darkness. Dread flooded his mind. His wife would now be fighting the most capable killer he had ever met in hand to hand combat, with a broom.

✳✳✳✳✳✳✳✳✳✳✳✳✳✳✳✳✳✳

22.

Torrential rains had caused the Charles River to swell, making its passage in winter possible. A thin layer of ice crunched underneath the bow of the runabout as the 65 horsepower motor pushed its way forward. Though the craft ahead was larger and faster, it had made no serious efforts to escape. The two vessels instead remained locked in an ever slowing game of cat and mouse.

Chase knew this river like the back of his hand and it was obvious the pilot ahead did not. More than once Rex had thought the other man would beach his Cadet, but the mariner had maneuvered each time. As the minutes passed and they approached his home Rex knew their trip was nearing an end.

It didn't matter how much rain fell from the heavens, the Charles River on the other side of Populatic Pond would be unpassable. He looked at Sarah who huddled under two large blankets. Her opaline eyes hid behind matte shadowed eyelids and she seemed to have fallen asleep.

Chase smiled as he turned his attentions to the narrowing waterway. The other craft had already moved into the pond. They would find out soon who was piloting the vessel. The inlet and outlet were very near each other and it seemed the other man would be continuing up the river. Rex reached under the bow ahead of him and felt for the service issued Colt M1911 he had hidden. Though he had never been in the service the weapon's dependability made it an easy choice for defense.

Rex reached to his left and picked some ice crystals from her long blonde hair. She hadn't said a word since leaving the city. Most women he had ever known would have complained the entire way. He moved his hand to her shoulder, shaking it as he spoke.

"Sarah. Sarah. Our little trip down the river is about to end. You might want to go ahead and wake up."

She stirred and lifted her head. Despite the frigid temperature her smile warmed him to his very soul.

"Mmmmmmm. I was having the most wonderful dream." She stretched her arms and sat up in the bright red seat. "We finished our dinner and went out for a night on the town."

"I'm afraid you missed our romantic trip down the river." Chase concentrated on the narrow passage ahead. Since his journey hours before, an odd shaped log had lodged in his normal route. "Maybe next time I can give you the guided tour Sleeping Beauty."

"I'm sorry, I was so sleepy." Her nose crinkled and her eyes squinted as she released a gargantuan yawn. "I guess everything was so exciting that it wore me out."

Chase smiled as he navigated the boat around the titanic log ahead.

"I know how that feels. Once that adrenaline runs through your body and is gone..." He paused sensing an abnormal smell in the air. "Once it's gone..." He paused again before backing the motor to idle. "Do you smell that?"

At that moment a torrent of large caliber bullets tore through the front of the runabout. Chase slammed the controls forward to their stops and the boat lurched ahead. Flashes from both sides of the river forecasted the projectiles that now ripped into the aft of the small vessel. He had thrown off their aim when he had slowed a bit and then sped up. They wouldn't be fooled for long.

Flames burst from the water in all directions as they gained speed and came past the now burning log.

"A gigantic oil drum."

Chase said the words aloud, but they disappeared amongst the din of gunfire and his protesting engine. A loud squealing noise accompanied a dark plume of smoke from underneath the rear of the craft.

"Come on baby, I just need you for a few more seconds."

Sarah sat to his left, her eyes fixed ahead. Chase grabbed her arm so she would hear his instruction and she returned his gaze. Instead of the fright he had expected, though, all he saw was anger and determination. Her turquoise eyes burned and reflected the flames which surrounded them.

"I need you to hold on tight. This ride is about to get real bumpy."

She responded with a determined nod and braced herself for impact. Chase pulled the wheel hard to starboard and then to port, submersing the bow of the craft as he made a 180 degree turn. Flames licked the side of his face, singeing his hair and stinging his eyes. The small engine protested once again as a flurry of bullets pounded into the maneuvering watercraft.

They had emerged onto Populatic Pond now and the lights from his cabin twinkled in the distance. On the bank to their left Chase could see one large flash of light firing in their direction with regularity. It seemed as if their enemies had concentrated most of their weapons on the riverbank, no doubt because the pond side could be difficult to traverse.

The bow of the 1934 Chris Craft Deluxe Runabout was now littered with holes and on fire. Chase pointed the nose of the wounded vessel into the machine gun fire coming from the shore of the pond and prodded the wounded engine for one last burst of speed. It responded.

More bullets slammed into the side of the craft and tall plumes of water joined the flames around the boat. Full automatic gunfire now seemed to be coming from every direction and Chase no longer maneuvered the runabout. Most of his enemies' now had a full side view and Rex was thankful that they seemed determined to fire their weapons on full auto instead of taking their time and aiming.

He possessed a fortitude most other men did not. While his unknown assailants let their adrenaline force them into improper technique, he steeled himself into making perfect decisions. The steep bank loomed ahead along with the machine gun nest. He would get just one chance.

In this area of the pond, near the river, the bottom came up fast. They were right on the edge of the thickening ice which layered the pond and Chase was going to use it to his advantage. It was now or never.

At the last instant before slamming into the foot thick ice he turned the wheel hard to starboard. The port side of the craft rose into the air and the runabout skidded up onto the shelf. The boat was unwieldy and tipped side to side. Chase spoke to himself.

"No. No. No. No. NOW. GET DOWN AND COVER."

He dropped the port side anchor, bringing the runabout in line with an old hickory tree that had dropped earlier in the fall. The boat flew into the air and crashed through the branches of the century old tree. His anchor ripped from its tie down and sticks tore at their clothes as the two huddled close to one another.

The chaotic ride seemed to last forever and then with a loud crash, it was over. No more gunfire shattered the night and the 65 horsepower Chris Craft engine sputtered to a stop. The soothing sound of the river gurgling nearby and the fires licking at its surface were all that permeated the winter landscape. Chase looked to the twinkling stars in the sky and rubbed the small goose egg on his head.

"I think this is my most exciting first date ever."

****

23.

Angela heard the chatter of automatic gunfire and made tracks back into the damaged building.

"Wait. Angela, you're unarmed. Wait."

She heard Leonard's voice, but did not heed his warnings. It didn't matter to her if she was going into a gun battle unarmed. George didn't have a machine gun, so that meant he wasn't doing the shooting. He needed help.

Evacuees still milled about in the lobby of the broken building. They made progress toward her husband slow and she shoved them aside, receiving dirty looks and protests. None of that bothered her, though. One thing was all that mattered.

George.

Another burst of gunfire erupted in the other room as she assessed the situation. Perhaps she would need a weapon of some kind.

"Does anyone have a gun?" She asked, receiving the attentions of a serious looking man nearby.

"Why would you need a gun ma'am? I'm with the President's detail and I suggest you evacuate along with the others."

"Don't you hear the gunfire in there? Aren't you supposed to be protecting the President? What are you, some kind of coward?"

"No ma'am." His delivery was terse. "The President tasked me with guarding the guests. His detail is with him in the basement. I'm out here. To my knowledge nobody has died out here yet and I'd like to keep it that way."

Angela looked at him and didn't see fear in his eyes. Until she had confronted him he had been performing his duty. She relaxed before continuing.

"My husband is in there. He is personal friends with The General and The President. I have to help him."

The man hesitated for a moment and then stepped aside.

"Thank you."

She flew past the guard and burst through an open door into the ballroom. A few yards away stood the assassin. He had finished putting on his coat, holstered his gun and was approaching the fallen Ahiga. The pandemonium in the other room had masked Angela's entrance and she took advantage. Grabbing a nearby broom she executed the only plan that crossed her mind. Screaming at the top of her lungs she charged.

"Get away from him. I'll kill you."

Her adversary spun around, a look of shock adorned his face even as she broke the wooden handle across it. She gripped the portion of the broom she had left and thrust it into the man's shoulder. He howled, but with the element of surprise gone, she was now at a disadvantage.

His massive left hand tore the makeshift weapon from her grip causing her to lurch in his direction. He laughed a maniacal laugh and used that momentum to deliver a vicious right to her jaw that sent the young woman sprawling. A wide yellowed smile pursed his lips as he reached for the pistol in his trench coat.

Angela could see he was not going to hesitate to kill her. George lay a few feet away, either dead or unconscious. Sadness flooded her mind and she fought the urge to cry as her soon to be killer spoke.

"You must be George's lady." He brought the handgun to bear on her even as he took notice of the wound to his shoulder. "It's a shame to kill a woman as beautiful as you."

A flurry of gunshots echoed across the otherwise serene ballroom. Angela covered her head with her arms, expecting each breath to be her last, but then the shooting stopped and she caught a glimpse of the Japanese gunman fleeing. The sound of footsteps replaced the gunshots and a strong hand touched her shoulder.

"Ma'am. Are you ok ma'am?"

Without saying a word Angela leapt to her feet and ran to George. He was unconscious, and had blood seeping from two large gashes on his head, but his pulse was strong. He would live. She looked to the man a few feet away who had saved her.

"Thank you. Did you kill him?"

"I'm not even sure if I hit him. He even stopped and picked up his other gun." His answer was a bit bashful as he hung his head a bit and toed the ground. "I've never shot at a person before."

Angela stood and walked over to him. She was tall, but had to stand on her tiptoes to kiss him on the cheek.

"Well, thank you for saving my life. Do you think you could watch him for a second? I'll be right back."

Before he could even answer she had taken off in a dead sprint and was out the ballroom doors. At the sound of automatic gunfire the lobby had cleared and she had no problem making her way outside. Leonard and Marilyn had begun walking in her direction and she met them, her voice coming in between gasps for air.

"Wh, Wh, Where is everyone else?"

"Don't worry about that." Leonard said. "What's going on in there? We were on our way to help."

"It's all taken care of. George is just fine and my friend is watching him. I'm going to grab a car. We need to…"

The squealing of tires interrupted her sentence and she recognized her would be killer's face as the Model 18 almost hit a crowd of people.

"Let me guess." Leonard had already taken Marilyn's arm and started toward their car. "We're going after that guy."

"You can follow me. We can do this better with two cars." Adrenaline surged through her veins, but her mind was clear. "I'm driving the Marmon."

✳✳✳✳✳✳✳✳✳✳✳✳✳✳✳✳✳✳✳

24.

"So explain to me again why I never knew that we had a machine gun at our house? Aren't those illegal?"

Lucille Chase didn't like being kept in the dark and she let her displeasure be known.

"I'm sorry dear, and they aren't illegal, just a little more difficult to own than before 1934. After the whole Dietrich Hoff debacle Rex and I thought it prudent that we all be prepared for some sort of possible retribution."

"Do you think that's what is happening?" Her displeasure turned to concern. "Are we being targeted?"

"I don't think so my darling." Alexei stroked his wife's long curled hair as he guided their Lincoln Zephyr into the snowy driveway. "It had to be about about The General and The President. I'll be right back."

Luce sat in the new vehicle and watched as her husband opened the garage door and retrieved a case from the rafters. She had seen it there dozens of times before, but had thought it housed a musical instrument, or some other device. It had never occurred to her that it was a Tommy Gun.

As he made his way back to the car she breathed deep the cool air that rushed in when he had opened the door. She supposed this small secret wasn't a terrible one. They knew she didn't care much for guns, though she accepted their usefulness in certain situations, situations such as these.

"Baby, why don't you go ahead and stay here?" Alexei had put the already legendary weapon in the trunk and taken his position behind the wheel. "I don't see any reason why you need to go anywhere that is dangerous."

"Oh, I see." Most women of the time would have agreed with him and spent the night at home baking pies or cookies. That wasn't her style. "You and Rex go out and do all the hard man work while I sit at home and knit you sweaters?"

"That's not what I meant at all." Alexei said. "This might just be dangerous work, my love. I'd die if anything happened to you."

She smiled and took his hand before replying.

"Well, if the boogeyman came to the house you have my machine gun, so what would I protect myself with?"

"Ha. I suppose that's true." Alexei chuckled as he slid the Zephyr's three speed transmission into gear. "Maybe you should take a peek in the glove box over there."

The rear wheels on the luxury vehicle spun, caught the pavement, and then spun again. Luce could feel the car move side to side as she opened the glove box to find a Colt M1911 semi-automatic pistol. She brandished the weapon in her hand, careful to point the barrel toward the front of the shifting vehicle. Alexei seemed annoyed, but she had become intoxicated with the powerful weapon in her grasp.

"We're stuck."

He had interrupted her train of thought.

"Huh?"

"We're stuck Luce. Here I was in a big hurry and I parked in a snow drift. We are stuck. Get behind the wheel darling while I go get something to dig us out."

"OK."

She had heard what he said, but hesitated a moment, studying the gun. The resistance of the slide surprised her and she saw that the chamber was empty, but that the magazine was full. A button on the side of the handle seemed the logical place to put a release, so she pushed it, and the magazine slipped out into her hands. Guns had never seemed of much use in her personal life, but tonight, well, tonight seemed different.

THE SENTINEL

She popped the magazine into its secured position and racked the slide, loading the 1911. Events of the day rushed through her mind as she set the safety and placed it on the seat next to her. The sound of her voice made the thoughts seem more real.

"I will kill to defend my family."

****

25.

"No, I swear it. I've known that young man since he was in diapers. It's just a coincidence that he plays for my favorite team as well, right Timmy?"

"He's not lying." Tim leaned back as he rubbed his belly. Between the two of them they had eaten three dozen oysters. "Where did you guys get those oysters from anyway?"

"Island Creek, and they were fresh this morning. Now don't change the subject. That kid they're talking about right now. He's what, your grandson?"

"No way." The old man laughed. "I told you, I'm 100 years old today. He's waaaaay too young to be my grandson."

"Well, if you're in here cheering against the Red Sox you had better have a darn good reason." She wiped her hands with a towel and addressed the younger of the two. "Another?"

"Sure." She dropped a few pieces of ice in his glass and retrieved a bottle of Maker's Mark from the top shelf. The amber colored 90 proof bourbon danced across the cubes as it settled and he swirled the glass before touching it to his lips. "Delicious. I love bourbon."

"Well don't love it too much. You still have to drive me home and I want to live to see tomorrow. I'll have another one too if you don't mind?"

The bartender was quick to oblige, but Wheat arched his left eyebrow before speaking.

"I know it's your birthday, but are you sure? I haven't seen you have more than one scotch in almost twenty years. As a matter of fact, I'm pretty sure it was your eightieth birthday when I had to carry you into your house covered in vomit."

"At least I didn't piss my pants on my fiftieth birthday."

"Touché."

The old man's retort and Wheat's reply had been quick as all three shared another laugh.

"OK, you do whatever you want. The wife is working all day at the hospital so I've got nothing but time."

"That's great, how is Candice doing?"

"She's good, thanks for asking. Still loving the new job, loving the hours, loving all of it. Life is just good."

"Loving the money too, no doubt."

"No doubt." Wheat chuckled as he sipped the bourbon again. "Hey, would you mind if I had a Guinness as well?"

"Uh, oh. It's time to start double fisting." She joked. It wasn't unusual for patrons to have a beer and a drink. "So tell me again how you two…"

The old man interrupted by slamming his fist down on the bar and they both gave him quizzical looks.

"What? Aren't you listening to the game? Your son just gave up a two run home run to Pedroia."

"The kid pitching is your son?"

Tim looked at his friend before replying to the bartender.

"Now you see why we have no option but to cheer for the Cubs today."

"I've been cheering for them my entire 100 years. I don't know what you're talking about."

The three shared another laugh as the bartender mixed ingredients in a tall silver shaker. She capped it with a cocktail glass and shook the contents. Seconds later she split the glass and poured its light blue liquid into three shots.

"Mind if I buy you guys a shot? I made it blue, just for your beloved Cubbies."

Wheat was a little worried, but all that left when he saw the look on the old man's face. He was like a kid in a candy store.

"If he's in. I'm in. To a hundred years."

"A hundred years."

The three spoke in unison, clicked their glasses together in the air, and poured the drinks down their throats. Wheat was the first to finish, the bartender a close second. A few moments passed and then the third glass hit the bar.

"You know, eighty years ago, I would have beaten you all."

"Well that's good because I would have been about negative thirty, and she would have been about negative seventy-eight."

"Ha, Ha, Ha, very funny."

They all laughed again before she spoke.

"I like you guys. You need to come in here during the day more often and keep me company. My name is Anastasia, but you can call me Annie."

"Well Anniestasia. This is my only bestest friend in the whole world Tim Wheat, but he's madly in love with his wife so don't even think about it." His heart warmed. Was it the liquor or because this young women was smiling at him? It didn't matter to him either way. "My friends call me RG2."

✱✱✱✱✱✱✱✱✱✱✱✱✱✱✱✱✱✱

26.

Katsuo lit another Lucky Strike and blew the smoke out his nose. The roaring din of automatic weapons fire had ceased and the more peaceful sound of ice crunching underneath his hull had replaced it. He smiled to himself and inhaled once again. They had expected more of a fight from his blonde adversary.

Rex Chase couldn't be blamed, however, since they had stacked the odds against him. Katsuo pointed his bow in the direction of the wrecked runabout and motioned for the others to follow. Eight small boats and one larger filled with elite commandos obeyed, firing up their motors and emerging from the shadows on the river's edge.

An acrid waft of smoke tickled his nose and caused him to sneeze. At first Katsuo had balked at the idea of bringing fifty of his most elite troopers, but then Izanami had shown him the reports from eighteen months before. Some of his soldiers had also seen the reports and begun calling the blonde Bostonian *howaito satan*. Japanese for "white satan."

Another smile curled across his lips. All it had taken to kill Lucifer was five type 96 machine guns positioned on the riverbank and one type 92 on the shore of the pond. The fifty troopers, it seemed, were superfluous. Perhaps the white devil had lost his edge.

To his left the larger Chris Craft Cruiser, with its mounted type 92, pulled alongside and they idled in silence toward the wreckage ahead. Nothing seemed to be moving. Perhaps he had lost a couple of men to the runabout's head on assault.

Katsuo held up his left fist and the other boats cut their engines. All was still. He scanned the shore with his eyes, but the fires on the water had ruined his night vision.

"OK. Let's get onshore." His men began unloading and he looked to his second in command on the cruiser. "Anori. I'd like you to..."

His comrade's head disappeared before he had even heard a sound and the deafening roar of the shoreline type 92 followed the hail of bullets. Katsuo's reaction was instant, and it saved his life. He dove headfirst onto the shelf of ice to his right, diffusing his momentum with a roll. Fire breathed from the Japanese machine gun and Takahiro scrambled to escape its wrath. White Satan, it seemed, wasn't going down without a fight.

****

27.

Squealing tires welcomed Chief back to the conscious world. He blinked his eyes hard as he wiped the blood from his face and got to his feet. The surrounding world was straight out of a nightmare, and his wife was nowhere to be seen.

"Hey."

George whirled on his feet, prepared to fend off an attack, but a friendly face met him instead.

"Take it easy. I'm with the President's detail." The other man had entered the room through the large hole in the wall. "He got away. I emptied my gun and I don't even think I hit him."

"Where's my wife?" Shin Shou was not number one on Chief's list of priorities.

"She's fine. She asked me to watch out for you while she ran back outside." The mammoth red-haired man offered his hand and George took it. "I'm Phineas O'Rourke."

"A good Irish name if I've ever heard one." A crocodile would have been proud in the amount of clamp down strength being exchanged. "I'm George Ahiga, but if you save my life, you can call me Chief."

"I'm not the person you need to thank." The vise-like exchange ceased as he continued. "Your wife came in here like a woman possessed and attacked that other guy with a broom. I think it might have even broken off in his shoulder. At the very least he has a nasty wound from it."

"That sounds like Angela." Chief rubbed the knot on his head. "Where are the rest of you guys?"

"I'm not sure. We were short four guys tonight because of a stomach bug so that took us down to a dozen men and two supervisors."

"How many men were in the President's immediate detail?"

"On a normal night we'd have had ten or eleven on the President, plus one supervisor, while the other supervisor roamed." O'Rourke scratched his head as he surveyed the room. "We're not prepared to deal with bombings, though. Most of our training involves taking down one man shooters and securing The President. I can't believe I didn't even hit that guy."

"Shooting at people is a heckuva lot different than paper targets." Chief patted the larger man on the shoulder. "So there's a good possibility The President's entire security detail is in that basement."

"Except for me."

"Except for you."

The dust had already settled in the room and though the evidence of chaos was everywhere, a few seconds of serenity passed. Far-off sirens began to wail as the Boston Police responded to the emergency. Chief stood still, gazing into the gaping hole in the floor. Feeble sounds of the wounded emanated from below.

"We had better get down there and see what we can do."

O'Rourke had spoken up and Chief was about to agree when the sound of squealing tires once again brought their attention to the fissure in the wall. The gleaming burgundy Marmon had come to a screeching halt just outside. Angela leaned across and opened the passenger door.

"Need a lift?"

Immeasurable feelings of love and relief swept over the young Navajo warrior as he found himself speechless. A moment passed, and then the Irish secret service agent broke the silence.

"He's driving a blue drop top Model 18. You go get that s.o.b. I'll coordinate everything here once the cavalry arrives."

"Thank you." Chief shook the other man's hand, picked up the 1911, and sat next to his wife in the luxury Marmon. His hand trembled as he cradled her face. Her smile is what made the sun rise every day. "I, I, I, couldn't help you."

"That's why I came to help you." Angela steadied his hand with hers. Her hair looked as if she had just stepped from the parlor and Chief drank in every line of her face. "Remember, we're a team."

"Forever and ever."

The two shared a quick, passionate kiss even while Angela put the vehicle into gear.

"He's driving a blue Ford convertible."

"A Model 18 according to Phineas."

"Who?"

"Phineas O'Rourke. You didn't have time for proper introductions?"

"I did not. It's a fine Irish name if I've ever heard one, though."

George beamed as he slapped his hand down on the dash.

"Do you have your own set of keys?"

"Doesn't every girl know how to hotwire a car?"

Chief clapped his hands as squealing tires once again dominated the night air and drowned his response.

"I love you more every day."

✱✱✱✱✱✱✱✱✱✱✱✱✱✱✱✱✱✱

28.

Under normal circumstances an unarmed assault on an enemies' machine gun position would be considered suicide. Sarah, though, had survived just such an attack. She looked to her right, but Chase was nowhere to be seen. Perhaps the violent crash had thrown him from the boat.

At that moment the roar of automatic weaponry again dominated the night. Now, though, the sound was different and she turned her head as she covered her ears. What she saw was mesmerizing.

A few yards away sat Rex Chase, his legs straddling the Type 92 heavy machine gun as it spewed lead. A long strip of bullets lay to his left and his shaggy blonde hair vibrated in time with the instrument of death. She watched as he methodically moved the weapon from target to target.

He started with the largest boat, but spent a scant few seconds on it. The nests on the other side of the bank opened fire, but it seemed Chase had already made them a priority. As soon as bullets had begun to pierce the air around her in every direction, their intensity began to lessen.

Rex Chase operated the purveyor of death with surgical precision. Whereas his enemies sacrificed accuracy for rate of fire, he let loose short, controlled bursts. She watched as he systematically eliminated their most imminent threats. Within fifteen seconds, silence had once again reclaimed Populatic Pond.

For her, time had slowed to a near standstill. It didn't seem possible that the man she had first met earlier in the night was capable of doing the things she had just witnessed. Then he was standing over her, his hand outstretched, a worried look on his face. Even in the darkness his bright blue eyes shone. She watched his lips moving, but her mind failed to process their message. He was so beautiful.

"Sarah. Sarah. Are you alright?"

The silent world to which she had retreated came into laser sharp focus.

"Yes." She cleared her throat, and delivered again with more force. "Yes. I'm fine."

"That's good because we have to go right now."

"Wait. Shouldn't we take that with us?"

Nearby the Type 92 sat silent, smoke still swirled from its barrel.

"Nope, it's low on ammo, hot as hades, and too heavy. We need to go."

"But, but, but..." Her mind was racing and her tongue couldn't keep up. "What if they start shooting again? How will we defend ourselves?"

A burst of tears flowed from her eyes, and she was milliseconds away from sobbing. Chase responded with a smile that melted her heart and eased her fears. Those eyes seemed to burrow into her very soul, and it felt comforting.

"Don't worry." He patted the M1911 tucked into his waistband. "I've got it covered."

Somehow, that seemed enough. Before she knew what was happening Chase had taken her hand and they were making a dash through the forest. The area was beautiful and she took notice of her surroundings. All around them the forest seemed to swallow everything, yet they moved like a knife through melted butter.

The only things that seemed to slow them were the occasional drifts of snow. Her lungs burned from the cold winter air and her legs began to protest. Just a few minutes had passed, but she could go no further, then they stopped. Sarah dropped to a knee, thankful for the respite, as Chase released her hand and peered from behind a gargantuan oak tree.

She had always considered herself to be in satisfactory condition, but as she looked at Chase she knew that not to be true. His breathing was deep and under control. Hers was coming in fits and she fought to manage it. Tears streamed down her face and mixed with sweat that emanated from her pores, yet he showed no ill signs from their exertions

They sat silent and still for two straight minutes and her breathing returned to normal. The unmistakable sound of foreign voices began to waft across the pond. It wouldn't be strange to hear a number of languages spoken in the area, but Japanese was not one of those. Sarah looked at Chase, but he didn't seem concerned over the sounds of their enemies regrouping. His focus was on the other side of the tree.

"Sarah. Sarah." She had been listening with such intent to the Asian men across the water that his hushed voice startled her. She snapped her head back around as he said her name a third time. "Sarah."

"Yes?"

"I think there are four of them up ahead. You stay right here and watch from behind the tree. Do you see that Plymouth parked next to the cabin?"

"Yes."

"Good. When you see me take the two guys in the Plymouth I need you to get to that garage over there as fast as possible. If I don't beat you, hide under the Packard. Do you understand?"

She was speechless. He was going to leave her alone in the middle of the woods. A thousand questions flooded her mind, but just one materialized in her voice.

"How did we get through the forest so fast? I saw brambles and briars everywhere."

He arched an eyebrow, smiled, and answered.

"I cut a little path this fall along an existing game trail. Don't tell George though, he likes to complain about how I always make him fight his way through the heavy timber. You know what to do?"

"Yes."

He squeezed her hand, kissed her on the cheek, and disappeared. A serene feeling rushed over her as she moved into position and peered from behind the oak. Chase was nowhere to be seen.

Few things surprised her in this world, but this man had managed to astonish her several times over the course of just a few hours. He was brilliant, handsome, witty, comforting, but most of all, fearless. During this entire ordeal she hadn't even seen a hint of trepidation in his eyes.

What happened next, on any other day, would have rattled the young woman. Machine gun fire again roared across the small body of water, however, she breathed deep and felt comfort. Rex Chase would keep her safe.

***

Chase had dispatched the first two guards within seconds of leaving his cover behind the mammoth oak. The two men had set themselves in a concealed position that predicted an assault from the road. Since Chase had come from the forest, their demise had been undemanding.

What was developing ahead of him now, though, was a more difficult assault. He had planned on using the Type 96 light machine gun from his fallen foes to defeat the two men in the Plymouth. From his new vantage point, though, the silhouettes of two additional men near the garage had become discernable. He needed time, but the voices crossing the pond became more centralized every second. His enemies were organizing.

Thirty yards and several snow drifts separated himself from the Plymouth. He had a fifty/fifty chance of crossing the space and dispatching the two men before they killed him. He would then have to rush around the back of the cabin before the two guards near the garage could kill Sarah. It wasn't foolproof, but it would have to do.

"Ok E.R.C. Let's do this."

Just then the sound of automatic gunfire thundered across the pond once again. Chase paused and saw the heads of all four guards turn away from him and back toward the pond. He couldn't have asked for a better scenario.

Even while high stepping through the knee deep snow he covered the thirty yards in less than four seconds. Neither man even saw what was coming as Chase slid to a stop outside the idling vehicle. The M1911 barked twice and the first phase of his plan was complete.

He rounded the corner of his cabin in full stride and sneaked a peek back toward the forest. Sarah was already three steps into her dash. Chase brought his attention back to the front. The report of his .45 caliber sidearm had alerted the other two guards. It was going to be close.

The automatic weapon crossing the pond continued its constant chatter as Chase bolted into the open. What he saw shot a wave of terror down his spine. The two guards had moved toward the front of the garage and now, with weapons raised, had Sarah within their sites. Rex had a seventy yard shot, with a pistol, but that was the hand dealt him.

He took a deep breath in, aimed, and hesitated. One of the Japanese soldiers had lowered his weapon while speaking in frenzied Japanese to the other. They seemed to be arguing and then turned as a pair. Rex stared down the sights of the 1911 as he met the soldiers' gaze. The men appeared startled but then brought their guns to bear.

Chase emptied the weapon's magazine. Fire belched from the five inch barrel as his hands steadied the cold steel. His first shot hit the larger of the two men in the side of the chest, doubling him over. The other man, though, managed to fire a few shots before Rex put him down.

He replaced the spent magazine, pulled the slide, and was back in the fight. He kept his gun trained on the two fallen soldiers as he advanced in a tactical fashion. Neither was dead, but neither still possessed their weapon. Rex was thankful the snow on this side of his house was inches deep instead of feet and he peered from the corner of his eye as he approached. Sarah stood frozen in the middle of the road.

"Sarah." He paused, but received no reply. "Sarah, honey. Where did I tell you to be?"

He didn't receive a reply, but saw her movement. Like a flash, she flew past and into the garage. A smile crossed his lips as he stood over the two fallen men.

"English?"

"No."

"Dono yo ni shinitaino de suka?" Chase spoke limited Japanese but the men understood. He offered them a choice in how they died.

"Watashi ga tata katte shinde shimau." Their reply was simultaneous and Chase could appreciate their courage.

"If you're going to die fighting boys I'd expect you'll want to get to it."

Both men moved as one in opposite directions and Chase recognized their ploy to divide and conquer. He fired with amazing speed and precision as two shots rang out within three tenths of a second. Both men went limp and their fight was over.

Chase looked to the pond behind him where the machine gun still wailed. The largest of the boats was using its weapon to carve a path through the ice while the smaller crafts followed. More men were coming to fight.

Chase weighed his options as he opened the door to the garage. Should they get in the Six and try to flee? Should they stay and fight?

"Sarah?"

Axl and Belle lay on the floor next to the Six whining. Chase was glad to see the intruders had left the animals alone. A small voice replied from under the vehicle.

"Just so you know. I don't speak a lick of Japanese."

****

29.

"Hang back a little farther baby."

"I know what I'm doing. This isn't my first high speed car chase."

"This is a low speed car chase and those are the kind I like. When were you ever on an actual high speed car chase?" George arched his eyebrow.

"Never mind that, he's turning."

Chief refocused his attention on the Model 18 up ahead. They had sniffed out Shou's trail eight blocks away from the ballroom and had been following ever since. Somehow Angela had known which way he was most likely to be going. Perhaps she had done this before.

"I would like to emphasize that I think we should hang back a little." Chief smiled as his wife shot him an icy glare. "It's just that traffic is pretty light tonight and we're just a hundred yards behind him. If he can drive as well as he can fight he'll be on to us before we know it."

Shou had turned onto a narrow thoroughfare, a long line of various shops nestled on either side. Angela made her turn onto the street, and Chief sensed danger. They had been too close.

"Stop the car." George said the words with absolute calm in his voice and when Angela didn't comply fast enough, he put his hand on her leg. "Please stop the car."

Colonel Howard C. Marmon had designed a brilliant luxury vehicle, but right now the sixteen cylinder engine sounded like a locomotive. Chief rolled down the passenger window allowing his ears access to the chill winter air. Their vehicle slowed to a stop as he trained his eyes on the scene ahead.

"Do you want me to…"

"Shhhhhh."

Chief interrupted his wife in a firm authoritative tone. Trees lined the desolate road ahead and workers had piled large mounds of snow on both sides. Paths leading to different shops and into the street weaved through the piles while access to alleys seemed open. Not a soul was to be seen, and George didn't like it.

"He's out there."

"How do you know?"

"The roads are too slick and we were too close. No way did he get to the end of the street. If you look to your left you'll see snow packed in the crossroads. He has to be out there." Chief noticed a slight trail of smoke wafting from an alley thirty yards ahead. He nodded in its direction as he spoke. "I'm going to check that out. If any shooting starts I want you to get out of here. This car is made of steel; it should keep you safe."

"I will not."

Angela's eyes burned with determination and George decided to use a different tactic.

"Fine, if any shooting starts stay out of the line of fire. The car should protect you. I'll be back before you know it."

Chief exited the vehicle, pulled the 1911, and made his way to a nearby mountain of snow. He peeked around the side nearest the shops and confirmed his suspicions. Protruding from the alley just ahead was the rear end and tailpipe of the Model 18. Exhaust drifted through the air and George contemplated his next move.

"You're lucky to be seeing me again."

George froze in place. How could Shou have snuck in behind him?

"I was just thinking the same thing."

Chief dropped to a seated position, while twisting 180 degrees. He strained to control the fall and within three tenths of a second had turned to face his nemesis, the 1911 pointed perpendicular to the ground. In his line of fire, though, was nothing but the Marmon. Angela's head had disappeared from view and Shou's laughter filled the air.

"Say goodbye to your woman."

Thirty yards away and on the other side of the street Shin Shou opened fire with the side loaded Type 100. Within seconds he had unloaded an entire magazine into the Marmon. Chief waited for the pause and hoped Angela had heeded his warning. When silence came, he made his move and what he saw seemed remarkable and impossible.

The Japanese killer stood atop a five foot high mound of snow, his automatic weapon reloaded. George had never seen anyone so well trained. Stepping into the street would be suicide, so Chief stopped and huddled against the snow once again. He needed a plan and he needed it now.

"Just so you know George. I have six more magazines filled to capacity over here. You will be dying soon."

"I have at least one bullet in my 1911. That should be all I need." George was stalling and Shou's laughter showed he was willing to play along. Chief poked his head up to look inside the Marmon. Angela was nowhere to be seen. "I was just thinking that was kind of a sissy move, you know, hitting me with a brick back there."

Shou's laughing stopped and once again the only sounds came from the throaty exhaust of the Marmon. Perhaps George had crossed a line. He peeked around the snow pile and Shin greeted him with a hail of bullets. They sailed mere inches off their mark and Chief was able to retreat to a safer point behind his snow fortification. At least if Shou focused the attack on him, Angela would be safe.

Chief took a deep breath and assessed the situation. Shou had him pinned down and he needed to move. The snow and ice made it difficult to do so with any speed and his adversary held superior firepower and positioning. Just then the roar of the automatic weapon filled the air again and George made a decision. He'd rather die fighting. Just as he stood to return fire something about the situation changed. At first he couldn't quite put his finger on it, but then it became clear.

The Marmon was no longer idling. All sixteen of its cylinders fired in perfect time and the exhaust roared. In less than two seconds its rear tires burned through the snow and caught the hardened surface underneath, propelling the five-thousand two hundred and ninety-one pound behemoth forward. Chief became a momentary spectator as the deep maroon vehicle raced ahead like someone had shot it from a catapult. Bullets smashed into its windshield and riddled the hood, but its advance would not falter. It was all happening so fast that, for an instant, Chief had dismissed an important part of the situation. Angela still was not behind the wheel of the car. It seemed to be driving itself.

***

At the first sounds of bullets Angela had huddled onto the floor just as her husband had instructed. She could feel the vehicle shudder as the 8mm projectiles struck it, but none seemed to penetrate on the first volley. She listened as her husband and Shou exchanged words. George was stalling. She could hear it in his voice.

THE SENTINEL

When the bullets began pouring through the windshield she made an instant and calculated decision. Her husband must have been at a terrible disadvantage or he wouldn't risk her vehicle taking this much fire. She had seen Shou climb to the top of the snow drift a few yards away so she gripped the steering wheel and muscled it into position.

"Here goes nothing."

Before she had even finished saying the words out loud she leaned hard against the accelerator while pulling on the stick with all her might. The aluminum motor roared, and since she had no way to depress the clutch, the floor mounted gear shift fought its assignment. A second passed and a tear rolled down her face. She had to succeed. Failure meant death.

All of a sudden, and accompanied by a loud bang, the transmission caught and the car shuddered as torque transferred to the rear wheels. Angela pushed her rear into the accelerator feeding the v16 even more fuel and causing the vehicle's tail to buck. She took her hands off the gear shift and instead tried to steer the vehicle in the direction of Shou. Everything happened in a matter of moments, but she moved with confidence and determination.

Then the car steadied and shot forward. Glass showered onto the seat ahead of her and she could see bullets tearing into the fine leather, sending small clouds of stuffing flying. A feeling of elation flooded her as she realized she had to be moving in the right direction if the bullets were coming through the windshield and impacting the seat.

A sharp pain in her back interrupted her elation. Even as the automobile slammed into the opposite bank the rear wheels clawed at the earth and snow below. Like a bull in a china shop the three ton vehicle fought forward. Then she heard an unmistakable thump, a noise on the roof, and saw a body fall past the passenger window.

Her pain seemed a million miles away. She had fulfilled the objectives of her self-assigned mission. Now it was up to George.

****

30.

Chase's logical retreat would be to his cabin home and garage. Katsuo knew it and had planned for it. Even as the heavy machine gun pounded at the ice ahead he recognized his chances of finding the young man alive were slim. He had placed his best six soldiers at the picturesque cottage and as they neared the shore he lit another cigarette.

"Cease fire." Katsuo barked the order and his men followed it. Glowing red, the barrel of the type 92 seemed to be a beacon showing the way. "Everyone ashore. Advance with caution and in teams."

Takahiro dismounted his river flagship and the sound of snow crunching under boots echoed across the grounds. He watched as his men seemed to move as a single living being. It reminded him of the flocks of mejiro back home. As a boy he had marveled at their ability to navigate as one.

"Sir." His highest ranking officer approached and spoke in a whisper. "Sir, they are all dead."

"Who is dead?" Katsuo asked as he took another drag of his Lucky Strike.

"Our men are dead sir."

He took in every aspect of the scene. His men stood shaken, looks of fear and confusion adorning their faces. None of them would admit it, of that he was certain, but the truth was behind their eyes. Katsuo smiled as he breathed deep the North Carolina tobacco.

"Burn it all."

"Now that isn't any way to say hello. It's your first time here."

Katsuo looked ahead and made out a shadow in the darkness.

"I just needed the light. I can't make out a thing from here."

"We apologize for that. Sarah, would you mind turning the lights back on for our friends? It's a switch right there on the wall."

A number of security lamps bathed the area in light and the Japanese fisherman now saw his quarry. He stood just outside of a steel entryway to the garage fifty yards away. This was going to be a slaughter.

"You shouldn't have brought your woman with you my friend. I take no delight in killing women."

"Are we friends now?" Katsuo could see the ear to ear grin on the other man's face. He was insane. "I don't even know your name."

"I am Katsuo Takahiro, and you are Rex Chase, and I am done talking."

"Easy there Kit-Kat. We have all the time in the world. What's your rush?"

"Kit-Kat? You'll have to forgive me Mr. Chase. It seems my English is lacking."

"Quite the contrary Kitty. You don't even have an accent. A Kit-Kat is a chocolate bar from England I read about. I'd like to get my hands on one of those. They sound like a real treat. You know I could..."

"Enough. I've had enough of your insults." Katsuo coughed as he interrupted. A deep seated anger broiled inside his belly. It was time to end this game. "I want every man here to..."

"You've had enough? He's had enough." Katsuo could see the other man's countenance and hear his timbre change. Before he had seemed happy, almost congenial, but now the fire of a warrior brimmed to the surface. "You come to my house and shoot up my boat, on my pond, and you've had enough? I tell you what Kit-Kat. You and all your men can go ahead and leave right now or I'll have no choice but to kill you all the way I did your friends. I believe the count so far is eight to nothing and I feel like I'm on a hot streak."

Katsuo smiled. The white devil was living up to the stories. It was going to be a pleasure killing him. Just then, though, a woman stepped from the small doorway ahead. She held a rifle and a small box of ammunition. His smile widened.

"If you surrender now I promise to just kill you. What do you think you are going to do with that old bolt action rifle anyway?"

"Well, the way I figure it is this. I have fifty rounds and there are about fifty of you guys. So that means it'll take me about three minutes to kill all of you with this Springfield M1903. I'm shooting a hundred fifty grain projectile at twenty-seven hundred feet per second. Since you guys are all about fifty yards away and the battle sight on this weapon is set to five hundred forty-seven yards my quick cipherin tells me to hold under twenty-four point seven four inches. So if you all want to die today, go ahead and stick around. If you want to live, I suggest you get back on those boats and get out of here."

A slight murmur went up amongst the men and anger swept through his body. They were rattled and he was perplexed. Chase's body language was free and easy, showing no fear of death. Katsuo shifted his gaze to the woman, Sarah, who stood by her man. She met his eyes, nodded and also showed no fear. She didn't even blink. His decision was simple and he gave the order.

"Kill them."

****

31.

Angela had created an opportunity where one hadn't existed before. She had saved them from certain death and Chief had no intention of letting her efforts go to waste. Before the Marmon even slammed into the Japanese assassin's perch George leapt into action.

Shou tumbled over the top of the vehicle and George attempted to speed his advance, but the ice crunching under his patent leather wing tips impeded all movement. They would not have been his shoe of choice for winter fighting. The other man was a mere twenty yards away and Chief stopped short, taking aim with the .45 caliber pistol. He steadied his arm and took a deep breath in, then blew it out.

Ahead of him, Shin Shou hit the ground, rolled, and came up firing. The move had been so fluid, smooth, and improbable that Chief hadn't calculated it into his shot. He squeezed the trigger once as bullets pounded the ground at his feet. Instinct and training took over as he moved left to avoid the fire, but the wing tips wouldn't hold their grip.

Even as he fell to the ground, Chief pulled the trigger over and over. He made no attempt to cushion his own fall, but instead focused on keeping his shots on target. Shin had exhausted his magazine and was on the retreat. That was something George needed to exploit.

His shoulder slammed into the ice hard, sending a lightning bolt of pain down his spine. That didn't matter now, though, as Shou was escaping. Chief retrieved the extra magazine from its position nestled in his lower back. It was a move he had practiced thousands of times, and within a second he was back in the fight. He had lost valuable time though, and Shin Shou wasn't wearing wing tips. The villain was out of pistol range in short order and George shuffled after the scoundrel, soon losing him behind one of the large banks of snow.

"Shinny, my buddy, my pal. Where are you?"

Roaring from the alley just ahead the Model 18's V8 engine anwered his question. The assassin was more mobile and was about to get away. Chief sprang into action. He would get one chance.

Every step was fraught with peril, but Chief didn't care. He had one goal, and he meant to achieve it. As the Ford's rear tires clawed at the ground and the mass production vehicle began to angle away he made one last effort to stop it.

He dove, and with his left hand grasped the vehicle's rear mounted spare tire. His feet dangled as the car picked up speed, and for a moment he considered tossing the 1911. It wouldn't do to be unarmed, though, so he fought to tuck it into his waistband.

George's left arm protested, pain shooting down its length and Ahiga grit his teeth. The vehicle was approaching twenty mph now and his feet were no longer of assistance. Chief threw his right arm onto the tire and in an instant pulled himself onto the automobile.

Not a second could be wasted and he knew it. George planted his feet on the back bumper and leapt onto the canvas top of the convertible. A burst of gunfire sounded and holes opened in the roof just ahead of his face. Maybe he hadn't thought this through. Another burst made a straight line starting inches from his waist and following his leg down the rear of the vehicle. This wasn't good.

He fumbled for the .45, but it was all he could do to hold onto the vehicle. Shin had begun swinging the car back and forth and the winter landscape caused it to careen across the road. Seconds passed and George held on for dear life expecting a lethal volley of bullets to end his time as a Model 18 stowaway. It didn't come.

Chief pulled himself forward and ripped at the canvas, making a hole large enough to put his head through. What he saw was good, or at least not as bad as it could have been. The Type 100 had jammed again and Shin fought to free the action. George saw his opportunity and he took it. He released his grip with his right hand pulled the 1911, and poked it through the hole. He wouldn't be able to aim.

"Hey Shinny."

Shou didn't look, but instead gave the souped up V8 a shot of adrenaline even as he continued to swerve like the madman he was. George held on for dear life with his left hand but began to squeeze the trigger with his right. He loosed four shots before everything changed.

Flying through the air was a singular and helpless feeling. Though he was moving at a high rate of speed, George could perceive everything that happened. The hot rodded Ford had slammed into a pole and he had lost his grip. Physics made it impossible for him to stay with the vehicle and he watched it move away. It had impacted just behind the right rear tire.

"At least he won't be driving that away."

The thought was clear and distinct. George pinwheeled parallel to the ground in a flat spin and he relished the icy air biting at his skin. If these were going to be his last moments he was going to enjoy them. The ground was coming up fast and Chief attempted to soften the blow, but control was not his. Darkness hit with permanent, instant, violence. George Thomas Ahiga was dead.

***

THE SENTINEL

Angela grunted as she squeezed from her hiding place inside the Marmon. By the time she exited the vehicle, George had already hitched a ride on the Model 18. She watched in awe as the vehicle careened out of control down the street. George's legs swung from side to side and gunshots rang out. Then it happened.

She had never run so fast in all of her life. Tears flowed even as she fought to control them. Her husband flew from the vehicle like a rag doll, his legs striking a nearby pole. The violence of the accident had hurtled him forty feet and he lay motionless.

Somehow she crossed the short distance, in high heels, without falling. Upon approach she slowed and slid to a stop on her knees. She could feel the ice digging into them and the warmness of blood trickling down her legs, but none of it mattered.

"George. George." His face was at peace and his hands were across his chest as if someone had staged them. She brought his face close, and though it was dark, could see the emptiness of death in his eyes. Grief poured over her as she fought to control her shaking. Tears rushed from their ducts and her body convulsed. No agony had ever prepared her for this moment.

Then a single gunshot once again pierced the air and all pain subsided. Angela felt her entire body go numb and her eyes blinked hard. She looked down and a large wound had opened in her chest. The ground came up to meet her and she blinked again as the pair of boots came alongside.

Though she felt nothing, the scope of her view changed and she could tell she was being rolled over. Above her stood Shin Shou, his yellow teeth gleaming in the night and the Colt m1911 in his grasp. He said nothing and she saw flame flash from the barrel twice. The bullets impacted her chest, but there was no pain. She fought to move as the Japanese murderer tossed the gun at her feet, but her arms and legs could not obey.

Though she felt nothing, Angela became more aware than at any other time in her life. Everything she had ever lived for lay dead to her left and everything she stood against was walking away. Evil had somehow triumphed over good. A great sadness passed through her and then a voice entered her head and with it came joy.

"Ma'am, my name is George Thomas Ahiga, and ever since I first laid eyes on you I knew we were meant to be married."

32.

Half of the commandos let loose a slew of bullets. They had learned their lessons at the river and were staggering fire. Brilliant golden streaks filled the sky in every direction and Chase put his arm around Sarah's shoulder. Though he had given her a brief lesson in scalar force fields, the amount of lead being leveled in their direction was daunting. He looked down at her and what he saw surprised him.

Fear was no longer evident in her demeanor. She had replaced it with a look of steady determination. Chase felt impressed and flattered at the same time. Either she had found an incredible amount of bravery in the previous minutes, or she had put her full trust in him. He had to shout his words above the din.

"I think they've had enough of a head start. Do you mind if I get to work?"

She handed him the M1903 and he took it with his left hand while cradling her cheek in his right. Her eyes softened as she tilted her head and he smiled ear to ear. Even as the heavy machine gun opened fire he felt as if no one else existed.

The sound of a tremendous explosion soon snapped him from his reverie. One of the commandos had thrown a grenade against their field a few feet away. Chase blinked his eyes and stretched his jaw. He was going to have to work on making his force fields sound proof as well. Five of the Japanese killers were attempting to come up his left flank and Chase brought the bolt action weapon to bear. He was now in the fight.

He wielded the military weapon with deadly accuracy. The men to his left had been the first to advance and they received gaping chest wounds for their bravery. Chase had fired five shots in less than seven seconds. Now came the tedious part.

He looked back to his right and Sarah had five more 30.06 projectiles in her hand. His focus was at its height and his fingers moved with purpose, pressing cartridges into the chamber. Ten seconds passed and he was back in the fight.

"Not bad E.R.C. At this rate we'll be done in three minutes."

The constant bombardment of enemy fire was making it difficult for him to see targets. His ability to peer into the darkness past the sea of yellow streaks was slight, but he brought the weapon up, aimed and fired again. In an instant the Japanese rate of fire lessened. He had silenced the big Type 92. Chase loosed four more shots, felling three more enemies.

"Here, I'll be right back."

Chase handed the gun to Sarah and pushed his way past her into the garage. The din outside faded as he made his way into the workshop. Since the field was up he failed to check his surroundings, and the chatter of automatic weapons sounded a few yards away. Instinct dictated his movement as yellow bands of light streaked the protective field. Chase dropped to his rear, pulled the Colt from his waist band and fired his final four shots. Two Japanese fell to the floor, a pair of mortal wounds in each man's chest. Chase gathered himself, retrieved what he had come for, and exited the building. Sarah greeted him at the door with a loaded rifle.

"Hold onto it for a second longer." Chase tapped the Remington Mark II Flare gun in his right hand. "I'm going to brighten things up."

People had been using signal flares since the invention of gunpowder, but on one of his flights earlier in the year Chase had met a man using illumination flares. When flying they were to be used as a last ditch effort to light the ground if all other sources were dark. Now seemed like a good time to use them.

He fired the gun into the air at an angle, and as the parachute opened, light bathed the ground 60 yards ahead. A momentary silence interrupted the chaos as all eyes turned to the sky. The sparkling apparition danced in the air as it rained sparks from its tail. It was almost mesmerizing.

Chase took advantage of the lull and fired two shots before his enemy snapped back into the fight. The flare would last four minutes and that was more than he would need. He and Sarah worked as a team and his rate of fire increased to twenty rounds a minute.

His previous breath hung in the night sky as he took in more air through his nostrils. Enemy after enemy fell, and with each came a clearer picture of the battlefield. Chase fired and handed Sarah the weapon again, but instead of reloading she shrugged. They were out of ammunition.

"Cease fire. Cease fire." Katsuo barked the order as he stepped from behind a large oak. That explained why Chase couldn't see him during the battle. "Cease fire."

The sound of gunfire subsided and an eerie silence filled the air. Sarah's breathing was the solitary sound Chase heard and it was comforting. His enemy approached, crooked yellow teeth cocked in a grin.

"Those are some fine energy fields you have. We didn't get a single round through did we?"

"Nope."

Chase responded as he surveyed the scene ahead. Dead bodies littered the ground and just five of Takahiro's soldiers remained.

"Well, I was told you wouldn't have anything like this." Katsuo turned his head side to side and seemed to be assessing his troops even as he spoke to Chase. "Boy, you did a number on my men."

"I'd say I'm up about fifty to nothing."

Katsuo laughed before turning and addressing his remaining soldiers.

"Do as I commanded earlier. Burn it all."

Chase laughed as he pressed closer to the energy field.

"It doesn't matter what you do Kit -Kat. You're not getting to us in here."

"No, I don't suppose I'll be able to. I heard some dogs barking in the cabin, though. I don't suppose they'll take to the heat."

Rex's heart sank. He had put the animals in the cabin to keep them out of danger. He had injected them the day before with the serum so that they could pass through the fields, and didn't trust them to stay during a firefight. His home had seemed the safest place.

"If you hurt my dogs..."

"You'll what? You wouldn't last two seconds outside of that fortress."

He was right, and Chase knew it. Except for his sidearm, Katsuo seemed to be unarmed, but the three men who hadn't gone to burn down the cabin kept their automatic rifles trained on Rex.

"I'll go inside and get the scalar weapon I was hoping not to have to use."

Takahiro's brow furled and he began pacing back and forth. Had he fallen for Chase's bluff?

"Go in and get it then."

Right then one of the soldiers came running down the hill from the cabin. He had Axl and Belle on leashes leading the way. The man was laughing like he had been having the time of his life.

"Sir, sir." His labored breathing came in fits as the two dogs danced at his feet. He laughed again before composing himself and saluting. "Sir, I found these dogs."

"Why did you bring them down here?" Katsuo asked.

"They growled and growled until we went inside. I thought we were going to have to shoot them, but then they just wanted to play. They're great."

Axl jumped on the diminutive Japanese commando as Belle whined for his attentions as well. The soldier's voice was almost jovial. It was as if he had forgotten Katsuo had ordered the animals burned a few seconds before.

"Isn't that wonderful?"

Takahiro's words left his mouth and Chase watched the scene ahead of him unfold in slow motion. Katsuo pulled an 8mm pistol from its holster, shooting Belle in the forehead. Rex fought every instinct to run from safety and help his animals. He saw the blood spray from the back of her head and heard her final yelp as she fell in a heap.

The young soldier dropped the animals' leashes as Katsuo continued to dole out wrath. Two shots entered the young man's chest and Chase took notice of his astonished look. Axl, who wasn't a stranger to guns, danced nearby, oblivious to the carnage. The firing of guns held a positive connotation for him. Takahiro's true nature was on full display as he showcased a maniacal laugh while taking aim at the gentle creature. Rex's hesitation had cost Belle, but he wouldn't lose Axl as well.

"Come on big dog. Let's go." Chase bolted from the sanctuary with a whistle and Axl responded. "Come on Axl..."

Rex Chase was fast, but the young golden retriever was like a blur. They had caught Katsuo off guard, but within a half second he spun and trained his gun in their direction. The other soldiers opened fire even as Chase approached his destination behind a natural depression in the landscape. Bullets tore at the snow around him and then he heard it.

A loud yelp followed by a guttural cry of pain interrupted the sound of gunfire. Chase slid to a stop just short of his goal to see his best friend of the last year and a half roll to a stop. He felt the heat of a bullet pass his ear, but somehow the danger seemed miles away. Rex Chase scrambled to his feet, pulled the flare gun from his belt, aimed, and fired.

The last of his illumination flares streaked across the ground and passed between the soldiers who ceased fire for the briefest of moments. Chase stood exposed and he didn't care. Without those two dogs he never would have stayed sane.

"Rex. Look out."

Her voice snapped him back to reality just as bullets pounded the ground around him once again. Chase moved like a cat and found himself marveling at his own mobility. He hadn't had a single problem with his hip. It had to be the adrenaline. Then, bullets stopped hailing around him.

A few seconds passed, and the echoing blasts of gunfire became more pronounced than ever. Rex stayed in position for a few moments longer, but when the sound of boat motors turning over reached his ears, he stood to survey the scene. What he saw was incredible.

Alexei Chase was advancing on the fleeing boats, his Tommy Gun pounding at their hulls. Another man Rex didn't quite recognize had a full auto weapon that he fired from the hip and breathed flames like a dragon. A third gunman approached from behind the burning cabin and death poured from his barrel. The three men alternated their fire until the water craft were out of range. Rex stood still, even as Sarah ran across the snow and embraced him. Anger burned inside his chest and he seethed as it boiled through his veins.

"He's going to pay for that."

****

33.

"For the record, nobody calls him RGII but himself."
Wheat laughed as he sipped from his Guinness. "The rest of us
just call him..."

"Wait, wait." The old man said. "I love this song."

The three new friends paused and listened to the music
playing on the overhead. Opening lines to Pearl Jam's *Animal*
flowed through the speakers as the old man sang along. After a
few seconds, the music faded into the background, a
commercial took its place, and he cleared his throat before
speaking.

"I always loved Pearl Jam. I don't know if they were my
favorite or Alice In Chains."

"You listen to Pearl Jam and Alice in Chains?" The young
woman's face scrunched as she smiled.

"I know I sure did in the 90's, but that was before your
time."

"He's a music lover, that's for sure." Wheat set his drink
down and addressed the bartender. "Two questions. Where's
the bathroom, and do you think you can keep him from running
off while I'm gone?"

"I think I can handle it." She pointed in the direction of
the lavatory and Tim exited the room as she addressed the old
man again. "I might be young, but I know a thing or two about
nineties music. My dad LOVED Nirvana."

"They were good. *In Utero* was an absolute
masterpiece."

"That's so strange." She laughed as she mixed a drink
for a server. "I have never met a man who got into grunge music
in his seventies."

"Well, I'm no ordinary man Anniestasia." He sipped the light brown liquid in his glass before continuing. "I've always loved good music. In the thirties and forties it was Bing Crosby, Bob Hope, and Judy Garland. In the fifties I loved Chuck Berry and Elvis. Of course the sixties were fantastic with The Beatles, Jimi Hendrix, and the Beach Boys."

"Hold on a second RGII."

Her face showed intrigue as she greeted another customer. Thirty seconds passed as she and the other man exchanged pleasantries and she got his order. The old man sipped his drink again. He hadn't had this much fun in a long time. It wasn't every day a beautiful young woman seemed interested in what he had to say.

"OK, I'm back."

"So Led Zeppelin was my favorite band from the seventies. The eighties were horrible. I kind of stopped listening to a lot of music because most of it was so bad, but then I got turned on to Guns and Roses, which led me to Metallica, and they saved that decade."

She laughed and it made him feel warm inside again. A surge of adrenaline coursed through his body and he felt fifty years younger.

"So we already covered the nineties so that brings us to the new millennium."

"It sure does. So what does a 100-year-old man listen to in the new millennium?"

"I kind of got into metal."

She laughed again and the man who had sat down next to him seemed to be paying attention as well.

"Metal?" Annie handed a drink to the silver haired patron who had just sat. "Have you ever heard of a man his age listening to metal?"

"I assure you I have not."

RGII felt like he was on a stage. It had been so long since anyone but Tim had joined him in serious conversation. He appreciated Wheat's company, but this was like kissing a woman you just met for the very first time. It was exhilarating and he tried not to act giddy.

"I like the technicality of playing intricate patterns at tremendous speed. It reminds me of when I was young and I would ride my motorcycle way too fast down a dirt road. You know, a controlled chaos."

"I understand. You like it because it makes you feel young." She was smiling at him again. "So who are your favorite metal bands RGII?"

"I have a few." He furrowed his brow and pretended to be lost in thought. This was fun. "I'd say Slipknot, Lamb of God, and Veil of Maya."

"Ugh." Annie slapped her hand over her face as she laughed out loud. "I had a boyfriend who listened to all of those bands. We saw Veil of Maya once, though, and I'll tell you this. They played *ID* start to finish live, and it was just like the album. I can appreciate the musicianship."

"They are fantastic musicians. I'd love to get out and see a band like that. So tell me Anniestasia. Who is your favorite?"

The young woman pursed her lips and placed her pointer finger at the corner of her mouth. Large dimples dented both cheeks and he studied the lines of her face. She was beautiful.

"I would have to say my favorite is Kanye West."

"Aghhhh. Kanye?" He rolled his eyes and feigned injury with a hand over his heart. "Kanye West couldn't rap his way into a whorehouse with a million dollar bill hanging out of his pants."

Both the silver haired man and Annie laughed at his remark. Alcohol had always loosened him up and he felt like he was on a roll now. He opened his mouth to speak again.

"Ice Cube wouldn't let Kanye West wrap his Christmas presents."

"Oh man, you've got him talking about Kanye again don't you?" Wheat returned from the bathroom and bellied up to the bar. "He's just jealous because he had a huge crush on Kim K."

"That woman does funny things to me."

The old man couldn't remember the last time he had this much fun. Across the bar a beautiful woman was enjoying his company. He had met a stranger and already had him laughing. His best friend sat to his left. It didn't get any better.

"Thanks a lot there old timer. After the day I've been having I needed that laugh."

"My hatred for men who steal my women has no bounds." The picture of the woman from his dreams popped into his head as he offered his hand to the stranger. "It's nice to make your acquaintance."

The silver haired man reciprocated the handshake, an ear to ear grin adorning his tanned and weathered face.

"My friends call me The Sentinel."

"That's an interesting name." The old man chuckled before continuing. "I'm Robert George Poppen the Second, but you can call me Bobby."

✱✱✱✱✱✱✱✱✱✱✱✱✱✱✱✱✱

34.

"Easy, boy. Just take it easy." Chase whispered as he knelt in the snow and cradled his wounded animal's head. He fought back a tear as the dog whined and licked his hand. "Just relax big dog."

Sarah sat next to him in the snow inspecting the golden retriever's wound.

"It looks like it hit him in the back hip, passed through the muscle, and came out the other side."

"Pack the entrance and exit with snow." Chase nodded as he replied, then whispered in Axl's ear. "You're gonna be OK. Don't worry. You're gonna be fine."

His pet replied with a whine as it laid its head back down on his lap.

"Are you OK son?" Alexei Chase had run across the snow covered yard and was out of breath as he approached. "I'm sorry we couldn't get here faster."

"What took you so long?" Anger tinted Rex's tone and he took no steps to hide it. "You should have beaten us here."

"If I had we would have had quite a run in at the road." The younger Chase relaxed.

"I'm sorry Dad. Did you see what he did to Belle?"

"I did. I also saw what you did to his men. All in all I'd say it was a pretty one-sided victory."

Though he knew them to be true, Rex found no solace in his father's words.

"Hey guys. Is everyone alright?"

The man stood just under six feet tall and donned a thick silver mustache. Rex felt as if he had seen him before, but couldn't match the face to a name. It was a rare occurrence when his memory failed him and he stood to shake hands as he replied.

"The Japanese and the dogs took the brunt of the action. Thanks for the help. I'm Rex Chase."

"I'm Al Scherzer. Glad I could help."

"OK. You're dad's neighbor. I knew I had seen you somewhere before."

"Yeah, I guess no one has ever introduced us. I suppose we've just seen each other in passing."

"Is everyone OK?" Luce Chase trudged through the snow and gasped when she saw Axl. "Poor Axl. Where's Belle?"

"She's lying up there on the ground. You must have missed her." Chase's voice quivered as his mother hugged him with one arm. "Mom, when did you get a Tommy gun?"

"I'm so glad you're OK. I didn't look at the ground much on my way over. I don't own a Tommy Gun, I borrowed this from Al."

"I've gotta say, she handled it pretty well." Al's face broke into a wide grin. "I should have given the B.A.R. to your dad, though. That thing was bucking like a wild mustang."

"Wait a minute, so mom was the third guy up there shooting?"

"You shouldn't call your mom a guy." Sarah attempted to lighten the mood and received a laugh from Al.

"You shouldn't have let her out of the car." Anger again rose in Rex's voice.

"I didn't have much say in the issue." Alexei Chase said. "She got it in her head she was going to help us fight and, well, you know your mother."

"Three guns are better than two." Lucille ruffled her son's hair. "Besides, I make decisions for myself."

"Well, I guess it turned out OK." Chase said. "Where did you pick up Al from anyway? He should have been at the party."

"I was." The middle aged Scherzer slung the Browning automatic rifle over his shoulder as he toed the ground. "I had a few too many Chivas. You know, that stuff has been real hard to find since that lousy prohibition. Every time I see it I just…"

"He drinks until he's asked to leave." Alexei said and the group chuckled in unison.

"Nobody asked me to leave. That bash was boring, so I went home. Your dad was lucky I was there too, or he'd have never gotten out of that snow drift."

"Or had two more guns," Luce said.

"So let me get this straight. You went home to pick up the Tommy gun and got stuck in a drift." Chase continued after pointing at Al. "He helped you out of the drift, even though he was too drunk to keep partying, but still sober enough to bring to a gunfight, with my mom, and wield an automatic 30.06?"

"I'm never too drunk to do that." Scherzer shifted the rifle to his left shoulder and pat the barrel with his right hand, a grin on his face. "I could shoot this monster in my sleep."

"OK." Chase leaned over and picked up his injured dog with ease. The retriever whimpered, but seemed to understand he was heading somewhere to get help. Rex began walking toward his father's car. "Dad, I'm going to put Axl in your car. Can you drop him at the vet for me?"

"I can."

"Thanks." Chase pursed his lips and fought his emotions as he walked past Belle. "Do you think you could take Belle too? The ground is too hard and I don't know when I'll be back."

"Yes."

"Thank you." Luce opened the car door and Rex placed his injured pet in the back seat. "I need to go check in with The General. Sarah, you're coming with me."

"Maybe I should call the veterinarian for you." Sarah said. "I doubt they are always prepared for gunshot wounds."

"Good idea. The phone is in the garage and the number is right next to it in the Wheeldex under Vet."

"What do you want us to do about the cabin?"

Forty yards away his home was ablaze. It was quite beautiful and Rex cast his gaze over the pond where the flames danced across the open water the Japanese had created. He needed to check in with The General. He needed to check in with George. He needed to get Sarah to safety. His 'to do' list was already full and that made his decision simple.

"Let it burn."

****

35.

"You are certain he is dead?"

"Yes ma'am."

"Did you check his pulse?"

"No ma'am."

"How can you be sure he was dead, then?"

"I have seen thousands of dead men. Trust me."

"Ok. What about his wife?"

"I didn't have the luxury of sticking around to find out, but I shot her three times in the chest at close range with a .45. She's dead."

Shin Shou detested reporting in on the telephone, though he detested reporting to a woman even more. Katsuo had kept her involvement in their operations clouded in mystery since informing Shou of her existence a few weeks before. His mentor had promised an explanation. That promise had yet to be fulfilled.

"I hope you are right. The Organization has meddled in our affairs too often. George Ahiga and Rex Chase have been most bothersome."

"I understand." Shin furrowed his brow. He struggled to hide the contempt in his voice. "What is The Organization?"

"Everything will come to light in due time Shin. Until then, I would very much like for you to continue your faithful execution of both my and Katsuo's plans. As a matter of fact, I have an errand I'd like you to run for me."

Shou swallowed hard. Until now it had been his impression that Katsuo Takahiro was his only superior and this woman was a separate party destined to remain in the shadows. Now she was issuing her own orders. His hesitation caused her to speak again.

"I understand your trepidation Shin, and perhaps I misspoke. These were contingency plans given to me by Katsuo, and not preparations of my own. You have done very well. I am just here to relay orders in his absence. He thought it would be best, in case something happened to either of you."

"I'm listening." Shin relaxed as her voice crackled across the wire. Perhaps she was a simple messenger. He made mental notes as she gave him his next set of instructions. He had already had a busy night, and it seemed his work was not quite done. At least he would have a little time to himself. His stomach growled and he realized he hadn't eaten any of the five course meal. It was going to be a long night.

****

36.

"It's great to meet you Bobby. Do you mind if I show you something?"

"I haven't had that much to drink." Poppen exclaimed and everyone laughed once again. "Whatya got?"

The Sentinel chuckled as he pulled a handheld electronic device from his pocket.

"I have to say, when I first got into town I was a little confused by the things I saw, but it's worked out. You shouldn't be too surprised by what I have here."

"Hey, what is that?" Wheat leaned over as the silver haired stranger placed the device on the bar top.

"It's gotta be the Galaxy S8 right?" Annie said.

"Not quite." The Sentinel manipulated the screen on the perceived smartphone. "Tell me what you think about this."

A three dimensional image appeared in the sky and looks of shock became apparent on everyone's faces.

"I didn't know they could do that," said Bobby.

"Me neither," said Annie.

"That makes three of us," Wheat concluded.

"Technology is amazing isn't it? Can you tell me what we're looking at here?"

"I'm not the math guy anymore. My mind doesn't quite work as well as it used to." Poppen shrugged his shoulders. "You'll have to ask Timmy."

"You know that Bobby. It's the solution to the E^8 equation. Well, it's part of the solution to the E^8. We've covered all of this before, remember?"

"Oh yeah. I worked on that a lot in college. It drove me crazy." Poppen shook his head as he passed his hand through the three dimensional projection. "Guaranteed A's if you solved the E^8. When did they solve that Timmy?"

"2007, maybe?"

"So you've harnessed scalar energy, force fields, and can travel the speed of light."

"Whoa, maybe I shouldn't have given you that drink." Annie laughed and the three men followed suit.

"You've read my old book. Did you get to read Tim's newest as well?" Poppen paused and received a shrug from the silver haired man. "Well, if you would have read Tim's latest book on scalar mechanics you would know that we've concluded that they are unfeasible. The solution to the E^8 is just too massive. Shoot, it would be the size of Manhattan if you put it on paper."

The Sentinel smiled before replying.

"You'd need a quantum computer."

"Ha. I don't even think one quantum computer would do it. You'd need several."

Wheat nodded his head in agreement.

"If you had one you might be able to power every single thing on earth, as long as it was stationary, but to calculate movement. That would take a whole army of quantum computers."

"I tell you what Bobby. What if protons didn't exist? What if gravity didn't exist? What if..."

The Sentinel kept on speaking, but Poppen's mind had shifted into overdrive. He felt like a teenager again and his head was spinning. Maybe it was the liquor, but he felt like he was going to pass out. Then everything became clear and imprinted in his mind in bold letters was a two line equation. When he spoke, his voice was hoarse.

"Anniestasia. Do you have a pen and paper I could use?"

"Sure Bobby. You gonna leave me a love note?"

Poppen smiled, but his mind was racing. His hands trembled as he picked up the writing utensil and began to put the equation to paper. This whole situation was surreal and he had a strong feeling of déjà vu. He finished his work and laid down the pen as Wheat leaned over his shoulder. The color on his best friend's face drained away and for a moment he was speechless.

"I'm missing something, aren't I?" Annie leaned over the bar to see what he had written.

"I wouldn't say you've missed anything most people wouldn't." An ear to ear grin adorned The Sentinel's face. "I doubt there are more than a few people in the world who even know what that means."

"Holy smokes Bobby." Wheat said. "This is going to change the world. I mean, the possibilities are endless: limitless free energy, unending light speed exploration, stasis fields, force fields, all kinds of fields."

"Time travel." The Sentinel said.

"Time travel." Wheat repeated.

The four sat in silence for a few seconds while they stared at the equation written on the paper. Poppen sighed before speaking.

"I'm going to miss you and that dog."

"What do you mean?" Tim said.

"Timmy, do you think you could watch Felix for a while? I'm going to convince our new friend here to take me on a ride."

"Not a chance." The Sentinel stood as if to leave. "I appreciate your help. Good luck gentlemen."

Poppen swirled the green cocktail straw in his glass, causing the ice cubes to interrupt the silence. He picked up the single malt scotch and sipped it even as The Sentinel walked away. He had awoken that morning a tired old man. Now his mind was working overtime and he was seeing things with more clarity than at any other point in his life. He crafted his next words with care and got straight to the point.

"Don't you want to know why I'm so old? It could be important."

****

37.

Thanks for the Memory played in the background and he found himself humming along with the tune. Shirley Ross and Bob Hope's voices wafted across the dense layer of fog and a smile formed on his face. They had seen the motion picture, "Big Broadcast of 1938" no less than ten times. She loved that movie and he loved her. He blinked his eyes hard, and the soup began to recede revealing shadowy figures hovering overhead. A slight panic gripped him, but just for a moment. If they meant to kill him, he would already be dead. Every second that passed brought more clarity into his mind and he became aware of a rhythmic pressure on his chest, like a small child was jumping up and down on it.

Consciousness was winning the battle against the darkness. His vision began to clear and feeling returned to his extremities. He was cold, and the man above, though blurry, had a white cloud puffing from his mouth that seemed to keep time with the chest compressions. A woman appeared and knelt over him. She brandished a needle and wielded the medical tool with superb expertise. He felt the instrument plunge into his arm and with it came an instant feeling of warmth along with a burst of energy. George Thomas Ahiga bolted upright. He was back from the dead.

"Take it easy Chief. I think you're going to be OK, but we have got to get you to the hospital."

The world was still sluggish to him, and a stubborn fog persisted, but George turned his head to the left, now recognizing the voice. He attempted to speak, but the words were difficult and came out slurred.

"L,L,L,L,Leonard. W,w,w,w,what happened? W,w,w,w,w, where's Angela?"

Chief could see the other man's pursed lips and determined countenance.

"We're doing everything in our power. Can you walk? Time is of the essence."

George didn't understand, but nodded his head. His legs had difficulty responding, but with Leonard's help he made it to his feet. The woman who had brought life into his body knelt nearby and Chief looked in her direction. Recognition flooded his mind and he retched in the snow. On the ground a few feet away lay his wife, stripped to the waist, one large and two small holes in her chest. The woman had smeared most of the congealed blood away with snow, but the scene was grisly. Chief could feel himself being swept from his feet. He vomited again, but then found himself seated in the front of a car.

George slumped in the leather seat and resisted the urge to be sick. Outside his wife lay in the snow and she seemed to be dead. He watched as Leonard scooped her into his arms and circled the front of the vehicle. Moments passed, and then the rear door of the sedan opened. His mind fought the fog and his body felt like a lead balloon, but Chief shifted in his seat to watch Angela's lifeless form enter. Leonard placed her body on the rear bench and Chief noticed another occupant in the cramped space.

"Wh,wh, who i, i, is he?"

"Shhhhhh. Don't worry. My wife is considered the best physician in the entire city," Leonard said. "I think she's going to be alright. He's just a friend of The General."

George acknowledged the elder who now held his wife's head with a nod. Leonard had backed out of the car and Marilyn now kneeled in his place. Before he knew it the vehicle was in transit and Leonard addressed him again.

"What happened to the Marmon? We didn't see it anywhere." Leonard's tone was almost nonchalant and George found it unsettling.

"I have no idea. What took you two so long?" Chief spoke to Leonard, but never took his eyes from the rear. Marilyn had removed items from a brown leather bag and was now rubbing a black powdery substance in Angela's wounds. His next words came in a whisper. "What is she doing?"

"I told you not to worry." Leonard turned and adjusted his rearview mirror. "She's the best."

What Chief heard next confused his injured mind even further. The unmistakable Navajo language quietly and rhythmically drifted from the back seat. He strained his ears, but could not make out the phrase. His wife's half naked form still lay motionless, but Marilyn now hovered over her. Dozens of questions flooded his mind, but he could manage to utter just one.

"What is happening? I don't understand."

"Everything is going to be OK George. Trust me. It is all going to be OK."

****

38.

The blast had rendered the wiry leader of The Organization unconscious. As the fog began to lift, he took notice of the surrounding destruction. Twisted steel columns groaned as they held their positions and debris lay scattered across the floor. Nearby, several rescuers carried an injured man up a makeshift ramp that ascended through the jagged hole above.

The General watched as the men disappeared. It was dank in the basement and he stood, testing his faculties. He breathed a sigh of relief as everything seemed to be where it had been before.

Voices echoed from the ball room above and he could sense they were approaching. One of the men was voicing his displeasure at the safety of the ramp. Another was urging the others to hurry. The voices were familiar and The General found solace in their approach.

"General? Are you down there General?"

"I am." His voice faltered and he cleared his throat before repeating. "I am."

"Are you OK? Stay where you are. We're coming down to help you out."

"Don't." The General's voice returned to its full authoritative timbre. "No sense in you boys risking your necks on that ramp. I can make my way out."

Though his back was stiff and his legs ached, The General made his way across the darkened room. Grief tugged at him as he stepped over the bodies of two dead secret service agents. Their sacrifice, judging by the distorted positions of their bodies, had been instant. He climbed the path to the upper level and crawled onto the floor where Captain Bryan Morris helped him to his feet.

"I'm sorry I couldn't get here earlier General, but I had to tend to my wife and daughter."

"I took care of Edith, Mary Anne, and Mary Margaret as fast as I could," said Patrick Castle.

"I took care of my wife and two boys first too."

"That's OK Bill." The General put his hand on the third man's shoulder. "I don't fault you boys for putting your families first. What's the word on the President?"

"A big redhead and a couple other guys carried him out of here, but he seemed to be fine. He was talking and giving orders." Patrick Castle said.

"Good." The General breathed a sigh of relief. "I guess that leaves me with an easy decision."

He scanned the other three men's eyes. They were all thinking the same thing. Captain Morris was the first to ask.

"What's that sir?"

"First thing is that I want you to pick up that camera over there. It might have some evidence." The General paused a moment before continuing. "We need a car. I'm going to sound the order."

39.

Chase's mind had been in overdrive since leaving his burning home. Every detail of the evening was etched into his brain and he scoured the information in his head for clues. Why kill the President, The General, and the Japanese diplomats? Why then stake out his house and bring more than fifty men? How did any of this make sense?

Without thinking Chase reached forward and turned on the radio. The once luxurious Packard Six was more Spartan a vehicle now, but one of the first things he had been sure to fix was the radio. He pushed one of the buttons and the dial jumped to 540 AM. A static filled voice saturated the cabin of the Six.

"Water is the only substance on earth that is lighter as a solid than as a liquid. Xylophones have eighty-three keys. Yellow Bellied Sapsuckers weigh two point eight ounces on average. Zucchini is often thought to be a vegetable, but is in fact a fruit. Asian Giant Hornets have a stinger a quarter inch in length..."

Chase let out a sigh, and for the first time in their drive Sarah spoke.

"What is this, some kind of trivia station? I've never heard of one like this."

"The General has sounded the order."

"What does that mean?"

"It isn't good. At least we know that he is alive." Chase turned a corner onto a snowy street. "I suppose Chief will hear this too. Maybe we should just head to The General's office."

"We're a couple of blocks from my place. Would you mind if I stopped and changed out of these clothes?"

Chase looked at Sarah. Somehow, through all the fighting, boat crashes, and blood she still looked radiant. Her bright opaline eyes shone and the cut of her dress accentuated her ample curves. He blinked before swallowing hard. Now was not the time to deviate from the plan, but like she said, it was just a couple of blocks.

"You'll have to be quick. Katsuo might have staked out your place."

"I just want to grab a couple of things."

The AM radio continued spewing facts over the next couple of minutes as they rode in relative silence. Chase rounded the block onto Sarah's street and his heart leapt. Parked in front of her house was the Marmon. He pulled in behind it and exited the Six.

"Hey, I'm going to run into the house real quick."

Sarah spoke, but Chase was busy looking over the Marmon. It looked like someone had put it through the ringer. They had smashed the front grill, the driver's side door had seen some action, and bullet holes dominated the front of the luxury vehicle.

"OK, but be quick. Tell George to get out here too. I want to know what happened here."

"You've got it." Sarah turned and took a few steps, then stopped. "Rex?"

"Yes." Chase popped his head up from the side of the maroon vehicle.

"How do you know that the radio call was real? Couldn't someone have faked it?"

Chase smiled before responding.

"We have a pretty simple code but not one that's easy to pick up."

"I know I didn't get it." She smiled and Chase felt almost as if it were a normal day.

"Alphabetical order. Each fact starts with the next letter in the alphabet, and every fifth fact is in fact, not a fact."

"That's a lot of facts, but I still don't get it."

"Doesn't everyone know that a Yellow Bellied Sapsucker's average weight is one point seven ounces?" He paused as a bright smile crossed her face. "On a normal day everything on that station would be true, and not always in alphabetical order."

"You have weird friends."

Sarah laughed as she turned and bounded up the steps to her house. Chase watched as she entered and closed the door. A few moments passed and then an awful thought pierced his consciousness. He crossed the small yard and leapt up the front stairs in less than a second, throwing open the front door.

"Sarah. Sarah."

"What?" Sarah came rushing from a back room, her dress off, wearing her underclothes and looking disheveled. "What is going on?"

"I, I, I," Chase stuttered and felt his face flush at the sight of the almost naked woman. She was exquisite. "I just realized that..."

He could see the startled look on her face before he even finished the sentence. Chase's instincts had warned him and now an attack from his rear was already underway. Someone was on his back, and that someone was heavy. A thick right arm wrapped around Chase's neck while another linked with the first and pulled hard toward the earth.

Chase felt immediate effects from the choke hold. It had happened so fast, and with such ferocity, though, that an avenue for escape did not present itself. Chase gasped for air as the attacker deprived his brain of blood and oxygen. The darkness was surrounding him and he fell to his knees, fighting its effects, but to no avail. As he felt the light leaving his body he took one last look at Sarah. Concern dominated her face, yet she made no move to help. Her words would be his last memory of consciousness.

"Don't kill him."

****

40.

"Do you have the prisoner?"

"I do."

"Do you have the stones?"

"No, they aren't here."

"That just won't do Shin." Her voice seemed different but still made his skin crawl. "We must have all of those stones and I believe Rex Chase is the key. He must live and so must the girl. I don't want her injured. Do you understand?"

"Yes."

"Good. Tell her they are going on a trip. You know where. Goodbye."

Shin Shou hung up the telephone and kicked the unconscious man on the floor.

"What did you give him?"

"Don't worry. Your boyfriend will be fine. I just need him to be a little more agreeable than usual." Shou sported a maniacal smile and his yellow teeth shone. "So he killed Katsuo and all of those men single-handed?"

"No," Sarah sat at the kitchen table, her hands folded in her lap. "I helped."

Shou paced around the table. His mind raced, though he knew his duty well. Whether Katsuo was still alive or not was of no consequence now. He had to deliver Chase and the girl to the pre-appointed rendezvous. Sarah interrupted his thoughts as she questioned him again.

"So what happens now?"

"You and your boyfriend are going on a little trip."

"Do you mind if I put on some clothes first?"

****

41.

Angela Ahiga lay unconscious in the drab hospital room. Under normal circumstances her bronzed skin would have contrasted against the pressed white sheets. Today, though, her olive complexion was gray and pale. She looked near death and Chief felt another lump forming in his stomach.

"She's going to be fine."

Marilyn put her hand on his massive shoulder and it pushed George over the edge. He fought the convulsions without success as he buried his head in the matron's shoulder. Her touch comforted him and she cradled his head even as tears poured down his cheeks. He wept unabashed for over a minute.

"Shhhhhhhhhh. It's going to be okay George. Everything is going to be okay."

Her words were soothing and the tears cathartic. Chief couldn't remember a time in his life where he felt more helpless. His wife was lying a few feet away and though Marilyn assured it would all be okay, he knew better. Angela had three bullet holes in her chest. The end must be near. He swallowed hard as he pulled away and wiped his eyes.

"Shou shot her in the chest three times Marilyn. You don't have to mince words with me. How is she?"

"Boy, you did take a blow to the head." Leonard came into the room, smacked George on the shoulder and smiled. "She's fine. Look for yourself."

George's mind raced. Why would they be saying these things? Doubt crept into his mind as he approached his wife, pulled down the blankets and peered under her gown. What he saw brought instant confusion and he searched for words.

"W,w,w,w,what did you do? I, I, I, saw the holes in her chest. You were in the back seat speaking Navajo and rubbing that black stuff all over her. You ripped off her shirt. I saw it. I saw it…" His voice trailed off as he replaced Angela's blankets and turned toward the others. "Leonard, you were doing something to me when I woke up. What was it?"

"That was just something my wife taught me to get the old ticker running again." Leonard's dimples sank deep into his cheeks and his grin extended ear to ear as he ruffled the younger man's hair. "Are you sure you're feeling okay? Maybe you should lie down and have my wife take a look at you."

"I'd be more than happy to give you a full checkup. As a matter of fact, it's a good idea if I at least get your vitals." Marilyn already had her stethoscope out and was rolling up George's sleeve.

"You do what you need to Doc."

Chief wasn't sure what was going on. They had been quick to change the subject back to him, but perhaps he had hallucinated his wife's injuries. He breathed deep as Marilyn listened to his chest, and offered no resistance as she took his blood pressure and pulse.

"Well, if I didn't know better, I'd say you'd just woken up from a nice nap." Her face was kind and her touch soothing. "Your blood pressure is one twenty over sixty and your pulse is forty-six beats per minute."

"I guess that must be good huh?" Chief rolled down his sleeve as she hung the blood pressure cuff back on the wall. "Leonard, have you turned on the radio at all?"

"No I haven't. Are you sure you're ready for that?"

"You heard the doc. Everything is just fine. I feel great, and if Angela is going to be fine…" Chief paused and looked at Marilyn.

"She is."

"Well, I don't see any reason for me to be standing around if we have work to do."

"OK."

Leonard strode to the bedside table where a Philco Model 41-255T sat, waiting for use. The table top device hummed as he turned the switch and electricity surged through its eight vacuum tubes. The super-heterodyne's speaker crackled and Leonard tuned to 540 hertz.

"Male emperor moths can smell female emperor moths from seven miles away. No word in the English language rhymes with month, or orange. Owls are the only bird that can see the color blue. Peanuts are an ingredient in nitroglycerin. Quicksand is found in all..."

The radio drifted to silence as Leonard turned the dial and the tubes began to cool. Silence dominated the room for a few seconds before George spoke.

"There aren't peanuts in dynamite, right?"

"Peanut oil is an ingredient in glycerol." Leonard's tone was stern, almost scolding. "Most birds can see the color blue. Some can even see into the ultraviolet range."

"What does all of that mean?" Marilyn said.

"It means I'm going to have to leave you in charge of my wife."

****

42.

A fire crackled in the hearth a few feet away. Katsuo reveled in its warmth and ignored the sharp pains in his hands and feet. The frigid evening and wet conditions had assured the discomfort, but Takahiro didn't mind. Somehow he had escaped the battle without being wounded. Not another of his men could say the same.

He watched as the remaining five warriors tended to each other's wounds. They were a tight knit group, and always had been. The loss of so many would be difficult, but they were handling it with astounding strength. Pride welled up inside of him as Katsuo pondered the evening's excursion. It hadn't been a total success, but hadn't been a complete failure either. The phone sounded, and he answered it on the first ring.

"Did you have an eventful evening?" Katsuo didn't answer as anger welled inside. "George and Angela Ahiga are dead."

Takahiro breathed in deep, flipped a Lucky Strike into his mouth and struck the flint on his zippo. The tobacco smoke filled his lungs and he blew it out before responding.

"Of course, that is excellent news. What of Rex Chase?"

"Yes, he gave you quite a difficult time, didn't he?"

"I suppose he did. He is the white devil." Anger welled again. "Perhaps you should get the information without my help next time. Did he have the stones?"

"No, and I don't believe he even knows of them. Did you get the information we needed?"

"Yes." The battle at the cabin had cost him almost all of his men, and though Izanami dismissed their deaths, Katsuo knew they could not be replaced with ease. "My men found his notes in the cabin. They confirm the Russian's calculations."

"Excellent. That is most excellent. That means the dam project is complete. It is a shame we could not have completed our more ambitious venture in time. Have you heard any more news from the detainee?"

"No. I think we need to follow my alternate plan." Katsuo had already set its wheels in motion without her permission. "It is well suited for our current situation."

"I will tell you what is suited for our situation." Her voice was sharp, even through the telephone. "Are you prepared for another prisoner?"

"Yes." Katsuo didn't savor his subservience to a woman, but she possessed something he held most dear. "Who is the prisoner?"

"Rex Chase is on his way to you. We will rendezvous at the station."

"Understood. What of my men?"

"Your men are injured?"

"Yes."

"Then they are of no use to us. Kill them."

****

43.

"You should have told me Izanami was more than a silent partner."

"She revealed herself to you?"

"No." Shin furrowed his brow. "I spoke with her on the phone. She gave me orders."

"Her orders are as good as my orders Shin. We are all working together to achieve a common goal and will reveal everything in due time. You must trust me."

"How can I trust you when you keep secrets?" Shin's anger boiled as questions swirled in his mind. "I know your final goal is Yasuhiro, but mine are different. I want…"

"Yasuhiro is of no concern to you." Katsuo moved close and Shin could feel the heat of his breath. Shou was not often intimidated, but trepidation crept into his mind. "I am still in control and our plans are progressing. Do not lose faith Shin."

"Of course." Shou bowed and stepped backward. "I did not mean to question your authority. I've brought you Rex Chase and killed George Ahiga. What is next?"

"You will report to the carrier and make sure our final preparations are in place." Katsuo stepped forward and laid a heavy hand on Shin's shoulder. "You are one of the finest soldiers I have ever commanded and our victory is near."

"Of course. Who will I be reporting to on the carrier?"

"It is time you met someone Shin."

✶✶✶✶✶✶✶✶✶✶✶✶✶✶✶✶✶

44.

Click click, clack clack. Click click, clack clack. Click click, clack clack. Click click, clack clack. The rhythmic beat of the 2200 pound steel wheels echoed into the night and served as a beacon of sound. Chase felt as if someone had beaten him with a sack of potatoes and he focused on the cadence.

His captor had bound his feet and blindfolded his eyes. He could hear and feel the train slow. Every minute that passed his senses became sharper, and as the train made its way back up to speed he had almost regained his full faculties. Questions flooded his mind.

Where were they going? Why was he here? Who had drugged him? Where was Sarah?

The door to his car opened and two voices entered. His mind was still fuzzy, but he recognized the man's intonation with ease. Chase strained his ears, but the woman's voice remained muffled. Perhaps she had on a scarf.

"Rex Chase. Are you awake? You should be awake by now."

"Is that you Kit-Kat?" Chase tested his restrictions, but they held tight. "I thought maybe I wouldn't see you again. Sorry for my dreadful hospitality before."

"I'm sure that you are." Takahiro said. "The drugs we gave you have made you thirsty, yes? Would you like a drink?"

Chase needed water, but that wasn't bothering him much. The hunger pangs in his stomach however had become a nuisance.

"To be honest Kit-Kat. I could use some supper. Do you have anything resembling a twenty-four ounce bone in rib eye?"

Sorry, nothing like that. If you'd like I could let my lady friend here feed you some dinner."

"Or you could untie my hands and I'll take care of it myself."

"Very good Mr. Chase. Very good. If you give me the information I need I'll go ahead and kill you right now instead of doing what I had planned. I'll even let her feed you first so that you die with a full belly."

"I'm not in the mood for torture." Chase responded in a matter of fact tone. "Whatya wanna know?"

"Where are the stones?"

"No idea."

"Where is Yasuhiro?"

"Nothing for two Kat. Do I still get dinner?"

Takahiro met his smart alec reply with a vicious blow to the left temple. The bed below cushioned its impact, but Chase winced at the pain and fought the darkness. Cloudiness returned to his head, but he managed a smile.

"Not gonna lie. That hurt a little. Now that I think about it, though, I have a couple of stones you might like to handle."

"Where are they?" Chase laughed at his own joke and the fact that Katsuo didn't understand. "What? What is so funny?"

Chase heard the muffled voice of the woman as she whispered in Takahiro's ear. A second later the Japanese madman delivered another vicious blow to Rex's jaw. He spit blood onto the bed, but smiled again, his teeth stained red.

"Your first one was better. Don't be sore at me Kit-Kat. You're the one who wants to handle my stones. Who is Yasuhiro?"

"YOU DON'T SPEAK HIS NAME. YOU NEVER SPEAK HIS NAME." Katsuo bellowed and Chase knew he had reached a critical point. It was better to ease back now.

"I don't know what you're talking about Katsuo. I'm starving and I've been on drugs for a while. How long have I been on drugs? Where is Sarah?"

"None of these things concern you." Katsuo had regained his composure, but hatred still filled his voice. "Feed him his dinner and put him back to sleep. We're done for the day."

****

45.

"I want to thank you all for getting here so quick."

George heard the General's words, but his mind was still at the hospital. Mere hours had passed since the explosion, but it seemed as if the night before was a lifetime away. It was now three o'clock in the morning and Chief's exhausted brain took notice of his surroundings.

General George Francis Reagan sat behind his gargantuan antique desk. His office in Washington D.C. was more formal and decorated than this Boston location. It was in that building in the nation's capital that he hosted meetings with public officials. The walls here were bare in comparison, and papers littered the cherry desk.

Seated in a semi-circle in assembled wooden chairs were a number of people. Chief was familiar with all but two and a couple others surprised him with their attendance. In his time with The Organization he had learned that its members oftentimes stayed in the dark regarding other agent's activities. It made deniability and ignorance viable excuses for lack of knowledge in case of capture, or governmental inquiry. The General, and perhaps Leonard, stayed apprised of everyone's role.

"George and his wife have been the leads on what we know so far, and I'll ask him now to brief us. How is your wife George?"

His mind had been wandering and Chief fought the lump in his throat. He looked at the other faces in the room and saw nothing but concern. Bryan Morris and Al Scherzer sat to his immediate left, and beyond them were Alexei and Lucille Chase. To his right sat Leonard and Patrick Castle with the old man from the car and a younger man he didn't recognize filling out the group.

"She is fine. The doc says she is going to be just fine. Have we heard from Rex and Sarah?"

"Not yet." A slight murmur amongst everyone followed the General's reply.

"I'm sure he'll be fine Luce." George made eye contact with his best friend's mother, but saw no fear. She was stoic. "I don't know a better man than Edward Rex Chase."

"Edward Rex Chase?" The old man had formed the name into a question.

"Yes."

"So you are Alexei and you are Lucille?" The old man's eyes were alive with curiosity and something about him seemed familiar to George.

"I'm sorry, sir, do we know you?" Luce said.

"Remarkable." The old man spoke to himself and seemed to be lost in his thoughts.

"I'm sorry everyone, but I have to interrupt." Leonard cleared his throat. "A lot of strange, exciting, and dangerous things are all happening right now. We don't have a lot of time, though, and I promise The General and I will keep all of you in the loop. I ask for your patience. George, will you please give us your briefing."

"Yep," Chief knew The Organization had secrets and that was part of the deal. "After Dietrich Hoff's defeat Angela and I took an assignment tracking the remnants of his empire. We knew he was affluent throughout the world, but, with the help of Will Idlewood, we were able to root around in his records. At first we hypothesized that without its figurehead, the empire would dissolve. Over the course of a few months, though, we didn't seem to see that happening. His holdings in the Pacific were the only business ventures that seemed to be affected. At first, it puzzled us, but then it became obvious that someone in Europe had succeeded Hoff. Their strength, however, didn't extend into the Empire of Japan. Japan's invasions of China and the Soviet Union further hindered our abilities to glean information from that portion of the world."

"Excuse me, if I might add something?" Al Scherzer said.

"Go ahead Al."

"The Soviet Union invasion has bothered me ever since I first heard of it. What was the purpose? Why would the Japanese sacrifice 50,000 men for nothing?"

"What are you getting at Al?" The General said.

"I remember hearing something come over the line one time about the Japanese kidnapping civilians. One of the raids was at a secret facility. The intelligence community considered the assault a massive failure since the empire suffered heavy losses and managed to extract just a few low level number crunchers. Chief, I've read your reports of Hoff's weapon. Maybe the raids were worth the risk if they got some much needed intellectual help?"

"That's very interesting Al. Hoff did kill most of his best minds." Leonard leaned forward in his chair listening to every word. "I'm seeing some correlations here. George, will you please continue?"

"Sure. Although we were striking out in the Pacific, in Europe we were getting close. Our friends in France, Amy Moreau and Eric Jorgensen, were hot on the trail. With the invasion of Poland in September, though, their schedules have become filled to overflowing. Since then we've been trying to track some of Hoff's business ventures here in the States, but whoever has filled his shoes is just as, if not more, cunning."

"What kind of business?" Morris said.

"The iron mine in Morocco is shut down and deserted, but earlier this year we learned of a small clandestine operation. It sprung up out of nowhere, and we didn't see it in time. They got what they wanted, loaded it onto what the locals referred to as a massive containership, and disappeared."

"Are they trying to build another weapon? Do we know how much of the ore they got?" Asked the young man to George's right.

"I doubt they are attempting a weapon. Without Bobby's equation it's next to impossible," said Alexei.

"Without the equation it would be force fields and devices which could move through them," the old man said.

"I don't understand." The General stood and paced behind his desk. "Why couldn't they make a weapon?"

"Without the equation, the mathematics to calculate variables in movement are gargantuan. In theory, you could build a weapon, but it would be a stationary, localized event." Alexei Chase was deep in thought.

"So it would be a defensive weapon, rather than offensive." George said.

"Yes, and prone to being disabled. The slightest change in position of any factored component would throw off the balance," the old man answered.

"Okay, thank you George." The General continued to pace. "Why try to kill the President?"

"The Japanese are ruthless s.o.b.'s," Al Scherzer was the first to answer. "It wouldn't surprise me if they attacked the U.S. any day."

"Shin Shou is ruthless, but he didn't seem reckless and we don't know anything about the other man who killed the Japanese diplomats. Killing the President doesn't further their agenda." George said.

"I talked with the building's owners, Mr. and Mrs. Prepot," The General said. "She said his name was Larry and that he was a nice boy. The woman seemed shaken up, but the husband appeared to be in his own little world. I felt bad for her."

"It makes a statement." Patrick Castle had been quiet, but stood as he spoke. His voice was authoritative, and when he had something to say, people listened. "As you all know, I'm in the business of making weapons, and it occurs to me that all you have to do to make this defensive weapon an offensive weapon is make it larger."

"Explain please," Leonard said.

"I mean, if you circled a house with the stuff, you could incinerate the house. If you circled a city, you could incinerate the city. If you circled a state you could incinerate the state..."

His voice trailed off and the room was silent for a few moments. Lucille Chase sniffled and adjusted herself in the uncomfortable wooden chair. Captain Morris stood and stretched his neck. The General continued to pace. Then the silence broke.

"Maybe they weren't trying to kill the President."

✳✳✳✳✳✳✳✳✳✳✳✳✳✳✳✳✳✳

46.

Moonlight danced across the ocean to the east and coastal lights flickered to the west as Shin Shou flew low over the Atlantic. Coastal winds were at a minimum and the water below resembled a flat sheet of glass. Comfort was not one of the aircraft's strengths, but there was no place else Shou would rather be. He was certain he didn't envy Katsuo's train accommodations. Shou was surprised to see him pick up Chase and the girl at the rendezvous, but it was clear Izanami was leaving little to chance.

Shin flicked his green cabin light on, illuminating the dash and bringing his artificial horizon into view. The original A6M schematics hadn't shipped with the feature, but for night flying Shin had added both it and a radio. His altimeter counted down the distance to the water below. As he passed through one hundred feet, he strained his eyes for the dull green markers he knew to be visible.

"Unidentified aircraft. Pull up. I repeat. Pull up." The voice crackled over his radio, but Shou ignored their attempt to help. "I repeat. Unidentified aircraft. Impact is imminent. Pull up. Pull up. Pull up…"

The man on the radio continued to repeat his command and being seen wasn't ideal, but it was of no consequence either. No matter how many times he had performed the maneuver it still brought butterflies to his stomach. It was thrilling, dangerous, and difficult. He relished every second and savored each sound as the water rushed up to meet him.

****

47.

"What makes you think that Robert?"

The General spoke the words, but for some reason the man's name triggered the light of recognition. A very old Bobby Poppen sat a few feet away. The truth of his identity lay behind the eyes. Everything else about his physicality seemed different, but George could see him now.

"Bobby? I don't understand. We buried you two years ago." Alexei Chase saw the same thing and George looked around the room as those who knew Poppen reacted. Morris was the only other who seemed surprised.

"Now is not the time for understanding. Everything will come to light in due time. Right now we need to get the ball rolling. Robert?"

"Yes sir." The General had asserted himself and George sat back in his seat, listening to the ancient Robert George Poppen. "You said yourself George that the Japanese had defected from the Hoff Empire. What if the explosion was a diversion to mask the assassinations of the other men at the table? Do you know who they were?"

"Of course." George said. "They were the owners of Nissan, Suzuki, Toyota, Kawasaki, and the Japanese Ambassador to the U.S. With them out of the way...."

A brief pause followed as George's voice trailed off.

"Do you think Shin Shou is their leader?" The young man George hadn't recognized spoke.

"I'm sorry, I didn't catch your name," George said, his hand outstretched.

"Bill."

"George."

"I doubt Shin is in charge," Leonard said. "It doesn't seem logical to send your leader in to do a dangerous killing like this."

"He's right." Scherzer said. "What about the kid who ran out the door?"

"We found him dead on the pier." The General said. "He had a single gunshot wound to the head."

"So who did Rex and Sarah follow down the river?" Lucille Chase was asking the questions now. "I'm not sure I understand what is going on here. Why would they fake killing the President and murder business owners?"

"Easy, to consolidate power." Leonard rubbed his eyes as he spoke. "Killing the President and The General would have just been a bonus for them. They've finished rebuilding Dietrich Hoff's empire."

****

48.

"Sir, come take a look at this."

"Whatya have seaman?"

Captain Michael C. Andover had cut his teeth in the First World War fighting German U-boats as a radio operator. He had enlisted at the age of 16 and after his service attended Annapolis. His experience in the field had given him an advantage against his classmates, which made his rise to Captain somewhat meteoric.

"Sir, it's a plane. It doesn't seem to be in distress, but it sure looks like it is going to crash into the ocean."

Andover squinted and focused in the direction the young man had pointed. The moon shone on the clear evening and its reflection danced across the gentle swells. Though it was night, visibility was excellent. Then he saw it. Less than a mile off and descending into the water was an aircraft with no running lights. The fool had fallen asleep.

"Radio. Issue a warning to that pilot to correct course before he crashes."

"Yes sir."

Andover smiled as he grabbed the binoculars he kept nearby on the bridge. Even at this hour the young radio man was full of energy. It reminded him of himself as a young man.

"Unidentified aircraft. Pull up. I repeat. Pull up."

The radio crackled as they awaited a response. Captain Andover rolled his neck and rubbed his eyes before peering back through the binoculars. He picked up the airplane in seconds since it hadn't altered course. Pulling a corpse out of the ocean was not how he wished to spend the rest of the night.

"Hit em again Jack."

The young seaman obeyed.

"I repeat. Unidentified aircraft. Impact is imminent. Pull up. Pull up. Pull up…"

Even as the young radio man repeated the warning over and over the captain could see it was to no avail. The plane's descent never deviated. He watched through the glass as it approached the water. Then it disappeared. He jerked the binoculars away from his face.

"What happened? Where did it go? Did anyone see?" Muted responses echoed through the cabin, but no one had seen the plane crash. "Bring us about. I want to find that wreckage."

Within minutes the USS Fox had changed heading and was steaming toward the crash site. Andover peered through the binoculars, but could not make out any wreckage in the water. Something seemed amiss, but he couldn't quite put his finger on it.

"Make your speed ten knots. Ahead easy. I want all eyes on the water."

He strained his senses, searching for any indication of the plane's remains. They should be right on top of the crash. Then he saw it, the aberration in the ocean which had bothered his eyes. Fifty yards ahead of the Clemson class destroyer waves broke against an unseen peril.

"Full reverse. Hard to port."

He pulled the binoculars down and a terrible realization flooded his mind. They were too close. The ship was going to run aground. It didn't make any sense, though. He had been patrolling these waters for years, and even in recent days had seen trawlers in the area.

"Reverse. Reverse. Reverse."

His men acted as a single unit and with lightning speed and proficiency, but they were too late. The 1190 ton destroyer slammed into the unseen obstacle which did not yield. Though they were traveling a mere eight knots the damage was instantaneous.

The collision threw men from their posts and cries of agony mixed with the sound of twisted steel. Andover fell to his knees and he fought to regain control. He had been unable to sound the collision alarm in time, but, unlike others had braced himself against the sudden stop.

The captain stood and what he saw was terrifying. His failure to recognize danger now showed in the mangled bow of the ship. Even as the screws flailed and the destroyer backed away, water poured into the hull. They had already listed several degrees and Captain Andover accepted the inevitable.

"Radio. Put out an S.O.S. All channels. All frequencies." A second passed without a reply. He turned to see the radio man unconscious on the floor. "Roberts."

"Yes sir."

"Get in that radio seat and put out an S.O.S."

Captain Michael C. Andover flipped a small emergency beacon switch before picking up the ship wide communication device. He thought for a few seconds what he would say to the men as he gave the order to evacuate. Chaos surrounded him, but inside tranquility warmed his soul. A bright light shone in all directions and its beauty was instantaneous. Then it was dark.

****

49.

"To use a euphemism of the Americans, we must strike while the iron is hot. Izanami, with the completion of the dam project we will…"

Consciousness began to put down roots in Chase's mind, though fantastic visions of light accompanied them. The drugs were having a hallucinogenic effect. Even as Katsuo continued to speak, he did not feel a call to action. He lay in a foggy state and found himself wondering what consciousness was. Even as his mind cleared and the words Takahiro was speaking became recognizable, he didn't attempt to formulate an escape plan.

Something was different, though, and it was this change that caused him to act. Gone was the click clack of the train tracks, replacing it instead with the drone of twin aircraft engines. He could feel the plane moving through the air, making slight adjustments as pressures changed. Flying was something that he had found addictive, and had been one of the few reasons he had left the garage in the last year and a half.

"Kit-Kat? Do you know what it is about the human brain that makes us capable of conscious thought?"

His hands and feet remained bound and his eyes covered, but he imagined Katsuo being startled by his question. The response he received seemed anything but alarmed.

"Izanagi breathed life into the islands of Japan. Allowing us to partake in the world he created."

"I'm not talking about religion. I'm talking about neurons and synapses in the mind." Chase's body ached, but he pushed the pain to the side. "What I mean is that even if you and I were twins conjoined at the hip, we would still have a different view of the world. The connections that our brains make, even though we would experience very similar stimulation, would not be the same. Perhaps I would see a rose and it would remind me of the time a bee stung me. Maybe you saw the same thing, but the rose reminds you of a time you went on a trip and saw a whole garden of flowers. You know, I'd even bet that dogs and cats have achieved a certain level of consciousness. You know my dog Belle, the one you killed, she would come up to me every day when I got home and a lot of the time..."

"That's enough of your blasphemous drivel. How dare you compare the Japanese race to that of a mere dog."

"You missed the point Kit-Kat. I was just saying that perhaps animals have achieved a certain level of consciousness. I'm pretty new to the science since I've just been thinking about it a few minutes, but if you and your lady friend wouldn't mind taking me to a library I'd love to read up on it. You know, I think you and I could become good friends. I mean, we got off on the wrong foot with me killing all your buddies and you killing my dog, but I think we can work through that. All around the world people are able to..."

"Your words bore me Mr. Chase. Izanami and I require your presence for a very specific goal. After that goal is reached, you will be dead. It doesn't matter how long you ramble on about the neuron doctrine."

"Izanami?" Chase dug deep into his brain. He had read a book on Japanese mythology once. "Didn't she eat a sandwich in hell and have to stay?"

"Izanami lives. She is with me even as we speak."

"Speaking in a figurative manner," Chase said.

"It is because of her that you are alive. I did not wish to feed you or give you water. She has tended to your needs with her own hands. You owe her everything."

Dread crept into Chase's mind. Katsuo Takahiro had just proved himself schooled enough to have knowledge of the neuron doctrine, yet blind enough to believe he traveled with, and took orders from a mythological being. Rex needed to change the subject.

"What have you done with Sarah?"

"See for yourself."

Takahiro jerked the blindfold off Chase's face and bright light filled the dark world in which he had been living. He squeezed his eyes shut for a few seconds before opening them. The flood of ocular information overloaded his senses and he struggled to focus on his surroundings. His mind, which had been making light in the dark, was now attempting to fight through the hallucinogenic effects of the drugs.

Katsuo stood over him, and in the tail section of the plane the back of a woman's head and shoulders poked above a seat. She wore her hair in traditional Japanese dress and five yellow flowers adorned the kanzashi. Her shoulders slumped and the left seemed a bit larger than the right. Chase stretched his jaw and blinked hard.

His eyes had almost adjusted to the light, but the sensory deprivation and drugs were inhibiting his ability to process. The fact that they were in a Douglas DC-3 aircraft was recognizable to him, but even as he tried to make out its interior features, he struggled. Then Chase saw her.

A few feet away, resting on a mattress was Sarah. Unlike him, she slept unrestrained, her long blonde hair draped over her face and he could see the steadiness of her breath as it escaped into the atmosphere. Her chest rose and fell in stable time. She seemed uninjured and he breathed a sigh of relief.

"As you can see Mr. Chase, young Sarah is doing fine, although she doesn't seem to hold her drugs as well as you. I've given you enough to put down a herd of elephants yet you continue to awake."

"Must be all that clean livin," Chase delivered the snarky remark, then his tone went cold. "If you've done anything to her I'll kill you."

"No need for idle threats Mr. Chase. It's time for you to go back to sleep, though. I have a lot of work to do before we land."

Chase started to protest, but it was too late. Takahiro had already plunged the delivery device into his arm. The numbing effects of the drugs coursed through his veins in an instant and he began to drift to sleep. Questions nagged his mind, though. Who was the woman in the seat? Where were they going? What were the stones Katsuo had referred to earlier? The darkness closed in and washed over him in waves. He entered a deep sleep, devoid of all conscious thought and the world, for him, no longer existed.

****

50.

Stepping onto the deck of the 7500 ton aircraft carrier was always a bit surreal. Shin Shou couldn't help but marvel at the feat of Japanese ingenuity. With a length of 168 meters and a beam of 18 meters its larger cousins dwarfed the ship, but its remarkability didn't lie in its size. Even the United States destroyer that now steamed toward them seemed to be similar in dimension.

"Would you like us to radio the U.S. ship and warn them away?"

"Of course he wouldn't." A woman's voice propelled itself from the shadows. "Shin wants to see them burn."

A sly smile crept over his lips as he strode across the deck of the ship. He had never met her before, and he didn't believe in the hocus pocus of Izanami and mythology. Katsuo had a keen mind, and Shou appreciated everything he had learned from the man, but the search for his brother sometimes clouded his judgment. He knew they had a few minutes before the destroyer would be on top of them and he needed to meet this woman.

"So you are a goddess?"

Shou peered into the darkness, but he still could not make out the features of the woman. She sat in a chair less than ten yards away where the ship's tower cast a deep shadow. He stepped forward to get a better look.

"That's far enough."

Two men stepped from either side of the goddess' figure. Submachine guns graced their arms and they were not Japanese. He stopped dead in his tracks before speaking.

"I don't understand."

"You are not meant to understand. You know what your role is, just like Katsuo knows his." A German accent tinged her broken English. "I'm much too old to be a silly goddess."

Though her voice did project significant authority, it also wavered. Realization flooded his mind. He had talked to two different female leaders on the phone and this woman was not Izanami.

"What should I call you then?"

"Mother will be fine. I've gone by that name for as long as I can remember."

"Okay, Mother. For me, this was the end of my instruction." Shou peaked over his shoulder, but the destroyer was still a short distance off. "Who gives me my next set of orders? Katsuo? Izanami? You?"

"If you would have killed Rex Chase and retrieved the stones your service would be complete."

"And you'd have me killed."

"Katsuo holds you in high regard and I appreciate all you've done," her tone shifted to that of a cold blooded killer. "But if you fail me again I'll have your liver."

"Your order is all that allows Rex Chase life. I could have killed him with ease." Shin seethed. "What am I to do now, then, Mother?"

"Tell me about my weapon."

"I reported to Katsuo..."

"And Katsuo reported to Izanami, who reported to me. Now I wish to hear from you Shin."

"We couldn't complete it by tonight, but it should be ready soon, perhaps tomorrow."

"That is fine Shin. I don't wish to use it until we have all the stones anyway. Tell me about my ships."

Shou didn't like being quizzed.

"You stand upon the first mobile platform. It is revolutionary in every way. Katsuo and I both had a hand in its development and now that we have consolidated Japanese industry with our vast natural resources we will commission a fleet. Along with our new fighter we will…"

"Your new fighter is already outdated. Tell me, what do you see around you Shin Shou?"

The question caught him off guard and he pulled a cigarette from his pocket. Lighting the tobacco gave him time to formulate a response. He breathed deep before answering.

"I see a wonder of Japanese industry. I see the brilliance of my countrymen. I see the power we have annexed with our work tonight."

"Wrong." Her laughter echoed across the deck even as the enemy destroyer bore down on their position. "What you see here is everything another man worked his entire life to create. What you see here is innovation realized by the blood, sweat, and tears of thousands, if not tens of thousands of Germans. What you see here is absolute victory."

She coughed and Shou could see her shifting in the overstuffed chair. The woman seemed out of place on an aircraft carrier.

"I'm not sure I understand. We…"

"Of course you don't. You're nothing but Katsuo's lapdog, recruited because your country had disowned you." Her voice heightened as the U.S. destroyer's engines filled the night air with their whine. "When The Organization killed our scientists and we asked the Japanese for help there were none that could rise to the task. We had to kidnap The Russian to finish the work." The destroyer was close now and she had to yell for Shou to hear her. "It was The Russian who designed the force field. It was The Russian who innovated their light bending properties. It was The Russian who theorized our functioning weapons system. You Japanese gave us these small boats, an outdated aircraft, and a slight boost in industrial strength. You're nothing. You're no one."

Shou turned at the sound of the USS Fox smashing into the inner field. The warship's metal screamed in protest as twisted steel succumbed to stress and the ship's beam buckled. A few seconds of absolute destruction followed, and then relative quiet returned.

Injured men cried for help and water rushed in through the gaping bow. Shou smiled at the carnage. Although the men on the crew had done nothing wrong he still marveled at the technological feats that had caused their deaths. Mother had attempted to put him in his place, but he knew otherwise. No one could fight like him. No one could fly like him. No one could replace him.

Perhaps Mother and Izanami had been using him before, and he knew they were using Katsuo, but now Shin Shou worked for himself. He would be Mother's thoroughbred for the moment, but she had underestimated his guile. Shin raised his left hand high in the air, his pointer finger raised to the sky. He hadn't thought of The Russian in some time. They had suffered enough.

With the drop of his hand the temperature between the inner and outer fields rose thousands of degrees, and dropped in less than one-one thousandth of a second. Shou squinted as the one hundred yard no man's land glowed a bright blue-green and then flickered away, leaving nothing inside its walls. Even the ocean water trapped within disintegrated leaving a dry wasteland circling the entire area down to the seafloor. Shou sneered as he turned and walked past the woman called Mother.

"I'd pay to see this show from the air."

****

51.

An angelic voice emanated from the nearby Commander 6d radio. *Somewhere over the Rainbow* was a mainstay of the station and Disparzio had no problem with the program director's choice.

"Man, I love Judy Garland. The things I would do to that woman."

Sergeant Ralph Disparzio was a first generation Italian American. His parents had emigrated from Sicily while he was still in his mother's womb and days after their arrival they celebrated his birth. Life had been difficult during the depression for their family, and work had not come easy for his father. The man had taught him a good work ethic, though, and when Ralph turned eighteen he had joined the army.

Disparzio was a natural leader of men. He had found his calling in the armed forces and just before his 21st birthday he achieved a promotion to sergeant. He and his men took an assignment on a small island in the Pacific and for the first time in his life he had left the United States. It was beautiful, the job was easy, and 80 degree weather on white sandy beaches greeted them at the end of every shift.

He was homesick, though, so when a general he had never heard of approached him about a job closer to home, with triple the pay, he had jumped at the opportunity. That was a decision he was starting to rethink. No sandy beaches were anywhere near his station. No beautiful women frequented the local establishments. Instead he spent day after day sitting at a desk listening to static on the radio. At least nobody ever checked in on him to see that he had his headset on over one ear while listening to music on the nearby Commander 6d radio.

"Someday da da da da da da, da da da da da da da da." Disparzio followed the melody with his voice but stopped as the song changed. "That's where... the human heart beats a hundred thousand times a day. The human heart beats a hundred..."

Sergeant Disparzio bolted upright in his seat, grasped his headphones in his hands and clutched them tight against his ears. He had been sitting in the same chair for months on end monitoring nothing, but that had just changed. A message had interrupted Miss Garland and as he strained his ears, waiting for it to play again, he heard nothing but the familiar sound of static.

Panic shot through his body as he began scanning the phrases written down in his binder. What had the message been? It was something about the heart beating all day long? During his training exercises they had given him partial messages to decode, but he was ready then. Stupid Judy Garland had distracted him from his duties. Then he saw it on his list.

The human heart beats 100,000 times a day. USS Fox. Call Washington D.C. Contact: Major Railey. 555-4892

Disparzio was all business now as he dialed the number on his rotary phone. The woman on the other end had him patched through to the major in short order and he waited as the phone rang.

"This is Railey."

"The human heart beats 100,000 times a day. USS Fox." Disparzio had never trained any farther than this before.

"One moment for verification." The authentication procedure seemed to last forever, but in reality took less than thirty seconds. Disparzio realized the radio behind him was still on, and he remedied the distraction just as the major came back. "Verification complete. 37.19198 by -74.918518 Lat 37 degrees 11' 31.128" Long -74 degrees 55' by 6.6648" Polar bear liver contains too much vitamin A and is toxic for human consumption."

The line went dead and the sergeant scribbled the information onto a notepad, even while he grabbed another nearby binder. He finished writing and scanned the second code sheet. Next to the line about polar bear liver was a phone number. Within seconds he had the phone dialed and an operator patched him through.

"General Reagan."

"General Reagan?" Disparzio's heart sank. He didn't realize whatever information he had obtained skipped straight to the head of The Organization.

"Yes."

"The General Reagan?"

"Yes."

"I'm sorry to call you so late in the evening, sir but I have an urgent communication."

"You were right to call me. What do you have?"

"I'm sorry it's so late, sir. I..."

"Stop apologizing young man and tell me what you need me to know."

Disparzio rattled off the information he had received and soon found himself blathering on about nothing. The General seemed to be taking the mild hysteria in stride, though, his tone never wavering.

"Excellent work young man."

"Thank you, sir."

"Goodbye."

"Goodbye, sir."

Just a few minutes had passed, but it seemed like he hadn't heard Judy Garland's angelic voice for days. Sergeant Disparzio leaned back in his seat and sighed. It was times like these he almost wished he smoked. Static emanated from the headphones as he placed both earpieces in their proper position on his head.

"Back to work Disparzio."

****

52.

"So, what are we going to do about my son?"

Lucille Chase had fought the urge to interject Rex into the conversation, but now she needed an answer. Earlier in the evening she had vowed to protect her family, and that was a promise she intended to keep. The surrounding men would not allow her to accompany on any of their missions, but she still desired to stay in the loop.

"Luce," Alexei took her hand, and it soothed the apprehension. "I'm sure he's just fine. You know, when I thought he was dead..."

"What do you mean you thought he was dead?"

"No, no." His calmness eased her dread. "This was when we were in France."

"I didn't know you assumed he was dead in France."

"My point is, Luce," Alexei cleared his throat. "My point, is that he wasn't dead. He's a grown man and capable of taking care of himself."

Lucille tried to quash the fear that rose inside, but it gnawed at her belly. They had worked hard their entire lives just to make his easier, but now he was in danger. She didn't like it, and there was nothing anyone could say to make it better. Rex Chase walking through the door was the only thing that could ease her anxiety. The phone rang and snapped her from self-pity. It was going to be a long day.

***

"General Reagan." The General answered the phone on his desk and took a seat while picking up a pen. "Yes... Yes... You were right to call me. What do you have?... Stop apologizing young man and tell me what you need me to know..." He shuffled through papers on his desk even as he scribbled on others. "Okay.... Yes... No... Tell him to keep doing what he's doing... Yes... I have it... I won't be leaving this room anytime soon... Yes... Thank you... Excellent work young man... Goodbye..."

The General hung up the phone and looked at the others in the room. Anticipation filled their faces. It had been obvious that he had just gotten vital information.

"A Navy ship just triggered an emergency beacon not far off the coast." The room remained silent and The General stood. "This beacon comes straight to us and is to be used as a last resort. In tests the devices continue transmitting whether on the bottom of the ocean or strapped to the end of an artillery shell, yet this survived seconds. George, it was right along the same longitudinal lines as you and your wife's report on the trawlers working up and down the coast. Do you remember what they were doing?"

"Communications for the Navy." George said. "They were laying communications cables for the Navy."

"OK. What do communications cables for the Navy have to do with a ship that is sunk so fast It just has time to flip our beacon and not issue a proper S.O.S.?"

"And the indestructible beacon is destroyed," Bill added as Alexei Chase nodded his head before speaking.

"Maybe they use a scalar energy field to mask some kind of ship?"

"Interesting," Poppen said. "The energy fields could be used to bend light around an object."

"Yeah, but that doesn't explain the indestructible beacon," Lucille said.

"It sure doesn't." Patrick Castle stood and began pacing. "George. How far up and down the coast do these cables go?"

"If I remember right the Navy had their own system installed on both coasts."

"Do you know if the Army had a similar project?" Castle continued.

"I believe they did." The General answered. "If I remember right we have a number of secure transcontinental lines."

"What are you thinking Patrick?" Alexei scratched his ear and wiped a bead of sweat from his brow.

"I was thinking that if I had numerous lines and buried cables made out of Castleinium surrounding the United States of America, I, well, I could incinerate the whole thing."

Silence dominated the room and Poppen was the first to speak.

"It's possible, but the math would be very, very difficult."

"How do we know they don't have the equation, though?" Lucille asked. "I mean, we can't be certain whoever has taken over Hoff's empire didn't find a copy lying around somewhere."

"They don't." Leonard had been quiet, but asserted himself. "It seems to me that if you had layers of these cables a person could also have layers of defense. If you were to lower one layer, a ship could pass, then raise the layer and incinerate it."

"But, wouldn't that be instant?" Willy said. "They did get off a short distress signal."

"Of course it would be instant, but if there's something I learned about Shin Shou it's that he likes to do his killing up close and personal." Anger flashed behind George's deep brown eyes. "I can imagine him watching them suffer a little before pulling the trigger."

"That settles it. George. If you are feeling up to it I have a trip I'd like you to lead."

"Yes, sir." George leapt to his feet and took the piece of paper offered by The General.

"You'll report to that man, and give him the numbers I jotted down. His name is Humboldt and you'll get further instructions when you get to him. Bryan."

"Yes, sir."

"Al."

"Yes, sir."

"I'm wondering if either of you guys feel like logging a little flight time?"

"Yes, sir." Both men said the words in unison and pride welled up inside of him. This tight knit group inside of The Organization had become his family. He'd give his life for each one of them.

"As for the rest of you, it's been a long day. Go home, get some rest and we'll start again around four tomorrow, or today, whatever it is."

Everyone began to stand and the General became aware of their weariness.

"Luce, would you mind doing me a favor?" George asked, and she responded.

"Anything my dear."

"I'd appreciate it if you'd go to the hospital and be with my wife when she wakes up. I doubt I'm going to be able to do it."

The Sentinel

"I won't leave her side."

****

53.

"What do you mean you don't know?" Shin Shou was furious. A large vein in his forehead protruded and it seemed as if it could burst from his body at any point. "Did they, or did they not, get off an S.O.S.?"

"I just can't be certain, sir. It seems lik..."

The gurgling sound of blood in his throat replaced the young sailor's words. Shin Shou had sliced the nineteen-year-old radio operator from ear to ear. He fell to the floor, clutching at the empty gash in his neck even as his body began to convulse. A maniacal grin accompanied Shin's wild eyes and men around the room seemed shocked. Shou delivered his next words in a calm and passive tone.

"Okay. Who wants to give me an answer to my question?" Terrified stares were all he received, so he addressed a young man a few feet away. "You. Did they, or did they not, get off an S.O.S.?"

"W,w,w,w,w,w,"

"W,w,w,w,w,w," Shou mocked him. "Spit it out. This is unbelievable. You know something? You're the second stuttering idiot I've met in the same amount of days. DID THEY GET OFF AN S.O.S.?...."

The young man snapped to attention and blurted a statement.

"The human heart beats 100,000 times a day. Sir."

"What in the world does that mean?"

"I don't know, sir. I just heard them transmit, sir."

Shou's anger boiled from deep within. He contemplated killing the second man as well, but thought better of it. He had proved his point and doubted anyone would challenge his command anytime soon. His wrist tingled from cutting the man so he flexed it. It wasn't every day you tweaked a wrist while slicing a throat.

"Is it possible for us to know whether anyone received the message?"

All eyes moved to the other side of the room. Mother's voice came through the ships communication system, but no one answered the question.

"You heard her." Shou paced and moved his eyes from man to man, resembling a tiger sizing up its prey.

"No, sir."

"No sir what?"

"No sir, there is no way for us to know sir."

"All of you leave the bridge before I have every one of you executed for dereliction of duty."

The men evacuated the tense area and Shin unleashed his frustrations. A nearby garbage can suffered first as he destroyed it with his foot. Then he proceeded to punch a chart cabinet over and over as he screamed at the top of his lungs. A full minute passed as he released the unrelenting anger and frustration and then he stopped. His thirst for violence quenched, he concentrated on the rise and fall of his chest. The beating of his heart and the steadiness of his breath were the only sounds in the room.

"Are you quite done with your temper tantrum?"

Her voice crackled over the speaker system and Shin's anger once again boiled inside.

"Maybe you would like to join me Mother?"

"No thank you Shin. I've been thinking about the things I said to you earlier, and I believe an apology is in order. I can get a little carried away sometimes."

Shou heard the words, and found the message confusing. She had made no bones about his country's uselessness. He decided to play the game.

"Of course I accept your apology Mother. We can all get a little on edge sometimes."

"We can. I could not have executed the beginning stages of the plan without you, Katsuo, Laurence, or your country. I am indebted to all of you and I wish to work together to further our goals."

Shou arched his eyebrow. The old woman was laying it on pretty thick. He knew how she felt and trusted her very little. Still, it wouldn't hurt to play along for now. He didn't know the full scope of the plan yet anyway.

"Perhaps you should depart the vessel Mother. The U.S. Navy will miss one of their warships even if nobody received their strange message."

"That would be a prudent move. We will sleep here and leave tomorrow evening. It's been a long day friend."

She was right, it had been a long day, but Shin knew that he wouldn't be falling asleep any time soon. A few things about their operation didn't quite add up. Mother, Katsuo, and Izanami had all given him orders. Which one of them was in charge? How had Katsuo agreed to all of this? Where would he be heading next? What was the ultimate goal?

All of the questions flooded his mind as he made the short trip to his quarters. He had no doubt Mother cared nothing about him or Katsuo, and he didn't care for her either. He had made enemies today, though, and still needed her to sort everything out. Until the picture became clear he would just have to play the game. He needed to speak with The Russian.

****

54.

It was the rank stench that first greeted him as he awoke. Chase breathed in deep the foul air and exhaled. He was still very drowsy, and his nose itched. He rubbed the affected area with the back of his right hand and noticed something about this airplane seemed different.

"Good morning sunshine." A grizzled, throaty voice emanated from across the dim room. "Boy, they had you juiced up when they brought you in here. I've never heard a man snore like that before in my life. I haven't been around too many folks as of late either."

Chase continued to scratch his nose even as he sat up on the hard concrete surface. It dawned on him that his hands and feet were no longer bound, and that he was no longer on an airplane. He rubbed his eyes as he tried to focus on the stranger with whom he shared a cell.

"Yeah, they've had me on quite a bender." His words came out slurred, but recognizable. "My name is Rex Chase."

"You can call me Tad." The man stood and walked across the spacious holding area, his hand outstretched. "You must be pretty important to get thrown in here with me in the super max wing."

Rex looked the man in the eye as he shook his hand. Tad looked emaciated, smelled repugnant, and sported an atrocious beard along with disheveled hair. The man was wiry, standing a touch over six feet tall, but not tipping the scales at more than 150 pounds.

"It's nice to meet you, Tad?"

"Baxter."

"Baxter. Good name." Chase took in every feature of the man, but managed not to stare. He didn't feel the need to embarrass him.

"I know I must be a sight. I'm sure I smell awful too. I'm afraid I haven't had a bath in quite some time."

"How long do you think you've been in here?" Rex shifted himself in his seat as he stretched his neck and rubbed his wrists.

"Oh, I don't know, a few months at least. It could be more though. I've kinda lost track of time." The look of dejection was apparent. This man needed medical attention.

"So what do you mean by super max? It looks to me like we have two guards, and no door." Chase raised his voice so the men outside could hear. "When I get out of here I'm going to snap their necks."

"Shhhhhh." Tad said. "They can do things in this room. Strange things. Magic things."

"Is that so? Tell me about them Tad."

"For starters," Tad hushed his voice and stood close. "They have an invisible door."

The revelation piqued Chase's interest. Until now he had believed himself to be the only name in scalar energy. That no longer seemed the case and he prodded the other man for more information.

"What else can you tell me Tad?"

"They can raise the temperature in no time at all without a fire, or hot air or anything. Once, they took me outside blindfolded and we walked for a few seconds. When they took the blindfold off and I turned around the entire building disappeared."

Drugs no longer inhibited Chase's thought process. Adrenaline shot through his body and sharpened his mind as the realization that Hoff's men or even Dietrich Hoff himself, was still furthering the science. It couldn't be Hoff, though, he was dead. Who, then?

"Tad, if you don't mind me asking, why are you here?"

"The same reason you're here I suppose, because of the stones."

Chase listened as Tad related the events of his life. He told the story about the grizzly bear, the man with the silver hair, and the thirty-nine magic stones. After that, the two boys had dedicated themselves to the study of the items. They had traveled the world collecting samples of various metals, and had even found four pairs of the mysterious objects.

"Willy was the brains behind all of it, though. I was along to help find equipment, and smooth things over with the locals when we got caught trespassin. Those folks at the iron mine, though..." His voice trailed off as the thoughts seemed to pain him. "Well, those guys at that mine in Africa just didn't appreciate us being there."

"Morocco?" Some things were starting to fall into place. "Was it a mine in Morocco?"

"Uh-huh." Tad had been pacing, but he sat down on the concrete pad. "Willy thought he was onto something with the stones. It had to do with them being made out of the same material as the iron in that mine, but somehow not being the same? I don't know. It was kind of over my head. Anyway, we asked permission and they wouldn't let us in, so we just snuck on in like we always would."

"Then you got caught," Chase said.

"Willy got caught, but I got him out of there." Tad smiled, a wide grin and proud look adorning his face. "I could talk us out of about anything, but there was this German fella there who seemed pretty hell bent on killing us. I sprung Willy, but they caught me, roughed me up pretty good, and then I got shipped here."

"So you met Dietrich Hoff?"

"Yep, that was his name. He was a mean s.o.b. You had the pleasure as well?"

"Yeah, you could say that." Chase chuckled before continuing. "I might have had a hand in his untimely demise."

"Well, I'm not much for killin folk, but that man was as evil as any I've ever met." Tad rubbed his eyes, scratched underneath his long beard and motioned toward the door. "I suppose I wouldn't mind killin those two outside the door either. They've tortured me more days than not."

Tad lifted his shirt and revealed a roadmap to his pain. Thick scars from deep cuts criss crossed horrific burns which encompassed his torso. Repulsion at the horrific sight flowed through Chase and he couldn't hide his reaction.

"I'm sorry." Tad lowered his shirt. "It seems like forever since I talked to anyone."

"You say you've been down here a few months?" Chase asked.

"I'd say at least a few months. It could be a little longer. Why?"

"Well, if you met Dietrich Hoff, then you've been down here at least a year and a half. Whatya say we get out of here and get you a hot shower?"

"Sounds great." If the revelation that he'd been captive for eighteen months bothered him, he didn't let it show. "How do you propose we do that? I told you they have invisible doors."

"It should be easy." Chase stretched his shoulders while flexing his lower back. He was still a little stiff from being bound and tied. "Guards. I'm starving in here. Can we get a little grub?"

****

55.

"Alright, Bobby, you have to explain to me how this is all possible."

Alexei Chase spoke the words. Most had gone home and gotten sleep, but he had stayed awake the entire night trying to comprehend what was happening. All he had for his deliberations, though, were questions.

"Well, Mr. Chase." Poppen had spent the night on the couch in The General's office and to his surprise felt spry. He leaned across the semi-circle of wooden chairs and handed Alexei a crumpled piece of paper. "Take a look at this."

"Call me Alexei." He took the paper, opened it and a look of astonishment adorned his face. "I, I, I, I don't understand. Do we have copies?"

Laughter filled the room as the mood lightened.

"Rest assured Alexei, we have multiple copies." The General had not slept either and he rubbed his right eye as he spoke. "Leonard, would you mind explaining a few things to everyone?"

"No problem General."

Leonard stood and prepared to explain himself for the first time to anyone but The General and the President. Around the room sat The General, Alexei Chase, Bill, Patrick Castle, and Bobby Poppen. He wished that Rex and George were present as well, but the time was now. He cleared his throat before he spoke.

"A number of years ago I accepted the task of protecting our interests. It is a job I have performed with great pride and I also enlisted the help of The General. Together, and with the blessing of the President of the United States, we formed The Organization you are all a part of."

Leonard reached into his front pockets and pulled out two shiny black objects. Around the room eyes followed his every movement as he manipulated the orbs. Bill, in particular, seemed to be paying special attention.

"You see everyone; a long time ago I used these two orbs to achieve a very specific goal." Leonard touched the two objects together and twisted them counter to one another. They leapt from his hands and began orbiting each other in the sky. The mood in the room changed to that of a state of shock and Leonard smiled. "Don't be afraid. It's science, not magic."

"I knew it." Bill stood and grabbed one of the circling black orbs from the sky. "You're him."

"I am indeed young Willy." Leonard ruffled the grown man's hair. "Go ahead. Do you remember what to do?"

"I haven't thought of much else."

Willy touched the stones together at their inscriptions, just as he had done so many years before. All eyes were upon him as the objects danced in flight. Then, the orbs ascended into the air, separated, and made a perfect box in the sky. Willy's heart was beating hard inside of his chest, but what he saw next confused him.

"I. I. I don't understand."

"I don't understand either, Willy." A puzzled look adorned Leonard's face.

"I'm with ya there," said Al.

"Me too," said Bryan.

"You see, thirty-nine of these objects exist. Nineteen pairs, and one 'master', if you will." Leonard leaned against The General's desk as he spoke. "If everything is normal the stones would show a three dimensional representation of their positions, but in recent times there has been interference."

"Interference? Are we looking at some kind of alien technology here?" Alexei Chase stood and waved his hand through the dark void projected in the sky. It seemed to waver a slight amount.

"Not quite Alexei," Leonard answered. "These are naturally occurring; however, when subjected to earth's atmosphere they do seem to break down over time."

"So they're broken?" Willy asked.

"I'm not sure, but I intend to find out. In the wrong hands, and with the right knowledge, they could be dangerous."

"Maybe someone just has them hidden in a dark room so you can't find them."

Leonard smiled before turning his attention to Bobby Poppen.

"Maybe, and with some significant knowledge of scalar energy. If they do, though, we need to get these last two into the hands of Rex Chase."

"Why Rex?" Alexei asked.

"It's hard to explain. Speaking of hard to explain. Weren't you going to tell me why you're so old Bobby?"

A sly grin crossed the old man's face and he rubbed the back of his hand under his chin as he spoke.

"What do you guys know about the multiverse?"

56.

Al Scherzer eased the controls of the F4F Wildcat to the east, banking slightly. It was only his second time in the plane but every passing moment he became more comfortable. He squinted as he massaged his right temple. The night before hadn't afforded him much sleep and paired with the scotch, his head was pounding.

Al shivered slightly as he peered down at the ocean below. Outside the temperature dipped into single digits and he felt himself pining for his normal runs in the Pacific. Truthfully, though, he almost preferred the cold to sweat dripping from his nose and condensation shorting out his instruments.

All of his senses were on full alert now and the pounding in his head seemed to subside. They should be at the drop site any minute and he wondered if it was the adrenaline or the Anacin he had taken earlier which eased his pain. He breathed deeply the cool air and relished every breath. Suddenly, and without warning bullets whizzed past his cockpit and he instinctively rolled the aircraft while simultaneously putting it into a hard banking maneuver.

A smile pursed his lips even as he concentrated with all of his might. Though his attacker was still unseen and his very life was in peril there was no place in the world he'd rather have been. His job was to escort the paratroopers to the drop and if he died performing his duty, then he would gladly die. He strained his neck, fighting the gravitational forces holding him back in his seat. Somewhere an enemy plane still loosed a withering stream of fire.

"Alright you sneaky s.o.b. Where are you?"

***

Bryan Morris yawned and stretched inside of the Wildcat's tight cockpit. His six foot two inch frame was right at the upper limits for a fighter pilot. He had spent most of the morning getting a feel for the experimental aircraft and instead of catching a nap in the afternoon he had studied its capabilities. They shouldn't meet a plane in the sky that could match the cutting edge design.

Spearheading a possibly hostile encounter was a mission he had been itching to receive. Running diplomats and ferrying members of The Organization around the globe had become tedious. He felt truly alive in the frigid compartment as he fixed his gaze on the water below. Their target and the paratrooper's drop zone should be visible any minute.

Out his window to the west he took note of the three Wildcats flying in formation. East of him three more took up station. With him in the lead they provided a formidable escort for the Douglas DC3 and its occupants. Their job was to protect and that was exactly what he planned on doing.

It seemed like he felt the attack before he saw it. Something was amiss and he brought his gaze to the east just in time to see Scherzer's plane maneuver violently toward the deck. Everyone had their own assignment in an air battle and they were performing flawlessly. A dogfight had begun and Morris scanned the skies for signs of their attacker. Adrenaline surged through his veins as he breathed deep the cool air and calmly transmitted.

"Keep doin what you're doin Al. Bogey is on your six. It's time to do some flyin boys."

****

57.

"I'm not joking fellas. We are really, really, really, really hungry in here."

Chase had been bothering the two guards for nearly thirty minutes about getting something to eat without receiving a response. The two men stoically held their posts without formulating a retort of any kind. Periodically they would cast a look in his direction, but their faith in the force fields was evident. Though he was genuinely hungry, dinner was not Chase's true goal, however.

He had been moving about the room as he distracted the two men with his chatter. Any time he approached the door they would monitor him more closely, but he knew the time would come. Neither man had turned yet as he neared. He reached out, and touched the nearest guard on the back.

"Hey."

Both sentries jumped into strategic position, but Chase had been too quick. Before either of them could respond, his hand flew back through the field and he already stood a few feet away. Rex took notice of the look on Tad's face, stopped, and attempted to make the same expression as he faced their enemies.

"What? What? What happened?" Chase turned to Tad. "Did you see what happened?"

"What was it Heinrich?" The larger of the two guards addressed the other Chase had touched.

"He smacked me on the back Rolph."

Rolph immediately relaxed, a wide grin coming to his face.

"You're getting jumpy down here my friend." He placed a large hand on Heinrich's shoulder. "Nobody can penetrate the force fields without one of these."

Rolph removed a thin metal piece from his pocket that resembled a playing card. He set it on the floor and approached the doorway. Chase saw his opportunity and approached as well.

"See buddy." He pushed against the invisible field, leaning his right shoulder into it while smacking it with his left hand. "It's solid as a rock."

Heinrich noticeably relaxed as well. Chase observed that both men had pulled Colt M1911 pistols and spoke with thick German accents.

"Können wir nicht sogar einige Stroganoff oder Spätzles?"

"We already know you speak German," Rolph smiled fiendishly as he leaned close to the invisible barrier, "and no, you can't have any stroganoff or spatzles."

"Careful Rolph." Heinrich still clutched the deadly .45, but had lowered it to his waist. "Remember, they told us to be careful."

Rolph was an alpha male, though, and Chase had made sure to lock eyes with him. Tad's torturer sneered as he and Chase stood face to face.

"I wish this barrier wasn't here. I'd love to go a few rounds with the white devil."

"Well, I'm not a genie, but…"

Chase delivered a right uppercut to the formidable German's jaw which lifted the man off the ground. The guard's eyes rolled back in his head, and Rex moved his attentions onto Heinrich. The attack had been so quick and delivered with such ferocity, that the smaller guard had not yet moved.

The mind numbing effects of the drugs no longer had an iota of control as Chase calculated his next course. Even as Heinrich brought the 1911 to bear Chase leapt to the right while delivering a shot to the guard's temple. The firearm barked once, but deflected off a concrete wall before ricocheting down the hallway. In less than two seconds both men lay in heaps on the floor. Chase picked up the two firearms and walked back into the cell. Tad had not moved, and his expression had not changed. Rex smiled as he offered his hand.

"So are you ready to get out of here or what?"

58.

"I have to say this, sir. We are not equipped to perform extensive rescue operations." The voice crackled across the radio and Chief's lips curled as he responded. A Captain had just referred to him as sir.

"We understand that Captain. If we don't land on your deck we should be nearby. Just don't let us stay in that water too long."

"Yes, sir. Is there anything we should be looking for while we're here sir?"

George furrowed his brow and clicked the button on his handset.

"Be careful out there, and keep your speed under five knots. You need to be able to stop on a dime." George failed to mention that they could all be incinerated at any second. "Good luck."

"Yes, sir. Good luck."

The Organization never ceased to amaze George Ahiga. Hours before he had been sitting in an office with The General and now he stood in the field with a dozen elite paratroopers, two naval vessels under his command, captains calling him sir, and the possible fate of the world resting on his shoulders. He had met the men earlier in the day and they accepted him into their ranks. It seemed his reputation had grown in the last eighteen months.

"So where's Rex Chase?"

The pilot had to shout above the din of the dual Pratt and Whitney R-1830 Twin Wasp engines and the question brought a smile to George's lips. His best friend's reputation exceeded his own.

"I don't know," George shouted back. "We got separated a couple of days ago and I haven't heard from him since. I'm sure he's figuring this whole thing out somewhere."

Ahiga peered at the dark water below. Their target area should be coming into view any minute, but the Atlantic's massive expanse still held its exact location secret. His thoughts drifted to his wife, Angela, lying unconscious in a hospital bed. It bothered him that he wasn't by her side, but she would want him to be here. A picture of her body riddled with bullet holes popped into his mind and he blinked hard while stretching his shoulders against their harness. He still found it difficult to believe he had hallucinated some of her injuries.

"You alright over there partner?" The twin 800 horsepower engines almost drowned out the pilot's deep southern drawl. "I don't need you up here anymore. You outta hop in the back and get your gear on."

"You got it." George extended his hand. "It was nice to meet you. Uh. Oh shoot."

"Jimmy. Jimmy Humboldt."

"Jimmy." Ahiga shook the other man's hand. "I apologize. I'm horrible with names. You sure you don't need help flying this thing back Jimmy? I bet I have at least one guy back there to help ya."

"Help? Me? You guys are the lunatics jumping out of a plane into the Atlantic Ocean. I don't see a thing down there."

"Ahhhh. We're going to land on a ship. Worst case scenario our boys pull us out in a few hours."

"Chyeah. You're gonna get cold, wet, or dead."

George squeezed himself through the tight compartment to the rear of the plane and began putting on his gear. What Jimmy and even the captain of the USS Fox didn't know was that the triggered device was a specialized distress signal sent to The Organization. Ahiga knew something was down there and it had attacked the Fox and could have incinerated it. He breathed deep through his nose as a strange feeling crept into his body. It was like he could feel Shin Shou.

Without warning, the plane lurched and George steadied himself using a nearby grip rail. He swung closer to the cockpit and leaned forward. The Wildcats no longer held their formation and Jimmy's grip on the controls had tightened.

"Everything alright Jimmy?"

"Somebody's doin some shootin out there."

Before the words had even left the pilot's mouth bullets tore into the rear of the lumbering troop transport. Ahiga snapped his head around to assess the damage. Three men suffered serious injuries. A decision needed to be made.

"We're getting off of here right now Jimmy. Thanks for the ride."

"Like hell you are." Humboldt's full attention was on the controls even as he contorted his body, searching for their attacker. "We're too fast and still a couple miles out. You keep those men strapped in and you'd better hold on tight."

George saw the young pilot push the DC3's controls to the stops and the Pratt and Whitneys responded to the increase in fuel. A few seconds passed and Ahiga looked through the cockpit glass. He couldn't see anything but bright blue sky.

"Five, four, three, two, one. Hold on boys. Yeeeeehawwwwwwwww."

George braced himself as Jimmy rolled the Douglas aircraft and positioned it in an inverted dive. The bright blue sky ahead transformed into the blackened seas below. His legs floated in the air behind him and blue/green veins bulged from his massive arms. He grunted from the stresses being put upon his body and tried to focus his attention on the instrument panel ahead.

They had passed through three thousand feet and were approaching two hundred seventy miles per hour. He was no aeronautical engineer, but he knew the aircraft was exceeding its limits. Seconds passed, but they felt like minutes and just when he thought he couldn't hang on any longer the plane rolled over.

"Keep hangin on."

George followed the pilot's command as the airframe shuttered under the duress. He looked ahead and saw a supreme look of confidence on Jimmy's face even though the plane felt as if it would rip apart at any moment. Ahiga marveled at the other man's skills when Humboldt threw the air brakes forward, deployed his flaps, and pulled up on the yoke. The plane recovered from its dive and hung in the air, losing 200 miles per hour in airspeed.

Chief's legs returned to the floor of the plane and he loosed his vise-like grips. He had never seen someone perform a similar maneuver and assumed he may never again. Jimmy's smiling face turned toward the aft of the plane and showed no ill effects from the drastic sequence.

"That's better. You boys just go ahead 'n jump now."

****

59.

"Why don't we pretend like everyone here is as dumb as me, and explain the multiverse that way." The General's tone was light, yet tinged with urgency.

Poppen took a deep breath and let it out as he stood. All eyes were on him and he could feel the tension in the room. It was exhilarating. He pulled a handkerchief and wiped his brow before speaking.

"This will be a little difficult to understand, but yesterday afternoon I was sitting at the Cantor Oyster House just up the street celebrating my hundredth birthday and I paid almost two dollars an oyster and fifteen dollars for a Glenlivet on the rocks."

"I can understand that you got ripped off yesterday. Happy birthday, by the way, but what does that have to do with anything?" Willy leaned forward in his chair as Poppen continued.

"Well, yesterday was a pretty special day. It was my hundredth birthday and I met Leonard for the first time. Oh, and I forgot to mention, 1915 is my birth year."

Poppen could see the perplexed looks around the room, but none seemed too surprised as he continued.

"You see, when I was a young man I fell in love with the game of baseball. Where I'm from, though, I'd just seen pictures of you and your wife." Poppen nodded in the direction of Alexei. "Where I'm from, the two of you died in a car wreck when I was just a young man. Rex Chase grew up on his own, started in the big leagues when he was seventeen, and set almost every single record in the majors. Most of those records are still on the books." Bobby closed his eyes and saw the numbers in his head. "Eight hundred seventy-two career home runs. Seventy-seven

THE SENTINEL

home runs in the 45' season and two hundred twenty-eight Rbi's in that same year. A career batting average of .394. He hit over .400 in fifteen seasons and collected four-thousand nine hundred and twenty-nine hits. He had five hundred thirty-three wins as a pitcher, over six thousand strikeouts, and walked four hundred twenty-two with a career e.r.a. of one point three two. People got hits off him if they were lucky. He was the greatest who ever lived and he managed to drink himself to death at the age of forty-eight. He hadn't even retired yet."

"Wait a minute. I assumed we were talking about some sort of time travel using scalar mechanics, but what you're speaking of is something different." Alexei stood and moved behind his chair.

"I am. What I'm talking about is the multiverse. You have your universe here. I had my universe there. A version of you, me, and everyone exists inside of each universe. In this existence I died a couple of years ago, whereas in my reality I have lived to be an old man. They all coexist at the same time and are difficult to bring together," Poppen looked in Leonard's direction, "but he knows how to do it."

"So it isn't time travel?" Willy said.

"No, it can't be. Any movement among the multiverse would have to be parallel. Right?" Alexei began pacing as he tried to wrap his mind around the concept. "Also, I thought that the math on this would be astounding without Bobby's equation, which you couldn't have Leonard."

Leonard smiled and nodded.

"The math on a multiverse jump is a lot easier. A quantum computer could have the calculations done in a few hours. On the contrary, it would take hundreds of them working for hundreds of years, without my formula, to perform actual time travel inside our current universe." Poppen scratched the back of his neck. "I'm guessing you don't have computers at all and we haven't even begun addressing the issue of the power involved."

"I see the power problem as a less difficult thing to explain." Alexei flexed his shoulders and rolled his neck. "We've all seen scalar energy in action. With the right amount of math muscle it's limitless."

"I consider myself a smart man, but I don't understand any of this." Willy said. "How can it even be possible for a man to survive a multiverse jump? I mean, wouldn't the speed, gravity, and external forces rip you to pieces?"

"Not if you were in a stasis field." Alexei interjected.

"Interesting." Poppen could feel his adrenaline pumping again. "This is all very interesting, considering no one has even invented this technology, and yet, here I am."

All eyes moved to Leonard who stood straight, an easy smile on his face. He brushed back his thinning silver hair and wet his lips. Everyone's eyes seemed to prod him for an explanation as he looked Poppen square in the eye.

"You still haven't explained why you're so old."

Just then the phone began to ring and the room let out a collective breath.

"Excuse me everyone," The General picked up the receiver and covered its mouthpiece with his left hand, "to be continued."

60.

An enormous plate of beef stroganoff sat in front of Chase as he sat back down to the table. He dug into the mound of noodles, shoving them in his mouth. It seemed as if he hadn't eaten in years. This was his third plate, which even for him, was a lot. Tad's running footsteps echoed down the hallway as he approached and entered the room.

"You're still eating?"

"No," Chase responded, his mouth full of stroganoff. "I'm watching the prisoners."

"Well, I have good news and bad news."

"Bad news first please," Chase said as he shoveled in the German variation of the Russian dish.

"The bad news is that this place is huge, and it's a labyrinth. I got so turned around I almost didn't find my way back."

"Not a problem." Chase tapped his temple with his fork. "I'm pretty good at remembering stuff. What's the good news?"

"The good news is that there doesn't seem to be a soul here. I mean nobody. Oh, and I found a telephone just down the hall."

"Very good, anything else?" Chase finished his third helping of the meal as Tad shook his head. "Can you believe they had stroganoff in here? On a side note, did you know that stroganoff is a Russian dish? This stuff is magnificent. I think I might have another plate. Are you sure you don't want anymore?"

"No thanks. One plate was enough for me."

"Suit yourself."

Chase stood and began to move back toward the stove where more food waited. Just then Rolph and Heinrich began to stir. Rex set down his plate and walked in front of the two men. They sat gagged and bound to separate chairs in the corner of the small cafeteria. Icy stares from both torturers met Chase as he spoke.

"You guys had this giant vat of food cooking over here the entire time and didn't even think about bringing us any?" Neither man reacted and Chase smiled as he began pacing. "Tad, how many times have you eaten stroganoff since you've been here?"

"I've never eaten anything but bread and vegetables. To be honest my stomach kind of hurts now."

"That's understandable." Chase continued to pace and pulled a six inch ice pick from his pocket, though his eyes never left their captives. "So the two of you think you can torture my friend, deny us stroganoff, and glare at me like I'm your dinner. Is that about right Rolph?"

Rex pulled the gag from the large German's mouth using the pick. Tad's primary torturer answered the question by spitting in Chase's face. Rex smiled as he let the mucous-filled liquid run down his nose and drip onto the floor. Seconds passed and tension in the room ran high. Just Heinrich's elevated breathing disturbed the moment.

Chase wielded the ice pick in his right hand, rolling it through his fingers. The steel flashed and blurred with the speed as Rex inflicted a solitary wound to the other man's neck. Rolph's eyes widened and he fought his restraints even as blood spurted from the punctured artery. Chase took a step back as the crimson liquid pooled on the floor. Thirty seconds passed and the guard was dead.

Without saying a word Rex began pacing back and forth in front of Heinrich. What lay in the more diminutive German's eyes, though, was not defiance. It was pure, unadulterated fear.

Chase approached and brought the cold steel of the ice pick down the other man's face, leaving a thin red trail of blood in its wake.

"I didn't appreciate Rolph's attitude Heinrich. Are you feeling more agreeable?"

The German nodded, his eyes wide.

"Good, why don't we get this gag out of your mouth then?" Chase removed the cloth before continuing. "How do we get out of here Heine?"

"I'm not sure."

He met the reply with speed and viciousness. Chase brought the ice pick down and buried it in the German's thigh, leaving the instrument in place. Heinrich howled as he continued.

"What I mean is they blindfold us when they bring us in. They blindfold us. They. They…"

"Shhhhhhhhh. Don't fight it Heine. Your endorphins will kick in. Where are we?"

"A power plant." Heinrich whimpered as he continued. "We're at a power plant just outside of Pekin, Illinois."

"Pekin, Illinois? What's in Pekin?" Chase asked.

"I,I,I,I,I don't know. P,p,p,please don't stab me."

"You're doing fine Heine. Why a power plant?"

"They don't tell me much, but I think it has something to do with hiding the energy."

"Why not do it in Chicago, or New York, or Los Angeles? Why Pekin?"

"If I were to wager a guess," Tad said. "It would be because of the remoteness. We saw it a lot in Hoff's dealings before. Small town bureaucrats are less likely to snoop around and want to know what is going on. They're just happy for the tax revenue."

www.timwheatbooks.com   246 | P a g e

"Interesting." Chase began pacing again. "Heine, I have a couple more questions for you if you're feeling up to it."

"Do I have a choice? They're going to kill me for this."

"I wouldn't worry too much about them Heine, Tad has a .45. How many times did this guy torture you Tad?"

"Hundreds." Hate tinged the malnourished man's voice.

"Tisk, tisk, Heine," Chase said as he leaned in close to the German. "Where is Sarah?"

"Who?"

"Where is Katsuo?"

"Who?"

"He's a stocky little Japanese man. Pretty hateful. Has a lot of anger issues. Oh yeah, and he's your boss."

"I report to Izanami or Mother."

"Izanami?" Chase arched his left eyebrow. "You've seen her?"

"Yes, sir."

"Who is Mother?"

"Along with Izanami she is all knowing and all powerful."

"Tell me what they look like."

"I,I,I,I don't know."

"Now, now, Heine." Rex tapped his finger on the pick.

"Please, no." Heinrich flinched, anticipating the pain. "What I meant was that I've met them, but it is always dark. Izanami is young and Mother is old and they know everything. That's all I know. I swear."

"Well, they didn't see this coming."

Chase tore the ice pick from Heinrich's thigh, causing the torturer to cry out. With speed and precision Rex guided the six inch rod through the man's cheeks and into the wall. The

German guard hung precariously attempting not to move or make noise.

"Tad, I'm going to make a phone call. I don't need him anymore, so I'm planning on leaving him nailed to the wall like that. You can do whatever you want, though." Chase took one look back at the hapless man as he strode from the room. "Hang in there Heine."

An eerie quiet filled the expansive hallway, the sound of Rex's shoes echoing off the thirty foot ceilings. Less than fifty feet down the passageway Chase found the room with the telephone and made contact within seconds. A familiar voice answered the line.

"General Reagan."

"Pekin, Illinois. Mother and Izanami are in charge. Katsuo is just the muscle and they're using scalar energy fields. We'r..." Someone cut the call mid-sentence, as he had suspected they might. Seconds passed and a feeling of solitude crept over him. "You OK down there Tad."

A single gunshot answered the question and footsteps followed. They approached and slowed just outside the door. Tad cleared his voice as he entered.

"I'm not much for killin folk."

"Me neither. We need to find Sarah."

"We need to find a way out of here."

"Don't worry about that Tad." Chase smiled as he approached the former prisoner and patted him on the back. "I've got a few tricks up my sleeve."

✱✱✱✱✱✱✱✱✱✱✱✱✱✱✱✱✱✱

61.

A dogfight was the ultimate test of flying skill and Scherzer pulled his plane from its drastic maneuvering. His still unseen adversary had broken off pursuit, but as Al turned back into the fight he saw something he hadn't thought possible. Two of the Wildcats were already on fire and the others seemed to be in disarray.

He didn't know any of the pilots on a personal level, but Captain Morris' reputation was not that of a coward. What he saw next affirmed that assessment. The enemy fighter had somehow injured two other planes and gotten into attack position on the DC3 with only Morris' craft in pursuit. A flurry of bullets loosed from the deadly enemy, but the captain pursued with dogged determination.

Scherzer cursed under his breath as he pushed the Wildcat to its limits. The battle was happening a thousand feet over his head which meant he was still thirty seconds away. Thirty seconds could mean doom for the paratroopers.

All of a sudden the lumbering passenger plane rolled onto its top and began a perilous inverted dive. Al watched in utter fascination as the troop carrier bolted past him in the sky. His distraction lasted mere seconds, however, and he hit the button on his mic as he resumed the fight against their lone assailant.

"Did you see that crazy s.o.b.? I'm not letting him out fly me."

THE SENTINEL

Morris fought to keep the nimble grey fighter in his sites as his eyes darted across the empty blue backdrop. Even as he worked the controls of the Wildcat and fought to protect the troop transport, questions flooded his mind. Was this their only adversary in the sky? Who was this pilot? Where had he come from? What kind of plane was he flying? Morris knew of no other aircraft with the capabilities being displayed.

Ahead, the DC3 rolled and performed a violent inverted dive. Bryan prepared himself to make the dive along with the larger aircraft, but the enemy pilot broke pursuit and began a steep ascent. Morris attempted to follow, but the other plane's maneuverability and climb abilities were far superior to his own. He put a few rounds on target and thought they had hit, but the enemy was soon out of range. He watched in impotence as the bandit strafed two more Wildcats.

"How am I gonna beat this guy?"

***

Shin Shou was enjoying himself and relished the opportunity to test his new airframe in live combat. His first two kills had come at the onset of the battle, though he had learned that his 7.7mm machine guns were not powerful enough to just bring down the American fighters. His plane was handling as he had forecasted, though his own lack of armor still brought him worry. He had never before seen the American warbirds he now fought, but if it was the best the United States had to offer then the Japanese would be assured air dominance.

Ahead of him another of the American planes plodded through his field of fire. Shou sneered as he selected the plane's 20mm cannon and fired, pounding the startled enemy pilot.

Shells tore into the airframe and crisscrossed the man's wing, but the stubborn plane refused to fall.

"I'll give them this. They have plenty of armor."

Machine gun fire flashed in front of the experimental craft and one round exploded his radio which shattered the cockpit glass. Icy wind stung his face and Shou cursed his complacency. His numerical disadvantage had slipped his mind.

Pulling back on the yoke and pushing his throttles to the stops Shou pushed the Nakajima Sakae radial engine to its maximum capabilities. He still marveled at the staggering rate of climb as he banked and found his quarry attempting to follow.

"Foolish Americans," Shou wet his lips as the frigid wind whipped through the cockpit. "If I had more ammunition, I'd prefer to shoot all of you down."

A sinister plan formed in his mind and he smiled as he eased out of the climb. The expert pilot brought the DC3 into view. It had separated itself from the fray and now antlike creatures seemed to be falling from its holds.

"Paratroopers?" Confusion filled his mind. "What kind of insane men would jump into the ocean? Unless..."

Shou spoke to himself and let his words trail off. Questions flashed through his mind as he brought the plane into a firing position on the defenseless troopers. Why would they jump from the plane? Did they know about the invisible carrier? What did that destroyer's message mean?

He stretched his jaw, breathed deep, and checked the American fighters to his rear. They were outclassed and two had lost considerable airspeed attempting to accompany him on his ascent. None of his questions would matter much in a few minutes anyway. He estimated he would have time for two passes before three of the American fighters caught up and decided to devote all his concentration to lining up the helpless paratroopers in his sites. A sinister grin crossed his lips as he switched back to the 7.7mm machine guns.

"Prepare to die."

****

62.

"So who wants to tell me what a stasis field is?" The General said.

"In theory, time, space, gravity, and everything we perceive, from a physical standpoint, doesn't exist inside of a stasis field." Poppen had been thinking about his most recent journey for the better part of the last twelve hours. "Once created, anyone inside of the field could travel anywhere, at any speed, without any noticeable effects."

"Or, if you entered a stasis field and stayed there you could live forever." Alexei said.

The phone rang and The General answered, listened for a few seconds, and then hung up. A wide grin adorned his face.

"Who was it?" Leonard asked.

The General held a finger in the air as he picked the phone up and dialed again.

"Brooke. Find out where that last call came from and get me Lucille Chase." Thirty seconds passed as the room waited. "Lucille? Lucille, this is The General. You'll be happy to know that your son is alive and he sounds just fine to me."

A collective sigh of relief echoed through the room as they listened in on the conversation.

"Thank heavens. Where is he?"

"He's in Pekin, Illinois."

"Was he OK? What did he say?"

"I'm not sure if he's OK, but he sounded fine. All he said was a few quick things before being cut off. I assume he was on a monitored line and just wanted me to know he was alive." It was a partial fib. A knock on the door interrupted his thoughts. "Lucille we have a lot of work to do here. I'll get ahold of you if I

get any more information... OK? OK... Sounds good... Goodbye."
Another knock on the door followed the first. "Come in."

A wiry young man strode into the room, a slight hitch in
his step, stopped midway, and stood at full salute. Leonard
grinned and The General almost seemed embarrassed.

"Samuel. I've told you before that we don't salute in
The Organization. Whatya got for me?"

"Yes, sir. I'm sorry, sir." Samuel James Radekar had
been a formidable young test pilot when a fire aboard his
aircraft had almost cost him his legs. The General's proximity to
the accident had afforded Sam the best medical care which
saved his lower extremities. He had been a member of The
Organization ever since. "I have the pictures you asked for, sir."

"Did you develop them yourself Sam?" Leonard asked
as the phone rang once again and The General answered.

"Hello...Pekin, Illinois is confirmed? Did they narrow it
down any more? OK. Thank you Brooke." The General hung up
the phone, a thoughtful look on his face. "Go ahead Sam. Did
you develop them yourself?"

"What's in Pekin, Illinois," Alexei interrupted, "other
than my son?"

"Don't know that," The General said. "Sam?"

"Yes, sir. I developed them myself, sir."

"Did you notice anything strange?" Alexei took the
manila envelope of pictures from the smaller man and began
emptying them onto the desk. Everyone huddled around as Sam
spread the pictures out and picked a few from the pile.

"We did get some good looks at the busser and the
Japanese dignitaries at the table, but I didn't notice anything
exceptional."

All eyes centered on the black and white still shots.
Over the course of the next few minutes slight murmurs

denoted their concentrated effort as the small group analyzed the find. Sam pointed out possible significance in a few of the photographs, but overall they seemed to be a dead end.

"It's her."

Focus shifted from the photos to Poppen. The one hundred-year-old man looked as if he had seen a ghost. His hands began to shake and his knuckles turned white as he grasped the candid moment caught on film. Leonard moved to put a chair behind the elder Robert Poppen.

"Who is it, Bobby?"

Poppen stared at the photograph a full thirty seconds as his mind attempted to make sense of the picture. He met the gaze of each man in the room before settling on The General.

"It's the woman of my dreams."

****

63.

An icy rush of wind met George as he was the last to exit the DC3. He felt the static line pull taut and he held his arms tight against his chest as the entire rear of his packtray tore away. The forces at work jerked him hard against his straps and he seemed to fall for an instant. Then the chute opened and his descent slowed. Ahiga scanned the sky below just in time to see the enemy fighter pass, machine guns ablaze.

His mind raced for options as the paratroopers continued their sluggish descent. They had jumped from less than 1500 feet, but he now wished they had been lower. He and the other soldiers drifted and a slight breeze pushed them as the dark gray killing machine made its way back for another run.

Helplessness filled him and Ahiga cringed as the bandit pummeled the men below. Under fire and out of options one of the professional soldiers cut himself free from his restraints. George contemplated doing the same. He would rather take his chances with the ocean below as well.

Then, something amazing happened. Ahiga rubbed his eyes as the man below fell less than fifty feet before stopping in midair. Without being told four of the other troopers steered in his direction and within thirty seconds George approached their defensive position in the sky. Not wishing to waste any time, he slashed at his parachute lines. His backup chute would have to suffice if he passed through the invisible field which rushed up to meet him. Almost in unison Chief cut the final cord and lit on the platform while muttering to himself.

"How'd I know I wouldn't just fly through this one."

Ahiga's mind raced. They had theorized this possibility, but now confirmation existed. Whoever had taken over the reins of Hoff's empire possessed an invisible stronghold a few miles from the east coast. He wasn't sure why the field worked on him since Chase had injected the liquid Castleinium in his arm, but that didn't matter now. Chief cleared his throat and met eyes with each of the remaining four men. They stood stoic and ready for battle.

"OK fellas. We have a few more seconds until he comes back around. Everyone listen to me and we'll get out of here alive." Ahiga could see the enemy fighter circling and his mind cycled through scenarios. "I'd guess we are about seven hundred fifty feet off the ground now. Agreed?"

"Yep." All four men answered in unison.

"That gives us plenty of time to pass through this field and deploy our chutes." George fumbled through his field jacket and located five of the syrettes he had taken from Chase's house while mumbling to himself. "I'm glad I stole these."

"Sir, I don't understand." The elite paratrooper's commanding officer stepped forward. "I've never seen anything like this before."

George looked below his feet at the barrier in the sky. It was different than the fields he had seen before and that troubled him. It didn't appear to be transparent. Instead, it seemed to be a representation of the ocean below as it shimmered and reacted to outside stimuli. Now, however, wasn't the time for sightseeing.

"Trust me boys. Rex Chase is my best friend, and he gave me these. Stab em into your leg, just like giving morphine, and we'll all pass through the field and deploy our chutes before hitting the water."

That seemed to be enough for the remaining men who all took a syrette. Chief could see their villainous attacker approaching, but his path no longer seemed to be in line with the men suspended in the sky. A quick scan of the area showed two Wildcats hot on his tail while a third attempted to get a passing shot. All three fighters had machine guns blazing and then it dawned on Chief.

"Pull up. Pull up. Pull up." Running across the color shifting force field was more difficult than he had anticipated and George stumbled as he waved his arms. "PULL UP...."

A hundred yards ahead and fifty yards below the Wildcats' bullets streaked yellow across the sky. Chief slid to a stop on his knees and dread flowed through his veins as he pleaded with the advancing friendly aircraft. Shin Shou's face became visible just as the enemy fighter disappeared into oblivion and Ahiga knew the three closest Americans were at a critical junction. He pulled an emergency flare from the cargo pocket of his jump pants and waved the flaming rod over his head.

Then it happened.

***

"Holy smokes. Did you see that?" were the last words ever spoken by Lieutenant Michael Colin Rafferty as the enemy fighter disappeared into thin air.

"Pull up. Pull up. All three of you get out of there."

Captain Morris issued the order, but it was too late. All three Wildcats slammed into the energy field but there was no accompanying fireball. Instead it was as if the barrier consumed them. Scherzer's voice crackled across the airwaves.

"We gotta take the fight up high boss. I'm not messin with that."

"Copy."

Morris pulled back on the yoke and flew in close to his wingman. If they were going to survive this encounter they were going to have to work together. They passed within a few hundred yards of the paratroopers lit on the mid-air platform below. He saluted and blinked his eyes hard as the men began disappearing into the unknown abyss.

"Don't see that every day."

✳✳✳

Chief closed his eyes and breathed in the ocean air. Twenty men had begun this battle a few minutes before and now, including the two remaining Wildcat pilots, eight survived. Jimmy Humboldt was out of harm's way by now, but George wasn't sure any of the rest could endure. If the enemy fighter didn't kill him and the other paratroopers then the Atlantic Ocean below would. The Navy wouldn't pass through the fields any better than the Wildcats had.

He gripped the Thompson M1A1 that had been slung beneath his right arm and turned to address the men. A smile crossed his lips even as the enemy fighter broke through the empty space ahead. The others had already made the dive. Chief pulled the protective sleeve from his own syrette with his teeth and examined the device.

"Here goes nothing."

Ahiga slammed the syrette into his right leg with the corresponding hand while his left gripped the release to a backup chute strapped to his chest. Faster than he had anticipated, the ground disappeared from beneath his feet and he was falling again. He scanned the skies in search of the troopers and spotted their deployed parachutes. What he saw next was unexpected and he pulled the reserve chute.

Below was the deck of a small aircraft carrier. His heart leapt at the idea of not taking a November swim in the Atlantic Ocean. Two of the troopers had already landed on the deck of the enemy ship and the other two were seconds away. Chief lined up the landing zone and moments later, joined his comrades who had taken up defensive positions near a large porthole. The four men gave him expectant looks and Ahiga tapped the stock of his Thompson as he spoke.

"I know I promised you guys a swim, but whatya say we take over this tub instead."

****

64.

"I'm afraid we have a slight glitch in our plans Mother." Izanami's voice tinged with trepidation and Katsuo studied the beautiful goddess as she received instruction.

"We've had a slight change in plans here as well." Mother's voice crackled through the receiver's small speaker and Takahiro could hear genuine concern in the voice. "We should advance into the final phases of our plan."

"Agreed." Katsuo listened as Izanami replied. The two women often treated him as inferior, but they had underestimated his intellectual capabilities. "What should I do with Mr. Chase and the prisoner?"

"Did you have a chance to interrogate Chase about his ability with the stones?"

"No, he was still under the influence of our drugs. I wasn't even aware that he had awoken."

"Interrogate him, then kill him. Since The Russian's calculations are confirmed, Rex Chase is of no matter. I have business to take care of. Goodbye."

Mother issued the orders and Izanami set the receiver back in its place. Her concern was obvious and Katsuo saw an opportunity. It wasn't often she seemed vulnerable.

Izanami had shown him many things since first meeting eighteen months before. Her knowledge of the stones seemed unparalleled and with that knowledge came the promise of Yasuhiro. He had recruited Shin Shou on her command in order to kidnap The Russian, but with the recent addition of Mother he wondered whose orders he had been following all this time.

"I thought Rex Chase was the key to finding Yasuhiro?"

"He was," she cleared her throat and continued. "We have come across new information, however, and his existence has become more of a threat than an asset."

"But you said he was the only way." Katsuo's anger bubbled inside. He wasn't containing it and he placed a cracked and weathered hand on Izanami's shoulder as he continued. "I recruited Shin Shou. We brought all the outliers in line. We fought battles and spilled our men's blood. We got you the contracts you needed. We have done everything you've asked, and now I'm asking that you deliver what you promised to me. Yasuhiro."

The Japanese immortal turned and took his hand in her own, bringing it to her cheek. She should have been afraid as she had witnessed his brutality on more than one occasion, but that is not what showed in her eyes. Katsuo met the goddesses' gaze and saw lust.

"Have patience, my love. I ask of you, patience." She pressed her body against his and nuzzled the small of his neck. "I can reunite you with your brother and we are close. Is there any way I can placate you in the meantime?"

Katsuo shuddered as her delicate hands moved across his body. He reveled in the physical contact he had denied himself for so many years and his thoughts drifted from his brother. Yasuhiro was his first priority, but it wouldn't hurt to take a little time for himself. His years of celibacy had become an afterthought months ago when such an exquisite member of the opposite sex had broken his defenses. He knew she used intimacy to control him, but his trepidations soon melted into the corners of his mind. Tomorrow would be a new day.

****

65.

The General leaned back in his chair, folded his hands behind his head and exhaled. Around him focused conversations on plans of action and the woman from the picture took place. His head was swimming with partial information as he struggled to organize his own thoughts. He rubbed his forehead as he leaned forward to address the group.

"Ok, everyone." Conversations ceased and all eyes focused on him. "Ok, everyone. So we suspected that they're using scalar energy, and Rex confirms that to be true. I should be hearing back from George within the day for more confirmation on that avenue. What is the consensus on the woman from Poppen's dreams?"

"We're in a strange part of the science here." Poppen said. "This multiverse Poppen could have met her and somehow through spooky action or something the imprint made its way into my mind."

"Wait, I thought your formula disproved spooky action?" The General asked.

"Well, maybe they can work together. Like I said, it's strange."

"What about the fact that the dreams you had of her were intimate?" Leonard asked and the others seemed to agree.

"I wouldn't say that they were intimate, so much. I mean we were in love in the dreams, but nothing intimate ever happened." The old man blushed as he shared with the others. "Perhaps young Bobby Poppen from this multiverse had some kind of tryst with the woman, or went on same dates, or shared a spot on the train. It could have been anything."

"Alright." The General's mind was racing, although he loved the thrill of command. "Robert, would you mind accompanying Alexei on a little trip?"

"No, sir. To be honest, ever since I came here I've felt wonderful, like I'm fifty years old again."

Everyone laughed as The General continued.

"Very good. I need the two of you to get down to Idlewood's and figure out everything you can on Katsuo, Shin Shou, Mother, and Izanami."

"Izanami?" Willy arched his left eyebrow at the first mention of the Japanese goddess. "Where did you hear that name?"

"Chase gave it to me. He says Mother and Izanami are the leaders and Katsuo is the muscle. What do you know about her?"

"Not a lot, other than she is a mythical being." Willy stood and began pacing. "After Morocco I spent a lot of time trying to find my brother and her name came up a few times. I always just thought it was some kind of mistake or that people were messing with me. But maybe with what we know now..."

"Maybe a member of Hoff's organization traveled through some kind of multiverse and brought a mythical being back to organize and head the empire?" A slight smirk adorned Leonard's face. "Not likely."

"Well, he's here, and I'd call that pretty unlikely too." Willy pointed at Poppen and the others received his retort well as all eyes moved back to Leonard.

"I don't know who she is, but wild conjecture doesn't help our cause." Leonard paused. "General."

"He's right. Bobby and Alexei, get down to Idlewood's and figure out Hoff's empire. I want to know all the figureheads involved and if you have time to look into Bobby's dream girl do that too."

"Yes, sir." Alexei and Poppen replied in unison.

"Willy and Leonard; I'd like the two of you to get to Pekin and figure out what is going on in Illinois." The General stood. "Patrick and Sam, you'll be here with me helping to organize this whole mess."

"You're just sending Willy and me to Pekin? It stands to reason that if they took Rex there then something important is happening. We could use a team, or two, or the army."

"With the war in Europe and the attack on the President, we're strung pretty thin right now."

"But this is what The Organization is tasked to do."

"You don't think I know that." The General's reply was terse and authoritative. "The fact of the matter is that a lot of our assets are overseas and even if I dispatched them all right now they are at least forty-eight hours away and I'm afraid this could be done before then. We just aren't prepared for a fight in Pekin, Illinois."

"What about Plan CF?"

The General ran his hand through his hair stopping to scratch in the back.

"Do you think we're that far along?"

"What's Plan CF?" Alexei asked.

"It is a highly mobile, highly trained…"

"Highly expensive and highly not proven to even work." The General interrupted Leonard's explanation and the silver-haired man nodded in agreement.

"They are all of those things. You see, Rex had the idea of creating a fighting force that could penetrate scalar shields using conventional weapons. Without Bobby's formula we had

THE SENTINEL

no reason to believe scalar weapons could still be used in battle." Leonard said.

"We knew about the iron so we equipped this group of men with state of the art weaponry designed using Castleinium. Couple that along with Rex's isolation of the element in an injectable solution and we have a fighting force able to penetrate the most sophisticated of defenses." The General said.

"The only real problem, though, is that all of this is theoretical." Leonard said.

"It's still untested?" Castle said.

"Yes," said The General.

"What does Plan CF mean anyway?" Willy asked. "I mean most of the time its Plan A, Plan B, Plan C..."

Leonard smiled and exchanged a glance with The General.

"Well, Plan CF was just a working name Rex gave to the project right at the start and it kind of stuck."

"We had planned on renaming the unit once it went operational, but it looks like that may be sooner than we had anticipated." The General shuffled a few papers on his desk, searching for something.

"Yeah, well what does it mean?" Willy insisted.

"The initial idea was that we would have to use this fighting force in the near future if everything was, well, to put it bluntly, completely f'd."

A round of laughter went up in the room at Leonard's explanation.

"I'd say that about sums up the situation." Castle laughed harder than most. "We're all grown men, though, you can say the word."

"He cannot." The General said. "In my office we act like professionals, not drunken sailors. How fast do you think Plan CF can be put into action?"

"If I remember right their equipment is already on rails. We were planning trials in Arizona in the coming weeks. I'd say the men could muster in an hour and be on their way in two."

"Are they still near Kentucky where my munitions plant is located?" Castle said. "That's where they got put together, right?"

"Yeah, they're still in Kentucky. I'd say they could be in Pekin at about the same time as Willy and I."

"Get on it Leonard."

"Done." Leonard stiffened his resolve. "What about the Army?"

"The President isn't going to deploy troops to Illinois when the Japanese just attacked him. We don't have enough evidence yet for me to even present that idea." The General breathed deep before continuing. "The Plan CF troops will have to suffice."

"If they are functional." Leonard said.

"If they are functional." The General conceded. "I also forgot that I was informed this morning about another one of our members going missing after the gala last night. We need to run that down too."

"We're sure she is missing and not dead?" Castle asked.

"She wasn't dead in the rubble and this one might not always follow the rules, but she sure would have checked in by now." The group seemed satisfied with The General's response as he spoke once again. "I have a couple of her people looking into that, though. We'll just have to monitor the situation from here. How long before you can be in Pekin?"

"Less than twelve hours and we should get there the same time as the Plan CF troops," Leonard replied.

"I guess you've got a flight to catch then."

****

66.

"Here Kitty, Kitty, Kitty, Kitty." Chase paused as he rounded another corner in the mammoth complex. He was certain someone had alerted Katsuo to Rex's phone call and the madman would savor a confrontation, if not the nickname. "Here Kitty, Kitty, Kitty, Kitty."

"I thought we were getting out of here." Tad trailed a short distance behind and fear was apparent in his voice. "I'm ready to be out of here."

"I know Tad, but I think my friend Sarah is being held here as well." Chase stretched his neck and rubbed his hip. From a physical standpoint he felt better than he had in ages and something else seemed different, but he couldn't quite put his finger on it. "I have to find her before I can go."

Tad's countenance changed at the mention of a woman in peril.

"Well, you didn't tell me that. Let's go get her."

Chase smiled at the man's determined attitude. After everything he'd been through, he still valued the life of a woman he'd never met above his own. Tad Baxter was a true gentleman.

"Don't worry buddy. I'll do all the heavy lifting. You don't even need to talk."

The new friends continued their search with Chase leading the way. He felt like a specific direction was drawing him in. It didn't make sense and he couldn't explain it, but he decided to follow his instincts. They didn't let him down.

"They're through that door." Chase pointed a long, lithe finger in the direction of a service entryway. "That's the one."

"How can you be sure? You haven't checked a single door since we left the cafeteria."

"I don't know," Chase said. "I just know."

"Good enough for me boss. What's the plan?"

Tad's exuberance after eighteen months of torture brought a smile to Chase's face. He gave the only answer that came to mind.

"Just get behind me, stay there, and everything is going to be fine. Trust me."

Chase strode toward the entryway ahead. A supreme confidence settled in his mind as adrenaline coursed through his veins. He paused and inhaled through his nostrils as he reached for the door handle. Never before had he felt more alive. His hands trembled and his stomach fluttered, yet he also felt an absolute sense of control.

"Weird," Chase mumbled to himself as he turned the door handle. "Here goes nothing Tad."

A thin streak of light pierced the blackness of the interior room as Rex gave the steel door a push. The expanse was massive and tall cylindrical pillars scattered throughout became discernible. Chase took a few steps into the expanse before looking back to check on Tad.

"You alright back there?"

"I've got a weird feeling."

"Me too."

"Mr. Chase." Katsuo's voice echoed across the walls and made it impossible to distinguish his position. "If you would be so kind as to close the door."

"Kit-Kat. Did you forget to pay your light bill or something?" Chase scanned the darkness but saw nothing. "It's dark in here."

"Just shut that door, and let me illuminate you." Katsuo's tone filled with confidence and authority. It was obvious he meant business.

"Go ahead Tad." Chase continued to peer into the darkness even as he motioned to the man behind him. "Close that door so we can be illuminated."

"Still feeling pretty funny about this." Tad's hesitation was momentary, but then with a loud bang, all light evacuated the room.

Chase furrowed his brow as he focused on the darkness ahead. At first, the lights were almost imperceptible. They seemed to emanate from the ceiling above and creep straight down in ever widening columns. Rex watched in awe as the tall cylindrical pillars came into illumination, mysterious dark objects passing in and out of the light.

"It's the stones."

Tad spoke in a hushed, almost reverent voice.

"Yes Tad." Katsuo's baritone echoed through the room once again. "I'd like to ask you about these stones Mr. Chase."

"First time I'm seein em Kit-Kat." Chase counted the pillars ahead even as he continued to scan the room for Katsuo's position. "I notice you've got twenty columns and thirty stones, though. It seems like you're missing a few."

"Very astute Mr. Chase."

"Call me Rex."

"Very astute Rex. Don't worry about how many stones we have. They are serving a purpose and their number doesn't concern you."

"Well, I've always been pretty good at counting." Chase's eyes had adjusted to the low levels of light and he could now make out a second-level balcony that encircled the room. Shadows of men lined the entire gallery and a sinking feeling crept into the pit of his stomach. Dozens of men surrounded them. "You know Kitty, one time when I was little I thought I'd try to count to a billion, but then I realized that even at four numbers a second it would take me something on the order of eight years to count that high. I mean, who's got the time for that?"

"Ah, yes. You are stalling." Katsuo's tone was light, almost jovial. "As I'm sure you have already noticed you are surrounded. I'll go ahead and tell you right now that fifty of my best men have Type 96 machine guns trained on your position. You have nowhere to run and nowhere to hide."

"Who's hiding here Kitty? Not me. I'm out in the open." Chase peered into the darkness. "Maybe you'd like to show yourself?"

"As you wish."

Light bathed the room and Chase shielded his face with his arm and squinted as his eyes adjusted. Fifty men with machine guns materialized from the darkness, but Chase noticed the stationary limitation of the rail mounted weapons which skirted the balcony. Ahead and twenty feet above stood Katsuo, a sneer evident on his face. Chase advanced through the room as he spoke, Tad in tow.

"Much better Kitty, thank you. Now, would these be fifty of the best men you had left, or did you have one hundred to begin with?" Chase brushed his hand against the Colt 1911 tucked into his waistband as he scanned the room for a tactical advantage. He found none. "I mean, if we're on a second group of fifty then these guys aren't the best, but if the first group, you know the ones I killed pretty much by myself, well, if they were a hundred strong then I guess these guys might still be pretty good. Either way, I'll accept your surrender at any time."

"Very good Rex." Katsuo's laugh boomed throughout the chamber and his men joined. "I must say your knack for stalling is magnificent. Have you found your advantage yet?"

"Just getting your boys all lined up." Chase paused as he neared the central pillar. This one position afforded a semblance of cover and he reached back and pulled Tad close as he stopped. "So when do I get to meet your boss? Excuse me. I mean bosses."

"Oh Rex." Katsuo's voice oozed with confidence. "I suppose even you have a boss. Does that make you any less in charge of your destiny?"

"I don't suppose it does Kit-Kat." Intrigue rose in Chase's mind. "Maybe you should go get Mother and Izanami and we can all just sort this thing out right now. I mean, I'd hate to kill you when it's them I want."

"Don't you worry about them Rex." Katsuo still stood obstructed in the shadows. "Right now you have me to deal with."

"Sounds good to me," Chase said. "What is it you're wanting from me anyway Kitty?"

"Oh, nothing much." Thirty feet ahead Katsuo paced on the balcony above. Darkness shrouded his lower body, but he became more visible as he moved back and forth. The pacing reminded Chase of a lion in a cage. "I'd love for you to give me the two stones you have in your possession and if that isn't too much, the location of the thirty-ninth would be appreciated."

"I'm tellin ya Kitty. I had never even heard of these things until a couple of hours ago." Chase leaned against the main pillar and felt its warmth. "It's quite the scalar energy setup you've got going on in this room, though. Here I thought I had cornered the market and it turns out someone else has beaten me to it. You know that Dietrich Hoff..."

"Silence." Katsuo's voice quivered with the command as it echoed across the room. "Your insolence is inexcusable. Perhaps you haven't found the proper motivation to comply."

Takahiro leaned to his left and with one arm pulled Sarah from behind a desk. She screamed and fought as he held her by the hair like a trophy. Her feet dangled and reached for the floor as he suspended the woman's frame in the air and ripped the pillow case gag from her mouth.

"Rex." Anger bubbled inside of Chase at the sound of her cries and he fought to control it. "Help."

"Katsuo." Chase pulled the two ice picks he had taken from the mess hall from his left pocket. An idea formed in his mind as he issued a stern command of his own. "Put her down."

"Oh, it's Katsuo now." Takahiro dumped Sarah's body to the floor and she fell in a heap. "It seems like I always have to hurt someone to get respect. Lucky for me, I rather enjoy hurting people."

"She'll be the last person you hurt."

In an instant Chase transferred an ice pick into each hand, touching the left to the main pillar while reaching for another nearby column with the right. He had calculated right and could span the distance. Confidence welled up inside of him as the energy seemed to flow throughout his body. Adrenaline pulsed through his veins and his senses soared to heights he had never imagined. His lips curled as he brought his gaze to the Japanese tormenter above.

"You shouldn't have done that Kit-Kat."

Time seemed to slow as Chase stood, his arms outstretched between the two posts. He almost expected the machine guns to open fire, but they were silent even as he began his maneuver. With lightning speed he brought his right pick down while maintaining contact with the left. He could feel Tad push closer against his back even as he maneuvered the instrument through the sky. Milliseconds passed and he prepared for the focused beam of energy that would soon emanate from the end of the purveyor of death. Then a second passed. Then another came and went. Chase dropped his arms and looked at the two benign ice picks he held. His shoulders slumped as Katsuo's laughter once again echoed throughout the room.

"What did you think was going to happen Rèx?" Takahiro's men once again joined him, filling the chamber with their catcalls. "Were you going to defeat me with a couple of puny ice picks?"

A collective roar went up and Chase reassessed the situation. It was not favorable.

"You can call me Mr. Chase."

The laughter faded and Katsuo dabbed at his eyes before becoming serious.

"Have it your way Mr. Chase." Takahiro pulled an 8mm Nambu pistol from his holster and pointed it at Sarah's head. "If you cannot locate the stones then none of you are of use to me."

"Wait." Chase's mind raced as his eyes darted around the room. His options were limited and without the scalar advantage he had counted upon having, would also likely conclude in both his and Tad's deaths. "What about Yasuhiro?"

Katsuo's guard dropped and he let his arm fall. The Nambu was no longer aimed at Sarah's head and Chase did the only thing he could think of to save her life. With speed and determination he pulled the Colt 1911 from his waistband while pushing Tad into the only covered position of the room. Rex stood exposed as he raised the forty-five caliber pistol and took aim at his quarry's head, pulling the trigger as fast as any human could.

Three shots barked from the weapon before the thunderous roar of fifty machine guns enveloped everything.

Chase saw Katsuo drop as the first wave of bullets approached at just over twice the speed of sound. A small sense of satisfaction crept into his mind even as one of the 6.5mm projectiles knocked the Colt from his grip. He dropped to the floor, his hands covering his head and arms in front of his face in a last ditch effort to protect himself from the inevitable.

Somehow, in that perfect moment in time, Mary Elizabeth's voice seemed to echo in his head. She didn't convey a message or even speak in words. It was a song. It was a beautiful song unlike any he had heard before. A supreme serenity enveloped his very soul even as he expected his body to be riddled with holes.

A second passed as the machine guns roared, and then two. Chase peered to his left, expecting Tad's body to be bloodied and beaten. What he saw was the opposite. Tad's six foot two inch frame stood at perfect attention as if he were reporting to roll call. Rex reached for the man in an attempt to pull him to the floor. He must have lost his mind.

"Tad." Chase's shout evaporated in the din. "Tad."

Rex noticed the other man's countenance and what he saw was unexpected. It wasn't panic. It wasn't fear. It was awe.

Just then Chase noticed a difference in the room as well. The warm yellow radiance of the scalar lighting had softened and now a powerful blue glow enveloped everything. He followed Tad's gaze above and blinked hard.

A perfect blue sphere hovered ten feet over his head. Its surface seemed cracked, like dried mud in the desert, yet somehow was also smooth like a mountain lake. Yellow streaks of light crisscrossed its expanse as the frightened Japanese warriors emptied their machine guns. Every bullet seemed attracted to the sphere and Chase stared down the muzzle of more than one of the weapons. Their projectiles raced in his direction and rerouted before the energy above swallowed them whole. Then the room went silent.

Chase's ears rang as he stood. A haze descended upon the room and the acrid smell of gun smoke filled his nostrils. The eerie silence somehow seemed louder than the machine guns had been seconds before and he reached toward the blue orb hovering a few feet above his head.

Then it happened. In a millisecond the blue sphere of energy flattened into a thin line twenty-four feet off the ground before disappearing. Machine guns separated from their mounts and men separated into halves. Chase watched as the soldiers' upper and lower bodies writhed independent of one another. Guttural cries of the condemned lasted seconds before conceding to a maddening silence interrupted by Tad's voice.

"H,H,H,H, How did y,y,y, you do that?"

"Do what?"

"Th, th, th, th, that blue thing. I,I,I,I, It came out of you."

"Ya got me Iad. I thought I'd need the ice picks." Chase's focus had shifted and a slight dread crept into the pit of his stomach.

"Sarah?" Silence greeted him as the smoke settled in the room giving him a better view of the balcony above. "Sarah?"

"Rex?"

Her voice seemed tiny and unsure, but it was her and Chase's heart felt as if it had skipped a beat. She stood and walked over to the rail as Rex crossed the room in a few quick bounds. Sarah's opaline eyes greeted him and Rex breathed a sigh of relief.

"Are you OK?"

"I'm going to have to get my hair done soon, but other than that I'm alright."

"How's Katsuo look?"

"Dead." She turned for a moment and then began climbing over the railing. "I'm going to dangle from here. Catch me?"

"If it got us out of here any faster, I'd catch you a dozen times."

****

67.

Shin Shou gritted his yellowed teeth and craned his neck as he searched for the two remaining fighters. The others had proven to be easy kills, but these seemed to have learned their lesson. They spiraled thousands of feet above and he guided himself into attack position.

The Japanese ace cursed under his breath as he took a fleeting look at the water below. Paratroopers were on the carrier by now and Shou did not intend to return to the floating headquarters. Killing all of his enemies was going to have to wait.

His aircraft gained ground on the lumbering Americans. He once again smiled a nefarious grin as he selected the 20mm cannon. This was a slight hiccup and in a few hours the loss of the carrier would be insignificant. Everything was going according to plan.

Ahead of him, the two planes split ranks and Shin decided to follow the aircraft to the east. He preferred the sun at his back if at all possible. Shou lined up his quarry and squeezed the trigger. Lead projectiles streaked across the sky and within seconds the first fighter was on fire. Unlike the men before, however, this pilot didn't seem to panic. The wounded aircraft banked in his direction and Shou passed nearby as its aviator stepped into the sky.

"Is he waving?"

Shou said the words to himself as he squinted at the man whose actions answered the question. He wasn't waving. He was throwing something. Shou rolled and banked hard as a shockwave impacted the rear of the plane.

"He threw a grenade at me." Shin laughed, bubbles of spit emanating from the corners of his mouth. "That crazy s.o.b. threw a grenade at me."

Bullets tore through the cockpit of the experimental Japanese aircraft and Shou jolted back into the fight. The other fighter swung around with more speed than he had anticipated possible and Shin was now under fire. He pushed the yoke in and to the left while giving full left rudder. The plane responded and Shou breathed a slight sigh of relief. The damage was minimal. He wouldn't be dying today.

"Time to finish them."

He spoke the words even as he put the nimble fighter through a dizzying series of ascents and turns. The American pilot attempted to match his abilities, but the man's machine was not up to the task. At the top of his final ascent Shin rolled the Japanese invention over and found himself behind the American.

"You've stalled my friend." Shin's sinister yellow smile crossed his lips once again. "You fought well."

He squeezed his trigger and reveled in the destruction as his 20mm bullets slammed into their target. Round after round tore at the airframe even as its pilot recovered from the stall and attempted to maneuver. Shin pulled back on the yoke as the two aircraft leveled, but he was not to be denied. Within seconds a dark puff of smoke emanated from the adversary ahead and the aircraft rolled, its pilot evacuating.

"It was a good fight."

Shin craned his neck as he searched the sky for the first pilot's parachute. He'd rather not fight these two experienced men again. Anyone who could fly that well and possessed the fortitude to step out of a burning aircraft while throwing a grenade was a man to be reckoned with. Two thousand feet below he found his quarry and banked to get into a strafing run.

"You almost made it."

The American seemed to hang in the air less than a kilometer ahead and five hundred feet from the water below. Shin's bloodlust boiled inside and his adrenaline surged once again. Piloting his aircraft had become second nature, but killing always seemed to satisfy his need for excitement.

Tracers streaked by the nose of his plane and the sound of several rounds impacting his airframe rattled his eardrums. Shin banked hard and pulled back on the yoke ascending at a dizzying pace. Within seconds he was out of harm's way and leveled the fighter while surveying the water below.

"Anti-aircraft fire. I should have known."

***

"Are you sure about this Captain?"

Morris pressed the button to his radio and released it. He breathed deep and let the air pass his pursed lips. Option after option ran through his head and perhaps if he had the time a more suitable plan could be devised, but as of right now, this was the only way. He pressed the button again.

"This is it Al," his voice wavered and he cleared his throat before continuing, "and we're just going to get one shot at it."

"Are you sure he'll follow you, though?"

"I know I would." Bryan brushed his hand across the MKII grenade secured in his jacket. He had always taken one with him into battle, but never thought he'd use it like this. "No sense staring into the sun if you don't have to."

"Ok, but for the record, I think you're insane."

The two men shared a laugh over the radio and then it was silent. Morris looked below and watched in awe as the enemy plane closed the gap with incredible speed. Nothing in the U.S. inventory could keep up with its performance capabilities.

"I'm going to count it down Al."

Morris's voice crackled across the airwaves and Scherzer's reply was almost instant.

"Yes, sir."

Captain Bryan Eugene Morris had been craving some sort of change in his life, but this wasn't quite what he'd had in mind. Right now he longed for the days of ferrying dignitaries and running errands for The Organization. That wasn't what today was going to be about, though, and he put all his focus on the advancing enemy below. They had to time all of this just right. He pushed the button on his radio.

"Alright Al. In five, four, three, two, one, BREAK."

Morris dropped the mic and pushed on the Wildcat's yoke with all his might while depressing the rudder with his right leg. He had noticed before that the American fighter held a slight dive advantage, but that was about it. He twisted and turned while trying to keep an eye on the enemy to his rear. He needed to hold on for thirty or forty seconds so Al could get the shot they needed, but the Wildcat was outclassed.

Bullets riddled the cockpit and engine compartment of the sturdy airframe and Morris once again checked his six. He could see the sneer on his pursuer's lips and despite his best efforts, knew the Wildcat's demise loomed. A fire broke out at his feet and he knew what needed to be done.

A calm came over him as he pulled the throttle back and put the plane in a slight bank. He undid his harness and then moved onto the canopy. Freezing winds whipped past as he steadied himself, clutching the pineapple grenade in his right hand.

"One Mississippi, two Mississippi..."

Bryan Morris had never jumped from a plane before, and this was to be unlike any jump ever attempted by another. He had pulled the pin, counted down, and stepped into the never while throwing the grenade with all his might. His chances of hitting the enemy were so miniscule as to be absurd, but something deep inside told him the plan was going to work. All he needed to do was get Al enough time to put some heavy fire on that little plane. It couldn't have enough armor to withstand much of an assault.

It all happened in an instant, and then he was falling through the sky. Morris had learned to fly in an age where bailing out of an aircraft was not an actual option and through the years had somehow managed to skip a lot of the training involved. His flight goggles pressed hard into his face as he fought to control the dive. Flight stability was key to releasing the chute. He knew that, and concentrated his efforts on gliding.

"It's just like a glider Bryan." He grunted the words as he struggled to control the descent. "Just spread your arms and legs and act like a glider."

After a few hard fought seconds, control became his and the ocean below came into focus. He had fallen thousands of feet and he grasped tight the parachute release.

"Here goes nothing."

The chute unfurled as designed and within seconds he floated on a cushion of air five hundred feet from the ground. Morris scanned the skies for signs of the battle above. What he saw chilled his bones even further. The second Wildcat was on fire and heading for the ocean, Al's chute was already open, and less than a kilometer away the enemy fighter was lining Morris up in his sites.

"Well, I sure don't want to get shot to death up here." Bryan pulled a razor sharp knife from his flight jacket and cut at one of the parachute's cords before stopping and looking at the ocean below. "I sure don't want to get in that water much either."

****

68.

"Are you seeing this boss?"

George had expected a fierce response from the crew of the aircraft carrier, but instead silence greeted them. All the normal sounds of such a large vessel were absent, along with its complement of aircraft. They explored the massive ship, uninhibited, and except for the lack of personnel, everything seemed to be in order. Ahiga had led them to the bridge and it was on their way they had stumbled upon a display of gore and macabre unlike any he'd ever seen.

"Ritualistic suicide." The words left his lips as one of the hardened fighters retched on the deck. "Shin Shou ordered them all to kill themselves."

"Sorry, sir. It's just..."

"Don't worry about it." Chief was fighting the urge to vomit himself. "I've never seen anything like this before either."

Men in combat often became immune to horrors that others would deem impossible to ignore. Headless corpses, men with shreds of bone and sinew hanging where an arm once existed, and entrails pushing their way through stomach wounds were not a rarity. This, however, was different.

Row after row of Japanese sailors slumped against one another, twisted looks of agony forever etched on their faces. Except for a handful of men piled in the corner, their throats slit, Chief recognized the deaths to be self-inflicted and simultaneous. George swatted at a fly as he first noticed the incessant hum of the countless insects' wings and the squeaking of an unknown number of rats. Entrails covered the floor and Ahiga lost his footing as he pushed his way past the deceased.

"We've all seen dead men before." George said.

"Not like this."

A murmur went up amongst the hardened fighters as they moved through the room and Ahiga concentrated on the task at hand. Such a sparse crew confirmed part of his fears. In order to run with such a small complement of men it had to be scalar powered. With that thought, though, came another. At least they stood a chance of sailing the ship out.

George opened the entrance to the bridge, stepped through, and the others followed. The last in line closed the door as Ahiga took notice of the equipment while surveying the battle raging outside. A smile crossed his lips as he looked to the deck below. He needed to act.

"Ok fellas. I've seen these controls before and we can operate this tub ourselves. Sergeant, how many men do you need to run that anti-aircraft gun down there?"

"Three to run it right sir." The man answered without hesitation and George trusted his judgment.

"Make it happen thirty seconds ago."

The three men exited back through the way they had come and Ahiga concentrated on the task at hand. Ahead of him the controls of the ship were a near carbon copy of the submarine he and Chase had piloted eighteen months before. His only problem now, though, was that Chase had read the German transcriptions then and the Japanese labels he now stared at weren't of much use.

"You don't happen to read Japanese do you?" Ahiga asked the remaining commando.

"I sure don't. This over here looks promising."

The man pointed at a set of controls that resembled the throttle on a large bomber or multi-engine aircraft.

"Push it forward."

The hardened fighter pushed the handle forward and they shared mutual disappointment.

"I bet we have to turn the engines on somewhere."

"Nothing jumps out at me on this panel. Whatya think? Should we just start pushing buttons?"

"Yep."

At first the two men pushed one button at a time, awaiting a response, but that became tedious.

"Hell, let's just push em all."

George smiled at the other man's impatience, but he was right. They didn't have time for this. Both warriors pressed button after button and Ahiga stepped up his efforts as one of the Wildcats burned above. A small speck fell through the sky and he followed it with his eyes even while pushing buttons. The parachute opened five-hundred feet from the ground and over a mile away. They had to get moving. Then, the Japanese vessel quaked beneath their feet and lurched ahead.

"Push those controls to their stops. How do you think we steer?"

The German submarine eighteen months before had possessed a traditional steering mechanism. Its Japanese counterpart did not. Ahiga scanned the panel before his eyes rested on what seemed to be a ball bearing sunken into the metal surface. He rolled the mechanism to the left and the ship below responded in kind.

"Hot dog." A hand clap accompanied the other man's joyful shout. "Now we're in business."

"Let's not count our chickens just yet."

Ahiga steered the carrier with his right hand while pulling down a very traditional looking mic with his left. The ship was fast and got up to speed in short order. George marveled at its capabilities as he noticed a gauge reading knots.

"Does that say we're nearing a hundred knots?"

The Sentinel

"I'm reading it the same way, so we're both crazy," George replied.

"But it doesn't even feel like we're touching the water."

George nodded as he focused his concentration on the battle ahead. The second Wildcat was on fire now and another parachute dotted the sky. He didn't know why their ride was so smooth and right now he didn't care. They had to stop that plane bearing down on their helpless pilot. He pressed the button down on the side of the mic as he spoke.

"Can you guys hear me down there?" The three soldiers manning the anti-aircraft gun responded with a trio of thumbs. "You need to shoot that plane down. Understand?"

Three more thumbs up was the reply and George smiled as he placed the mic back in its cradle. A slight wave of guilt washed over him as he realized he was enjoying himself. He didn't have time for that now, though, and he steeled himself to the task at hand.

"Come on girl." Ahiga patted the console with his left hand. "Just a little more."

Then the entire ship lurched and Ahiga braced himself. The Japanese carrier's speed reduced eighty knots in a matter of seconds while a massive spray enveloped the bridge as well as the men below. George looked to his right in time to see the other man's body slam against a bulkhead. He recovered as the ship steadied itself in the waves.

"What just happened?"

"We passed through the fields." He looked below and the three commandos were dragging themselves back into fighting positions. "They still don't have Poppen's equation. Even though we were moving we were still using the stationary power from the fields. It's all about them."

The other man shrugged as Chief picked up the mic once again.

"If you boys are ok down there we could use some anti-aircraft fire."

They responded by firing the Japanese gun at the plane five-hundred meters distant. Fire streamed from the barrel as the men below led the enemy aircraft. Round after round hurtled through the air and the plane's survival amazed him.

"Keep giving it to him boys," he murmured. "Shoot the son of a gun down."

Then, the plane turned, ascended at a sharp angle and leveled out of range. Chief steered the ship in the direction of the pilot now entering the water. He was going to be cold.

"Pull that throttle back and meet me down on deck. We've gotta get that guy out of the water."

The commando obeyed and the two men beat it down to the deck. Ahiga looked at the sky above and could see the other chute steering in their direction. He should be able to make it without a water landing. That was good and George met up with the three men who had warded off their attacker.

"We've got a ladder right over there we should be able to bring him up on." One of the men led Ahiga toward the edge of the ship just as Captain Morris ascended over the side.

"I thought maybe you'd need a lift. We stole this pile a ways back. Who else is up there Captain?"

"Al." Morris shivered, glad his minutes in the frigid Atlantic were over. "I figure he'd prefer landing on the deck if that's alright with you."

George's smile somehow widened further.

"I'm not sure if we have the room, but we'll see what we can do."

****

69.

"Wait. The stones. Why aren't we taking the stones?"

"You said they weighed about nine pounds each. That's three-hundred and twenty-four pounds. We have to forget about them for now."

"Shouldn't we take some of them? Maybe you can make one of those blue things to save us." Sarah said.

"We can't go back now."

Chase could see the disappointment on Tad's face, but the tortured man put forth no more objections. The three escapees moved with purpose and Rex held Sarah's hand tight while Tad trailed a few steps behind. Her beauty was undeniable and Chase felt himself wondering what it would be like to bring her back to the pond. His mind drifted as he thought of his beloved Belle and the burning of his home. Axl was certain to lose all his fur from separation anxiety. He had spoken with the General, but what about George, Angela, Leonard, Marilyn, and his parents? Questions flooded his mind as he navigated the massive complex.

What was Mother and Izanami's endgame? With Katsuo dead did that change things? What was the exact purpose of the stones?

"Which way now?"

Sarah's voice interrupted his daydream and he surveyed their surroundings. They had emerged into a large open area. Brilliant sunlight shone through huge skylights in the ceiling fifty feet overhead. Seven exits were available, but Chase knew which one to use.

"Over there."

He pointed as he moved with a purpose, Sarah in tow and Tad a short distance behind. They burst out of the elaborate compound and Rex braced himself for the cold Midwestern weather that awaited them. To his surprise, though, the temperature outside reached ninety degrees. The sun shone, birds chirped, and flowers held in full bloom. It made no sense.

"November in Illinois is a lot warmer than I'd anticipated. What's going on?"

"I'm not sure." Chase's answer was the absolute truth and he scanned the sprawling industrial yard for an escape vehicle. To his surprise they hadn't run into a single guard or any other personnel. "They must be able to control the temperature using scalar fields."

"That's right Mr. Chase."

Katsuo's voice was powerful for a dead man and all three escapees turned in unison.

"The Harley with the sidecar thirty yards away looks like our only mode of transportation." Chase whispered to the others. "Follow my lead."

"Do you have secrets Mr. Chase? I must say I'm rather shocked at what you did inside. You'll have to show me how you did that."

Chase squinted as the sun reflected across the glass exterior of the atrium through which Katsuo had exited a short distance away.

"My only regret is that I didn't get you too Kit-Kat." Chase prepared himself for the dash to the motorcycle. "It looks like I might have nicked you a bit though."

Blood streaked both sides of Takahiro's face, but the Japanese warrior seemed to pay it little mind.

"It's more than a nick. I'll give you kudos for your speed and accuracy with a pistol." Katsuo wiped the blood using his right hand. "I think you spun me with the first shot to my left ear, hit me once straight through my cheeks, and one off the top of my head. I should thank you though. It appears by shooting me you saved my life."

"Well, I want your demise to be extra special, not run of the mill like all the other men you've sent my way." Chase began moving in the direction of the motorcycle and Sarah and Tad followed. "Unless you've got a few more to throw at me I think we'll be leaving."

"So soon? Well, I guess I can't blame you. I've been a horrible host. Are you sure you wouldn't like to talk a while longer. I have some friends on their way right now. I'm afraid we just weren't quite prepared for you to get out of that room. You must be the true white devil."

"Thanks for the hospitality Kit-Kat, but I think we'll get going."

Chase turned and sprinted to the 1930 Harley Davidson 74 ci Model VL. The olive drab paint shone like the day it had come out of the factory and Chase barked orders as they approached.

"Tad, you get in the sidecar and Sarah is behind me. If we have a proper road out there this baby should be able to get us up to seventy miles per hour or so."

"Out there?" Sarah questioned.

Chase smiled as the Harley's seventy-four cubic inch engine roared to life. He wished he had some goggles like the men he had seen at the track, but he didn't see any around. With his arm outstretched Chase pointed a quarter mile ahead.

"You see that shimmer up there? If I were a betting man I'd say that's a modified light bending scalar energy field that makes this entire place invisible from the outside."

"And the outside invisible from us," Tad said.

"You got it." Chase confirmed.

"How are we going to get through it?" Sarah yelled as Chase revved the Harley's engine.

"Leave that to me. You all set over there Tad?" The emaciated prisoner responded with a thumbs up and Chase popped the clutch while goosing the throttle. "Hold on tight. Here we go."

The overloaded 530 pound Harley lurched forward, its twin pistons pumping. Acceleration was slow and Chase became aware of another sound besides the overtaxed engine. Bullets whizzed past the two-wheeled vehicle and streaked a bright yellow while being absorbed by the fast approaching field ahead. They were traveling sixty miles per hour now and Rex adjusted the side mirror to get a look at their pursuers.

"Looks like Katsuo wasn't lying when he said he had some friends coming." Chase said. "We've got at least a hundred men on our tails in twenty Jeeps. Do either of you know the landscape around here at all?"

"No. They brought me in blindfolded." Sarah shouted.

"I remember seeing a river or creek pretty nearby to the west," Tad said.

"Perfect."

Now, at least, he had a plan and it hadn't come too late. Chase pulled hard on the bike's handlebars and its tires bit into the fine gravel roadway. Sarah's grip tightened as the machine slid sideways, attempting to follow its master's order.

Rex's senses were alive and his focus laser sharp. Every muscle in his body fought the machine below which in turn fought back with ferocity. The turn complete they were now heading due west and approaching the field.

"Here goes nothing."

All three passengers of the over-taxed Harley held on tight as the cycle burst through the shimmering field of energy.

Chase had expected to emerge into a cold winter landscape, but instead arrived unharmed in another warm zone. It was bleak and contained no flowering plants or leaved trees, but warm nonetheless. Maybe Illinois was mild for this time of year.

"I thought you said there was a river up ahead," Chase yelled as he pressed the Harley's throttle all the way to its stops.

"I'm certain of it," Tad said. "Look, there's the power plant over there. We're heading the right way."

Chase took notice of the facility which hadn't been visible before. Something seemed out of place and he couldn't quite put his finger on it. Then, without warning the scalar field they had just passed dematerialized and Katsuo's men flooded through. Rex felt himself leaning forward, urging the side-valve engine to give him more speed. He blinked hard as he attempted to make sense of the situation.

"Two fields." He shouted to no one in particular. "They have an inner and outer set of fields."

A hundred yards away the outer barrier approached and Chase detected its shimmering base. Why hadn't he thought of that before? It would make sense for them to have one field to hide the massive scalar facility and the stones while an outer field could protect the entire sprawling complex in case of an emergency. Rex felt a slight surge of pride. It felt nice to be such an emergency.

Seconds had passed and the bright streaks of light again appeared in front of them. Chase looked to his right and Tad's smiling face gave him comfort. He looked to be having the time of his life. Sarah's vice-like grip hadn't let up and Rex assumed she didn't share the men's zeal for the impromptu motorcycle adventure.

Two feet of snow and freezing temperatures greeted them as they burst through the outer field. Chase shivered as the frigid wind bit at his face and chilled him to the bone. He hadn't thought it possible, but Sarah's grip tightened and she buried her head in his back. The Harley bucked as its rear tire attempted to find traction in the winter landscape.

True to Tad's word a stream appeared a half mile away. Chase held the throttle wide open and aimed for a small bridge that seemed to span the creek. Thirty seconds passed and as they neared Chase noticed something out of place. The bridge was out. He came to a stop feet short of the outer bank and checked their rear. The outer field still stood and Katsuo and his men seemed to have broken their pursuit.

"What now boss?" Tad asked.

"I don't know." Chase shivered as he scanned the shoreline. Visibility was good and another crossing wasn't in sight. "Is everyone ok?"

"I'm fine." Tad said.

"I'm cold. We'll die out here Rex." Sarah's words rang true and an eerie silence settled on the group. "At least back there we stand a chance."

"At least the wind isn't blowing." Chase gave Sarah a strange look. The suggestion that they go back hadn't set well with him and Tad's displeasure was also apparent. "I think we can jump this."

"Slaughter Creek," Tad said.

"What?"

"Slaughter Creek," Tad pointed to a dilapidated and weathered sign at the edge of the decrepit bridge. "Let's hope it doesn't live up to its name."

"I don't intend for it to. We can jump it."

"Not with this stupid sidecar."

"Are there tools in that toolbox? We could have this thing off in no time."

Chase asked the question and Tad delivered a full complement of tools as Sarah stood nearby shivering. The two men went to work and the sound of steel on steel mixed with their grunts and groans as the VL's bolts fought removal. A few minutes passed as they detached the car. Just then the nearby scalar field dematerialized and the roar of Katsuo's vehicles filled the sky.

"Give me your 1911 and jump her over. You'll never make it back in time." Tad said..

"No way. We're all getting out of here." Chase replied.

"Don't be stupid." Tad reached into the larger man's pocket and took his weapon. "I'll take cover behind this fence row. With all the snow piled up they'll have to get pretty close to get me. I'm too weak to handle that bike anyway. You have to go now."

Rex couldn't argue with Tad's logic and he breathed a slight sigh of relief as the Harley's engine fired.

"Let's go."

"I don't know Rex. We could die." Sarah said.

"What? We'll die for sure if we stay here. Now get on."

Sarah obeyed but Chase wondered where the brave woman from the cabin had gone as he prepared to depart.

"You fight like hell Tad. I'm going to figure something out."

The v-twin engine roared as Rex fed it fuel. He retraced his tracks in the snow and the gap between he and their pursuers shortened. His brain calculated their approximate weight and how fast they needed to be going to jump the creek.

"Slaughter Creek." He said to himself as he spun the bike around and gave it full throttle. "Here goes nothing."

The VL was more responsive with the loss of the sidecar and third passenger. Its rear tire clawed at the gravel beneath the impacted snow and shot forward. Chase took another look in his mirror and Katsuo's Jeeps were having a little trouble finding good traction in the snow as well. In seconds the half broken bridge approached as they shot past Tad who hunkered in the snow behind the fence line.

They hit the wooden remnants of the bridge at fifty miles per hour and Chase saw that he had calculated their need for speed wrong. They were way too fast and overshot the other portion of the bridge by twenty feet, landing hard. The bike wavered, but Rex handled the machine and brought it to an abrupt stop.

A sudden burst of guilt flowed through his body. They could have jumped the bridge with Tad on the back. It would have taken a little longer run, but it would have been possible. Katsuo's men approached the edge of the creek and Chase watched as Tad attempted to stay hidden in the snow. His footprints were a dead giveaway, though, and Chase knew it. He had one option

"Baby, I'm gonna need you to hop off real quick."

★★★★★★★★★★★★★★★★★★★

70.

"So what is it you fellers are needin from me?" Wade Richland spoke in a thick southern drawl.

"I just need to borrow the Stearman from you for a little reconnaissance work." Delays were holding up the Plan CF forces and Leonard was itching to get eyes on the power plant. "You still have the Stearman, don't you?"

"Shooooot. That there aeroplane is in tip top shape. I been doin a few moderations to her here and there. She'll get ya where ya need ta get safe and sound."

Richland had served with distinction as a pilot underneath The General in WWI. A machine gun had disabled his Curtiss and he had crashed behind enemy lines. The downed pilot eluded German forces for days, surviving on water from mud puddles before surprising a lone soldier and stealing his uniform. When he emerged from enemy lines three months later he had sabotaged countless attacks, gathered vital intel, and assassinated a number of high ranking officers, all without speaking a lick of German.

"Leonard tells me you've got quite a story from the war." Willy made small talk as they walked across the farm yard to the barn. "What made you move to Manito afterward?"

"Shoooooot. I ain't done nothing in that war but preten like iyas deaf n kill some Krauts. I moved to Manito to run liquor down the river. There she sits."

Wade had opened the sliding doors to the barn and all three men squinted as their eyes adjusted to the dim conditions. Rays of light shone through cracks in the siding and particles of dust floating in the air accentuated their effect. Leonard peered ahead and laughed as the unmistakable form of the biplane came into view.

"What have you done to her Wade?"

"Well, first thing I done was tear that engine down and fix it up right. You know those boys in the factry must never have flown a plane before. They come outta there..." Wade paused as the other two men's laughter had gone from loud to uproarious. "What you boys laughin so hard at?"

Forty feet ahead sat a bright purple Boeing Stearman Model 75. The 220 horsepower Continental R-670 powerplant gleamed more than the day it had left the factory five years before, and the glossy violet paint shone. It looked more like a museum piece than a functioning unit and Willy took notice of one of Wade's additions.

"I've just never known a man to have a purple plane with a Browning Automatic Rifle mounted in the rear seat."

"Well, he's always had a thing for guns," Leonard said. "I'm not sure about the purple, though."

"That's what yer whoopin an hollerin bout?" Wade rested his hand against the immaculate flying machine. "Shooooot. Holly told me she'd take up flyin if I painted her purple. So I's painted her purple."

"Of course. How is Holly? She must be married. Maybe a few little grandkids running around?"

"Nah. She don't have much time for boys." Richland circled the rear of the aircraft. "She got one of them masterin degrees from the University of Illinois and now all she does is walk round here talkin bout blue jeans n breedin chickens n makin sweet corn taste better whilst bein drought resistant."

"Blue jeans?" Willy said.

"You know. We all got them jeans n pass em to kin?"

"Genes." Leonard chuckled. "Like Gregor Mendel."

"Yep. She talks bout that feller sometimes."

"I've never heard of him, but I know what you're talking about now." Willy eyed the B.A.R. before continuing. "What made you mount this monster on here?"

"Well, like he said," Richland pointed a gnarled finger at Leonard. "I like my guns n if I'd a had one a these in tha war them Krauts woulda had their hands full. I got a storage compartment in there with fifty mags."

"Fifty mags?" Leonard said. "What do you run into out here that warrants that? Also, you know those are illegal now, right?"

"Shoooooot. I don't suppose the sheriff is a itchin too much to come an get em. I ain't served no warrants myself, but I'd rather not need fifty mags for the gun then need em n not have em." Wade laughed as he continued. "Got another fifty n a rifle in the back a my truck along with tha Tommy, prolly somethin in ma boat too. I's never hadta use em when I'sa runnin the lightnin, but near everyone knowed that I had em. Like I said before; better safe than sorry."

"Well, I don't think we'll need all that firepower, but I'd still like to take her out for a little recon if you don't mind." Leonard hopped into the pilot's seat. "I haven't sat in this chair in a while."

"Shoooot. It'll come back to ya." Richland pat the side of the aircraft. "You fellers gave me this old girl anyway. I suppose you borrowin it once every five years won't hurt any of us."

He couldn't have been more wrong.

71.

Poppen took a look back at the 1938 Chrylser Imperial which had just dropped them at their location. He had lived the last day in utter fascination of the events which had transpired. This world was not unlike what he remembered from his youth. Everything was almost identical. The cars, the clothes, the language, the music, and the people were all the same. It was astounding and he struggled to wrap his mind around it all.

"My goodness you've aged young man."

William Rodger Idlewood was seventy-seven years of age, but you wouldn't know that by looking at him. His gait was not that of an old man, and his thick silver hair made him seem younger. He had been a good friend of The Organization since its inception and his skills as a forensic accountant had proven vital in the uncovering of Dietrich Hoff's financial holdings. Poppen took the outstretched hand and the vigor of the handshake surprised him.

"I apologize sir, but I don't believe I've had the pleasure."

"Well, you may not have met me, but I've met you."

"I'm surprised you recognized him so fast." Alexei Chase said as he offered a hand to Idlewood. "It took me a little while."

"It's all in the eyes my good friend. It's all in the eyes." Idlewood cleared his throat as he turned and ascended the steps to his office. "Well, I know you guys didn't come to chit chat and I'm not that interested in how he got to be so old, so why don't you tell me what we're working on."

"I don't suppose our goals are all that different than they were last time." Alexei said. "Someone has taken over Hoff's organization and we need to figure out who and why."

"Sounds easy enough. What else?"

"Well," Poppen met eyes with the other man. "I've been dreaming about this girl..."

****

72.

"Idiots. You are all a bunch of idiots." Katsuo slammed his fists onto the front dashboard of his Jeep as it came to a halt thirty yards from the creek. His quarry had already jumped the old bridge, and the new bridge was miles away. They had escaped and he stepped out of his vehicle while dabbing at the dried blood on his cheek. "Who is head of security in the complex?"

Men clamored from their vehicles and took up defensive positions around Katsuo and the lead Jeep while three scouts advanced to the edge of the creek, but no one answered his question.

"I said. Who is head of security in the complex?" His voice boomed and a small lieutenant reported to his side.

"I believe I am the ranking officer sir."

Katsuo pulled the Nambu from his holster and shot the young man in the temple. A few seconds passed and all was quiet. His temper had gotten the best of him, but that didn't matter.

"Who is next in command?"

Another small lieutenant reported to his side.

"I believe I am sir."

"Is anyone back in the complex to secure it?"

"Yes sir, but they've killed most of our squad leaders and ranking officers in the last few days sir. I'm afraid the few left in the complex are rather green." The lieutenant's report was timid, but seemed honest.

"When we get back I want their response times drilled until they have it right. They don't eat. They don't sleep. They don't go to the bathroom. They don't breathe until they can raise and lower the fields immediately upon receiving my command."

"Yes sir."

The lieutenant snapped to attention and saluted. Katsuo's focus, however, had already moved elsewhere. Rex Chase still sat on Takahiro's personal motorcycle. He had always wanted a Harley Davidson and had purchased the gleaming machine a few months before. Katsuo walked toward the creek passing the sidecar and tools on his way.

"There are two people on the other side of the creek." He shouted loud enough for Chase to hear. "I want the other one found."

Just then gunshots rang out at the edge of the water. Two Japanese soldiers had approached the edge and gotten shot for their troubles. Their bodies slumped in the snow as Takahiro's men returned fire on the unseen enemy. The lead scout had reacted by throwing himself flat in the snow.

"Cease fire. Cease fire." Katsuo's order echoed through the group of soldiers and within seconds the shooting stopped. "He's behind that little fence row. I think my Type 92 should flush him out."

Katsuo climbed in the back of the Willy's Jeep and chambered the automatic weapon.

"I don't care how much snow is in front of you. This thing is going to shred you at thirty yards."

Katsuo sneered as he prepared to gun down his former prisoner. It had to be Tad hiding behind the snow and he couldn't have much ammo left. All was quiet except for the sound of a small biplane lumbering past overhead. Then, the buzz of the small plane joined the unmistakable protests of the v-twin's engine.

Rex Chase and the prized 1930 Harley Davidson VL had taken a short run up to the bridge and already flew through the air ahead. The bike landed hard on the lead scout's position and the snow thrown in his face muted the agonizing screams. Katsuo watched as the entire event lasted a few short seconds. Nobody fired a shot and then Chase was behind cover.

A smile curled across his lips. His day had just gotten much better.

"Thank you for joining us Mr. Chase. I wish very much to kill you myself."

****

73.

"Well you know what they say Kit-Kat. You can wish in one hand…" Chase let his voice trail off even has he took up position next to Tad. "How much ammo do we have left?"

"How much ammo do we have left?" Tad's voice was incredulous. "Are you kidding me? They have a hundred men and machine guns. What were you thinking?"

"More like ninety-seven men now." Even Rex was second guessing his own decision. "How much ammo?"

"I don't know. See for yourself."

Tad handed over the two Colt M1911s and Chase removed the magazines. The situation could have been worse, but they were out gunned and out manned. He mulled options in his head even as Tad spoke.

"Well, how many?"

"Thirteen."

"Well at least my torturing friends were kind enough to have one in the chamber with full mags."

"That's seeing the brighter side of things."

"We could use one of those blue thingy's shooting out of your hands right about now. I'd love to see that again."

"Well, the thing about that is…" Chase shifted his weight underneath himself and craned his neck to see what their Japanese tormenters were doing. "The thing about that is, well, I don't know how."

"Perfect," Tad said. "I know the only super-hero who doesn't know how to use his secret powers."

"Super-hero? You read comics?"

"I sure do. Superman. Arrow. The Crimson Avenger." Tad's eyes lit up. "It was the only luxury they afforded me in that hole."

"How about Batman? Did they give you Batman?"

"Nope."

"Oh man. When we get out of here you're going to have to read every copy of Batman. It's about this guy name Br…"

Machine gun fire interrupted their discussion as bullets hailed around them. Both men covered their heads and Chase snuck a look to the sky. No blue energy materialized and streaks of yellow light didn't seem to show any protection over their position.

Two men attempted to flank their right side and Chase put a bullet in each of their heads. A slight lull in the automatic gunfire brought another tentative assault around the left and it took Chase five more bullets to put them down. Eight shots remained in their arsenal and the situation was becoming more desperate by the second.

"During the next break in machine gun fire we hop on the bike and make a run for it." Chase cupped his hand over Tad's ear to make sure he heard him. "I think we can get back across from here."

Tad responded with a thumbs up and it caused Chase to smile. His spirit and bravery were undeniable. Across the creek Sarah huddled behind a fallen tree where Chase had left her. He couldn't make out her face but he intended to return to the woman he hoped to pursue when all this was over.

Then came the respite in fire from the Type 92 and Chase prepared to run. The absence of the machine gun's roar, however, revealed another sound. Chase turned his gaze to the sky once again to see a purple Boeing Stearman Model 75 lumbering along, the silver hair of its pilot gleaming in the sun. Behind him another man stood, a mounted Browning Automatic Rifle in his grasp. The unmistakable chatter of the automatic 30.06 spewing lead from the sky brought a new ray of hope.

Chase peered from their hiding spot and saw the Japanese soldiers in disarray.

"You thought it was cold down here Tad. Be thankful you're not up in that purple monstrosity."

"I think that's my brother."

"Well he's saving our butts." Chase mounted the Harley and turned the engine over. "I say we do our part to advance the effort."

Tad wrapped his arms around Chase's waist and squeezed.

"Consider my effort advanced and butt saved."

****

74.

"How ya doin back there Willy?"

Leonard's voice was lost to the wind that whipped past the Stearman's gleaming indigo fuselage. The two men hadn't been in the air more than a few minutes before spotting Katuo's army of Jeeps on the horizon. It had become evident they were in pursuit of someone when Rex Chase's unmistakable blonde hair and lithe physique jumped the creek on a motorcycle. No sooner had the man soared to safety, though, than he had jumped back to the other side and taken up cover behind what looked to be a fencerow and pile of snow. Leonard had communicated that they would provide cover and Willy had started firing the Browning.

"Glad we have all this ammunition back here. Swing me around a little to the port."

"Will do. Concentrate your fire on personnel. We don't have enough firepower to take out all the Jeeps."

"How about that big bast…"

No less than a dozen rounds tearing through the heart of the underpowered and overweight plane interrupted Willy's sentence. Leonard grunted as he rolled the nimble aircraft onto its side and descended in an attempt to gain speed. He hadn't checked to make sure his partner had engaged his safety harness but a quick peak over his shoulder showed the other man had taken proper precaution.

"Did you see where that came from?" Leonard craned his neck at the battle scene now raging behind them, but the undeniable bark of the B.A.R. overpowered his voice. He smiled and waited for the magazine swap. "Where do ya need me Willy?"

"It's that big bastard in the middle." Willy flexed his fingers, coaxing blood into the extremities as he loaded the deadly weapon of war. "He's got a gun bigger than ours."

Leonard brought the Model 75 around and took notice of the machine gun below. All other members of the battle seemed to be in disarray, but that one gun being wielded with deadly efficiency. He would fire a burst into the fencerow and then a burst into the sky. Bullets whizzed by and Leonard ducked. They had to take that gun out.

"I'm going to dive right at him and then pull up broadside so you can get a good look."

"He'll get a good look too," Willy said.

"Well, I'm going to need you to get him before he gets us." Leonard began the maneuver before adding. "Shoot em straight my boy. Shoot em straight."

With that he tipped the biplane's wings to starboard and brought the Stearman into a steep dive. The airframe shuddered as they passed 130 miles per hour. If his memory served it couldn't handle much more speed. He needed a few more seconds, though, and Leonard felt a lone bead of sweat trickle down his face.

"How did that not freeze?"

He said the words aloud but the frigid winds whisked them away. Seconds passed as The Sentinel focused all his energy on the task at hand. He had spent his entire life preparing himself for the moments that lie ahead and he intended to fulfill his duties. No man would stand in his way. He wouldn't allow it.

"Hold on Willy."

Leonard pulled back on the stick while applying full left rudder. The Stearman fought the assignment, its 220 horsepower radial engine beating the prop against the cold winter air. He had pushed the airframe to its maximum capabilities and an iota of doubt crept into his mind. Then the plane righted itself and seemed to float perpendicular to the land gunner's position.

"Get him Willy. Get him."

Willy had opened up with the Browning before the words had even left his pilot's mouth. Spent 30.06 shell casings rained from sky as the young men changed magazines, losing little time. Leonard watched as bullets tore through the rear of the Jeep, but the unyielding fire from below continued.

"I have six magazines left. What do you think…"

A loud bang, accompanied by a loss in power brought all of Leonard's attentions to the controls of the plane. The last volley of bullets from the machine gun below had pierced the engine separating one of the seven pistons from the crankshaft. Unbalanced, the radial power plant now destroyed itself. They were going down and Leonard knew it.

"I'm going to have to put her down Willy."

"I'm going to fire off the rest of these rounds if I can."

Leonard smiled and wondered if young Tad had grown up with half the moxie of his brother. With speed and deft skill he powered back the seven cylinder Continental engine and within seconds they were gliding. Willy's B.A.R. roared from the rear, but Leonard's ears heard just the delightful sound of rushing wind. They had no chance of making a soft landing and as he surveyed the ground ahead few viable options presented themselves. They were going to crash and the creek loomed ahead.

"Well, Leonard," he mumbled to himself. "Here goes nothing."

75.

Bobby leaned back in the rickety office chair and rubbed his eyes. They had been working for hours and the information was streaming in. He rather enjoyed the hunt, but not as much as Idlewood. The other man was like a bloodhound in his search for knowledge.

"I'd give my right arm for the use of the internet right now."

"The what?" Idlewood peered over the top of his glasses which rested on the end of his nose.

"It's a great way of sharing information. All the world's knowledge is stored in one place and everyone has access from their homes."

"Huh. Sounds dangerous. So any John Q. could just hop on the internet at his house and learn how to make chlorine gas?"

"Yeah, I suppose he could."

Idlewood joined Poppen in leaning back in his chair and also rubbed his eyes.

"Boy, aren't we a couple of old timers. Why don't we go ahead and run through what we have already?"

"Well, I'm afraid it's not a lot." Poppen shuffled some papers as he gathered his notes. "If it weren't for that fancy car of hers we'd be up a creek. Thanks for that tidbit Alexei."

"What?" Alexei Chase was pouring over files Idlewood had collected on Hoff and his empire, including several boxes Charles Gorney had sent over from England. "I'm sorry. I've been chasing my tail over here a bit. It seems like Hoff's empire has been busy since his death."

"No problem. I was just thanking you for telling us about the Marmon. All we know about Sarah so far is that her father was a rich industrialist based out of Boston who went by the name of David Horowitz."

"So her last name is Horowitz?" Alexei asked.

"I don't think so," Idlewood said. "I can't find a single record of any Sarah Horowitz born or owning anything, anywhere, at any time. I'm certain she hasn't paid any taxes."

"Perhaps her father changed his name to make it more American. When we moved to the States we changed from Chasiliov to Chase. That happens more often than you'd think."

"I don't think he did," Poppen said. "Up until his death, which isn't recorded, business transactions and taxes bearing his signature show it as Horowitz. Here, look at this."

He showed a paper with the man's signature.

"So she doesn't have her father's name," Idlewood said.

"She's never had her father's name," said Poppen.

"Or her father also had a different name," Alexei said. "It wouldn't be the first time a businessman held more than one identity. He could have gotten into something shady or tried to hide money from an ex wife. Do we know what he did?"

"Cables." Poppen and Idlewood answered in unison.

"Cables?" Alexei asked.

"Yeah, like the kind that made the transatlantic cable or hold up the Golden Gate Bridge. Huge, industrial cables." Poppen stood; his back ached from the wooden seat.

"Strange." Alexei said. "Do you mind if I see some of those signatures?"

"You got it." Poppen handed over the documents and moved toward the boxes near Dr. Chase.

"What are you thinking Alexei?" Idlewood asked.

"Hold on." The elder Chase dug through a box as he rifled through papers. He stopped and held a lone note in the air. "Aha. There we have it. Horowitz Industrial Cabling, a division of Dietrich Hoff Incorporated."

Alexei was proud of himself, but the elders continued to dig through the boxes he had made his own. They seemed unimpressed at his revelation and he was a little hurt by it.

"Come on guys. Her father worked for Hoff. That's a big deal, right?"

"I suppose," Poppen mumbled. "I had kind of already figured something like that since the company didn't skip a beat upon his death, continued filing taxes, and kept supplying cable."

"Me too," Idlewood said.

"Well what are you fellas looking for then?"

"Got one."

"Me too."

Both gentleman held a single document from different boxes. On their surface they seemed unrelated, but their implications were the same. They came together at William's desk, each laying down their evidence.

"Alexei, bring over that one of yours," Poppen said.

The senior Chase obeyed, laying his paper in line with the other two. Dietrich Hoff's signature graced Idlewood and Poppen's papers whereas Chase's held the signature of a David J. Horowitz. He stood still, studying the two men's eyes, but saw no evidence of what they were thinking.

"Wanna let me in on this fellas?"

"The d's are the same."

"Yep, and so are the h's and o's."

"I don't understand," Alexei said.

"David J. Horowitz and Dietrich Hoff are one and the same." Idlewood stepped to another nearby box and began digging through it. "I've got something else in here too."

"Are you sure?" Alexei looked at the signatures and saw the resemblance. "So Sarah's father is Dietrich Hoff?"

"Maybe. Maybe not," Poppen said. "She could have had a real father that Hoff used as a cover for business deals or any other number of scenarios."

"Here it is." Idlewood's eyes were alive and he seemed prepared to dance a jig as he crossed the room and exited. A few seconds passed before he poked his head back through the entryway. "Are you guys coming?"

Alexei and Poppen laughed at the other man's zeal before crossing the room full of books and entering a dim area that housed three chairs, a chalkboard, and a projector. William was moving with a purpose as he strung the 16mm film through the movie projector's guides.

"I came across this one day a while back," he explained as he worked. "It's dated November 7, 1914 and labeled *D.H. and S.M. play with rocks*."

"November 7, 1914 is Rex Chase's birthday," Poppen said.

"So it is," Alexei smiled. "You are a fan."

"I love baseball," Poppen conceded as the grainy, full color picture began to form on the chalkboard.

"Alexei," Idlewood cleared his throat. "Do me a favor and pull down that screen."

Dr. Chase performed the duty and the color film came to life on the white screen. He retreated in awe as the other two men studied the moving pictures accompanied by sound. Neither seemed impressed.

"I didn't know anyone had invented this in 1914," Alexei said.

"They hadn't," Idlewood said. "Like I said I came across this a while back. It seems that Dietrich Hoff's father, through an American bank, loaned George Eastman money way back in 1888. With a little further digging I was able to find that Hoff also had a major interest in the Agfa company out of Germany. These two companies had very similar ideas when it came to kodachrome technology, but Hoff liked it so much he kind of held it back for his own personal use. Gorney says he has thousands of hours of this home movie stuff back in England. If it weren't for that infernal war we'd have gotten more out of Germany."

Poppen stared at the screen ahead. High definition television, Imax theaters, and handheld devices had been the norm for him a few days before, but all this regression in technology was wonderful. A euphoric feeling spread through his body and he shivered with the excitement.

"What is it we're looking for?"

"Give it a bit. The first part is a little damaged so we can't understand the audio, but from what I can gather Dietrich Hoff is at his estate in Germany playing in the yard or something."

On the screen stood Dietrich Hoff, but instead of his customary scowl a jovial grin adorned his face. Alexei had met the man for just a moment, but the vision on the screen didn't resemble the person from his memory.

"Come here you silly little girl." The voice was unmistakable and Chase found himself wondering who held the camera. "Stop for a second and show me what you are playing with."

"I don't understand what it is we are looking for here. Maybe if you told me wh…" Poppen's voice trailed off as the little girl entered the scene. Her green dress mimicked the lush German grass, which seemed odd for November in the Rhineland. Hoff scooped up the little girl and she squealed in delight before presenting the villainous man a set of two black stones not unlike the ones Leonard had shown them less than twenty-four hours before. "What is…"

"Shhhhh," Idlewood said. "No talking during the movie. It's almost there."

Poppen's jaw dropped as the little girl mimicked Leonard's previous movements and the two stones began circling each other. Hoff's demeanor changed in an instant and he approached the camera before the video changed to a horseback riding scene with two unknown participants. Idlewood stopped the projector and rewound a few seconds before pausing the movie on one certain frame. Between Hoff's elbow and ribcage was the happy, still face of the little girl. Her blond hair and opaline eyes shone in the sun and Poppen stared in disbelief as he repeated the same words he had used in The General's office.

"It's her."

****

76.

Mother sat a few feet away and Shou studied her gnarled fingers and weathered skin. It was hard to believe she still possessed the mental faculties to lead their multi-national outfit, but her mind remained sharp. He formed a slight grin as her countenance changed. She had scheduled them to leave upon his arrival, but then insisted on staying for this special phone call.

"Are you sure it is finished?" Her voice wavered and Shou detected the emotion. "Thank you."

The old woman turned and the tears in her eyes surprised Shin. Weakness was not what he expected and she looked even older. The moment passed, though, and she stood with the aid of her two large guards.

"Tell me Shin, have you ever lost someone you love?"

"Love is a weakness I cannot afford," Shin said. "Look at what it has done to you."

Without blinking Mother moved her face close to his, her guards flanking either side.

"I should have you killed."

"I could snap your neck before they even knew what was happening."

Shin's yellow grin dominated his face as he looked down at the woman. She replaced her display of weakness with utter defiance and anger, but it was too late. He held the advantage even as one of the guards touched his left arm.

More out of instinct than any malice toward the man, Shou pulled down on the guard's outstretched hand while delivering a vicious blow to his right temple, knocking him unconscious. The second man reacted quicker than Shin had expected, but he wasn't as fast as the Japanese killer. Shou ducked the right cross aimed at his ear and delivered a brutal elbow to the overmatched sentry. He heard the air rush from the guard's lungs and circled his back, wrapping two large arms around the man's neck.

"You think that these are the men who protect you?" Shin snarled as he met the old woman's unyielding gaze. "Without me you are nothing."

With that he pulled his arms opposite directions and snapped the larger man's neck. The body beneath spasmed before it became limp. Shou stepped over the fresh corpse without breaking Mother's gaze, stopping inches from her face, but she showed no fear. All emotion had drained from her pitted and craggy face as she wore a blank stare.

"Now you think you will kill me as well?"

Her voice was calm as Shou looked for any lingering sign of weakness and saw none. She still seemed in control and Shin thought better of his actions. His loyalty lay within, but for now Mother could have her way.

"I wouldn't think of it Mother. I just didn't care for your dogs putting their hands on me."

"I'll have them replaced. It seems they weren't the best anyway. Tell me something Shin. Are we in danger from the capture of the carrier?"

"I doubt it." Shin said. "The carrier was a prototype and base of operations, more integral to our long term-plans. We'll have plenty of time to build more once we carry out the next stage."

"What if the Americans have figured us out?"

"Even if they have it's too late. We have already won. They just don't know it yet."

Mother's smile was superficial. The weariness she had displayed before returned and Shin contemplated killing her. He had an ingrained respect for his elders, however, which caused him to think again. She would live.

"Come Shin. Fly me to Pekin so we can end all of this."

"I just have to make a quick phone call to speed us on our journey. I'll meet you at your plane and then escort you on."

A few hours ago Shin had never seen his superior's face, and now that he had, his respect for her had further dwindled. She ruled with an iron fist from afar, but somehow her enemies hadn't realized she was a feeble old woman. Shou dialed the number as he studied the crumpled piece of paper in his hand.

"Hello."

"I need to speak with The Russian."

"This is he."

"How can I be sure?"

"When you liberated me I pissed my pants when you slit my wife's throat and murdered my children."

"Of course," Shin smiled and stifled an evil laugh as he recounted the experience. "I apologize for that again. Your wife did try to shoot me, though."

"She did. What can I do for you?"

"I wanted to be certain your decipher of the transcriptions was still the same."

"It is."

"And you're sure the transcriptions from the other two are of no matter."

"They are not. I can extrapolate their instructions from the other thirty-six. Are you certain Mother…"

"Excellent." Shou interrupted as his hair stood on end and a wave of exhilaration passed through his body. "We'll have the world at our fingertips soon my friend."

"Everything is going as planned." The Russian's voice wavered before continuing. "How are the final stages of the dam project?"

"They are proceeding." Shou knew nothing of a dam project so he prodded the man for information. "Are there any final instructions?"

Shou listened as the man detailed another plot of which Shin had no knowledge along with a second revelation. Izanami was more cunning than he had previously surmised. He hung up the phone and walked to his awaiting Zero. Mother and Izanami had their plans and now Shou had his own. The best part for him, though, was that he could wait until the last minute to play his best hand. Except for Katsuo, everyone had underestimated him his entire life and it seemed even his mentor had been keeping secrets. No one could be trusted.

"It's time to finish this."

****

THE SENTINEL

77.

"You're certain." The General's voice exuded stress and he cleared his throat as the man on the other end of the line stated his case. "Well, if you're certain then you need to find out what they're up to, and I mean yesterday." He paused again as the other man added more tidbits of information. "Do you have proof of that?... No, I mean solid proof... The company did what?... And you're sure?... In that case I'm sending George your way and then you're both off to Pekin, or Manito, or wherever they are... Yes... Yes... No, I'll be more certain when I find that out... Yes... Yes... Good luck to you as well. Goodbye."

The General hung up the phone and rubbed his left hand down the center of his face before cradling his chin. Alexei Chase was no alarmist, but the revelation he had just unloaded on The General was nothing short of life changing. His decision to dispatch the men of Plan CF had been the correct choice. Not briefing the President had been wrong. He picked up the phone and dialed. A few short moments later he had the leader of the nation on the line.

"Mr. President... Yes, sir... Yes, sir... I know we've known each other a long time... Yes, sir... But you are the president sir... Yes, sir... I believe The Organization has stumbled onto something huge sir... Yes, sir... I know, sir... Listen to me, sir..." It wasn't often that The General ordered around his longtime friend, The President of the United States, but the man wasn't listening. Silence dominated the line as The General continued. "It is my firmest of beliefs that the United States is under attack by an enemy more dangerous than The Empire of Japan or The Third Reich. Our true enemy is well-funded, well-trained, and possesses the capability to obliterate our country from the map. I need you to mobilize the army under my command."

The President met his request with more silence as Patrick Castle and Sam entered the room once again.

"Yes, sir… Yes, sir… Thank- you sir… I won't let you down sir…" The General hung up the phone and addressed the two men while still completing the motion. "Whatya got fellas?"

"Not much," Sam said.

"He's trying to build it isn't he." Patrick Castle's face was ashen and The General nodded.

"He, or she, or whoever might have already built it, and we paid for it. The Army and the Navy and whoever hired Hoff Inc. to circle our country with Castleinium." The General was furious and he fought to control his emotions as the phone rang once again. "Yes." He snapped. "George. You're calling a couple of hours early. I need some good news. What do you have?… Yes… Uh-huh… You're sure?… Yes… It was unarmed and they're all dead?… Yes… Yes… OK, give me a second."

The General retrieved a map from the edge of his desk and scanned its face.

"It looks like they have planes where you are. Commandeer two of them and if the base commander has a problem with it have him call me… Yes… Yes… After that I need you to get to Washington and pick up Poppen and Alexei and get to Manito. I have control of the Army now, but we need all the men we can get there as soon as possible. I want you to link up with Leonard, Willy, and I hope Chase. If everything has gone to plan they'll be at Wade Richland's. Do you remember it?… Good… Yes… Yes… No, if they didn't load the carrier with planes I'm putting it on the back burner for now. Did you see anything that indicated there were more?… OK… Yes… Well, make sure you're debriefed by Alexei and Bobby, they have a lot to tell you… Use your best judgment… I plan on leaving in a few hours… Yes… Yes… Good luck to you as well… Bye."

The General hung up the phone once again and expectant looks from both Sam and Patrick greeted him.

"I need the two of you to find this woman." He pulled a picture from under a stack of papers. "You know her name, and now you have her face. I need her back right now."

"I, I, I'm not a detective." Patrick Castle said. "I'm not a detective."

"Me neither," said Sam. "Don't you have someone better?"

"I have a lot better, but today they are all being used elsewhere." The General stood, circled his desk, and put a hand on the rich tycoon's shoulder. "Today I need you to be detectives. She's important. Even more so now than ever before."

A knock at the door interrupted their conversation and The General moved to answer it.

"Hello there," he said. "How are you feeling?"

"Oh, I suppose I'm alright," the old man said as he struggled to carry a heavy briefcase. "They didn't get it right the first time so we're all still here."

The General laughed and took the heavy case from the old man.

"What do you have in here anyway? Bricks?"

All four men laughed in unison as The General set down the briefcase and Sam helped the old man to a chair.

"How is your wife?" Patrick Castle said. "She seemed shaken up before.

"Oh, I suppose she's alright," the old man sat and shifted in his seat before locking eyes with The General. "I suppose she's doing just fine."

The General looked into the deep brown eyes of the old man expecting to see confusion brought on by dementia, but instead he saw hatred and evil. In his years of experience in battle it was a sight he had seen more than once and the old man exuded the quality, but only from the eyes. John Francis Reagan became uncomfortable in his own office.

"What is it I can do for you?"

"Die."

An explosion rocked the second floor of the decades old building. Sam had been standing almost on top of the case and was incinerated in an instant. Patrick Castle tumbled through the air. A corner of The General's desk shielded him from part of the blast.

Time seemed to slow for The General, however, as his eyes remained locked with the old man's. His attempted murderer showed no fear, no remorse, and didn't so much as flinch as the flames engulfed his body. The General watched the man burn in absolute serenity even as the flames rushed in his own direction. The shockwave from the blast hit and threw him like a doll against the outer wall of the complex. His conscious mind rushed through scenarios of how this had become possible. Nobody had ever blindsided him before and it had now happened twice within a matter of days. The fight would continue without him, but death seemed a certainty. As the darkness closed in, flanked by brilliant flashes of light his mother's voice accompanied him on his journey.

"Angel of God, my Guardian dear, to whom God's love commits me here. Ever this day, be at my side, to light and guard, to rule and guide... Angel of God, my Guardian dear, to whom God's love commits me here. Ever this day, be at..."

John Francis Reagan breathed his last breath and donned a peaceful smile. Then he died.

****

78.

Fuel ignited in perfect time as the V-twin's pistons pumped with furor. Chase shivered and fought the front forks of the decade old bike. It took all of his effort and concentration to keep the fishtailing motorcycle aimed at the bridge ahead. They weren't at the optimum angle, but that couldn't be helped.

He shifted gears as the duo made their mad dash to safety a few yards ahead. Bullets impacted the ground in front of them causing snow to cascade all around. Chase shook his head, cupped his bottom lip upward, and attempted to melt the thin layer of white powder which covered his face. He blinked hard as the combination of wind and snow stung his eyes.

"Ten seconds Tad," he shouted over the howling wind and unyielding machine gun fire. "Just ten more seconds."

The other man responded with a squeeze and Chase dug his feet into the bike's pegs. He would have to time the jump to perfection in order to make it. Traction was less than ideal and he knew the landing was going to be close.

Above, the Stearman continued to pound away at the men on the ground, but for reasons unknown it hadn't stopped the occasional flurry of automatic gunfire in Chase's direction. Rex heard a loud bang and peered at the sky above. Smoke bellowed from the Stearman's uncowled radial engine and the unmistakable sound of an airplane losing altitude at a perilous rate now dominated the battle.

They were three seconds from the jump now and Chase poised his body for maximum exertion. His timing was going to have to be perfect or they didn't stand a chance. The muscles in his arms bulged and he flexed his fingers. He felt Tad tense and Rex crouched, his legs bent, ready to spring like a cat. Every bit of energy he could muster would be needed, and then it happened.

Less than a second before the jump Chase felt the bike's rear end shudder as three 7.7 mm projectiles slammed into the frame. He fought a losing battle and every muscle in his body tensed as he struggled against the sideways momentum of the impact. Rex pushed off with his legs as the VL rocketed over the wooden precipice. It was evident that the duo would fall short of their goal and he pushed the bike away.

Chase's arms flailed in the air, grasping at nothing in a feeble attempt to gain a slight sense of control. The water below was rushing up at incredible speed, its uninviting cold a foregone conclusion. Rex fought the urge to continue wind-milling his arms, instead holding them down at his side. He needed to hit the water straight and flatten out in order to best protect himself.

A sharp pain shot through his side and he felt his body spin and begin to tumble. Time slowed to a near standstill as Tad passed through his field of vision, followed by water, then snow, trees, and sky. He was falling out of control and moments away from impact when a dull thump echoed in his ears followed by an intense ringing.

Nobody had ever shot Rex Chase in the head before, and as he tumbled the ringing in his ears subsided and for the second time in thirty minutes a supreme serenity enveloped his very soul. It was a feeling to which he was beginning to become accustomed and not an iota of fear entered his thoughts. Tad held his concern. Sarah held his concern. Leonard held his concern. Then it was dark.

✶✶✶✶✶✶✶✶✶✶✶✶✶✶✶✶✶✶✶

79.

Death rained from the sky above and Katsuo cursed. His thirst for blood had blinded him to the disarray being perpetrated by the small biplane. All around him men clamored for cover even as the other two machine guns sat unmanned and silent.

"Get on those Type 92's," he shouted, but no one heeded the order. They had lost complete combat effectiveness and Katsuo mumbled to himself as he lined up the plane in his sites. "I asked for 1000 men and I got 100. This is what happens when women run military operations. Jin."

"Yes, sir." The driver of his Jeep was still in the fight.

"Get me the ammo out of those other two Jeeps. I'm running low."

"Yes, sir."

Jin sprinted from the Jeep and Katsuo let loose a flurry of 7.7mm shells into the sky. He walked the line of fire into the biplane's fuselage thankful for at least one fearless soldier. He hadn't thought of tracer rounds for the weapons, but Shou had insisted. Katsuo was happy for the markers now as they made shooting the slow moving aircraft a breeze.

The momentary respite in fire as Takahiro reloaded brought his attention back to the ground. Chase and Tad had mounted the VL again and started another dash for the bridge. Katsuo loosed a flurry in their direction and received a violent answer from above. Bullets tore through the seats to his right and left while more projectiles slammed into the area Jin had vacated. Takahiro brought the gun around, took careful aim, and released a full seven second burst at his tormentors in the sky.

Underneath his feet the Jeep's frame shuddered at the constant rate of fire. Blue-green veins seemed to burst from the robust Japanese man's arms as he fought the machine gun's violent display of power. His muscles burned and sweat poured down his face from the exertion and then a puff of smoke emanated from the plane's engine.

Katsuo swung the Type 92 back around. Chase and Tad were feet from their jump and Takahiro squeezed the trigger without the luxury of aiming. The first rounds impacted five yards from the rear of the Harley's back tire, but the tracers made it easy to adjust. Like he had done with the plane above Katsuo marched the projectiles up the back of his prized American made cycle.

He paused as the bullets slammed into his machine and the two men soared through the air. Rex Chase flailed his arms in an attempt to steady himself and Katsuo smiled as he pulled the trigger once again on the deadly Type 92. Escape was not going to be an option.

Round after round streaked through the sky and Katsuo's smile soon turned into a fiendish grin as his projectiles found their mark. Rex Chase's body went limp and pin wheeled through the sky. Takahiro released the vise like grip on the Type 92 just in time to hear the slap of his enemy's lifeless form on the water. He looked to the south and his grin widened even more. The small biplane hit the ground and the clatter of metal being twisted echoed across the creek.

"Where is my ammo?" Katsuo asked as his driver approached.

"I'm sorry sir, but there wasn't any ammo in either of the other vehicles," Jin said between heavy breaths.

"They didn't fire a single shot. Those imbeciles came to a fight with no ammunition? Take me to the edge of the creek."

Jin occupied the tattered driver's seat and guided the wounded Jeep forward. Katsuo's men, their skyward tormenters disabled, had begun to regroup at the edge of the creek. Takahiro looked at them with disgust as a few took some initiative in spraying the water with bullets.

"Cease fire." He gave the order as Tad flailed in the frigid water below. Rex Chase's body was floating face up and showed no signs of life. Takahiro smiled as the girl screamed and entered the water, swimming with all her might. "Take them prisoner and bring me the body of Rex Chase. I want to examine it myself."

Rex Chase and company had once again killed half of his forces and Katsuo didn't plan on leaving anything to chance. The girl gasped and cried as the soldiers fished her from the water. Tad floundered, but fought the men who attempted to once again take him captive. Takahiro admired the prisoner's willingness to fight. If only half of Katsuo's own men had the same enthusiasm they would have won the battle with minimal casualties.

Takahiro shivered and squinted his eyes as a lone vehicle approached from the west. It was an International Harvester pickup truck he had seen in the area before. A local must have heard the commotion and come out to investigate. Local officials would be along in short order and Katsuo trained his gun on Chase's unresponsive form.

"Get the girl out of there," he said. "I'll take care of the other two."

Three of his men had already begun dragging the beautiful young woman up the side of the creek and four others discontinued their pursuit of Tad and Chase. Katsuo breathed deep the cold winter air. He would appreciate the warmth of the scalar compound in a few short minutes. First he had two more victims to claim.

Jin's head exploded, sending bits of brain and skull cascading across Katsuo's face. He blinked hard and wiped the blood from his cheeks and forehead. One of the other man's eyeballs hung from the left grip of the heavy machine gun and Takahiro released his grasp on the deadly device. Bullets slammed into all parts of the Jeep sending plumes of stuffing from the seats into the air.

Katsuo looked in wonder across the stream. A man and woman stood in the open, alternating their machine gun fire. The Japanese soldiers once again retreated and Takahiro contemplated doing the same. His men were worthless in battle and his ammunition was low. He pushed the lifeless body of Jin from the driver's seat with his boot and slid into the spot. The Jeep's engine was still running and Katsuo retreated, though nagging questions crept into his mind.

Who were the men in the plane? Where had they come from? Who were the couple on shore? Why wouldn't Rex Chase just die? He flexed his shoulders and spun the Jeep around. A few yards away men loaded the captured woman into another Jeep and retreated as well. Katsuo shivered again, but harder than before. Everything would be over by this time tomorrow anyway. They had one day to go.

****

80.

"So you told The General we busted our planes up and this was the best he had available?" Al ducked his head underneath the wing of the Bell YFM-1 Airacuda as Bryan stood nearby studying the flight manual. "Did you even tell him about the flight capabilities of whatever it was we just went up against?"

"He told me it was the closest, best option available." George circled the massive fighter. "The little guns on that plane couldn't shoot these two things down anyway."

"Chyeah." Scherzer grumbled to himself as he continued his pre-flight check of the plane. "A lot of good all this firepower and armor does us if he's always on our six."

"Did The General say what we're up to now?" Morris looked up from his manual. "I mean we just found a Japanese aircraft carrier a few miles off the Eastern Seaboard. On another note, these things are experimental, they've built twelve of them, and they call for a crew of five. I'm counting, one, two, three of us."

"To answer your questions in order. Yes, The General gave us orders. No, we're not doing anything about the carrier, which, by the way, we parked right over there." George smiled as he pointed to the east and the other two men turned their heads. Their arrival had been something of a fiasco, drawing the attention of no less than three full bird colonel's and two high ranking generals. "Last, we're going to pick up a couple more people right now."

"So we'll have enough crew to man one of the aircraft." Morris dismissed Ahiga with a wave of his hand and buried his nose back in the manual. "I'm going to know how this thing works anyway."

"For that, Captain Morris, I am grateful."

"Not me." Scherzer said. "I'd be grateful for a big bottle of scotch right now, but that's about it. Where are we headed anyway boss?"

"The two of you are headed straight to Manito, Illinois." George stretched his back and yawned. "They have a little landing strip just to the north of town and a man named Wade Richland lives nearby. We'll rendezvous there."

"So, who's flying this?" Bryan arched his eyebrow as he pointed to the other aircraft.

"I am, of course." George grinned ear to ear. He loved surprising people. "I've logged a little over five-hundred flight hours in the last eighteen months. I got tired of always having to wait for a ride."

"If it's all the same to you, and if I'm not overstepping my bounds, I still think it's more prudent if we stick together." Scherzer had finished his walk around and slapped the nose of the plane. "You never know who we're going to run into out there, and I'm not real keen on just landing at small town airstrips with weird looking fighter planes."

"Sounds like a plan to me." Chief joined the other two men in a short round of laughter. "Right now these weird looking things are going to take us to Washington and then on to Manito. You fellas can just fall in behind me and we'll be there before you know it."

****

81.

Bobby Poppen stood and stretched his back once again. If there was one thing that had never changed about airports it was that they made no comfortable seating available. Hours had passed since they had left William Idlewood's office and his mind had not stopped racing since. Alexei, however, seemed immune to it all and snored, his head hanging over the back of the wooden chair.

"You wanna have a drink?" Poppen kicked the other man's foot and he popped upright. "Let's have a drink. I'm bored."

"Do you have vodka?"

"Ha. I don't have anything, but I saw a bar on our way in."

"Well, it looks like we have a few hours before we're scheduled to be picked up." Alexei took notice of his watch. "I suppose we could sneak in a couple of snorts."

"I'm sneaking more than a couple." The two men began walking as Poppen continued. "We've found out that a multinational conglomerate of bad guys may be planning on incinerating the United States. Hell, I'm all for getting on these planes and heading to Europe."

"It isn't much better over there Bobby." Alexei said. "Don't forget that they might also possess other mobile weapons of unimaginable destructive capabilities."

Poppen tapped a long bony finger to his temple.

"As long as we take good care of this old head of mine they shouldn't be able to expound upon those, though, right?"

"I wouldn't think so." Alexei and Poppen had a working theory of what Hoff's organization was attempting. "You never know, though. What do you think they were up to with all of the shipbuilding?"

Before leaving Idlewood's the three men had uncovered a massive naval construction budget which seemed to funnel through one of Hoff's Russian subsidiaries. The construction sites, though, were not identifiable. Idlewood had chalked it up to the Russian's poor record keeping.

"I suppose if you circle the United States with cables made of Castleinium and then incinerate it you'll need a navy." Poppen opened the door to the run down establishment and Alexei walked through. "I don't buy into the idea that it didn't leave a paper trail, though."

"Welcome gentleman." The bartender greeted the two men as they bellied up to the bar. "What can I get for you?"

Bobby looked around and realized that he hadn't had the slightest hint of a hangover.

"Whatya got in the way of Glenlivet?"

"I've got Glenlivet."

"Perfect." Poppen laughed and Alexei joined him. "What are you having my friend?"

"Vodka. Lots of vodka."

"You've got it fellas. You have a preference on vodka? On the rocks?"

"Rocks for me."

"Smirnoff on the rocks please, and keep em coming."

****

82.

Chase blinked his eyes hard as a beautiful voice hummed the words to Dorothy Field's and Jerome Kern's classic, *Just the Way You Look Tonight*. She was right there and he could almost hear the soft pitter-patter of the snare and easy strokes on the hat. What was happening? Was he dreaming?

"Mary Elizabeth?" The hoarseness of his own voice surprised him and he cleared his throat. "Mary Elizabeth?"

"Shhhhhhhhh. Take it easy. Everything is ok, but they shot you."

"Yeah. People keep shooting at me." Chase breathed deep and the acrid taste of smoke caused him to smack his lips. "How did you get here Mary Elizabeth?"

"Shhhhhhhhh. My name is Holly. We'll get you to the doctor as quick as we can, but one of your friends is hurt pretty bad. My father is seeing to him first."

Chase's faculties increased tenfold. The vision of Mary Elizabeth standing over him dematerialized and a stunning young woman took her place. She dabbed at his head with her right hand while compressing a rag on a bloody wound to his side with her left.

"Is Tad OK?" Chase attempted to sit up, but he was stiff and a lightning bolt of pain streaked down his side.

"Take it easy I said. Daddy fished you and the other fella on the motorcycle out of the water. He's just fine, but you took a bullet to the side and a grazer to the head. It doesn't look too bad, though, and your side has already stopped bleeding."

"I've been a fast healer as of late."

Chase propped himself up on his arms once again and took notice of the woman tending to his wounds. She was drop dead gorgeous. Braids held her long sandy-blonde hair on either side of her head as her deep brown eyes exuded a kindness not often seen. He blinked hard again making sure he saw her right. Then it hit him.

"What about Sarah? Where is Sarah?"

"She was screamin and hollerin to beat the band. I tried to tell her not to, but she jumped in the water after you fellas anyway and those Japanese boys pulled her out the other side. She should have known better than to jump in that water. It's too cold."

Rex shivered as he first took notice of the frigid temperatures. The sun was beginning to set and the wind had picked up. He was feeling a touch better as his mind continued to clear. Why would Sarah have jumped in the water? It was stupid of her and he cursed under his breath.

"What about the airplane? What happened to them?"

"That's what all this smoke is about." The beautiful young woman pointed along the bank of the river. "Daddy's over helping them as best he can. One of them is hurt pretty bad I think."

Adrenaline coursed through his veins and Chase jumped to his feet. The pain in his side was manageable and though his balance was a little uneven he began walking toward the wreckage. A sinking feeling grew in his belly as he neared the twisted metal flying machine. Tad and Willy stood a few feet away while the girl's father tended to the silver-haired man lying motionless in the cockpit.

"Are you Rex?" The man's southern drawl was thick and Chase wondered why the girl didn't also possess it. "He's been askin for a Rex?"

"I am."

"I'm Wade Richland." The man extended a bloody hand and Chase took it. "I'm sorry son, but he's in pretty poor shape."

THE SENTINEL

Leonard lay amidst the twisted wreckage. His lower body disappeared into a small mass of metal while a broken wing strut pierced his upper body through the stomach. The Sentinel's chest shuddered as it rose and fell. Chase swallowed hard and fought tears as he kneeled next to his fallen friend, wiping the blood from the man's eyes, which fluttered open.

"Do I look as bad as I feel?"

"Worse." Chase let out a quick breath and smiled at Leonard's reaction. "I'm going to get you out of here and get you fixed up, though. We'll get your wife on the phone."

"No. No. You keep those butchers away from me. Nobody works on my dead body but Marilyn."

"You've got it. Nobody but Marilyn."

"Good. How are Willy and Tad?" Chase looked to his right and the two men both gave him a thumbs up. They were concealing their excitement at being reunited. "They're fine. Don't worry about all of us. We're fine."

"But that's my job. I'm The Sentinel. I worry about all of you."

"What can I do to help?" Chase disregarded the man's last comments. "I'll do anything you need."

"Can you get into my coat pocket?"

Chase looked at the bloody leather bomber jacket and reached into the nearest pocket. Inside he found two smooth, egg shaped stones. His eyes grew large as he felt the weight in his hands and rubbed his fingers across the objects.

"Where did you get these?"

"It's a long story. The stones aren't stones at all. They are pure energy and a concentrated form of what you've named Castleinium..."

"You're the man from Tad's story." Chase said.

"I am."

"Then you killed a grizzly bear with your bare hands, brought it back to life, then brought their father back from the dead as well."

"I used a knife." Leonard paused and smiled. "None of that is important anymore. My time as The Sentinel is coming to an end. You are the one Rex. You are the one who will take my place."

"I have no idea what you are talking about." Chase's head was swimming. "You're going to make it. We're going to stop Katsuo and Mother and whoever else tries to destroy the world, and then everything will just keep going on like before."

"Shhhhhh. Listen to me. Feel the stones in your hands. Hold them close to your chest. Can you read their inscriptions?"

Chase held the objects close and took notice of the abnormal writing on their surface. They were warm and he could feel their energy pulsing through his body. The inscriptions almost seemed to pop off the surface and though he couldn't read them he somehow knew what they meant.

"I can't read them, but I know what they say. This is strange."

"Good, good." Leonard smiled again as he released a deep breath and closed his eyes. "It will all be ok now."

"Wait. Leonard." Chase placed a hand on his mentor's cheek and the silver-haired man's eyes fluttered open once again. "What do you mean? I'm The Sentinel? Of what?"

"It's inside of you." Leonard raised his left arm and poked the young Rex Chase in the chest. "The energy is inside of you. In your genes."

"Is that why I've been so hungry?" Chase felt Holly kneel beside him. She seemed concerned. "Leonard?"

"It's why you've been so hungry. It's why your hip and shoulder have healed so fast. It's why those gunshot wounds will be better in a few hours. It's why you've had a little trouble controlling your temper. You're the key to it all."

"Are you saying that he has a gene that produces unlimited energy?"

Holly interjected into the conversation and Chase gave her a bewildered look.

"You've always been a smart one," Leonard said, "but you're wrong. The energy is unlimited. It is a biological process, though, and our bodies will wear out. Be mindful of your anger Rex. You wield more power than you understand."

"I stabbed a man in the leg and cheek for no reason earlier." Chase's nostrils flared as he closed his eyes and attempted to understand what was happening. A lot of the prior days' activities now seemed to be falling in line: the hunger, the healing, the indiscriminate ability to kill, the life-like visions of Mary Elizabeth, all made sense. Then it hit him and his eyes flew open. "This all began when I injected myself with the Castleinium solution. What have I started?"

"Don't worry." Leonard's breathing had become shallow and weak. "The solution gave you a boost, but most others will not be able to biologically manufacture..." His voice trailed off as his body began to spasm and his face twisted in agony. "Use the stones." Another round of spasms followed as the man fought for every last breath. "Stop them."

Leonard's body shook as his eyes rolled back in his head. Chase wept and Holly rested her cheek on his shoulder as tears poured down her face. Rex accepted the solace, taking her head in his right hand while embracing her with his left arm. Leonard had been like a second father to him the last eighteen months and he couldn't bear the thought of life without him. Then something remarkable happened. Leonard's body stopped shaking, his eyes burst open, and all pain seemed to leave his body as he spoke his final sentence.

"I never found out why Poppen is so darn old."

The Sentinel was dead.

****

THE SENTINEL

83.

International Harvester's half ton D2 pickup was one of Rex Chase's favorite designs to come from any manufacturer in 1938. The company had paid special attention to both design and functionality and that was something he could appreciate. Its suave lines intertwined with a smooth running Green Diamond 214 C.I.D. "L-Head" Engine and three speed transmission. It was a fine automobile.

As the vehicle rumbled down the road, though, Chase's mind wandered. Next to him sat Tad and Willy, huddled underneath a blanket Holly had given them. The brothers were happy to see one another despite the loss of Leonard, and that was understandable.

Rex stretched his legs and slumped down in the bed of the pickup truck. Unlike the Baxter boys he was warm. He could feel the energy from the stones coursing through his body and he now contemplated his next move. The General had to have backup on the way by now, but Leonard, Willy, Wade Richland, and Holly didn't seem like a true force to be reckoned with.

Chase lifted his bloody shirt and rubbed his hand over the bullet wound just under his left rib cage. The projectile had passed through his back and left a large hole in the front. That injury seemed more closed every second and Rex shut his eyes, imagining the energy healing his body.

Questions flooded his mind. What was the purpose of The Sentinel? How could he perform a job when he didn't even understand its duties? What duties had Leonard performed? Were there others who could manufacture Castleinium in their bodies? Was he some kind of mutant?

A large bump in the road bounced him up in the air and his butt slammed back into the bed of the truck. He turned and Holly smiled at him through the truck's rear window.

"Sorry."

She mouthed the words and Chase smiled while responding with a thumbs up. He found her to be intriguing and beautiful, but Sarah was his priority in women now. Rex closed his eyes once again and a picture of Mary Elizabeth burst into his mind's eye. Every inch of her being showed in perfect detail from the fleck of green in her right eye, to the two dimples nestled in her lower back. She would always be there.

Chase burst from his reverie and prepared for anything as the truck slowed and Richland laid on the horn. In one fluid motion Rex brought his face to the front while hopping to his feet and bringing the B.A.R. to rest in a firing position atop the pickup just as it came to a stop.

"Is that any way to greet your best friend?"

Chase left the Browning right where he had placed it and leapt from the D2. George Ahiga had been his closest friend since they were boys and it seemed like an eternity since they had seen one another. Tears streamed down his face once again as he picked up the stocky Navajo in a bear hug.

"Easy there fella. You're getting blood all over me."

"You'll live Chief. I see you brought the cavalry. Plan CF?"

"That I did. Plan CF."

Rex looked around at the fighting group of men. Plan CF consisted of a full company of soldiers numbering two-hundred men. Those two hundred men boasted twenty-five jeeps, ten M2 light tanks, and three Grumman F4F Wildcats. Every metal component of every vehicle consisted of Castleinium and the men had all been injected and supplied with the isolated syrettes Chase had developed. They had trained hard to become a mobile and efficient fighting force and now they were just that. It was the first time Rex had seen them assembled and a chill ran down his spine. He had envisioned and developed this.

"Edward Rex Chase."

"Dad." Chase turned to his left and covered the twenty yards to his father, picking him up in a bear hug much the same as he had Chief. "Where'd you come from?"

"I was over by that tree, taking a pee."

"I hope no one charged you a fee. Do you like to ski? I like to eat brie." Chase and his father shared a laugh. "Is that Captain Morris and Al Scherzer I see over there? We could use a couple of good men to fly these Wildcats."

"It's nice to see you again Rex." Morris approached and extended a hand and Chase shook it.

"Glad to see you're alright." Al nodded at Rex's stomach as he spoke. "None of that's your blood, right?"

"Some of it's mine. A lot of it is Leonard's."

The sound of men working on their vehicles and preparing for battle rode the cold winter air. Chief sniffled and wiped his nose. Alexei scratched his ear and spoke.

"Is he in the back of that truck?"

"I couldn't even get him out of the plane and he doesn't want anyone but Marilyn to touch his body." A fury broiled inside of Chase, but he breathed in through his nose and then blew the anger out. "It was one of his dying wishes and I intend for it to be kept. We need to get on the phone with The General right away. He'll be able to get a hold of her and we need to figure out our next course of action tonight."

"About that," Ahiga drug his toe through the dirt as he spoke. "We haven't been able to get The General on the phone, and reports are that there has been an explosion."

"An explosion?" Incredulity dominated Chase's voice as he processed the information. "So, bad news piled on top of more bad news. Hey Wade."

"Yeah."

"Do you mind if we get in the house and maybe get something warm to drink? Maybe we can wrap our heads around this a bit and decide what we're going to do next and who's in charge."

"Just from lookin at all these fellers right here I'd say you're in charge."

Chase looked at the men surrounding him. He considered them all his friends and in no way saw himself as superior, but you could see it in their eyes. They were looking to him for guidance.

"Well, in that case. Let's get in the house. These guys look cold."

"Holly. Get summa that chocolate cocoa stuff brewin, and some coffee." Richland shrugged his shoulders and scratched his head. "I dunno what we're gunna do with all these boys out here though. I guess they'll hafta sleep in the barn."

✱✱✱✱✱✱✱✱✱✱✱✱✱✱✱✱✱✱

84.

"Why am I hearing about this now?"

Mother let her anger show and Katsuo decided to play dumb.

"I didn't know about it until we were on the train. Perhaps it is Izanami with whom you have a problem?"

"Izanami. Even the two of you must realize by now she is no deity."

"Then why did you present her to us that way?" Shou said. "I haven't even met her."

"You've met her. You Japs are just so traditional and mythological." Mother paced back and forth, her gait interrupted by a slight drag in the left leg. "We thought it prudent to convince you to join us. I will get you Yasuhiro, though, you can be certain of that. Now stop changing the subject. You can't expect me to believe that Sarah kidnapped her biological mother just to wear a big wig and try to fool Rex Chase on the plane."

"Sarah is Izanami?" Shin said.

"Of course she is. Katsuo, answer me."

"So Amy Moreau is Sarah's biological mother?" Katsuo feigned a lack of knowledge. He and Shou had arranged the kidnapping. It had served multiple purposes, all of which were coming to fruition, though Shou was just now becoming privy. "I had no idea. How could I have known? Shin?"

"Maybe you shouldn't have kept us in the dark on so many things." Shin held his hands out to either side and shrugged his shoulders while showcasing his toothy yellow grin. "We are as trustworthy as it gets."

"Why Moreau is here is of no matter anyway," Katsuo said. "We need more troops Mother, and we need them now.

Rex Chase knows we're down to our last few, and he'll be bringing an army with him. I told you I would need a thousand men."

"Let them come. You fools seem to forget that we hold all the power, and we couldn't exactly sneak a thousand Japanese soldiers into Central Illinois anyway. By the way, what happened to your face?"

Katsuo seethed at being labeled a Jap and a fool as he touched his own cheek.

"You are the one who is foolish to underestimate this man. He has defeated us at every juncture against the greatest of odds." Katsuo's voice raised to the level of an orator as he spoke. "Izanami witnessed him create the same energy we wield so precariously from the palms of his own hands. He is dangerous."

"Tell me again why you didn't see it?"

Mother stopped her pacing and smirked as she delivered the line.

"Because he had already hit me three times with a .45 caliber pistol at forty yards before a single one of my men could fire a shot."

Katsuo was furious and it showed in every facet of his demeanor as he approached the old woman, grabbed her by the neck, and pinned her against the wall.

"Kill her." Shou seethed.

"We did everything you and Izanami asked and I still have not met my brother again. Give me one reason I should allow you to live."

"Because I am the only one who will help you find him." Mother's voice was frail and Katsuo released his grip. "Sarah doesn't hold the secret. Shou doesn't hold the secret. I am the one who can give you what you so desire."

Mother turned and exited the small room and Katsuo let his anger simmer. It felt good coursing through his veins and he contemplated everything that had happened. Shou stood nearby and Takahiro regretted not keeping his fellow Japanese warrior more informed. Mother had insisted on anonymity, as had Izanami, and he had agreed. The previous days' and weeks' events must have been even more unsettling for him.

"I apologize for keeping so many secrets Shin."

"You forget Katsuo. I moved through the same corrupt Imperial ranks as you. Maybe I'll surprise you. I think we've put ourselves in an advantageous position though. Amy Moreau was a nice touch."

"Thank you."

"She's in quite a huff." Sarah entered the room and Katsuo took in the sight of the beautiful woman. He regretted ever allowing her to wield her sultry charms on him. "Shin. It's so nice to meet you."

"Shut up." He said the words with force and could see the hurt in her eyes. "Don't give me that look."

"Katsuo." She ran her left hand down his arm while circling behind him and rubbing his neck. Her voice lowered and Katsuo could see the look of surprise on Shou's face. Her left hand sneaked down his side before coming to rest near his zipper. "What can I do for you to help ease this tension?"

"You could start by no longer lying to me." Takahiro pulled her arms away from his body and grabbed her around the throat. Her legs dangled in the air and he grinned at her helplessness. "Should I call you Izanami, or maybe Serena, or perhaps Sarah? Do you even know who you are?"

Katsuo felt the air rush from his body as she delivered a vicious kick to his private parts. He couldn't help but laugh even as the pain coursed through his body and doubled him over.

Takahiro looked up just as she attempted to kick him in the face, but he blocked the maneuver and she fell to the floor. Gone was the helpless, sultry, eager to please goddess. He had seen this woman before when she had helped kill his men on Populatic Pond.

"You don't know how to reunite me with Yasuhiro any more than I do. Admit it."

"I admit it." She stood as fire shot from her eyes. "I am the one who has put my life on the line over and over. I could have died on the river. I could have been caught when your men didn't fire on me at the cabin. I jumped a river on the back of a motorcycle in the middle of the snow."

"You had the stones to protect you."

"I did in the beginning, but not today."

"After everything you showed me and everything you promised, I expected more. You should die."

"Kill her." Shou said.

Katsuo stood over Izanami and contemplated killing the woman who first promised him Yasuhiro. She was a liar, but no fear showed in her eyes.

"Take it easy boys. I coordinated communications. I put people together to get the job done. Do you think what I have done is simple? Mother is the one with the information you desire Katsuo, but she loves me. I can control her."

"Ha."

Shin had been standing nearby watching the entire sequence of events while his mind raced. Even Katsuo had underestimated him, but that would no longer stand. He still held no trust for either of the German women, but Takahiro was an honorable man. His only weakness was the quest to be reunited with his brother. Shou twisted the omamari around his neck before making his play.

"The two of you think you're so smart and the rest of us are so stupid." Shou was going to put all his cards on the table and he addressed Katsuo first. "You think that Mother knows how to get you to Yasuhiro? Wrong. Her son might have had an idea, but she is just an old woman out for revenge." He pointed at Sarah next. "You think that you can control that insane old bat? She just sent her husband on a suicide mission."

"My grandfather died a hero." Sarah said.

"Shin..."

"I'm not finished yet." Shou began to pace as the volume of his voice raised. "You picked me for this job because I am a superior aviator, a competent fighter, and have an ability to see the big picture. You've attempted to keep me in the dark at every turn, and yet here I am, more informed than either of you. I know the two of you kept me in the shadows on the dam project, but do you even know how to use it?" He could see the bewildered looks in their eyes and it fueled him. "I've been on my own since I was a little boy. Nobody ever looked out for me, and even when I thought I had risen to a point where I would be taken care of some bureaucrat had to pull the rug out from under me. I owe this opportunity to you Katsuo, but you were wrong to trust them over me. I can tell you how to see your brother again. I am the key."

He paused for effect, and decided that perhaps he would gauge their responses. The two stood silent for a minute before Katsuo spoke.

"I don't understand Shin."

"Neither do I."

"Of course you don't."

Shou was glad he had let them speak. They were now captive to him. He was their new leader and Mother would never get it back. Shin began pacing once more as he closed his eyes to tell a story.

"One of my earliest missions against the Soviet Union was a smash and grab. I had been on a few of them before, but it was the first I had led. Do you remember it Katsuo?"

"We needed mathematicians, but the mission failed. You brought us one good mind."

"Ah yes." A yellowed smile dominated his face as he continued. "I remember the disappointed speech you gave me. We lost thousands of good men and gained almost nothing. I was sick about it and many a Russian soldier paid for your lies. The man I grabbed in that mission, though, turned out to be a very special man. He was, in fact, the exact objective of the mission. I doubt Mother told you that, but when I became informed about our secret carrier and other plans it all reminded me of the reams of data we gathered from his remote workshop. The Russian is the brains behind Mother's plans and was working for her son before his death. He is the one who can show you the way to your brother, and he is the one who has cracked the secret of the stones. Mother's plan is archaic and small minded."

Shin breathed in deep as adrenaline pulsed through his veins. The story had brought all his frustrations and anger to the surface. They had underestimated him for the last time.

"Only I have the full trust of The Russian. With me we will rule the planet. Why settle petty disputes by destroying the Americans when we can subjugate them all?" He paused and his heart leapt as he saw the utter shock in their eyes. "I WILL BE THE FIRST EMPEROR OF THE WORLD."

****

85.

"So you see, when I cross-pollinate the different varieties I end up getting a sweet corn that fixes sugar at a much higher rate while still holding onto the drought resistance capabilities of the inferior tasting corn."

Holly had been explaining genes and their evolution to the men although few of them knew why. Her knowledge impressed Chase and he had learned that she had studied at the University of Illinois. Wade Richland was a country boy through and through, and she was not just beautiful, but smart. He seemed to be running into a lot of those girls. Rex smiled and clapped as she concluded.

"Well done. Well done indeed."

The other men joined him and her cheeks turned a bright shade of crimson as she picked up dishes from the table.

"Come on guys. I know when you're patronizing a girl. You're all just lucky I'd made such a big batch of cookies. I knew we were going to be having a few visitors, but not this many."

"I apologize for the inconvenience ma'am." Chase stood and took her hand in his, kissing it and her cheeks turned an even darker shade of red. "You're as brilliant a cook as you are a geneticist."

"She's not a bad shot with that Tommy Gun either." Willy added. "She had those Japanese fellas on the run for sure."

"I wish I could have seen it." Chase hadn't taken his gaze off the gorgeous young woman and a sudden wave of guilt passed through him. He cleared his throat before speaking again. "Anyway, we have some business to take care of. Katsuo is down to less than fifty men. I think we need to get in there as soon as possible. Do you have a plan in place Major?"

Major Julius Maximillian Prentice was a first generation American whose parents had emigrated from Greece while his mother was still pregnant. He had risen through the ranks in the army and when the opportunity to work for The Organization had arisen he had pounced upon it. Plan CF was his life and he knew the men inside and out.

"We have schematics of the power plant itself and I look forward to a debrief from you about the interior of the complex. Our men are more than capable of putting down fifty dissenters with ease."

"I'll give you my brief before bed." Chase rubbed his eyes. He was getting tired. "I'm assuming you guys haven't just been sitting around while I was taking drugs and riding motorcycles. Whatya got for me?"

His father and George led the descriptions of the previous days' events. Chase heard about the ring of cables surrounding the country as well as the light bending force fields surrounding the carrier. The consensus was that Mother intended to burn the United States to ash. Rex yawned as a strange feeling came over him. He turned to see an old man walking through the kitchen into the dining area where they sat.

"Bobby?"

"I look a little worse for wear, don't I?" Poppen smiled upon meeting his idol. "It is an honor to meet you."

"I, I, I'm at a loss." Chase stood and laughed as he crossed the room and hugged the old man who was one of his best friends. "You died."

"You can give me a real hug. I'm old, not a china doll."

The room erupted in laughter as Chase picked up his lost friend and gave him a proper hug. His mind raced and Leonard's last words made sense. Why was he so old?

"Why didn't anyone tell me about this?" Chase pulled a chair out for Bobby who took it. "I mean, this is a big deal. What are we talking about? Time travel? Light speed travel? Come on guys. Talk to me."

The room erupted in laughter once again as Chase fired off question after question without allowing anyone the time to answer. All thoughts of tiredness left his body as he wrapped his mind around this wondrous puzzle. Bobby Poppen was back.

"What do you know about multiverses son?"

Alexei Chase spoke the words and Rex was off and running with it before the sentence even ended.

"A lot more than anyone else here I suppose, except maybe Bobby. I get it though. It makes sense, especially with what you've been telling me about dual force fields with light bending properties and high performance carriers that lose all speed."

"Well, I'm glad it makes sense to you," Ahiga said, "because I have no idea what you're talking about."

Men agreeing with Ahiga accompanied another round of laughter.

"I suppose if you had two of those fields you could make the inside field a stasis chamber while the mass between the inner and outer fields acts as a delivery device across the separate universes. It would all be pretty static." All eyes shifted to Holly and they could have heard a pin drop. "What? I took physics in college."

She blushed once again and Chase grinned ear to ear.

"I couldn't have said it better myself, but where did you guys get the power to do that?"

"The power isn't the problem." Alexei stood and joined Holly at the sink, picking up a towel to help her dry. "The real problem is in the math."

"You're right there," Chase joined his father and began putting dishes away while the other men at the table fidgeted, ashamed they had not offered a hand. "Even with a stationary set of fields, you would need Poppen's equation, but he was on the other side. Tell me we have that equation."

"We have that equation," Poppen smiled. He didn't feel the slightest bit guilty for not helping. "I wrote it down for you so you couldn't forget."

Chase read the Poppen Equation for the first time and the synapses in his brain responded by firing at three times their normal rate. Doors opened that hadn't been there before. The impossible would soon be possible.

"This, this, this is amazing Bobby, but it still doesn't explain how you got here."

"Or why he's so old," Chief said.

"That too," Rex conceded.

"The only explanation I have for it was that it would take a quantum computer."

"Yeah, that would do it, and I suppose they have those in 2020, or wherever you're from, but here in 1938 we're lacking in quantum computing supplies. I just don't get it."

"That's a secret that died with Leonard."

Ahiga said the words and a somber silence fell over the room. Just the slight clanking of dishes as Chase put them away interrupted the solace and Rex used the moments to think. So much had happened and so much more needed to be accomplished. He had an edge now, though. He had two of the stones, and he knew what to do with them. He had the Poppen equation and he knew how to use it too. Katsuo, Mother, Izanami and whomever else were in for a rude awakening tomorrow.

"I have one more thing for you Mr. Chase."

"Don't call me that Bobby. We've been friends for years."

"It's about Sarah."

"What about her?"

"She is Dietrich Hoff's kidnapped daughter. She is Izanami. She is Sarah Marie Moreau, biological daughter of Christian and Amy Moreau."

"Who is missing." Alexei added.

"Correct."

Chase paused as he set a dish in its place. It made sense now. He knew that something had seemed off when he had seen the back of Izanami's head on that plane. That set of slumped shoulders was the same pair he had seen leaning over to dip a towel in cool water in France. It was the woman who had broken his fever and warned him not to hate. If he hadn't been so delirious from the drugs he would have found out Sarah earlier. He owed Amy Moreau his life and he knew Katsuo had her.

"She's in the compound and I'm going to get her out. Everyone get a good night's sleep. We attack in the morning."

★★★★★★★★★★★★★★★★★★

86.

Brilliant streaks of orange, purple, and yellow reflected off the cirrostratus cloud formation twenty thousand feet overhead. The dawn of a new day gained ground on the barren Central Illinois November landscape, revealing the Plan CF fighting force in position and ready to advance. Ahead, the innocuous outer field shimmered and Chase kicked a mound of powdery snow as he glanced at his watch. It was 6:35 A.M.

"Whatya think Major?"

"I don't see a soul." Major Prentice peered through a pair of field glasses before removing them from his neck and stowing them in the back of his Jeep. "The men are ready and briefed. We are all waiting on your order."

Chase breathed through his nostrils, letting the cold November air provide oxygen to his body. A monumental argument with Chief and his father an hour before had him sitting the invasion out. Major Prentice and his men would storm the complex. Major Prentice and his men would attempt to apprehend Mother, Sarah, Katsuo and Shou. Major Prentice and his men would finish the job Rex Chase considered his own.

His father and best friend, however, had been correct. With Leonard's death and The General out of contact he was the acting leader of The Organization. Chase adjusted his M1 helmet before squeezing the stones nestled in his jacket pocket. They were warm and a sense of power flowed through his veins.

"I'm dying to be out there with ya Major." Chase looked at the sky above. Leading from the rear wasn't his style. "Take em in."

"Yes, sir."

The order went out and the steady sound of idling diesel engines increased tenfold. Chase breathed through his nostrils again, relishing the scent of the mixture of fuels. It reminded him of their brief time in the German tanks outside of Hoff's ballroom.

"Penny for your thoughts?" Chief had taken up station alongside Rex who smiled before responding.

"I was just thinking about a couple of crazy kids who took on two, fifty millimeter guns with FG42's and then hijacked German tanks equipped with a hundred five millimeter cannons so that they could blow a hole in a multi-million dollar mansion."

"Chyeah." Chief smiled. "I'm glad we never got the bill on that one."

****

87.

"Mother. Mother." Katsuo spoke in a hoarse whisper so as not to startle the old woman. "Mother. They are here."

Katsuo had worked with Linda Hoff, her husband David and granddaughter Sarah for eighteen months now. He was not a stupid man and had known Sarah was no deity for quite some time, but some of the things he had seen had caused him to believe. Aligning Japanese interests once again with the Hoff Empire had been necessary to appease these women, but as Takahiro watched Linda struggle out of bed he knew her usefulness was past.

"Let me help you."

"I don't need any help."

She slapped his hand away and Katsuo smiled, though it was too dark for her to see.

"As I predicted Rex Chase has arrived with a formidable force, although it is smaller than I had imagined it would be."

"Rex Chase this. Rex Chase that." Mother stepped behind a traditional Japanese folding screen Katsuo had presented her as a gift. "David sacrificed himself to cut off the head of The Organization. The others will fall in line and be lost without him."

"You are foolish." Anger built in Katsuo's stomach. "Have you forgotten that it was Rex Chase who killed your son?"

"You don't need to speak of my son," she said. "Rex Chase was under orders from General John Francis Reagan. He was the brains behind everything The Organization ever did. Without him, they are done." Mother finished changing clothes and stepped into the light. "Just because this child has bested you a few times you are now so scared. It doesn't suit you."

She turned her back on him and Katsuo seethed.

"It is never sound strategy to underestimate your adversary. I am advocating that we proceed with caution. Their force is formidable and far exceeds the defenses our fifty men can provide."

"Have you forgotten we are surrounded by impenetrable shields of energy? Have you forgotten we are hours away from obliterating the Americans the way you always wanted? Have you forgotten about the years of abject racism and sub-human treatment? You of all people should want Rex Chase to witness these events. After this we will find the remaining two stones and then I can reunite you with Yasuhiro."

"Is that why we need the stones?"

"If you get me the final two stones, I'll get you Yasuhiro."

She pulled back the shades on her window and the morning's first light flooded into the room. A slight adjustment in the fields allowed them to see out, and Katsuo squinted as his eyes adjusted to view the force which now advanced on their position. Mother was a fool, but he was not. He had not forgotten about the years of racism and sub-human treatment, but he also planned on living through the day. Rex Chase had penetrated their shields before and Takahiro assumed he could do it again.

Katsuo glanced through the window before following Mother out of the room to the main control facility. A new plan formulated in his mind and he needed to speak with Shou in private.

"I'm coming brother. I'm coming."

****

88.

"It's a little different than the last time huh?"

His father's voice interrupted the waning sounds of diesel engines as Rex fidgeted with the stones.

"I just can't get over this feeling that I should be up there with them."

"You're not Alexander the Great. You can't just lead from the front anymore."

Chief said the words and Rex relaxed even as the forces ahead advanced.

"Alexander the Great? Somebody has been doing some reading." The three men shared a laugh before Chase continued. "It just seems so strange. They're up there about to head into battle and I'm back here with you two, a redneck, his beautiful smart daughter, and a hundred year old man."

"She is a sight," Alexei said.

"Smarter than me," Chief added.

"It just feels like we're missing something. Like... It's too easy." Something inside him screamed that he should be with the men, but his intellect told him otherwise. They were right. He had responsibilities now and should be protected. "Major Prentice has it handled, though. I know he's the man for the job."

"So, what is in store for the stones?" Poppen joined the group of men.

"Yeah, what do those inscriptions mean anyway?" Alexei asked. "Are they some kind of weapon?"

"No, they aren't a weapon at all." Chase craned his neck and picked up a pair of field glasses to better monitor the company's advance. "They're more like a protective shield when in pairs and activated, but at the same time they are also a window."

"Yeah, Leonard mentioned something like that, but they weren't working. Maybe he didn't have them activated right." Poppen said.

"Somehow I doubt he didn't understand their function, since I know Katsuo and his men are able to raise and lower the inner field. Katsuo did have them in a darkened room, though," Chase said. "You could see what they were seeing; it was just that they were seeing blackness."

"Makes sense," Chief said. "So what happens when you get them all together?"

"I don't suppose I'll know until I get them all together."

"Sure wish Leonard was still around for that," Poppen said.

"He could have told me about all of this a thousand times, though, but he didn't. For some reason he felt like it was something I needed to do myself."

"Like a parent."

"What?"

"Like a parent teaching their children." Alexei put his hand on Rex's shoulder. "I must have told you a thousand times not to touch the stove when you were little, but you kept trying anyway. One time I warned you, but let you go ahead and do it anyway. You burned your finger a little, but never did it again. Leonard was just saving himself time."

"Huh."

Chase continued to peer through the field glasses. Not a soul attempted to repel the Plan CF troops. All was quiet. It was too quiet.

"You know, I've been thinking a lot about the USS Fox. What happened to them is bugging me." Chief broke the momentary silence.

"You guys didn't tell me about the Fox." Chase brought the glasses down. "What happened with the Fox?"

"They sent out an S.O.S. which got cut off and then they disappeared."

"They disappeared?"

"Off the face of the planet," Chief said.

"Where did this happen?"

"In the same spot where we found the carrier."

Chase dropped the glasses on the ground and took off in a sprint. His focus was pristine and his mission clear. All iota of doubt had left his mind, but it was too late.

Molecules between the inner and outer fields of the compound leapt thousands of degrees and held steady as a brilliant blue ball of energy materialized from nothingness. The ground seemed to pulse with the radiant azure death as men and machines obliterated into nonexistence. Chase shouldered his rifle and stood in awe as he witnessed the silent carnage. The orb towered thousands of feet in the air. It was magnificent. It was a massacre. He had allowed it. Then it was over.

"Everyone at the Jeep right now."

Anger coursed through his veins: anger over his leadership error, anger he hadn't recognized it earlier, anger he hadn't had every bit of information. He breathed in deep as he heeded Leonard's advice while meeting eyes with every person at the rear of the Jeep. Two minutes passed as he allowed his emotions to subside. Anger would not control him.

"We should have seen that coming. It was a stupid mistake and I will not let it happen again. From now on, if I say

I'm going to lead from the front, then I'm going to lead from the front." Chase paused as a single Wildcat landed, taxied to their position, and killed its engine. "You made it Captain."

Bryan Morris dismounted and approached the lone vehicle.

"I can't say the same for Al. He got caught in that big blue thing. What was that?"

"I want you to hop right back in that plane, take Wade with you, and go back for the other Wildcat. If anything gets out of here in the air I want you to follow it. How is your eyesight?"

"Did you know that Makai tribesman from Kenya can see what someone is doing at over a mile and can recognize who it is?"

"No, I didn't."

"Well, it's about as good as that."

"Perfect. I want you to fly high. From what I hear he's nimble and fast. Your service ceiling should be well above his. I just want to know where he's going. Wade, how about you?"

"Shooooot. I's can see a pig fly at a thousand yards. Come on Holly."

"Nope." Chase overruled the father. "I need her here. I'm already going to be asking too much from a hundred year-old-man."

Richland's mouth opened to protest, but instead he kissed his daughter on the forehead and joined Morris who had already fired the Wildcat's engine. The duo taxied away as Chase continued.

"Here is what is going to happen. Chief and I are going in alone."

"But won't they just fry you with that blue thing again?" Holly asked and Chase answered.

TIM WHEAT

"They'll try, but like I said, once activated, the stones act as a protective shield. An outer field is created by focusing scalar energy using Castleinium mined from the earth, and the stones create an inner field which protects those inside from a blast focused between the two. The more Castleinium there is in a structure or person, the larger the outer field."

"And the more stones you have, the larger the inner field," Poppen said.

"Right Bobby. That's why there were thirty stones when they imprisoned us inside the power plant, and that's why it was so warm in there and the flowers were blooming and leaves were on the trees."

"What?" Chief said.

"When we were escaping the compound earlier all the plants inside the first field were in full bloom, and it was warm."

"Of course," Alexei said, "because it's a stasis field, everything within is ageless."

"You've got it," Chase continued, "and the reason they had thirty stones before was because they were using some to protect the carrier. When the stones were no longer aboard and activated it was no longer protected."

"So they could have fried me at any time?" Chief asked.

"Maybe they like you."

The group shared a brief laugh as the tension eased. Minutes before evil had shaken his confidence to the core, but now he laid out his plan with supreme poise. It wasn't perfect, but time was of the essence. Whomever was in the power plant had shown their capabilities and Chase believed it was just a matter of time until they annihilated the United States. He wasn't going to let that happen.

✳✳✳✳✳✳✳✳✳✳✳✳✳✳✳✳✳✳

89.

"You know they're going to try to burn us alive when we get in the kill zone."

"I know."

"You're sure those two little stones are going to keep us safe?"

"Shoot, I don't even think I need them anymore when we're this close to all that Castleinium. My body will act like a shield all by itself."

"So you're invincible?" Chief asked.

"Not quite. By factoring into the Poppen equation how much injectable Castleinium I administered myself and assuming it hasn't deteriorated, I should be able to exude a natural field when surrounded by this much of the isotope." Chase said. "Once we get away from all of this, though, that could change."

"So what happens when we get away from here?"

"It depends on a number of things I could measure in a lab." Chase theorized. "I'll be as mortal as any of you. Over time, though, and depending on the saturation rate of the isotope my body could become its own field anywhere."

"And you could travel through time, approach light speed, and be invisible on a whim."

"I bet it will start with the ability to fly."

"Without a plane."

"Yep." Chase grinned as the prospect of natural flight sparked his imagination. "It's better if you hold the stones now, though. You know, in case we get separated."

The two men walked at a steady pace and George laughed as Chase offered him the stones.

"Take em if you want em Chief, but do it now. These things are heavy."

George stopped dead in his tracks. They were a few feet away from the outer field.

"You're sure they're activated."

"Just as sure as I am that we won't need them."

"How much is that in percent?"

"More than fifty." Chase paused, a sly grin crossed his lips. "At least fifty-three or fifty-four."

"Shoot, I would have been fine with fifty-one."

George pocketed the heavy objects and stepped across the invisible barrier. Chase hurried to catch up as he took notice of his childhood friend. Both arms almost burst from the seams of the field jacket and inches of tanned skin showed above his boots. Rex's smile widened as he took up position next to the stocky Navajo.

"Did you and Bobby get your uniforms switched up or have you hit a growth spurt?"

90.

"Who?"

"Rex Chase and George Ahiga."

"Give me those."

Shin Shou grabbed the binoculars from Katsuo's hands and brought them to his face. Much to his amazement Rex Chase and George Ahiga strolled across open ground to the south. It was like they were two old friends on a Sunday stroll.

"You assured me George Ahiga was dead." Annoyance tinged Mother's voice. "How else have you failed me Shin?"

"They're inside of the outer field." Shou turned and spoke to the man running the control panel. "Hit them again."

"What do you think you're doing?" Mother's tone had gone from annoyed to angry. "I'm in charge here."

Shou shot her an icy glare and repeated the order.

"Hit them again."

The young man obeyed Shou's second command and a cool blue hue bathed the room. Shin watched through the window while keeping tabs on Mother out of the corner of his eye. Her stoic gaze peered ahead and her hands balled into fists. Shou smiled before turning his head to speak again.

"Alright, that shoul..."

"Look." Sarah watched a few feet away and now pointed to the yard below. "Look."

Shin blinked as he turned to face the window again and what he witnessed boggled his mind. Rex Chase and George Ahiga walked unharmed across the courtyard toward the atrium below. Chase even skipped a few times as the fledgling security force surrounded the two men.

"What did they...How did they..."

TIM WHEAT

His voice trailed off and his fury boiled as Mother laughed. Shou's anger needed an outlet and there was but one logical place for it to go. He pulled the 8mm Nambu from its holster and shot the soldier running the control panel in the face. The young man fell to the floor and cried in agony as Shou crossed the small room, put his boot on the hapless man's chest and fired four more times.

"Over did it a bit, don't you think?" Katsuo said.

"When I give an order I don't expect to repeat it."

A fleeting calm filled the room as a crimson pool of blood inched from under the control station. Mother was the first to speak.

"They just walked right through it. What are you going to do now Shin?"

Shou looked to Katsuo who nodded and moved in behind Mother.

"Shin was wrong to supersede your authority, but you were about to issue the same order." Mother turned and faced the hardened fisherman and soldier as Takahiro continued in a controlled tone. "I told you we needed more men and you didn't give them to me. I warned you Rex Chase was dangerous and you ignored me. When they come inside you say your piece and then I'll take over. You brought me in to deal with men like this."

"Perhaps we should turn America into a wasteland right now," Mother said. "Then they'll have nothing to fight for."

"If you kill everyone they love you won't live through the day." Sarah said.

"These are the men who killed your father Sarah." Mother's tone was incredulous. "Do you suggest we let them go?"

"I suggest that when you sent fifty men to kill him and me in Massachusetts we walked away unscathed." Sarah glared at Katsuo who smiled and shrugged. "I suggest that he escaped your inescapable prison, killed more of our men, and came back for more. I suggest perhaps he is more than we can handle without all the stones. We should leave and live to fight another day. The dam project will allow us to…"

"Coward." Shin said. "Do you even know how to use the dam project? Do you believe Mother is still leading any of this? Look around yourselves fools. She is an old woman with no son, no power, and no future."

Tension was at an apex in the room as the command structure crumbled. Distrustful looks passed from person to person and Shou met eyes with each before landing on Katsuo. Even his most trusted mentor had attempted to keep the transportation device hidden, but Shin had proved himself worthy of the cat and mouse game all were playing.

"She's not wrong. We still don't have the final two stones and it makes little sense to risk our lives now."

"Hey Kitty." Chase shouted from below and interrupted the stressed conversation. "I hear gunshots. Is everything OK up there? Anyway, I don't know if you're in charge, or your mommy, or the fake goddess, or maybe even Stinky Shoe. The fact of the matter is that I don't even care. You ought to call these guys off out here, though, before we have to kill them all. They look like they're sixteen."

"Then again," Katsuo seethed. "I'd rather enjoy seeing Rex Chase's corpse."

91.

"What do you mean they are all leaving?"

"Am I speaking a foreign language? I mean they are all leaving."

Bobby smiled as Holly handed him the field glasses. Along with Alexei they had driven to the south and circled back around, penetrating the inner field thirty seconds before the blue death. Poppen's heart seemed to beat against his chest bones, but he felt alive as he peered through the magnifying tool.

"Huh, they passed right through it and now all the guards are leaving. Just like Rex said they would."

"Just like he said they would." Holly's smile was contagious and the other men joined.

"So you up for a hike old timer?" Alexei put his hand on Poppen's shoulder as Bobby dismounted the Jeep.

"I haven't been on a hike since I've turned a hundred, or am I twenty-three?"

"Don't look at me," Holly said.

"Me neither," Alexei chimed.

"Oh well, I guess it doesn't matter either way." Poppen began walking toward the massive complex ahead. "I hope you guys remember how he told us to get in. This place is huge."

****

92.

Rex navigated through the glass atrium, down the hall, and into the unlit room. He and Chief now stood in the middle swallowed by absolute darkness. Seconds passed and then a minute without a sound.

"I'd give my life's savings for one of those wooden thingy's to stick under that door," Chief said. "That'd give us a little light to see."

"Hey Kitty." Chase cupped his hand to his mouth. "Here Kitty, Kitty."

"Very good Mr. Chase." Mother's voice emanated from the darkness. "We all think you are very funny."

"And who are you all?"

"I've been told you ask excellent questions." The old woman's voice seemed familiar, but Chase couldn't quite put a finger on it. "Do you know who I am?"

"Well, right now I can't even see my hand in front of my face, so no, I don't know who you are."

"I apologize Mr. Chase. I was also told you would be well informed. Perhaps your lack of information could have saved a life today."

Rex fought to control his rising anger as the faces of each man in the company rolled through his mind.

"I suppose we can share blame for the death of my men."

"Oh, no, I can't share blame for that. Shin ordered their deaths. I was referring to the death of your beloved General Reagan."

Chase's mind raced as he pondered the possibilities. The General had not been in contact and there were reports of an explosion, but his death was not yet a certainty. She could be bluffing.

"I just talked to him an hour ago. Early bird gets the worm I always say. Also, I'm not sold on daylight savings time for you folks here in the Midwest. I mean, we coul…"

"Silence." Mother's voice trembled and her anger satisfied Chase. "He is dead. I know that he is dead."

"How?" Chief joined the conversation. "Did you kill him yourself?"

"No. Bring up the lights."

Mother issued the command and soft yellow light bathed the room. Chase's eyes were able to adjust and he scanned the previous battle zone. The stones were no longer present, but there was a surprising lack of damage. Many of the pillars suffered superficial holes and the walls matched, but the room was intact. Someone had even swept and dusted.

"The place looks great guys." Rex noticed they hadn't replaced the machine gun posts above. "Your maid service did an excellent job cleaning up in here. I mean, I've known…"

"You stall and you stall." Mother's voice became louder as she approached on the balcony above. Chase had guessed there to be an antechamber behind and he could see her enter and walk into the light. "I know your general is dead because my husband, David Hoff killed him."

"Linda Prepot," Chase said. "I'm guessing that would make you Linda Hoff and I doubt if I'm stretching too far when I assume Rick was your son?"

"Who is Rick?"

"You've heard his affinity for giving people nicknames." Sarah entered the room and Chase's heart sank. She had fooled him. "What was mine again? The fake goddess? Not your best effort."

"Sometimes I deliver. Sometimes I don't."

"I still don't know who Rick is."

"Dietrich. Rick. Get it Grandmother?" Sarah's voice was playful. "She's getting a bit on in age."

"From down here I'd say she's about a hundred and eighty," Chief said. "How am I going to explain this to my wife Sarah? You're going to break her heart."

"I enjoy your wife's company. You boys did kill my father last year, though. It's time you pay."

"Your father?" Chase's tone shifted yet again. "Dietrich Hoff killed your real father. His name was…"

"Silence." Linda Hoff's voice carried more weight than usual, though it seemed more tense than he remembered, and an easy smile crossed Rex's lips.

"The truth is out there Linda, and something tells me it's a lot closer than she knows."

"Well done Mr. Chase."

"Call me Rex, Kit-Kat. It's nice of you to join us. You've got a little something on your cheek right there. It could be a piece of cake or something. I don't know."

Katsuo had stepped from the other room unnoticed and Chase peered into the darkness behind the balcony. He tapped a quick message on Chief's leg and received an instant response. The two had learned to communicate via Morse code as boys and this wasn't the first time it had served them well.

He tapped: *Shou in shadows: stop Moreau is kneeled: query*

Chief replied: *Confirmed Shou: stop Confirmed Moreau: stop*

"We might as well get on with the main event then." Linda's voice had a nervous tinge to it and Chase noticed a slight look of bewilderment on Sarah's face. "Are you ready for your country to burn Mr. Chase?"

Before Chase could even respond Katsuo pulled the 8mm Nambu pistol from its holster and shot Linda Hoff in the back of the head. Her aged body fell to its knees before crashing face first into the ground. No electrical pulses fired. No darkness closed in around her. The matriarch of the Hoff Empire was just dead.

A genuine look of horror along with speckles of her grandmother's blood now dominated Sarah's face. His mind raced as the coup developed before their eyes. Plans were changing and he tapped on Chief's leg.

Katsuo is boss: stop save Moreau is mission: stop give up stones is ok: stop

Chief shot him a look after the reference to the stones, but tapped back.

Use our guns: query

Follow my lead

"Look fellas," Chase took a step toward the balcony as he spoke. "I don't know what kind of little family dispute you have going on up there, but why don't you just give us Amy and we'll be on our way."

"I'd like to inform you that I had my men wire this entire room with RDX in anticipation of our visit today. I am prepared to die, are you Mr. Chase?"

"I'd rather not Kit-Kat," Chase noticed a door at his two o'clock open, and he waved his hand in an attempt to call off the other portion of the mission, "but I'm no soothsayer. I'd settle for just you dying."

"I can still incinerate the U.S. you know. Shin and I would prefer to see you suffer though."

"Yeah, that's where you're wrong." Chief took up station to Rex's right and winked before continuing. "After I stole your carrier The General had a little talk with The President and they thought it prudent to shut down the grid. Did you know that every substation and cable relay area has a disconnect? I know I sure didn't, but I guess that's why they get paid the big bucks and you and I are here shooting old ladies in the head."

"W,W,W, What are you saying?"

Katsuo's voice filled with doubt and Chase seized the initiative.

"He's saying they've shut down your main continent killing weapon. You're out of the genocide business."

"Sorry Kit-Kat."

Chase smiled at his friend's use of the nickname.

"They wouldn't dare shut down power to the entire nation." Doubt had crept into Katsuo's voice and Chase fueled the flames.

"It'll just be a bit longer. A lot of the country folk have had electricity in their homes for about ten years or so anyway. They'll be fine."

"We still have her." Shou dragged a whimpering Amy Moreau by the hair as he entered the light near the balcony's edge. "We still have the stones and we still have the dam too. You're looking well for a dead man."

Shou addressed Chief directly who shifted his weight before answering.

"You know what they say about bad pennies Shinny."

"Sarah."

Amy's voice was desperate and she kicked Shin who dropped the woman. She covered the ground to Sarah in less than a second, falling to her knees as she wept.

"Sarah Marie Moreau. My daughter Sarah."

Chase could see tears welling in Sarah's eyes and couldn't help but feel bad for her. She had been kidnapped and brainwashed and now it was all falling apart.

"They told me you were a dream. I saw you once at that ball. You tapped fath... umm... Dietrich on the shoulder. It confused me, but I saw you get dragged out and then they told me you weren't real. I, I, I..."

The two women embraced and sobbed. Katsuo stood nearby and sneered while Shin rubbed his arm. Somehow this was part of their plan.

"Kill them both."

Shou uttered the words and Katsuo's Nambu 8mm rose. Rex knew Chief would be reacting and he threw his right arm in front of his friend.

"If you kill them I won't help you find Yasuhiro."

Katsuo's motion stopped and his head cocked to the side as he seemed to be studying Chase. Just a few steps away, pure, unadulterated hate was shooting from Shou's eyes.

"He's lying. The Russian and I can help you find Yasuhiro. Kill them both."

"I noticed you don't have the stones circling the pillars anymore." Chase rubbed his left hand down the side of one of the smooth limestone supports. "It's too bad too. It turns out I have a knack for these things."

Chase held out his hand and Chief delivered the two stones. Rex placed their inscriptions together, turned the objects counter to one another, and let them go. They began to form a pattern in the air.

"That's what they call an infinity symbol fellas. Watch this."

THE SENTINEL

Rex grabbed the lead stone with his right hand and held it in place as the corresponding orb tapped it three times in short succession. A great feeling of satisfaction crept through his body as he noticed the two Japanese killers had become distracted. The two stones made a box in the sky and then a perfect vision of a cockpit materialized from nothingness.

"It's beautiful."

Shin spoke the words and Katsuo's mouth was agape. He seemed speechless as Chase manipulated the stones while tapping a message to his friend

What dam query

No idea stop

"Cockpit. Cockpit. Cockpit. Cockpit." Chase spoke the words as he received Chief's reply. "If I didn't know better, I'd say someone is taking these somewhere."

"In an airplane." Katsuo's demeanor had done another one-hundred and eighty degree turn as he brought the Nambu to bear on Shin Shou. "You told me you loaded them into my boat."

"Why would I put them on a stupid boat when they'll be out of the area today by plane?"

Shou's tone was incredulous as he pulled an identical Nambu 8mm from his own holster and crossed the room. Katsuo continued to track the man with his gun, but the elder Japanese was not the object of the younger's lust for death. Chase yanked his Colt 1911 from its holster just as Shou started to pull the Nambu's trigger, but Ahiga was quicker.

Chief's hands were a blur and Rex heard the first shot which buried itself in Shou's thigh. The Nambu barked almost at the same time, but the Japanese hitman's aim faltered. Chase hurried his first flurry meant to impact Shin Shou's head and put three rounds off the back wall. He took careful aim as the young aviator raised the Nambu once again.

Chase breathed in through his nose then let the air out. Katsuo was emptying a full magazine in Rex's direction, but it didn't faze the fledgling Sentinel. He wasn't sure who or what he should protect, but it was going to start with the two women clutching each other in fear on the balcony above. Yellow streaks of light materialized all around him as he squeezed the trigger and the dutiful report of the 1911 reached his ears. Another bevy of sounds joined the sudden free-for-all and Chase picked them out one by one. An explosion, the crumbling of concrete, the twisting of metal, and the initial cries of the wounded were all separate audible entities and accompanied by a sensation he recognized well. He was falling.

"I guess they didn't get the message."

✵✵✵✵✵✵✵✵✵✵✵✵✵✵✵✵✵

93.

"Alright, this is the middle one right here," Alexei whispered. "Let's get around the corner and I think we're all set."

Alexei, Holly, and Bobby Poppen were in an anteroom behind the main chamber where Rex and Chief stood. RDX connected to a plunger now skirted a number of support columns for the balcony above. Holly spoke in a low voice as they snuck around the corner to relative safety.

"I don't understand why he doesn't just walk right up to Katsuo and punch him in the face. They can't shoot him right?"

"Unless they have Castleinium bullets he'll be protected," Bobby said. "They still could annihilate the U.S. though."

"That's why he can't just..."

The muffled sound of a single gunshot popped from the balcony overhead and Bobby froze in his tracks.

"Wait." The elder Chase peeked around the corner and spotted a doorway leading into the other room. He worked the handle, cracked the door, and used his shoe to prop it open. "Now we should be able to hear a little better."

Bobby continued around the corner as the conversation in the other room became audible. The plan required them to wait until Katsuo, Shou, Mother, Izanami, and any other nefarious characters were on the balcony and then collapse it to the floor below. Rex and Chief would then subdue the remaining villains, collect the stones, and they would all ride off into the sunset.

"I think he's trying to tell me something." Alexei whispered the words before ducking behind the door. "I think he wants us to hide."

"We are hiding." Holly said.

"Well, I don't know. You take a peek." Alexei moved and the beautiful young geneticist peered through the crack in the door. "Whatya think?"

"You should have left your shoe on," she replied and Poppen muffled a laugh. "Other than that it looks to me like he's just telling us to wait a sec."

"That's what I had planned anyway."

Bobby Poppen's blood pressure had been a problem since his fifties and a smile crossed his lips as he thought about what his doctor would say about today's exertions. He closed his eyes and relished every breath as if it were his last. In his hands rested a plunger attached to a number of explosive charges. Two days ago he was pissing his pants and watching dog shows with Felix. Today, though, he was on covert missions tied to mass genocide and global domination. The world was a strange place. Then, a flurry of gunshots echoed through the crack in the door.

"Blow it now."

Alexei's tone was short and his voice authoritative. Poppen twisted the t-shaped grip, pushed the plunger to its stops, and carnage followed. The relay complete, energy pulsed down the connecting wire igniting the caps and blowing the RDX. In an instant fire enveloped the room in every direction and the floor began to crumble beneath his rear. Robert George Poppen II was one hundred years old, free falling in an explosion, and a solitary thought ran through his mind.

"I'm going to miss that little dog."

****

94.

Chase blinked hard, cupped his hands against his ears, and stretched his jaw. A sharp ringing faded as he struggled to his feet and surveyed the room. Katsuo's RDX had exploded in concert with their own, causing the floor to fold into the basement. Rubble fell from the ceiling above and Rex marveled the entire structure had not collapsed.

Nearby, Chief struggled to his feet. His oldest friend blinked hard and Chase shook his head again in an attempt to clear the cobwebs. Dust settled in every direction as a familiar voice cut through the fog.

"You're hurt." Chief was yelling and pointing at his head, but Rex's mind was cloudy and he didn't understand. "You're hurt."

In surreal fashion Rex Chase put a hand on top of his own head to find a six inch piece of twisted Castleinium implanted in his skull just above the right ear. He felt no pain and very little blood seemed to emanate from the wound when, before thinking, he pulled the offending material from its hold.

"No." Ahiga shouted.

Chase's hearing had almost returned to normal and he fell to his rear as Chief rushed to his aid. Blood gushed from the now open wound as Rex stared at the foreign object resting in his hand. His friend manhandled him into a resting position on the floor and Chase could feel Chief applying pressure to the wound.

"Come on buddy. You're not dying on me like this."

Rex Chase had no intentions of dying. Twelve hours before a machine gun had hit him in the side and that area healed in hours. Endorphins surged through his body and he could almost feel the wounded area restoring itself. Within thirty seconds, his mind sharpened and his faculties began to return. He sat straight up, looked an astonished Chief straight in the eye and spoke.

"I think I'm ok. Let's finish this."

****

95.

Katsuo had not lost consciousness at any point in the explosion and its aftermath. His mind filled with fog, however, and he drug himself against a surviving support beam. As the dust settled and his faculties returned the seriousness of the situation began to sink in.

He had fallen thirty feet, but luck had been on his side. The RDX he had set focused on the room below which had thrown those on the balcony in the air. They had received little of the shockwave from the blast itself. No rubble had fallen on him, and he had no significant injuries of which to speak. Shou grunted a few feet away as the aviator attempted to recover. The man's right ankle enflamed and a large goose egg swelled above his right eye.

"Are you ok Shin?"

"I'll live."

That was good enough for Takahiro as a single burning question imprinted itself on his mind. Who had detonated the explosives? The answer presented itself less than ten meters away as a trio of intruders were dusting themselves off near Sarah and Moreau. All were uninjured. Katsuo stood to his full height and holstered his pistol which had remained in his grip.

"We'll kill them all with our bare hands."

****

96.

"Bobby. Bobby."

Poppen's eyes opened to the sight of Holly leaning over him. A concerned look dominated her face which was filthy. She smiled a perfect white grin as he reached full consciousness.

"If this is heaven I'm glad we came together. Beautiful women always get treated better than me."

"Bobby." She blushed and extended her hand which the old man took. His bones ached as he rose to his feet, but considering the circumstances he was none the worse for wear. "I think we used too much."

"You're not lying." Alexei Chase stood a few feet away. "Are you ladies alright?"

Poppen shifted his attentions to Amy and Sarah Moreau. The reunited mother and daughter had fallen together in a heap. Sarah acted dazed as she kneeled over her mother's still form.

"I think she might be dead."

Sarah's lip quivered and Poppen stared at her in amazement. She was dirty and her hair tousled, but the woman was a perfect representation of the girl in his dreams. He stepped in her direction and then Shou kicked her from behind.

"If she's not dead already she will be soon."

Shin's voice overflowed with hate and Poppen stepped over Sarah, his brain pumping endorphins to his body.

"Not if I have anything to say about it."

"Oh yeah old man?"

"Bobby?"

Poppen was face to face with a man who had no qualms in ending his life, but confidence oozed from his delivery as he failed to break eye contact with the villain.

"Yes Sarah?"

"Bobby Poppen? It's Serena. How are you so old?"

"I've heard that a lot. Did you say Serena?"

"She's had a lot of names my friend." Katsuo stood a few feet distant. "As a matter of fact I gave her a few new ones myself when we were intimate."

"I picked you for more of an impotent kind of guy," Poppen lowered his voice and touched his nose to the stocky Shin Shou's. "I'm a hundred years old and could show her a better time than either of you."

Shou's breath was atrocious and Poppen held no illusions that he stood a chance against the trained fighter. In the distance, however, Chief and Rex were getting to their feet. He needed to stall a few moments longer.

"Very good old man." Katsuo said. "He is as talented a staller as Mr. Chase. The Moreau's die first."

All the air left his body as Shou delivered a crushing right cross to Poppen's ribcage. Out of the fight, he collapsed to the ground and gasped for breath as the two Japanese killers moved as one. Alexei Chase was a sizeable man and fought well, but within seconds the duo had subdued him and he lay motionless nearby.

Poppen watched as Shin Shou picked Sarah up by the hair. Her feet dangled inches from the floor and she screamed as a maniacal laugh emanated from within the killer. It had all happened so fast that they had mistaken Holly's hesitation for fear.

She surprised Shou with a well-placed chunk of concrete to the back of the head which sent him sprawling as he lost his grip on Sarah. The two crashed in a heap onto a nearby pile of rubble as Holly raised the concrete to strike once again. Katsuo was too fast, though and had reacted with lightning speed. Before she could strike he had tossed her against the wall like a rag doll.

Amy Moreau regained consciousness at some point during the melee and now struggled to her knees. Poppen watched in horror as Katsuo was the only man left standing. He pulled the 8mm pistol from its holster and pointed it at the middle-aged woman's head.

"No."

Poppen's eyes grew wide and Sarah screamed as she dove to save her mother. He had never seen anyone murdered on their knees at point blank range before and the moment was surreal. Three gunshots rang out.

****

97.

Chase moved with a fluidity and speed he had never thought possible, delivering a shoulder to Katsuo's midsection just as the killer discharged his weapon. The two tumbled together as Takahiro's back took the brunt of the fall and Rex put a vice-like grip on the Japanese maniac's wrist. More gunshots fired against the wall as the two struggled for position.

Both men fought with furor and the older man's conditioning impressed Chase. The Nambu was empty and Takahiro released the weapon, which bounced across the floor. Every offensive move countered, Chase struggled to find an advantage, but the weathered Japanese fisherman was gaining the upper hand. Katsuo rolled hard to his left, putting Chase on his back while delivering a vicious knee to Rex's groin area. A lightning bolt of pain exploded in his stomach and he released his grip on the opponent.

A few seconds passed and he expected the attack to continue, but it did not. Chase breathed deep and looked around the room. Katsuo and Shou were nowhere to be seen. His father was regaining consciousness a few feet away. Bobby Poppen was down, but seemed ok. Holly was standing to dust herself off. It was then that he heard it. It was the sound of a mother's utter despair.

****

98.

Chief was two steps behind Chase and three steps to his left. Shots rang out as he lowered his shoulder in an attempt to knock Shin Shou from his feet, but the young Japanese ace sidestepped the attack. Even with an ankle three times its normal size he was light on his feet. Ahiga slid to a stop as chunks of metal and concrete dug into his knees, then turned to face his adversary.

"I've been looking forward to this Shin."

"It will be a pleasure to kill you again."

"You've got a pretty nice shiner above that eye. It might be a little hard to see."

The maniac smiled, pulled a knife from his dungarees and sliced the engorged area. Blood spurted from the cut as it relieved the pressure. Crimson liquid streaked down the side of his filthy face before pouring onto the floor and Shin smiled a yellowed, bloody smile.

"That's better."

Shou and Ahiga circled each other as Katsuo and Chase fought nearby. Chief's instinct was to help his friend, but George knew how dangerous Shou could be. Even with an injured ankle and limited vision, it would take all his skill to defeat the capable enemy.

"That was an excellent maneuver your pilot made over the Atlantic to get you off the plane. I bet a few men lost their lunches to that." Shin grit his yellowed teeth. "I thought you were all insane, just jumping into the ocean like that. I assume that was you anyway."

"You assume right, and we're not as insane as a man who orders an entire crew to disembowel themselves."

Chief looked for an advantage, but saw none. Shou sneered, pushed off his uninjured foot, and attempted to take out Ahiga's left leg. Chief reacted with speed, flattening his body against the attack and pulling his right hand under the attacker's left armpit. Blue-green veins bulged from the two men's arms as the exertion caused sweat to pour from Ahiga's face.

They were physical equals when it came to strength and Chief grunted as they locked arms and went to the ground. He could feel that Shou held an immediate advantage. Ahiga jockeyed for position, but Shin countered every move. The Japanese killer had a thick arm wrapped around the Navajo's neck and oxygen soon became in short supply. Stars burst at the corners of his vision and he gasped as the blood flow to his brain was interrupted.

"Shhhhhhhhhhhhh." Shou was on his back now. "You'll feel no pain. It will be..."

In a last ditch effort to survive Ahiga gripped a large piece of concrete in his left hand. He interrupted Shou's sentence and delivered blow after blow to the man's temple. It took four shots before he felt the grip lessen, and then, before the fifth, it released.

Chief scrambled to his feet, though the sudden rush of blood and oxygen to his brain caused him to wobble. Shou was no longer near and Ahiga turned to see him snatch the two stones from the sky and scramble up a fallen steel beam to the remaining floor above. He was escaping.

✶✶✶✶✶✶✶✶✶✶✶✶✶✶✶✶✶✶

99.

"Help her." Amy Moreau wept and tears streamed down her face. "Somebody help her."

Chase was the first at her side and he knew that the situation was dire. Sarah lay on her back, her face ashen, and three large exit wounds through her belly. Rex tore at her shirt and she coughed, causing blood to flow from the injuries. Chief knelt at his side and Holly did the same.

"Did Leonard ever say anything to you about some black stuff that can heal this sort of thing?" Chief whispered the question and Chase could see the hurt in his friend's eyes. "I saw them use it to save Angela. They tried to tell me I made it up, but I saw them."

Rex's silence answered the question as Amy looked to them again for help.

"What are you doing? We need to get her to a doctor right now. Do you have a plane outside? Where is The General? Where is Leonard? They can help her. I know it."

"Shhhhhhhhh." Sarah's voice was weak and her eyelids fluttered as she took her mother's hand. "It's alright mom. It will be alright."

Holly began crying and tears rolled down Poppen's face. Chase pushed against her belly and she cried out in agony. The blood continued to pour out of her body and he wiped it away with his hand.

"I can't help her." He admitted to the room. "I can't help you."

"It's OK." Though her skin had paled and her breathing was shallow, her opaline eyes hadn't dulled and Chase could still feel himself getting lost in them. "I'm so sorry for everything I've done. I'm so, so, sorry."

"Don't be sorry honey." Tears streamed down Amy's face as she attempted a smile. "We'll take care of everything."

"I was having the best of times at the gala." Sarah addressed Chase and he swallowed back emotion. "You are the single most incredible man I've ever met. I wish it could have been sooner."

Sarah Marie Moreau took her last breath a freed woman. It seemed a vicious web of lies and deceit had defined her entire adult life. The love of her true mother and the affection of Rex Chase had brought her from the darkness into the light. She blinked her last blink and a solitary tear rolled down her cheek. The eldest daughter of Christian and Amy Moreau was dead.

****

100.

"I'm sorry to have to say this, but we have to get after Shou." Chief broke the full minute of silence. "He grabbed the other two stones on his way out."

"Where do you think he's going?" Alexei asked.

"I don't know."

"All I heard him say was that he was getting out of the area." Amy wiped a tear as she offered the piece of information.

"We're not going after Shou." Chase sighed as he took one last look at Sarah's lifeless body. "Dad, if you're OK I need you to help Bobby, Amy, and Holly get back to the Richland place. Chief and I are going after Katsuo."

"Are you sure son? That cut on your head looks pretty serious."

"I'm fine dad. We're going to need the Jeep, though, so you'll have to find something out there."

"Did you hear me say that Shou had the final two stones? He could be anywhere within a few hours and we'll never have another chance to be this close."

"What do you know about The Russian?"

"Who?" Alexei said.

"When Shou was reassuring Katsuo he said that he and The Russian could help him find Yasuhiro. I want to know who The Russian is."

"So we're going after Shou."

"Do we stand a chance against him in an air battle?"

"I don't know."

Chief's face showed doubt and Chase recognized it.

"He's that good?"

"He's that good."

"Then we let Wade and Bryan shadow him like I planned before." Chief made Rex's decision simple. "It doesn't seem like The Russian will be in the States so we should be fine for now. Now we just need a boat."

"Why a boat?" Holly asked.

"Katsuo said he was leaving in a boat." Chief said. "That's why, right?"

"That's why." Chase smiled at his best friend. "Do you know where we can get one?"

"My father drove to Detroit in 1932 to watch Gar Wood race." Dust and dirt streaked Holly's face and accentuated her brilliant white smile. "When he got back he decided to put two V-16's in a 1929 Gar Wood Triple cockpit. Well, he tried to make it look just like the America VIII, so he had to rebuild the boat a bit. She'll do every bit of a hundred miles per hour on a smooth day."

"Gar Wood huh?" Chase hadn't followed the multi-millionaire inventor's racing career, but had heard of his exploits on the Detroit River and The Miss America series of boats. "No machine guns?"

"Don't worry. I haven't looked, but if my dad owns a vehicle, he equips it with machine guns. Just one place to put in nearby too. Even money Katsuo's heading the same way we are."

"Then let's get going."

✳✳✳✳✳✳✳✳✳✳✳✳✳✳✳✳✳✳

101.

"It would have been nice to know about the sabotage to their incineration device before we were in that room."

Chase shouted over the constant protest of the Jeep's engines. Temperatures soared into the thirties and made the dirt road muddy, if not impassable. Holly's driving was exceptional, though, and he looked at his oldest friend as the man responded.

"Well, I just didn't think of it before."

"You didn't think of telling me about a plan that had disabled one of their main threats to the United States? A weapon so huge and powerful the entire country would be obliterated in less than a second?"

"No, I literally had not thought of it yet." Chief grinned and held on as Holly maneuvered the Jeep through a muddy hole. "Do you think The President could order the grid shut down and it would just happen? I thought you were a genius."

"So it was a bluff?" Rex grunted as the Jeep bounced along a dry portion of the terrain. "Remind me not to play poker with you any time soon. Any sign of Katsuo?"

"I've been in his tracks the entire way." Holly yelled as she downshifted in preparation for a bend in the path. "No local would be using this road today. It'd take ten more minutes, but the paved road around is easier."

"How much farther?" Chief asked as Holly navigated through a thick line of trees.

"Almost there."

The vehicle burst from the tree line and machine gun fire greeted them. Chase ducked as the projectiles slammed into the engine block of the sturdy automobile. Within seconds smoke bellowed from beneath the hood and Rex reached for the manual shifter, forcing the transmission into reverse.

"Floor it Holly." He screamed above the din. "We've gotta get to the trees."

Chase looked to his left expecting the beautiful young geneticist to be slinking below the seat in an effort to find cover. What he saw, however, was the exact opposite. She sat within view, her left hand on the wheel as her right arm draped over his passenger seat. Two large caliber bullets impacted the seat inches from her face sending stuffing flying through the air. Her expression, however, never wavered. Her brow furrowed, eyes pointed to the rear, she guided the dying vehicle to the trees.

"Now what boss?"

Chase exhaled as the machine gun fire lessened and became sporadic. A hundred yards away the unmistakable sound of a powerful marine engine now dominated the landscape. Katsuo was furthering his escape.

"Where is the dam?"

"What?" Holly said.

"Where is the dam?" Chase repeated. "Shou said something about a dam earlier and Katsuo seemed none too happy about it."

"The army corps of engineers just built a dam a few miles upstream," Holly said. "There isn't much to it, though. The river bends left, then right, and you're there. In dad's boat you'll make it in a few minutes."

"That water looks cold." Chief had ducked behind the seat in the back of the Jeep and he dismounted the vehicle as Katsuo's boat sped away. "That water looks real cold."

"You planning on going for a swim?"

"Every time I get in a boat with you we go for a swim."

Chase smiled and patted the side of the bullet riddled vehicle as he opened the door and stepped out.

"Well, it doesn't look like the Jeep has anything left in her. Holly, let's get to the boat."

The three trotted up the beach together, Holly in the lead and the men a short distance behind. A hundred yards ahead three boats sat in their slips, none of which seemed impressive.

"I thought we had a speedboat unlike any other?"

"Those aren't daddy's." Chase squinted and peered up river as the sound of Katsuo's fleeing craft waned. Holly jogged past the slips and threw open the doors of a covered dock which jutted into the river. Chase and Chief followed as she flipped on the lights. "That's daddy's."

Chase could feel his jaw drop as the boat's brilliant Philippine mahogany decking shone under the lights. The long sloped nose of the watercraft followed sleek lines past the engines to twin seats in the rear. Just as Holly had promised, the dual V-16 engines gleamed, their thirty-two exhaust pipes extending into the air.

"I've never seen anything like it."

"Where did he get the motors?"

"He built them," Holly announced. "He read all about the ones Harry Miller built and even met him once over at the Indianapolis 500. I don't think they ever even watched the race. They just sat and talked about engines the entire time. Daddy came straight home and built these two one-thousand one hundred and thirteen cubic inch supercharged beasts. They put out eighteen hundred horsepower each and will rev at six-thousand rpm every day of the week. We could take a nap and still catch Katsuo."

"He's going to kill us when we get his boat all shot up." Chief said.

"Not as much as if we got his daughter shot up." Chase extended his hand. "Holly, we've put you in too much danger already. Thank you for your help, but it's just Chief and I from here on out."

She ignored his hand, instead grasping him in a tight hug before pulling back. Chase looked into her deep brown eyes as every fiber of his being told him to kiss her. He hesitated, however, as something inside him resisted.

"Holly," Chase stammered and he could feel his face flush. "I, I..."

She kissed him deeply and he closed his eyes. Waves of relief passed through his body as he allowed himself to relax and for those brief seconds, nothing else seemed to matter. It was easy and natural, yet exhilarating. Then Holly pulled away, her brown eyes sparkled and her bright white smile gleamed.

"Don't you want to know where the machine gun is?"

102.

Shin Shou descended through fifteen thousand feet. He had spent more than three hours at thirty three thousand feet, the service ceiling of the capable fighter. Above stretched a never ending sea of blue while below the checkerboard of the American landscape grew.

He performed a number of maneuvers to assure no one followed him and checked his six one last time before committing to a landing spot. Within minutes he lined the fighter up for final approach at the small country airfield. Shou landed the plane on the smooth dirt surface without a bump and taxied toward the small facilities lone hangar. Two men walked from a large building as he approached and Shin decided to shut down. As he climbed from the aircraft the first man addressed him.

"What in tarnation do you think you're doin, just comin on down here without even askin permission on the radio?"

Shou dismounted the plane and spoke in accented broken English as he put his hands together and bowed.

"So sorry most honorable American friend. I no have radio and plane is broken."

"Gee ma nee Christmas." The man's southern drawl was thick as both man laughed. "Randy. We got ourselves a genuwine Jap out here."

"Sank you. Sank you."

The other man scrunched his nose and made a face like a rat as both repeated the phrase over and over. Shou bristled as he looked to the skies above. A plane flew low miles to the east, but it was moving the wrong direction. He was certain the aircraft posed no risk and smiled as the two men continued to mock him.

"And to think, I was planning on letting you live."

"What?"

Shou leaned over and pulled a knife from his boot and the two men smiled.

"If it's blood you come for, then its blood you're gonna get boy." Randy spoke his final words as he brandished a Smith and Wesson .357. "Come on and get ya some."

Shin rubbed the back of his blade along the cut just over his eye as he sized the two men up. Randy was the smaller of the two, a bit on the heavy side, and balding. The other man was tall, lean, and seemed to be in fighting shape. Most days Mr. No Name would receive attention first, but Randy had a gun. Shin made his decision.

Shou moved with speed as he ignored the protests from his cramped legs and injured ankle. Gunshots rang out, but no pain followed their report. Shin brandished the knife in his right hand as he moved left. His six inch blade sunk into the fat man's neck and he brought it around, almost decapitating the bigot. Blood streamed from the vicious wound and spurted on Shin's face. The unremorseful killer dabbed at the viscous liquid with his finger and then stuck it in his mouth. The skinny man vomited as he witnessed the horrific event.

"What's your name?" The skinny man wept and hesitated in answering Shou's question. Shin paced as he ran his finger across the sharpened blade of his knife. "I suggest you answer my questions."

"L,L,L,Luke Walters. What do you want?"

"I'm asking the questions Luke Walters. Is there anyone else inside?"

"No."

"Anyone who is going to miss you or our fat headless friend Randy?"

"No, sir. We both live out here alone."

"No mommas or wives or kids?"

"No, sir."

"Well, then I'm sorry. Your corpse may be rotten before anyone finds you."

Shou relished the look of horror that crossed his victim's face as the man fought for survival. He was a powerful adversary and fought well, but within seconds Shin's blade found its mark, severing the carotid artery. Blood spurted from the wound as Luke Walters gasped before falling backward to the ground. Shin flashed a fiendish yellow grin, relishing the idea that it was the last thing the ignorant American would see.

"If you would have just been kind..."

Shou walked to his plane, started its 950 horsepower radial engine and taxied into the hangar. It had been a long day and he rubbed his neck as he parked the experimental fighter. Tomorrow he would begin his journey to rendezvous with The Russian. Tomorrow would be the beginning of their partnership against The Organization and the rest of the world. Tomorrow everything he had worked so hard to achieve would be one step closer to fruition. He closed his eyes and leaned his head backward in his cockpit as he spoke to himself.

"Tomorrow will be the dawn of my new life."

****

103.

All thirty two cylinders fired in perfect time and Chase marveled at the feat of marine engineering. Their throaty roar echoed down either side of the muddy river as the mahogany monster passed seventy miles per hour. Just ahead of the massive engines Chief held on tight as he manned the single B.A.R. which Richland had custom mounted. Rex smiled as startled waterfowl fled the speed boat's path. A day earlier he had considered Wade Richland a simple country boy. Today he considered the man a genius.

"We have to be getting close." Chief yelled over the din of the engines. "She said it was a couple miles and right after the bend."

Chase knew his friend to be correct and yet he wished their pursuit had been a bit longer. Driving the 3600 horsepower craft would be addicting. As he rounded the second bend, however, his wishes changed. The cylinders on the left motor began to change timbre. Then, the motor locked.

Rex fell hard against the wheel even as he brought the throttle down. Chief folded in half as the boat lurched and he held onto the B.A.R.'s mount to keep from being thrown into the water. Stresses the wooden craft could not long survive pulled at its very fiber and the mahogany planks groaned. Even as he fought the rudder to gain control Chase took notice of the oil pressure gauge. They had none and he shut down the engines.

Relative quiet returned. Chase stretched his jaw and collected himself. His chest hurt and he had sprained his wrist.

"What happened?"

Chief seemed little the worse for wear as he began bailing water from the hapless craft.

"We lost oil pressure." Chase said.

"Or we never had any to begin with. It would make sense he had these beauties winterized."

"Well, either way, the right engine is still good." Chief was right about the winterization. "We can push forward. I can see the lock about a quarter mile ahead."

"Whatever keeps me out of this water." Ahiga said. "I've got what looks to be a quart of oil floating up here by my feet."

"Put it in."

Chief picked up the lubricant and took a step toward the massive engine block.

"You've got it boss. Keep an eye out for Katsuo. I don't see him at the lock and I don't think we passed him. Lots of good places to hide out here tho…"

Just then, the familiar sound of a high powered marine engine coming to life echoed across the river. A hundred yards to their stern Katsuo's Chris Craft Cruiser burst from hanging tree cover. The villain's form was unobscured as the front window of the pleasure boat lifted open to reveal both him and the barrel of a machine gun.

Chase fed the still functioning engine fuel as he worked its custom ignition. The remaining V-16 fired and Chase pushed the throttle to its stops just as Takahiro's Type 92 began breathing fire in their direction. Bullets tore into the mahogany and Chief's B.A.R. began to bark.

On a normal day Richland's custom behemoth would outrun and outmaneuver the Cruiser, even with one engine. Today, however, that one engine was devoid of life giving oil. It was a matter of time until it failed. Chase fought the wheel as the boat's desire to turn in circles almost overpowered his ability to steer.

THE SENTINEL

"How many rounds do we have?" Chase shouted as Chief reloaded the automatic 30.06. "I think I'm going to beach."

"Not enough." Chief said as he slammed the breech shut on the weapon. "Beach it. I'm still not keen on getting in this water."

Rex's arms burned and his sore wrist protested as he battled the overpowered watercraft. The V-16 whined and objected to the exertion but Chase needed a few seconds longer. Chief poured round after round through the B.A.R. changing magazine after magazine until he threw up his arms. They were defenseless.

Rex had been steering in the direction of the beach near the lock, but without return fire Katsuo's type 92 would have their boat shredded before they made it. He had to make a decision and it had to be now. Chase killed the taxed engine just short of their destination.

All was quiet as Katsuo's boat slowed and maintained its distance twenty yards away. Rex looked at Chief who rolled his neck left to right while swinging his arms side to side. Chase tapped on the boat's hull.

Going for a swim: stop

"Figures." Chief answered out loud, a wide grin dominated his face. "You never think about my needs."

"It seems you boys are dead in the water." Katsuo had exited the Cruiser's cabin and now the two boats drifted downriver. "I used all my ammunition down below. I'll have to finish you from the upper mount. You boys forget to give her oil?"

Katsuo's fiendish grin was noticeable as Chase formulated a last ditch effort to survive.

"She's a beauty though wouldn't you say? Did you know Wade Richland designed these engines based on…"

Chase tapped a message to Chief as he stalled Takahiro by giving the full specs of the boat and engines, adding some blustery by-lines and interesting details he had read about Gar Wood.

Damaged engine fuel lines near your position: query

Yes: stop

Spill fuel jump in water: stop

"…and because they had both beaten the starting gun by more than five seconds the judges disqualified them. I tell you what Kit-Kat, those were some crazy times back then. I mean, I was just doing eighty on this boat and I couldn't imagine doing one-hund…"

His tactic had succeeded as the sound of Chief diving into the water interrupted the impromptu speech. Katsuo's diabolical smile widened further at Ahiga's perceived act of cowardice. He laughed as he spoke.

"Even your friend knows death is near." Takahiro's voice lowered as he aimed the roof mounted Type 92 in Chase's direction. "I've been looking forward to this moment Mr. Chase."

"Call me Rex."

The pungent smell of specialized high octane fuel wafted into Chase's nostrils as he swirled the liquid below with his foot. He sneezed as he tore the nearby ignition switch from its housing and the two wires which followed were a blessing. Rex ripped them from their solders, crossed the wires and sparks began to fly as the power plant roared to life.

Fire enveloped the air around him as fumes ignited and spread to the mixture of fuel and water at his feet. Chase slammed the throttle to its stops and pulled hard to starboard on the wheel. His momentum carried him in the direction he had planned and the custom racer lurched ahead as he dove into the water, bullets from the type 92 raining around him.

Chase pushed for the bottom as the icy river swallowed the light from above. His orientation eluded him for a moment. He had either dove beneath the bullets, or they had stopped. Then, a bright flash emanated from above and a shockwave hit him in the chest. Rex let out a grunt as the muddy bottom of the river softened his descent. The shock had pushed him fifteen feet lower in a fraction of a second.

Chase blinked hard and attempted to gauge his position, but the opacity of the water was nonexistent. He kicked hard off the bottom and swam into the current. If his hastily perceived plan had succeeded he would surface upstream from the wreckage. If it had not, he would be gunned down. A few seconds passed as he swam.

Rex surfaced ten yards away from the free floating wreckage now downriver. Katsuo's boat was ablaze and the custom twenty-eight foot Gar Wood, having served its purpose as a makeshift torpedo, slipped under the surface. Ten yards upstream Chief was struggling and Chase sliced through the water to his friend's aid.

"Need a lift?"

"Talk about déjà vu," Ahiga said.

"Did you see Katsuo jump?"

"I was backstroking for a while and then I worked on my breaststroke. I had time for a couple of fingers of scotch..."

Chief's body shuddered from exposure and his voice trailed off as Chase took the muscular man in his left arm. Ahiga's lips were blue and he was shaking, yet Rex himself felt no ill effects from the glacial temperatures. They had ended their trip upstream thirty yards from the lock and Chase pushed for the relative safety, though his friend needed warmth and he needed it soon.

Using a powerful side stroke Chase reached ahead with his right as both legs scissor kicked. A long service area extended downstream from the dam itself and he steered them in its direction. Onshore a man stood holding out a long rescue pole, a curved hook at its end.

"Reach for the hook fellas and I'll pull ya in." He shouted.

Chase reached for the device and within seconds the man helped them ashore. Chief's respirations were slow and shallow. His body was fighting the state of shock, but hypothermia would soon set in.

"Most days I use this thing to fish junk out of the water." The enthusiastic young man exclaimed. "Who would have thought I'd get to save three people in one day. What happened out there and what are you maniacs doing on the river on pleasure boats in the middle of winter?"

"Three people?" Chase looked up from his friend to question the young dam worker. "Who else did you help out?"

"A pretty rude Japanese fella was in about the same shape as your friend here a few minutes ago. He just stormed past me into my little shack back there and started drinking all my coffee."

"What's your name?"

"Terry Graffton. What's yours?"

"I'm Rex Chase and this is George Ahiga." Chase looked beyond the man to the small building nearby. Katsuo glared at them through the glass. He was pale from the exposure but seemed none the worse for wear as he exited the building on a dead run for the dam. "I'm going to need you to take care of my friend here while I go have a talk with my rude friend up there about his manners."

****

104.

Chase took off in a sprint. His hip, which had given him trouble ever since he had jumped from the Six eighteen months before was no longer a hindrance. His focus was sharp and his body was warm. Katsuo didn't stand a chance.

Fifty yards ahead the Japanese madman was quick, both for his age and for the amount of punishment his body had just endured. He had suffered in the water, as had Chief, but Katsuo Takahiro fought on. Chase put down his head and put on a burst of speed just as Katsuo slid to a stop behind a large array of antennas.

"Stop right there Rex Chase." He said. "Stop right there or hundreds of thousands will die."

Chase came to a stop twenty feet short of the brutal killer. He breathed in through his nose, relishing the clean country air. Boston could sometimes smell a bit, well, like a city.

"What is it you think is going to happen whenever you do what it is you plan on doing?"

"I thought you knew everything Mr. Chase."

"How many times do I have to tell you this Kit-Kat? Call me Rex." Takahiro fought to control his breathing, but the exertion of their dash had brought color to his face. He was recovering and Chase looked for an advantage. "I've never claimed to know everything, but I do remember your nickname. Heck, I use it every time we have our little heart to hearts."

"Very good Rex." Katsuo laughed as he held his hand over a series of buttons on a control panel meant to regulate water flow through the dam. "I am a few keystrokes away from opening a portal transporting myself far away from here. The energy dissipation will kill you along with hundreds of thousands of others in the immediate area, much the same as you performed in our chamber once before. I've been meaning to ask you how you did it?"

"Don't know." Chase leaned over and rubbed his hand in the dirt while palming a golf ball sized rock. "I just got lucky with that one."

"Lucky." Katsuo leaned his head back and laughed before becoming serious. "If you leave now I'll continue on without using the..."

Chase threw the oblong stone from a short-armed side position with all his might. The innocuous piece of sedimentary rock whistled as it traveled the twenty feet to Katsuo's ear at one-hundred miles per hour. It struck the fisherman and he stumbled backward as Rex closed the gap and buried his shoulder in Takahiro's stomach. Both men hurtled through the air, tumbled to the ground together, and fell from the dam into the turbulent water below.

Shock from the icy water was minimal and Chase gripped Katsuo around the waist as the dam's wash tossed them about. Thirty seconds passed, and then a minute, and they were clear of the wash, floating in calmer water. Takahiro had gone limp seconds into the ordeal and Chase lightened his grip.

Katsuo kicked for the surface and Chase grabbed him by the leg. A serene sense of calm passed through his entire body as he realized he felt no cold and his lungs were not screaming for air. Rex Chase closed his eyes, tightened his grip and manhandled the muscular, strong swimming, man of the sea. He dove further and further as the Japanese killer kicked at his face. Blow after blow landed to the top of his head and temple, but Chase shrugged off the effects. He could feel the energy pulsing inside. It was magnificent.

"Rex."

The voice startled him and Chase opened his eyes to peer into the murky water. Mary Elizabeth was a few feet away and he reached to her with his free hand. She smiled as he opened his mouth to speak, but got nothing but a mouthful of muddy river water.

"Shhhhhh." She reached out an apparition's finger and placed it over his lips. "I've missed you."

Chase longed to reply, but instead he stared as brilliant streaks of light exploded around the corners of his vision. Mary Elizabeth's head cocked to the side as she leaned forward to whisper in his ear. Rex yearned to feel her breath as she spoke.

"You're not immortal Rex. You need to breathe."

In an instant Mary Elizabeth dematerialized and Rex Chase became aware of his lungs' need for air. He had lost grip of Katsuo at some point in his reverie and The Sentinel was in danger of drowning. He kicked hard with his legs and stroked with his arms. In a matter of seconds his head burst into the air and he vomited an entire lungful of murky river water. Fifteen seconds passed as he sputtered and coughed while tears streamed down his face. Then he saw him. Thirty feet away Katsuo drug himself back onto the service outcropping.

"Katsuo."

Frozen, exhausted, and almost drowned, the diabolical villain and willing killer looked back and sneered as Rex shouted his name.

"Now you will all die."

Rex kicked hard for the nearby land, covering the span of water in less than ten seconds. As he scrambled to his feet, though, another vision burst into his head. Chief was fighting with Katsuo.

Rex blinked hard as the combination of exertion and oxygen deprivation caused him to become very dizzy. He stumbled forward and vomited again, his stomach and lungs rejecting the abuse they had just received. Thirty seconds before he had been invincible, but now he fought to utilize his faculties. He put one foot in front of the other as his dazed mind attempted to regain control. Somehow Takahiro had fought his way past Chief and the Navajo struggled to his feet as Chase approached.

"I've been getting my butt kicked all week."

Chase smiled as the two fought to run after Katsuo.

"Where is Terry?"

"I left him on the phone with the President. You should have seen his face when I dialed him direct."

"Good idea. He'll send everyone."

"What's the plan with Katsuo?"

"I don't know."

"Stop right there." The two men limped to a standstill thirty feet from Katsuo who belched and wretched as he punched numbers into the keypad. "I just have to put in one more number. Don't come any closer."

"If you're going to do it, then just get on with it."

Chase laughed at Chief's comment as he fought to control his breathing.

"I wouldn't if I were you," Rex said between gasps. "You'll never survive."

"The Russian assures my survival and your destruction." Katsuo was hesitant but also determined. "He has deciphered the code of the stones and with their power we will soon rule the world."

"That's what this is all about." A realization swept over Chase and he cursed under his breath that he hadn't seen it before. "The Russian has used the four of you to gather the stones for himself. Shou is as good as dead once he delivers them, just like you if you push that button. The Russian no longer has any use for your services now that the empire is reunited. Do you believe in the afterlife?"

"What is that supposed to mean?"

"Because that's the only way you'll ever see Yasuhiro again." Chase saw the hardened look in Katsuo's eyes at mention of the name. "He must have been very important, but he is lost to you in this life. So go ahead and push that button if you believe. Otherwise surrender to us and I'll see that you receive better care than you afforded young Tad."

"You make a convincing argument." Katsuo jutted his lower chin as he donned a maniac's grin. "By pushing the button I am assured of your death, though, and I want to know you are dead."

Katsuo pressed the final keystroke and a cylindrical beam of blue energy a precise twelve inches in diameter descended from the sky above. His maniacal grin transformed into an awe inspired gaze as a deep azure light bathed the once simple Japanese fisherman. Takahiro breathed deep as he tilted his head back to absorb the energy's warmth and power.

"Get behind me." Chase's voice was authoritative and Chief obeyed. "Here goes nothing."

Chase stared straight ahead as the beam grew to a diameter of ten feet. Katsuo stood in the middle reveling in its magnificence, but soon his joy turned into fear as the blue energy overwhelmed his senses. His fear grew as the blue energy intensified in magnitude, its infinite power burning the man who had summoned its wrath.

Katsuo Takahiro spent his final moments in undeniable agony and his face twisted with the pain. His clothes burned as the skin melted from his body revealing bone and muscle. He screamed in pain but his vocal chords were no longer capable of producing sound. The blue energy seemed to pulse and Rex Chase observed the empty sockets which once held the eyes of Katsuo Takahiro. Then it happened.

The Japanese madman's remains exploded as Rex brought his hands together in a praying configuration six inches in front of his face. The massive blue wall of energy expanded in exponential fashion as he twisted his hands counterclockwise to one another and shaped them as if he were holding an invisible sphere. Thirty feet away a perfect round ball of energy six feet in diameter appeared from nothingness.

Sweat trickled down his nose and his body began to quake from the exertion. He grunted and tightened his midsection as every iota of his being concentrated on the task at hand. The blue wall of energy slowed its expansion and Rex brought his hands closer to his body as the wall of death approached.

A deep humming sound grew in magnification until the vibration rattled him from the inside out. His ears felt like they would explode and as the blue cylinder of energy just kissed the tips of his knuckles it ceased to advance. Its beauty was undeniable and it pulsed again as if it were a living, breathing being. Chase narrowed his eyes, pushed his hands further from his body and cupped them together.

Brilliant white light shot from dried mud-like cracks in the surface of the sphere as the blue energy collapsed upon itself. The low humming sound increased in pitch at an alarming rate until it reached the opposite end of the spectrum. Chase's arms shook and his veins bulged as he fought to control the supernatural actions yards away. He yelled at the top of his lungs as the piercing sound of the energy's collapse threatened to leave him deaf.

"Enough."

Chase moved forward as he flattened his hands together and held it with all his might. The sphere consumed the blue energy before collapsing upon itself. It retracted to a diameter of twelve inches as Rex hastened his movement forward. He approached, breathed in through his nostrils and blew it back out. Something deep inside told him this was what he needed to do. Rex Chase separated his hands, stepped into the pulsating blue sphere, and prepared to do his duty as The Sentinel. This is why he was here.

"No."

Chief yelled and lunged toward his friend, but the energy field surrounding Chase wouldn't allow passage. Seconds turned to minutes as Rex stood as if frozen in time. The azure ball of energy faded and Ahiga watched as it dissipated. Moments passed and it no longer seemed to exist. The sound of rushing water dominated the now serene landscape.

"Are you ok?"

"I'm right as rain." Chase turned, a huge smile on his face. "Did you see that?"

"Did I see it?" Chief's voice was incredulous. "I just don't know what 'it' is."

"The Russian didn't tell Katsuo that he would need the stones to create a stasis field so that he could pass through the portal." Chase said. "Well, someone didn't tell Katsuo. It could have been Shou, but I doubt it. Anyway, without a stasis field he was unprotected and torn to pieces."

"What about you?" Chief said. "I thought you said you wouldn't be protected out here away from all the Castleinium."

"I took an educated gamble, assuming this energy is the same energy as my body is creating. Therefore, according to the Poppen Equation there is a certain amount of energy my body should be able to absorb whereas other people, such as our good buddy Kit-Kat, are torn apart. Oh, and I also assumed they had this dam built out of a certain amount of Castleinium, not to mention they probably had it all hooked into the grid."

"An educated gamble and assumptions of madmen's actions." Chief laughed as he put his arm around his friend. "Why don't we get warm and you can tell me more about all that while we decide what to do with my good friend Shin Shou?"

"Do you think they have any good places to eat around here? I'm starving."

****

105.

Birds chirped at the first signs of light and in the distance the repeated calls of a rooster awakened him from his slumber. Shin Shou sat up and stretched as he wiped the sleep from his eyes. He yawned as he set his feet on the wooden oak planks that covered the floor.

The previous days' exertions had worked him to the point of exhaustion and the uninterrupted night of sleep had rejuvenated the flying ace. He went about his normal morning rituals as he found a small sack of oats in the kitchen. Oatmeal was one of his favorite breakfasts and he devoured several helpings after preparing it on the dead men's stove.

Shin stepped from the house a new man and he checked on the stones as he prepared the experimental craft for flight. They were in their place and accounted for and that brought a smile to his face. He had fueled the night before, but with each journey came a pre-flight checklist and he went about the work.

The aircraft taxied from the relative darkness of the hangar into the light and Shin brought it around to the runway. Flies swarmed the bodies of the two dead men and a slight odor wafted in his direction. Shou smiled as he passed the fallen bigots.

"See you later boys. Thanks for everything."

With that, Shin Shou eased the throttle forward and felt the weight of the yoke as the plane bounded down the dirt runway. Within seconds he achieved take-off speed and the nimble fighter lifted into the expansive blue skies. Shou looked at his gauges and all seemed well. He climbed to thirty thousand feet and leveled out before taking a look at the skies around.

The air was smooth and the wind whistled as it whipped past the cockpit.

Shou had perfected the art of relaxing as he flew and he inhaled the life-giving oxygen from his mask. Then, a flash caught the corner of his left eye. He turned his head and saw nothing. Then another flash caught the corner of his right eye, accompanied by the unmistakable sound of bullets slamming into his fuselage.

The experienced pilot relaxed and pushed the yoke forward while working the left rudder. His plane responded by entering a steep dive. On his right an American aircraft sped past while bullets continued to whiz past his cockpit. Shou concentrated with all his might as he stressed the airframe to its maximum capabilities.

Metal groaned and his controls fought his commands as he passed through four-hundred miles per hour. He had descended fifteen thousand feet in a little over forty seconds. Anyone who had followed would have to be a madman. Shou reached the maximum capabilities of his aircraft and he struggled to recover from the dive. He grunted and beads of sweat ran down his face as he regained control enough to level at ten thousand feet. He ripped the oxygen mask from his face and searched the skies with fervor. Bullets slammed into the rear of the craft and he gave the Sakae radial engine a boost of fuel while pulling back on the yoke.

Shin kept a hand on the controls as he returned the oxygen mask to his face while searching the skies to his rear. Below two of the American planes he had fought in the previous battle took up station. They followed, but not at a steep rate of ascent. Instead the aircraft weaved back and forth crossing each other's paths every so often. A few minutes passed and Shou leveled out at twenty-thousand feet. He watched in anger as

the two planes broke off their pursuit two thousand feet below
and continued their weaving path through the sky. The
Americans had learned a lesson of some kind. Shin grinned as
he selected his 20mm cannons and put the nimble fighter into a
dive.

"I hope you're down there George." Shin seethed. "I
really do."

✹✹✹✹✹✹✹✹✹✹✹✹✹✹✹✹✹✹

106.

"Are you sure you want to go through with this?"

Rex held the transmit button on his radio as he awaited his friend's reply.

"Don't have much of a choice now, do I?"

"We could always call Bryan down from above."

"Negative." Captain Bryan Morris' voice crackled across the radio. "This big old bird is supposed to be flown by five experienced airmen. I have a physicist, a geneticist, a hundred year-old-man, a WWI pilot with an itchy trigger finger, and two of Abraham Lincoln's sons."

Laughter echoed across the airwaves as everyone shared in the joke.

"You're sure about our plan though, right Captain?"

"For everyone's sake, I sure hope so. I know we don't want to be descending from way up here, guns blazing. Poppen already looks a little green."

Chase and Captain Morris had talked about the enemy fighters' capabilities the night before. The F4f had a certain advantage in service ceiling and seemed to handle better in a dive. That was the first phase of the plan which they had already executed. Since they hadn't shot Shou down in phase one they now moved onto phase two.

Shin Shou held most of the advantages in a dogfight. He was superior in skill. He was superior in top speed, rate of climb, and rate of turn. He was also far superior in range with at least double the distance. What the Wildcat exceeded at was superior armor, self-sealing tanks, and armament. Chase and the Captain had adjusted their strategy to focus on those.

Morris had first checked in the day before just north of Amarillo, Texas and Chase and the others had begun their journey west without knowing their final destination. Morris and Richland had both refueled once while managing to evade detection and the Captain had radioed their position to Air Force bases along the path which had ended a hundred miles east of San Diego at a small airport in the desert west of Mexicali.

Chase had picked Captain Morris as his wingman for the plan, even as he had seen the disappointment in both Chief and Richland. It was Morris, though, who suggested George would be a better pick. He had more recent experience than Richland and the Airacuda would take significant skill to handle if they needed phase three of the plan. Rex had conceded to Morris' wisdom as he felt most comfortable with Chief at his side. They just fought better together.

"Well, my friends." Chase clicked on the button on his handset once again. "We're down here playing sitting ducks. Whatya say..."

"He's diving."

Morris' voice came across the radio and all joking ceased as Chase spoke again.

"Stick to the weave George. Don't deviate. Stick to the weave no matter what."

"Roger."

Chase watched as 20mm rounds rained from above. Shin's fighter descended at a high rate of speed and passed between the two Wildcats. Chief's plane had taken a beating on the initial pass, but his flight path had not deviated and Chase gave him a thumbs up as they crossed paths once again. Shou made a sharp turn below and come up fast, settling in on George's tail once again. Chase watched as round after round pumped into the rear of the plodding aircraft. Rex fought the urge to engage and instead followed the weave as Chief's plane finished the long turn. It worked.

As the two Wildcats converged Shin Shou was within Chase's sites. He squeezed the trigger and loosed the full fury of his six browning machine guns. A flurry of rounds buried themselves in the fuselage of the enemy plane and Chase removed his mask. He smiled and waved as he flew past the Japanese ace. Shou broke off his engagement, rising a thousand feet in twenty seconds.

"How ya doin over there George?" Chase radioed.

"You know. Getting shot at. Tryin not to blow up. Stickin to the plan. Same old, same old."

"He's diving again."

Morris' voice came over the radio as bullets once again pierced the sky. This time, however, Chase received the fury. Rex grinned as he realized Shin had taken the bait.

"Get him Chief."

"Roger."

Shin Shou took up station on Chase's six and pounded him with the 20mm cannon. The Wildcat shook as rounds buried themselves in the sturdy airframe and Rex found himself leaning forward in the cockpit as if that would convince his plane to finish the turn faster. Seconds seemed to last minutes as the barrage continued and then Chase saw him.

From his port Chief bore down on the smaller plane, his six Browning machine guns firing on full auto. Chase craned his neck and watched as his lifelong friend put every round on target, many of which hit the fighter's delicate non-sealing tanks. A fire erupted from the left wing and Shin Shou was going down in a hurry.

"Alright, let's get down there. If he gets out alive I'd rather not find out what The Russian has him doing with those stones."

✼✼✼✼✼✼✼✼✼✼✼✼✼✼✼✼✼✼

107.

"Why won't you fight?"

Anger flowed through Shin Shou's veins as he leveled his superior aircraft after a one-thousand foot ascent. Below, Rex Chase had just crippled the experimental plane and Shin watched as Chase and his wingman continued their lazy path through the sky.

"Come up here and get me you cowards."

Shin screamed the words as he ripped his oxygen mask off his face and dove once again. He squeezed the trigger of the 20mm cannon and put a bevy of fire onto Chase's plane. Shou pulled from the dive with supreme expertise and settled fifty yards from the rear of the American craft. Dozens of rounds pumped into the aft of the other man's plane and yet it continued to plod along its course. It was as if it was leading him somewhere.

Bullets tore into the side of Shin's experimental fighter and he looked to port in time to see George Ahiga's face smiling as his sextet of automatic Browning's decimated the Japanese flying machine. Shou cursed, pulled back on the yoke, and attempted to use full left rudder in order to turn into his opponent and out of the range of fire.

Something was wrong, though, and he looked out the window to see his wing on fire. One of the sacrifices they had devised to make the aircraft more nimble was to lose weight by not using self-sealing tanks. Shin was beginning to reconsider that advantage.

The Baja Desert below was an uninviting, inhospitable terrain and Shin grinned a toothy yellow grin as he descended. Under power and in control he landed the craft on the smooth desert surface. He shut down the radial engine and grunted as he lugged the heavy stones from their storage compartment.

Sweat poured down his face as he arranged the stones in a pattern The Russian had advised. He pulled a measuring tape from his pocket and measured their distances with precision as not two, but three planes circled above. They were coming to get him and as he finished his preparations all three planes landed nearby before taxiing the remaining distance. Rex Chase was the first to shut down his engine and throw open the cockpit of his fighter.

"Shoe string." Even Shin grinned at the nickname. "This is a heckuva place for a get-together. Wouldn't you rather just give me those before you hurt yourself?"

"You are the ones who will die." Shou longed to brandish his knife and slice the man's throat, but the others approached as well. George and Chase would make a formidable team. "I see you brought others to witness my ascension."

"What ascension?" Chief squinted and shaded his eyes with his right hand as he looked to the sky. "Anyone see a fiery chariot?"

"What was it you called me before?" Shin said. "A sissy? I believe that was it. I believe you hitting me on the head back there with the concrete was a sissy move George."

"Well, I felt like I owed you one Shin Splint."

"Good one."

Chase offered the congratulations as the others joined him in laughter.

"Your insults don't matter to me." Shin said. "In a few moments you will all be dead and I will be on my way to being the first EMPEROR OF THE WORLD!"

"Take it easy Horse Shoe." Holly joined in on the name calling and Chase met her gaze. She winked at him before continuing. "You're gonna blow a gasket before your ascension."

"You joke and you tease." Shou looked at the surrounding stones as he pulled the final pair from his pocket. "Now I will show you my undeniable power."

"Wait." Chase stepped forward. "I don't think you want to do this Shin. The Russian is just using you like he used Mother, Sarah, and Katsuo. What do you know about him anyway?"

"How dare you question our partnership?" Anger coursed through Shin's veins. "Together we will rule the world."

"Yeah, yeah, yeah, but in what universe does that happen?" Chief stood at Chase's side as the two confronted the Japanese killer. "I mean, you double-crossed Mother who double-crossed you who double-crossed Sarah who double-crossed Katsuo while double-crossing Chase. There's not a lot of trust."

"Be quiet. With a twist of these stones I will become the most powerful man on the planet."

"If you do it, you will die like Katsuo did." Chase concentrated on the pattern Shin had laid into the desert. He couldn't read the inscriptions but somehow it all made sense and he knew how to stop it. He felt Chief slink backward as he continued. "You see, the stones are not a weapon. They are a portal, a window, or a mode of transportation. If you twist those two stones then tap them twice you will die."

"How did you know I was to tap them twice?" Shou's curiosity rose. "I didn't say that."

"Because I can read them Shin." Chase said "If you…"

Even as Rex spoke Shin started the sequence. Chief was a blur as he hurtled his body toward Shou, but he was too late. All thirty eight stones rose into the air as Shin and Ahiga tumbled outside of the jagged circle. The Japanese aviator regained his footing and countered the stocky Navajo warrior. A deep rumbling emanated from the sky above as the stones arranged themselves in a geometrical shape in the sky, but the two men fought through the distraction.

"Chief." Chase looked at his childhood friend who paused. "Get away from him."

George retreated and Shin stood alone as the thirty-eight objects began to float in his direction. He watched as they descended upon him, each stone moving to an assigned space on his body. Shin Shou donned a menacing smile as the shiny black objects did their work.

"Do you see?" His voice raised in both pitch and volume as he spoke. "Do you see? They have chosen me. Their power has chosen me. NOW I WILL ASCEND TO MY PROPER PLACE IN THIS WORLD! YOU WILL ALL BOW TO ME!"

His body covered by the stones, he began to rise into the air. Chase watched in fascination as the man floated ten yards away and equally high. Shou's arms pressed against his sides and his legs dangled toward the earth.

"This is different than the last one." Chief had rejoined Chase at his side.

"It's going to stay that way."

Then, the rumbling gave way to a sharp cracking sound and lightning seemed to emanate from inside of Shou's body. The Japanese aviator's face twisted in pain as the electrical pulses coursed through his frame. Without warning the stones expanded at an exponential rate, taking with them pieces of Shin Shou. His final moments were agonizing as they tore him into thirty-eight separate pieces. The crackling of energy almost drowned out his screams, but Chase could still hear their mournful song. Shin Shou's eyes flew open in separate areas of the sky as another burst of energy flowed through them and the stones collapsed. His body pieced together for a moment and Chase witnessed the man's terror before a bright burst of light caused everyone to shield their eyes.

In an instant the rumbling stopped, the lightning ceased, and the Baja Desert was back to inormal. A curious lizard approached and Chase watched as it climbed over the tip of his shoe. Last week the world had been a much simpler place.

"That's what happens when you defy gravity without a stasis field."

Bobby Poppen had exuded reservation since the beating he had taken at the hands of Shou, but he spoke nonetheless.

"Is that the same gravity that doesn't exist?"

Chief smiled as he asked the question and Chase looked around the group. They were not rattled. They were not scared. They were The Organization and he was their leader.

"It is indeed my friend. It is indeed. Whatya say we head back to Boston?"

✱✱✱✱✱✱✱✱✱✱✱✱✱✱✱✱✱

108.

"I once asked General John Francis Reagan if he thought I would have made a good soldier. He replied, 'Frank, you couldn't fight your way out of a piss soaked paper bag. You're better off back here with the rest of the politicians cackling about like a bunch of old maids.'"

A brief wave of laughter passed through the gathered crowd of two-hundred fifty thousand and Chase allowed himself a smile. That sounded like The General.

"He was an exceptional leader. He was an extraordinary judge of character and talent. He was courageous in the face of tremendous danger. He was a man to be looked up to and counted upon. To me, though," The President of the United States choked on his words as he cleared his throat and attempted to deliver the next line. "To me, though, he was and always will be, first and foremost, my friend."

Rex scratched the side of his head, removed his sunglasses, and dabbed at the corner of his eye with the sleeve of his tuxedo. His mother Lucille offered her left hand and he took it. Alexei stood by her side and Chase marveled at the funeral's attendance.

A quarter of a million mourners had gathered for the presidentially declared state funeral. Every protocol afforded a president or former president was being heaped upon the first head of The Organization. Women wept and men dressed in their Sunday best did the same without embarrassment.

He had been a hero to Americans everywhere and a leader to countless soldiers. Over the previous days Chase had met with hundreds, if not thousands of The General's former troops. Each had recounted similar stories of their beloved leader. His presence on this Earth would be missed.

"Thank you."

The President finished his speech and left the podium. A reverent silence hushed over the crowd and Chase extended his hand as the man struggled to walk.

"I'm sorry for your loss."

"We have a lot to talk about young man." The President leaned against the two men who flanked either side. "Tomorrow."

"Tomorrow, sir."

State funerals often dripped with tradition and followed rigid protocol, but The General's wishes superseded those procedures. He had directed his body to be buried in a government issued casket, the same as one afforded any of his fallen soldiers. He had also ordered that there be no procession or Taps played over his gravesite. Chase smiled as The General's voice echoed in his head.

"I don't want the saddest doggone song ever written played when I die. Just put me in the ground and be done with it."

"So what do we do now?"

Chase snapped from his reverie as Chief extended a hand. He breathed deep, took the offered hand, and pulled his lifelong friend in for a tight hug. Rex shook as he fought to control his emotions before releasing his grip and stepping back.

"You're going to take that wife of yours home and get her some rest." Chase smiled as he embraced Angela Ahiga. "You look beautiful. How are you feeling?"

"I feel great." Angela stunned in head-to-toe black and a brilliant smile shone from beneath her veil. "Marilyn told me I just took a pretty bad knock to the head. I don't even have a bump, though. George told me what happened with Sarah too. I'm so sorry for everything. If I hadn't…"

Angela began to cry and Chase stepped in.

"Don't worry about any of that now. She pulled the wool over everyone's eyes, but at the end I think she was the person we all knew. It's great that you're feeling better. I hear you gave everyone a scare, including my friend Phineas."

"A good Irish name if I've ever heard one."

Alexei Chase made the remark as he and Lucille joined the growing group along with Tad, Willy, Bryan, and Bobby.

"I met him that night." Chase shook hands with the other men as he continued speaking. "It seemed my pacing back and forth in the lobby had him concerned. I might never have made it in there if he hadn't asked me what I was doing. What do you hear about Patrick and Amy?"

"She's already on her way back to France, and he's resting in the hospital." Alexei said. "We almost had to strap him to the bed to keep him from coming."

"That's good. Speaking of better Tad, you're looking better already."

"Thanks a lot. I went and saw that doctor you told me about and felt better pretty much the same day. She's a miracle worker."

"I told you she was the best." Chase moved down the line. "Willy, I see you are none the worse for wear from your crash."

"Nah, I wish I could have helped you more, but Tad needed me."

"He did indeed. Captain Morris, I'd say we'd have been in a bit of pickle without you the last few days. Thank you for your service."

"Not a problem." The two men shook hands. "I'm here when you need me."

"Thank you." Rex hugged his mother Lucille who shook as she wept in his arms for a full thirty seconds and a hush fell among the small group once again. "It's OK mom. I've got you. Everything is going to be OK."

"I know." Lucille Chase took a step back before continuing. "I thought you should know that once it was clear Angela was going to be OK I had Belle buried out at the pond, and Axl is waiting for you at our house. I don't think he likes living in the city, though. He spends most of his day staring out the window."

"If you let him take a couple laps in that river he'd love you forever. That dog is a swimmer."

A chuckle went up amongst the group as Chase shook hands with his father.

"What do you have planned for the old man over there?"

"Yeah, what about me?"

"Bobby, you and I have a lot of work to do, right after I figure out what all that work entails."

"I don't suppose you could hop across and pick up my dog Felix for me?" Poppen said. "I'm missing that little guy."

"If you know how to do it, I'm all ears."

"I think we need to figure out where those stones disappeared to first."

Bobby spoke the words and heads nodded around the circle. Chase looked at each of the men and women. The Organization's leadership had hit the ground running.

"Tomorrow, everyone." Chase met each person's gaze as they looked to him for guidance. "We'll get started on all of this tomorrow."

TIM WHEAT

"What about us?" Holly flashed a smile as she and her father approached. Chase envisioned the kiss they'd shared and a tingle ran down his spine. "Daddy and I want to help."

"I'm going to have to brush up on my genetics before all of that. I don't like it when people speak over my head." Chase smiled as her deep brown eyes locked with his blue. He shook her father's hand as he spoke. "Wade, I sunk your boat, but I promise we're going to fish those monstrous engines from the river. You're going to have to tell me about those. They were amazing."

"Can't say I was real happy bout that." Wade's drawl seemed less pronounced. "How'd you know to take oil with ya anyway?"

"About that." Chase shifted as he took a step back. "They might be locked up when we find them."

"Geez Louise." Richland slapped his hand over his forehead. "You killed her."

"She's not dead, just resting." Chase said.

"On the bottom of the Illinois River." Chief added.

"It sure is." Chase smiled at Holly who cocked her head and blushed. "I'll add it to my list."

The group disbanded as each bid the others farewell. Chase thought about each person's specific role in The Organization. He compared how The General had used them with how his own personal knowledge of their abilities had evolved. Filling The General's shoes was going to be a monumental task.

"You know, given enough time even the tiniest fraction of a second's difference in the spin of a universe would cause its occupants to age at a rate different from those in another."

Chase said the words aloud, but received no response. He turned and approached a nearby couple who feigned an engrossed conversation.

"That's why Poppen is so old."

"I told you he would spot us." Marilyn giggled as she hugged Chase. "I'm sorry for the subterfuge Rex, but he's supposed to be dead you know."

"You could have told me."

Rex Chase looked at the man standing within arm's length. His silver hair reflected the sun and his tan skin glowed.

"You had to do it on your own." Leonard grinned and hugged Chase. "It was something I couldn't help you with."

"I saw you die." If Chase had learned anything over the course of the last days, weeks, and months it was that the impossible was becoming possible. "You were dead."

"I wasn't quite as dead as I let on."

"I have so many questions for you."

"Maybe you should be asking my wife."

Marilyn smiled and Chase could feel the confusion spreading through his body. Questions fired into the forefront of his brain, but he asked the first, even though it was the most ludicrous.

"Are we aliens?"

"Aliens?" Marilyn giggled as she took the two men's arms, one on each of side, and guided her escorts away from the crowds and down a deserted sidewalk. "Well, I'm human, though I can't speak for the two of you. Maybe we should find some place a little more private."

✱✱✱✱✱✱✱✱✱✱✱✱✱✱✱✱✱✱

Postlogue

The servant listened to the tune being whistled by his employer and he paused before approaching.

"It's a beautiful day Comrade Moskchenko. Is it not?"

"It is indeed."

"I brought your favorite, a Tuxedo No. 2."

The servant placed the modified martini drink in his employer's hand and watched the diminutive Russian swirl the gin, vermouth, maraschino liqueur, and bitters.

"Strange weather we are having though." The servant looked to the sky as he turned to leave. "If I may ask, Comrade Moskchenko, what was that tune you were whistling? I've never heard it before."

"What makes you say that?"

"Well…" The servant's mind raced. His employer could be a bit mercurial. "I guess because I've never heard it before."

"No, no." His employer leaned back in the beach chair. The sound of waves lapped against the nearby shoreline as he sipped the popular cocktail. "What makes you say that about the weather?"

"Well, sir." The servant crafted his words again. He would have been better served keeping his mouth shut. "It is the middle of November, it was negative three degrees yesterday with three feet of snow on the ground and today it is eighty degrees and you are relaxing on the beach with a cocktail."

"Quite right." Moskchenko let out a small chortle and the servant observed the man reach into a leather satchel, extracting from it two jet black stones. "Rhapsody in Blue."

"Sir?"

THE SENTINEL

"The song I was whistling before is a George Gershwin tune that was popular when I was spending time in Germany in the 20s. It's called Rhapsody in Blue."

"Of course, sir." The servant watched as his employer placed the shiny objects back in their place. Something was different about him today. "Will that be all, sir?"

"That is all," Mikhail Oleg Moskchenko paused a moment, closed his eyes and breathed deep the clean country air, "for now."

www.ingramcontent.com/pod-product-compliance
Lightning Source LLC
Chambersburg PA
CBHW051538250626
47157CB00001B/101